Date: 3/12/19

GRA KAMIYA V.3
Kamiya, Yuu,
Clockwork planet.

# CLOCKWORK PLANET

Yuu Kamiya & Tsubaki Himana

Illustration: Sino

PALM BEACH COUNTY
LIBRARY SYSTEM
3650 Summit Boulevard
West Palm Beach, FL 33406-4198

Hearing a loud rumble, the soldiers all turned toward the source. Toward a building that had been sliced up like a jigsaw and collapsed into pieces. Amidst the roar of the collapse, a clear voice sounded like a music box.

"—Your attention, please." Standing before the collapsing building, the girl in a black dress gave an elegant bow. Crudely mimicking her big sister's gesture, the young girl beside her in red and white armor bowed as well.

"How are you all faring on this day? I am the First of the Initial-Y Series, RyuZU YourSlave."

"U-umm... I'm the Fourth of the Initial-Y Series, AnchoR the Trishula, o-or the One Who Destroys. N-nice to meet you."

It all began with the greetings from the two legendary automata.

That something was the last incident in this chain of events. A grand conclusion that tied all of the preceding incidents that had occurred together under one neat name. It was also the very first of the incidents in a chain of numerous others that would shake the very foundation of this world.

This grand incident was what would later be known as the Uprising of 2/8. But it had another name. And that other name was the Second Ypsilon.

In this year, on this day, at this hour, in this second... 5:59 AM Japanese Standard Time, on February 10th in the 1016th Year of the Wheel...

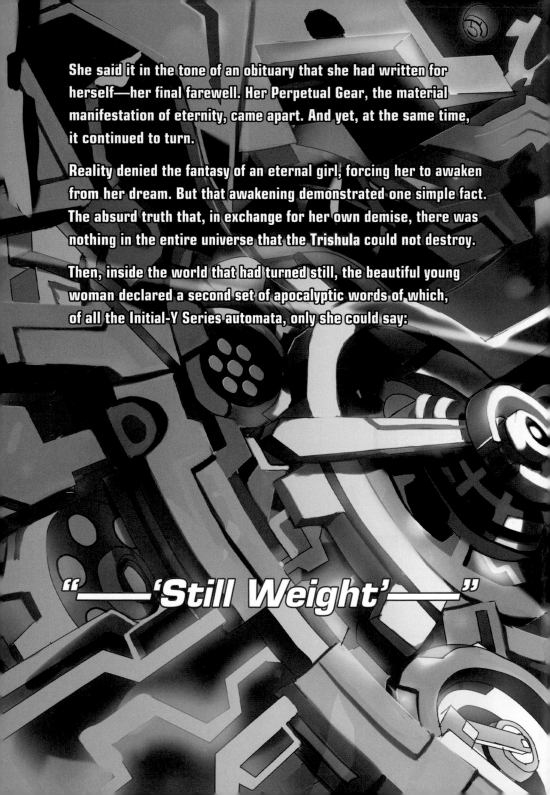

She said it in the tone of an obituary that she had written for herself—her final farewell. Her Perpetual Gear, the material manifestation of eternity, came apart. And yet, at the same time, it continued to turn.

Reality denied the fantasy of an eternal girl, forcing her to awaken from her dream. But that awakening demonstrated one simple fact. The absurd truth that, in exchange for her own demise, there was nothing in the entire universe that the Trishula could not destroy.

Then, inside the world that had turned still, the beautiful young woman declared a second set of apocalyptic words of which, of all the Initial-Y Series automata, only she could say:

# "——'Still Weight'——"

# contents

# CLOCKWORK PLANET

Presented by
**YUU KAMIYA** *and*
**TSUBAKI HIMANA**

*Illustrated by*
**SINO**

Seven Seas

**novel club**

CLOCKWORK PLANET, VOLUME 3

©2014 Yuu Kamiya, Tsubaki Himana
Cover illustration by Sino

First published in Japan in 2014 by Kodansha Ltd., Tokyo.
Publication rights for this English edition arranged through
Kodansha Ltd., Tokyo.

No portion of this book may be reproduced or transmitted
in any form without written permission from the copyright
holders. This is is a work of fiction. Names, characters, places,
and incidents are the products of the author's imagination or
are used fictitiously. Any resemblance to actual events, locales,
or persons, living or dead, is entirely coincidental.

Seven Seas books may be purchased in bulk for promotional,
educational, or business use. Please contact your local
bookseller or the Macmillan Corporate and Premium Sales
Department at 1-800-221-7945, extension 5442, or by
e-mail at MacmillanSpecialMarkets@macmillan.com.

Seven Seas and the Seven Seas logo are trademarks of
Seven Seas Entertainment, LLC. All rights reserved.

Follow Seven Seas Entertainment online at
sevenseasentertainment.com.
Experience J-Novel Club books online at j-novel.club.

TRANSLATION: fofi
J-NOVEL EDITOR: Andrew Hale
COVER DESIGN: Nicky Lim
INTERIOR LAYOUT & DESIGN: Clay Gardner
COPY EDITOR: Cae Hawksmoor
PROOFREADER: Jade Gardner
LIGHT NOVEL EDITOR: Nibedita Sen
EDITOR-IN-CHIEF: Adam Arnold
PUBLISHER: Jason DeAngelis

ISBN: 978-1-626929-36-4
Printed in Canada
First Printing: November 2018
10 9 8 7 6 5 4 3 2 1

## Interlude / 06 : 05 / Reviver

LET THERE BE no doubt about it.

The universe was askew from the very beginning.

We were all born into this world before we could even stand. Wailing desperately and floundering in our frail bodies, fearing both the unknown and the threats in front of us, we asserted our existence and managed to survive by racking our meager brains.

All the while wondering...

*Where did we come from?*

*And where are we going?*

We invented God out of anxiety and fear. We forged philosophy as a means to guide pure reason. We discovered mathematics as a tool to predict things. Timidly, fearfully, we began to write our own history.

Ending the world several times over along the way.

The Earth, which had once been flat, became a sphere. We, who had once been at the center of the universe, became a satellite to the sun. Upon mastering the laws of gravity, humanity took to the skies. Eventually, we used our humble reason to ascertain the five fundamental forces and managed to lay our hands on the throne of Truth at last.

By applying knowledge, language, and violence, by flooding the world with blood and tears, we repeated the cycle of joy, anger, and sadness. Hurting an unfathomable number of people, leaving them writhing in desperation...

We recreated our world time and time again.

We rewrote our history. And by doing so, we managed to prolong humanity's existence.

In the end, it was a futile effort.

That day, that hour, that moment, everything vanished along with our ephemeral dreams. On that day, the Earth was destroyed, the world came to an end, and the universe was reconstructed. And humanity was taught a lesson. Our legacy was erased. The path we had chosen was a foolish mistake. All our worries and suffering had been for nothing. The knowledge we had accumulated was worth no more than trash.

Humanity, which had been at Truth's doorstep, was thrown right back to its infancy. The universe was the model garden of a mad god, and in its design we were nothing but babbling babes.

However, we must ask ourselves: if everything is vague, uncertain, absurd, and filled with contradictions... just the whim of a god... then does this world really exist at all?

A thousand years later...

· · ● · ·

Twenty planes tore through the dawning light, high in the skies above Akihabara Grid. With their whirring rotators and loudly clanking gears, they seemed like steel birds of prey. The pilots of these seventh-generation tactical fighters were the Seventh Aerial Squadron of Tokyo's military. Also known as the Sakamuro Squad.

They were the most powerful aerial force that Tokyo's military possessed. These twenty fighters had launched from a base in Yokosuka Grid and were headed straight for Akihabara.

They had only one objective.

"Destroy the enormous unknown weapon that appeared in Akihabara Grid."

"Eat shit and die," Captain Sakamuro spat out, tearing through the morning at a supersonic speed.

He had been rudely awakened past midnight and ordered to be on standby. The order to sortie had *finally* come at dawn: they were to take down an enormous unknown weapon, just like that.

"Hey AWACS. Want me to stick a cruise missile up your ass to wake you up?" he threatened, half-seriously. The captain was infamous for his short temper.

"Watch your mouth, Captain. That was an official order."

"I'll make you shit yourself."

"I'll only say this once more, Captain. This is an official order. The Seventh Aerial Squad is to promptly destroy the enormous unknown weapon—which we're tentatively calling 'Yatsukahagi'—that appeared in Akihabara Grid."

"Hah," Captain Sakamuro snorted. "Are you stupid? You've gotta be. Only an idiot would take me as a fool."

"Captain!"

"Hey stupid, listen up. I don't know what this Yatsukahagi is, but you're telling me that an enormous weapon suddenly surfaced right in the middle of Tokyo? What was our security force doing? Jerking off and falling asleep on the job?!"

"The security force has already been decimated."

Sakamuro sank into silence. Visual data was sent to all pilots through the transmission line. The image of an enormous mechanical spider, big enough to squash buildings with its feet. Akihabara engulfed in flames.

"Everyone, it's as you can see. This is a very real threat. The destruction of Akihabara Grid would spell the end of Tokyo, which in turn would spell the end of Japan. Pilots, give your all for the nation!"

"..."

"Also, Captain Sakamuro, you'll be court-martialed for your behavior after the operation. You're excited, right?"

"Hah, yeah. I'd be thrilled to go."

*If I can make it back alive, that is!* Captain Sakamuro nearly yelled in a rage, barely swallowing his words at the last second. The captain couldn't afford to say such a thing in the resonant transmission where his subordinates could hear. Irked, Captain Sakamuro struck the canopy of his unit with his fist.

*An enormous unknown weapon that appeared at the heart of the capital out of nowhere, huh? What a joke.*

*No one knew of this thing's existence? If you expect anyone to believe that, then maybe try cleaning out your ears, because you've got shit where your brain's supposed to be.*

*Someone knew. At the very least, the top brass did. Both what this thing is and its objective.*

*If that isn't the case, then why the fancy name for an unidenti-fied enemy object that could simply be called 'the target?' They came up with that gem pretty damn fast for a pack of numbnuts caught with their pants down!*

*It's obvious.* Captain Sakamuro gritted his teeth so hard that it wouldn't have been surprising if some of them cracked. *The target assaulted Akihabara Grid, and Tokyo's security force intercepted it. And they failed. Was their failure a part of some plan? Or did they screw up somehow? In any case...*

*Our job is to clean up after some bed-shitter's mess!* Captain Sakamuro howled internally. It was just a hunch. However, it was an analysis that proved exceedingly accurate.

*Tokyo's security force is no joke. They aren't a force that could be crushed so casually. They're among the strongest in the nation. That generous budget and high-level training isn't for nothing.*

*And yet, as far as I could tell from that image, they were annihi-lated, and without even leaving a single scratch on the enemy at that.*

*And so the politicians, the wretches that they are, decided to shove the responsibility onto the air force.*

*Their thinking was beyond childish. "Well, the security force couldn't do the job, so let's try throwing the air force at it next." How simpleminded. If they really think that we can do what the security force couldn't, then they're beyond help.*

*The security force had resonance cannons at their disposal.*

*In theory, a resonance cannon was the strongest wieldable*

anti-ground weapon. *If even resonance cannons couldn't scratch the target, that would mean it either had armor that could withstand cannon shells or some kind of mechanism to neutralize them.*

Captain Sakamuro had no way of knowing what that mechanism could be, but there was one thing he *could* say.

*Even if I slam all of my unit's cruise missiles into the target, the chance that they would have any effect is—*

"Everyone, you'll soon be arriving at the mission area. All units, prepare for battle!"

"Roger," Captain Sakamuro replied with a disgruntled sigh. *I'll follow orders. That's my duty as a soldier. However, according to the brass, the target's armaments, number of cannons, and firing range are all unclear. In that case...*

Sakamuro sneered.

"Storm One to all units," he announced to his troops, adjusting the headset's mic. "Switch to Formation Delta. We're going with a 'burst and run.'"

He had chosen Delta because it was a triangle formation, it was a measure to avoid the worst-case scenario of having all his units caught in the target's line of fire at once.

"Blow your load from maximum range then skedaddle."

"Captain?!" the AWACS operator barked. "You haven't been given orders to use such a tactic. Don't decide things by your—"

"Tactic? If you're gonna call, 'destroy the mysterious enormous weapon' a tactic, then how to execute that order is under my jurisdiction! Filthy armchair tacticians can go ahead and keep their mouths shut!!"

*I'll obey your damn orders. That's my duty as a soldier. However, above all, I have the responsibility not to let my subordinates die in a futile engagement.*

"All units, do you read me? Obey my orders. I'll take responsibility for this."

"Captain!" the AWACS operator yelled in furious exasperation.

"Storm Two, roger," the squad's vice-captain replied, ignoring the operator. "All units, switch to Formation Delta."

"Roger."

With that cue, Sakamuro Squad switched to Formation Delta.

"Seventh Aerial Squad! You bastards!" the AWACS operator roared through the transmission line. Then, all of a sudden, his voice cut off.

The AWACS aircraft that had been flying above them exploded.

"Wh-what was that?! Don't tell me—"

"Oy, you've gotta be kidding me... The target shot down AWACS?!"

Captain Sakamuro looked at his sonar before trepidation could spread any further among the squad.

Seeing the enormous response that came from way off in the distance, he clicked his tongue and shouted harshly: "All units, adopt evasive maneuvers as you turn around and disperse! Ignite your afterburners and retreat at maximum speed! We're in the enemy's firing range!!"

"R-roger!"

Unable to conceal their disquiet, all squad members of the

seventh obeyed their captain's orders and turned around, tracing a wide arc. Captain Sakamuro couldn't conceal his own alarm either.

*Shooting down AWACS first? Cheeky bastards...*

The enemy had shot down their AWACS, flying twenty thousand meters above them, from outside the range of their cruise missiles. It was obvious what that meant. It was a brazen *provocation*, as if to say, "You've all been inside our firing range for a while now."

Enduring the overwhelming strain of the G-force on his body, Captain Sakamuro turned his unit around like everyone else and ignited the fuel compressed by the rotors in the afterburner.

"Ngggh!" The shock of accelerating to Mach 5 slammed him forcefully against his seat. He gritted his teeth through overwhelming pressure on his body. Then the unit in front of him exploded into pieces.

The valiant men of the Seventh Aerial Squad stared at it wide-eyed.

"Storm Three has been shot down! I repeat, Storm Three has been shot down!!"

"What... what the hell is this?! What was he shot w—" someone cried out in the transmission line, cut short.

Something flashed by.

"How would I know, you wanker!" Sakamuro howled as the units of his retreating squad blew up one after another.

*They were being fired upon from more than 18,000 meters away—the maximum range of a cruise missile. Hitting our AWACS, an aircraft 20,000 meters above us, that can take evasive maneuvers at hypersonic speeds? For a single unit... no, even for several units working in conjunction, to have such absurd anti-air capabilities is impossible.*

The reality of the situation was that the units of his squad were being shot down. Forget striking back, they couldn't even evade the enemy's attacks. They were being annihilated.

Just then, his instincts told him to do something inexplicable.

"Dammit!!" Following his gut without hesitation, Sakamuro released the limiter for the angle of the plane relative to the horizon and pushed the joystick all the way forward into a nosedive.

He was engaging in a forbidden maneuver. Something a pilot should never do. His vision stained red as fierce "upward gravity" made his blood concentrate in his brain.

A condition known as "redout." Those who experienced it could end up dead. However...

"Ngh...ngggghh!!"

The intense impact that scraped the back end of the unit proved his instinct right. He had managed to avoid the attack by a paper-thin margin.

The moment he processed that, the captain returned his unit to level.

"Fuck off!!" he shouted through a fierce, throbbing headache. "I'm flying at five times the speed of sound here! Why can't I see it coming?!"

An attack that came from behind as he was flying at Mach 5. Even considering the relative speed, from his frame of reference, the attack couldn't even be seen at Mach 5.

It wasn't a laser, nor was it a resonance cannon shell. If it had been one of those, there was no way he would have been able to evade it. *There's no doubt about it. This is artillery.* It was abnormal and hard to believe. It was impossibly fast and accurate. A magic bullet.

*An artillery shell that couldn't be cognized even while moving at 1,650 meters per second. Against something like that, the entire squad will be shot down before we can leave its firing range, damn it!*

"Storm One to all units! Eject! Abandon your unit and bail out—right this second!!" Captain Sakamuro yelled into his mic.

"R-roger!" the surviving squad members replied.

Captain Sakamuro waited to see them do as ordered before pulling the lever by his own feet.

"Urggghhhh!!"

The canopy opened, and he was ejected with his seat.

Because he'd been flying at Mach 5, the still air hit him like a brick wall. Feeling like he really might lose consciousness this time, Captain Sakamuro twisted his face and stared across into the distance.

Not at Akihabara Grid where the target was but Kasumigaseki Grid. The location of the National Diet Building.

"You damn pigs! Just what kind of a monster did you bastards pick a fight with?!"

Right on cue, as if it had been waiting for the Seventh Aerial Squad the whole time...

Countless flashes of light arced through the dawning sky and landed in Akihabara Grid.

*Ahh, so if both Tokyo's security force and the air force are no good, then next up would be...*

Captain Sakamuro sneered. *What a simple-minded idea.*

Those flashes of light had come from Tokyo's defensive cannon tower, which sat atop the peak of Mt. Fuji and was armed with ultra-long-range artillery batteries. It was Tokyo's anti-ground anti-air trump card, whose main purpose was to protect the Pillar of Heaven in Tokyo.

"Feeble-minded pigs," he sheered, feeling beyond hatred as he took it all in. "You'd better have your next excuse prepared already."

He opened up his parachute mid fall and felt a hunch that was more like a conviction.

The countless falling stars that lit up the dawn sky in their descent toward Akihabara... most likely, even those wouldn't be enough.

· · ● · ·

Weak vibrations ran through a dimly lit, narrow room.

It had low ceilings and countless monitors affixed along the walls. A thick glass tube was strung around the perimeter of the multi-tiered floor. Inside, blue-white lightning would flash now and then.

There were around thirty people in crisp military uniforms standing in this room. All of them had their eyes focused on the monitors and gauges before them.

"Enemy signals have ceased. We've shot them all down. I'm also receiving confirmation that we've been hit by Tokyo's defensive cannon tower," one of them reported. Everyone gulped. "We've been hit eight times but have suffered zero damage."

The room filled with feverish enthusiasm. It felt like cheers might break out at any moment. Facing his subordinates, the large old man sitting in the chair nodded.

"Good."

"Phased array radar, radar lock, infrared sight, railgun, magnetic shields—all stable."

"Remaining power at 12%. That's still 2% over what we would need to finish recharging the railgun on schedule. Requesting permission to reduce the power being fed to the FCS by 30% to conserve energy."

"Granted." Giving that brief response, the old man—Gennai Hirayama—sighed deeply.

"What a magnificent showing, Your Excellency," said the young man standing beside him in a slightly shrill voice. "To defeat the famous Seventh Aerial Squad this easily!"

"It was the obvious outcome," Gennai replied, leaning back in his chair.

Really, the outcome of the engagement could not have been more obvious. Humanity had once wielded this power, the easiest form of energy to freely utilize in this universe. In current society, where everything had been replaced with gears, researching this technology was a crime in and of itself. It was electromagnetism, the scientific theory that united three of the five forces in the universe: the electric force, the magnetic force, and the Coulomb force.

Before this weapon, the culmination of humanity's lost knowledge of electromagnetism, all clockwork weapons were nothing but toys. Thirty years ago, Gennai had designed this weapon himself, convinced of that fact.

The mobile composite electromagnetic assault weapon, Yatsukahagi. It had its origins in a government project. As far as its name went, the decision to keep its official name the same as its code name during development came down to both Gennai's sentimentality and his sense of sarcasm.

"Foreign countries will be forced to acknowledge the validity of our research on seeing this result," an officer ventured.

"I wonder. It's nothing more than the obliteration of a single squad in the end," Gennai muttered.

"Hardly!" said another young officer. "Annihilating Tokyo's security force is an achievement that no country can ignore!"

"I agree, Your Excellency. I mean, even Tokyo's defensive cannon tower couldn't touch us!"

*True,* Gennai thought. *I knew the resonance cannons of the security force wouldn't work on us. After all, it's impossible to crack magnetic plating via sympathetic vibration.*

*However, Tokyo's defensive cannon tower is a traditional projectile weapon.* It was Japan's defensive trump card in the case of an enemy invasion: a battery of recoil-based semi-automatic cannons. Their magnetic armor—materialized through constantly coupling iron atoms—was sturdy, but even so, on paper it had been fifty-fifty whether their armor could withstand shelling from Tokyo's defensive tower. Gennai had won that gamble as well. And on top of it all, they had obliterated a veteran aerial squad that was fairly well known, even abroad.

"At this point, there's nothing in Tokyo's military arsenal that can stop us!"

"Ahh... yes, you're right." Gennai nodded, surveying the faces in the control room without a smile. Everyone was lost in the moment, thrilled.

*I don't care about that.*

*In the end, this is nothing but another case of "an eye for an eye." We're the same as the government. We've simply repeated something that humans have done since antiquity.*

*We never change. Aren't capable of changing.*

*But, if that's the case, what about "Y," the one who remade our world?*

*This planet continues to turn normally, properly, consistently... but also abnormally, improperly, and inconsistently.*

*What was the true identity of the one who created this ultimate contraption—the Clockwork Planet—with hands no different from yours or mine?*

*He tore down everything that humanity's brightest had managed to accumulate by dedicating an unfathomable amount of time to understanding the laws of nature. One day, out of nowhere, he shoved his incomprehensible, unbelievable truth right in the face of all humanity.*

*And the one who succeeded in that feat was a mere human. A humble clocksmith.*

*Don't make me laugh! Who would believe such a story? Who could accept it? In declaring his ideas to be the one and only truth in this wide universe, he demonstrated an arrogance that would put even the gods in the heavens to shame. An insolence that would flabbergast even the demons of hell.*

*You're telling me that the one who pulled that off was human? A member of our species? We creatures who have been squirming about on the Earth's surface for thousands of years?*

*On that day, I became convinced the answer to that question was a resounding "no."*

*Humanity never changes. It's something like karma at this point.*

*However, "Y" overturned all our human assumptions. Arrogantly, insolently, he twisted the universe askew.*

*There's no way that was the feat of a mere human. Calling it vile would not do it justice. If there is someone who could execute such boundless evil, that person must be a being that transcends morality.*

*Well, if that's the case, I can accept it.*

*I don't care whether he's a god or a demon. If he's a monster whose existence transcends human understanding, then there's no way for us to defy him. If he chooses to delude humanity in a dream for all eternity, in a world he made himself when the old one had been on the verge of collapse, then that's all there is to it.*

*There's no way that we mediocre humans can oppose a transcendental being. As such, while I was disappointed by history and thrown into despair by the world, I thought that it would be fine if I lived out the rest of my life in resignation.*

*That is, until I saw that boy touting about one of "Y's" automata...*

As everyone in the room was zealously eyeing the next target, convinced that they had nothing to fear, Gennai's moss-green eyes clouded over.

"Now then, 'Y,' just you try to stop me..." he muttered to himself, sounding almost like he'd gone mad.

*The world you created beyond the boundaries of good and evil in your arrogant insolence shall be crushed by mediocre humans in the midst of our own self-destruction. The weight of humanity's unchanging karma.*

*Swallow that fact as you answer me, wretched monster.*

*You who recreated the world. Just what are you?*

*A malevolent god? Some demonic transcendental being? Or nothing but a haughty human?*

*Show me your true self, with the world you created on the line!*

•  •  ●  •  •

In a workshop in Akihabara Grid, a blonde-haired girl—Marie—sat against the wall with her feet outstretched. Her mind wandered aimlessly. Her emerald eyes had lost their luster.

*This situation is like a wild fantasy. One that everyone has entertained in their mind at some point. Being left behind in a world that's been destroyed for one reason or another. The premise of a B-movie.*

*With neither food nor water, and the tools of civilization all broken, the only things that you can rely on are your own knowledge, body, and comrades.*

*I see.*

*It's only natural that such a premise would be labeled B-class—it sounds totally unrealistic. No screenwriter has ever actually experienced the end of the world. They don't have a clue how such a scenario would actually play out.*

*Reality isn't so simple.*

*Reality always far exceeds the human imagination. Unreasonably. Absurdly.*

Halter was collapsed on the floor before her, his entire body giving off smoke. Marie laughed scornfully, emptily. She held on to the screwdriver in her hand. Another one was dangling from it, attached where their metal ends touched, as if they were glued together.

*The tools of civilization are broken? The only things you can rely on are your own knowledge, body, and comrades?*

*Don't make me laugh—this is the reality of a violent, non-negotiable, worst-case scenario calamity. The situation is completely hopeless.*

Marie let out a sigh that seemed to expel her very soul.

"Uwah! Why's it so hot?!" a short boy yelped as he leapt up. "The hell?! What's going on here? Wait, why are my headphones so loud?!"

The boy—Naoto Miura—tore off his headphones and threw them away. He screwed up his face as if enduring some intense pain, and then, noticing Marie's listless gaze, he asked the obvious question:

"Wh-what happened?"

"Good question." Marie smiled. "If you're okay with conjecture, then my answer is: we were hit by an electromagnetic pulse." Her voice sounded lifeless.

Perplexed, Naoto knit his brows together. "An elec-tro-magnetic... what'd you say?"

"..." Marie didn't even have the strength to retort. With a languid sigh, she held up the two screwdrivers, stuck together. "Everything... absolutely everything...has been destroyed. Do you get it now?"

An exceedingly, unbelievably powerful EMP had magnetized everything.

*No, if that were the end of it, things wouldn't be so bad,* Marie thought. Most likely, the heat from the EMP's electromagnetic induction melted the more delicate clockwork parts like nanogears, wires, and springs.

The only things left were some tools made useless by magnetism. Nothing but broken clockwork remained.

Processors, cars, the lighting, and the door lock of the room... even these screwdrivers were broken.

"Should I put it in simpler terms?" Marie said, opening her hand. The screwdrivers made a dull clang as they hit the floor. "Now that everything's been magnetized, we can't even do something as simple as leaving this room!"

Clockwork technology was vulnerable to magnetism. This had been pointed out long ago. That was why humanity abandoned electromagnetic technology: they had no choice but to do so.

However, even if the Planet Governors at the North and South Poles intercepted the electromagnetic waves that poured in from space, fully eliminating electromagnetic waves from the planet was impossible. As such, anti-electromagnetic technology to protect clockwork devices from the influence of magnetic fields had been continuously researched as a topic of extreme importance.

In light of the current situation, you could see why it was so important. In short, everyone living on this planet just had all of their knowledge and technology sealed, without exception.

Forget fixing the broken clockwork—there weren't even any tools you could use. The people in Akihabara Grid were like birds with their wings plucked off. No, if that were the case, things wouldn't be this bad. If you plucked a bird's wings off, it would still at least have its legs.

Even if Marie was a genius, she was helpless if she couldn't apply what she knew. In a world where everything had been replaced with gears, this was the reality. It was the absolute worst-case scenario.

"What should I do?" Even such a thought was too optimistic.

"What can I do?" There was absolutely nothing left to suggest an answer.

Marie recalled something that surpassed her current B-movie, disaster film situation. An absurd, ridiculous movie from ancient times. Her lips formed a lifeless smile.

The premise of the film was that the world we live in was just an illusion. That the true world had perished long ago. Humans were only permitted to live inside a dream, their brains connected to machines.

*It's ridiculous. I'm well aware of that. However, if that were true, this situation would suddenly make a lot more sense.*

*Now then, what can I do?*

*When my consciousness is stuck inside a dream?*

*In a world where I literally can't move my arms and legs, where everything is a fantasy. How can I escape the dream, armed with nothing but my brain?*

*When everything I see before me is a lie?*

*And among all those illusions, the one that gives me true despair is the thought of how great it would be if it really* were *an illusion.*

Marie turned her eyes toward one of the thick-paned windows of the room.

Outside, she could see the nightmare responsible for this situation. The towering object that was blocking out the sun. An absurdly enormous mobile weapon. The monster had wiped out everything, and now it was standing there like a symbol of despair.

"Wha... R-RyuZU?!" Naoto cried out.

Marie turned her gaze back in his direction. Naoto was looking at a silver-haired girl who was collapsed on the floor. Panicking, Naoto leapt towards her. He tried to lift her up in his arms.

"Ow! Huuuh?!"

The moment he tried to touch her, he recoiled. At last, he realized the source of the heat that had woken him. Naoto paled, his face flushing pure white.

RyuZU was wallowing in a sea of blood.

At least, the half-melted, glowing metal panels of the floor were hot enough that you could mistakenly see it that way. The reason for that was RyuZU herself. Her very body was what was emitting enough heat to melt the iron in the floor.

Naoto almost collapsed from terror.

"Hey, where's AnchoR?!" he yelled in a trembling voice. "Old man Halter, too! And that babbling head..."

Marie answered silently, motioning with her eyes. Following her gaze, Naoto found Halter, whose body was smoking, limp on the floor. Next to Halter, he saw AnchoR collapsed like a puppet with severed strings. She was completely still. Finally, there was Vermouth's head. Eyes vacant, settled by Halter's feet.

"Were you listening? I told you, didn't I?" Marie said, as if reciting content of a bad dream. "Everything's been broken..."

A stillness like the ocean depths settled over them.

"Don't mess with me..." Naoto clenched his teeth together and pulled Marie up by her collar. "Then we have to hurry up and repair them. You can do it, can't you?!"

Marie didn't offer any resistance. Naoto shook her. She smiled at him faintly.

"Sure I can... if I could just demagnetize them. Erase their magnetic field."

"Then what are you sitting around for?! Get your ass—"

"And how would I go about doing that?" Marie asked quietly. The tone of her voice shut Naoto up. Meeting his gray eyes, she continued: "Ignorance is bliss, isn't it, Mr. Naoto? I'm envious, really."

*Of course, in theory, I know how to demagnetize something. If clockwork can become magnetized, then it can become de-magnetized.*

For Marie, an ex-Meister, tuning magnetized clockwork was a simple task. She could do it with her eyes closed. The idea was simple: either apply an alternating electric current through the material or force it against an opposing magnetic field until its own charge faded away. That was all there was to it. Marie was well-versed in both the methods and procedures.

However, in order to even begin...

"Electricity is absolutely necessary! Understand?! That shitty weapon fired off a damn EMP in a clear, brazen violation of the international treaty!!" Marie lamented.

Naoto let her go, daunted. Marie sank back down against the wall. She was completely lost in thought.

*Ahh, but of course. No country or organization actually adheres to that treaty.* The wireless EM transceivers inside Halter and Vermouth's artificial bodies were also in clear violation. But that was beside the point.

"You can tell with those bizarre ears of yours, can't you?! That EMP *completely destroyed* Akihabara Grid! Well?! Just how exactly am I supposed to get out of this room?! How am I supposed to get my hands on the demagnetizing equipment?! Would you mind explaining it to me in simple terms so that I can under-stand?!" Marie was shouting. By the end of her tirade, her words had become mixed with tears.

It was impossible.

Marie knew, in theory, how to generate electricity using gears. However, it was impossible to control that electricity precisely enough for demagnetization. Simply having that knowledge, much less testing it, was a crime. And as far as legal demagnetizing equipment went, they were managed as strictly as level 4 pathogens. Such technology wasn't something that Marie, a civilian, could freely access. Not to mention, there wasn't even any demagnetizing equipment that could work on a human-sized machine, much less municipal grids.

*Just for argument's sake, even if I went to an EM management facility and stole some demagnetizing equipment, I'd still have to carefully demagnetize the clockwork parts one by one. The protective shell around Halter's brain should hold on for a while longer, but even so, there isn't enough time.*

"What am I thinking? I can't even get out of this room," Marie muttered, hanging her head.

*In just one move... has the enemy really rendered me this powerless? All the knowledge, all the skills that I've carved into my flesh and bones, neutered by just one move.*

*Now that feels like a lie for sure.*

Tears streamed down her face. Suddenly, she heard the sound of glass cracking.

Startled, she raised her head to see Naoto slamming a chair against the window. A second time, a third, a fourth... the cracks in the tempered glass grew larger.

"Argh!!!"

With one last hit, the window smashed to pieces. Perhaps he

had swung too hard, because the chair flew outside, slipping right out of his hands.

"All right. Let's see, so we've got RyuZU, AnchoR-chan, old man Halter... and the talking head, but I guess we can just carry him in our hands. I'm going to lower them down one by one, so... is this the eighth floor that we're on? Well, in any case, find me something like a cable or cloth that's long enough to reach the ground."

"..."

Marie watched, dumbfounded. Naoto clicked his tongue impatiently.

"Argh, fine, forget it! Keep grumbling over there then. Just stay out of my way!" Naoto yelled, turning towards RyuZU.

Hands outstretched, he reached towards her body. It was hot enough to melt the floor.

"Wha... wait a sec!" Marie called out.

Naoto grabbed hold of RyuZU's body.

"Ngggggggggh!"

His face twisted, and the stench of burning human flesh reached Marie's nose. In spite of that, Naoto casually lifted RyuZU up in his arms as if he didn't feel a thing.

"What are you doing?! Are you insane?!"

"Shut up! Dead weight can sit in the corner and keep its mouth shut!" Naoto howled, moving RyuZU away from the red-hot floor. "I don't know why, but I get the feeling that RyuZU can't be left where she's lying!"

Yelling through agonizing groans, Naoto gently lowered RyuZU down on her back on a cool part of the floor.

It'd be an understatement to say that RyuZU's body was in terrible condition. A large chunk of her abdomen was entirely gone, which seemed to suggest a good number of her parts had vaporized on melting. You could see distortions in her frame as well. The damage was such that not even Marie could repair her on the spot.

Ordinary automata would be discarded without a second thought. It wasn't merely a question of having the necessary tools, Marie would also need a ton of extremely expensive replacement parts. However, at the same time, Marie felt certain that something didn't add up.

*After being exposed to temperatures high enough to melt metal, and for such a long time... this is all the damage that was done?*

Considering that its parts had vaporized, RyuZU's abdomen should easily have reached several thousand degrees Celsius. However, despite being subjected to such high heat, no parts of her clothes, artificial skin, or her hair were damaged. She looked practically unscathed aside from her totaled midsection.

*No, in the first place,* Marie wondered, doubt taking hold in her mind. *Could electrical impedance really induce enough heat to wholly vaporize clockwork parts?*

"Guh!"

Naoto shook his head for focus as he rose. He didn't seem to pay any mind to his burnt skin or the clothes that were now glued to him by sweat. He gathered things like cables and wires, anything stringy that seemed structurally sound, and began to tie them together.

"What... are you planning to do..."

"Can't you tell by looking, Miss Genius?! If the door won't open, then we'll get out through the window!"

This room was a workshop. It was made to be airtight. Not a single speck of dust could get inside. If the door to such a room wouldn't open because its autolock had been broken, then what?

One could just smash the fixed window and get out that way. That was all there was to it. However...

"Right, so we escape, and then what?"

Naoto whirled around in frustration. There was a clear tint of contempt in his eyes.

"I'm gonna get outta here! Then I'll find a way to 'demagnetize' things somewhere! When I do that, I'll be able to fix up RyuZU and AnchoR-chan, and old man Halter as well! I guess, while I'm at it, what's his name, Vermouth?! I'll fix him up, too!! And then...!!!"

Marie had never seen him make such a bloodcurdling expression before. Saying there was murder in his eyes wouldn't do the vehement glint in them justice.

The culprit behind everything.

"I'm gonna stuff the bastards who did this to my wife and daughter in a kettle and boil them alive," he shouted, glaring at the enormous weapon trampling through Akihabara's streets. "Is that good enough of an answer for you?!"

"..."

"If you're not gonna help, then at least keep your mouth shut and stay out of my way!"

*Does this guy really not understand the situation?* Marie thought, but at the same time, she found she was content with his answer. *I'll admit, right now, I've fallen so low that I couldn't even think of escaping through the window. Even an idiot could come up with something like that...*

"You sure can talk, eh?" she said. "With Akihabara Grid magnetized and its gears literally sitting still... the number of ways to get to a neighboring grid are pretty limited. Do you realize that...?"

"Hey, at least I'm doing something! How's grumbling going to change anything?"

"Yes, you're right. Really, it's just like you said, isn't it?!"

*I must admit that rushing into things like Naoto is far more commendable than anything I've done so far.*

Naoto seemed surprised by her reply. He faltered for a moment. Marie slapped her cheeks with both hands and stood up so she was peering directly into Naoto's face. His ashen eyes were as radiant as always. No, even more radiant than usual, in light of the grim situation. Even with things as they were, Naoto still hadn't given up on anything. That was what his eyes were saying. Nothing. Not a single thing.

*Just for now, I'll follow your lead.*

"First, we should go to the rendezvous point that we agreed on with the other Meisters. Grid Ueno. Although, now that one of Tokyo's grids has stopped functioning, it surely isn't going to be easy to get there, as there's no one in Akihabara right now. Under normal circumstances, it would have been possible to use the restricted connecting bridge between the two grids, but..."

Marie felt a strange sensation. Seeing Naoto smile at her, his eyes narrowed and his face relieved, she felt something deep inside her heart grate.

"Confirming that the magnetic field has dissipated. Ending emergency sequence. Booting in normal mode."

Naoto and Marie turned around with a start at the quiet voice.

"That really surprised me!"

AnchoR. Blinking her wide eyes in astonishment. She tilted her head slightly.

*We're the ones who are surprised...*

Before that thought could even run through Marie's head...

"Thank gahhhhhhhhhhhd! So AnchoR-chan was un-harrrrrrrRRRRmed! Daaaaammit, I almost had a heart attack y'know!" Naoto leapt towards AnchoR, joining her in a mutual embrace.

"Ah?! No! I don't want you to die, Father!" Taking his words literally, AnchoR pulled him into an even deeper hug with her dainty arms.

"Don't worry, I won't die! After all, RyuZU is fine as well. But really, I was on the verge of fainting from worry, you know."

"Was it AnchoR's fault? Is AnchoR a bad girl?"

"No! You're a really gooood girl! Oh, you! Papa's still here because you're alive, you know! I might have seriously considered suicide if your gears weren't turning!"

"Even though Father almost died because of AnchoR, Father survived... because of AnchoR?"

Watching the idiot and that automaton together, Marie was at a loss for words.

*What's going on here?*

*Was she seriously able to withstand the EMP?*

*The same magnetic field that pierced right through Halter's anti-magnetic shielding and melted his parts in spite of his Breguet next next-generation military cyborg body?!*

*Is it dumb of me to be surprised by the capabilities of the Initial-Y series at this point? No, wait, if that was the case then why was she nonoperational? No, wait, wait! More importantly, what did that idiot just say?!*

"Naoto, just now... you said that AnchoR's gears were turning...?"

"Yeah, that's right. Her gears were turning the whole time. That's why I was able to stop myself from committing suicide."

"If AnchoR was moving, then RyuZU must have had a reason for heating herself up," he continued, as if saying something obvious. "Or so I thought, but it wasn't like I had concrete proof. That's why I was so desperate to do something. But you kept grumbling..."

Naoto petted AnchoR's head.

*The reason she heated herself up...?* she thought, ignoring him.

Something clicked in Marie's head, but before she could formalize it, AnchoR said apologetically:

"I'm...sorry... for the 'prickly countermeasure' umm..."

It seemed like she didn't fully understand her own functionality—actually, it seemed like she didn't understand it at all.

"I think I was in an emer-gency... 'hea-ting' se-quence...?"

"..."

Marie felt like she was going to faint.

*Ahh right, there's "one more way" to demagnetize things. I'll admit, I did forget about that in my moment of distress, but give me a break.*

*Normally, that method is absolutely impossible. Even if it was possible, no one would ever willingly utilize it, much less set it to automatically execute.*

"Demagnetization through the application of heat. Demagnetizing yourself by heating yourself up to the Curie temperature? You seriously did that?" Marie yelled. "You've gotta be kidding meee!"

Curie's law.

Magnetized materials completely lost their magnetic fields once they exceeded a certain temperature. In short, one just had to heat them up. It was an exceedingly simple method.

However, it was also a last resort. Actually, it would normally be out of the question, failing even to serve as a last resort.

As clockwork parts heated up, they warped and eventually melted. The Curie temperature was different for each part of a clockwork mechanism, and the wider the range of temperatures, the more likely the system would break. Gears and wires that had lost their strength due to the heat would perish—it'd be strange if they didn't.

*And even if that were possible, AnchoR should have shut down when the EMP hit. In that case, just how did her heating mechanism continue to operate?!*

"So basically, it's possible to demagnetize things by applying heat," muttered Naoto, ignoring Marie's struggles. "AnchoR slowly raised her core temperature with her frictionless Perpetual Gear over time while RyuZU deliberately shut herself down by converting all her power to heat in one go. Is that right?"

AnchoR abruptly stood up.

"B-big Sister!" she yelled, hoarse with panic. "That's bad, Big Sister can't cool herself d—"

"Don't worry, AnchoR, I got that feeling somehow. So I already moved RyuZU to a cold area on the floor!"

"Father, you're amazing...!" AnchoR exclaimed in admiration. Noticing the burns on Naoto's hands, her expression completely reversed, eyes drooping sadly. "But doesn't it hurt...?"

"Ah ha hah! If it's for the sake of my wife and daughter, burns like these ain't a thing!" Naoto declared his fortitude with a manly smile, just like a real father putting on a brave face in front of his child.

*He really is amazing.* Marie thought as she watched, dumbfounded. *So amazing, in fact, that I can't even understand it anymore. He's weird.*

*The situation had far exceeded her imagination.*

"Yeah... yeah. Demagnetization through the application of heat..." Marie muttered softly.

She wasn't satisfied with that answer.

She couldn't comprehend how it was possible.

However, there was something about the way Naoto and AnchoR marched on, leaving her behind and stunned, that...

A feeling of stark emptiness washed over her. Marie picked up the talking head that had been lying on the floor.

*For now, I should do what I can, too.*

"Well at any rate, let's get out of Akihabara Grid first and foremost," she said, and hurled the disembodied head at the red-hot spot on the floor.

· · ● · ·

"You rotten whore! My brain nearly cooked, you know?! Is your head just as loose as your crotch?!" Vermouth shouted as the gang ran through the stilled Akihabara.

"My, so you're alive. I was almost certain that you had failed to demagnetize," Marie answered coolly, without stopping.

Beside her was AnchoR, who was carrying RyuZU, and a panting Naoto trailing slightly behind. Leading the way, Marie carried Vermouth and Halter's heads under each arm. Vermouth was confused.

"Huh…? What's going on here? Why is the master a talking head now, too? Oy, Phantom Princess, explain yourself! What the hell do you think you're doing?!"

Marie ran past a streetlight and slammed Vermouth against its pole to shut him up. Halter's artificial body had been too damaged for repair and was far too heavy to carry, so Marie had been forced to settle for saving just his head.

*I feel bad for Vermouth,* Naoto thought. *Because he was still asleep, there's no way he could've seen the way Marie's face looked when she removed Halter's head…*

"Ah, it was a bad time to ask that old man," Naoto managed awkwardly through ragged breaths. "But anyway, you really were fine after all?"

"Huh? Ahh, you're the guy who was with this absolutely rotten princess. I'm fine? Where the hell did you get that idea? First, I might die any time now, maybe even within the next three seconds. I have no way of knowing, my oxygen gauge is askew. To add to that, it's looking like my right eye's crushed, so I can't see color all that well either. The very fact that I can still hold a conversation with you must be a miracle. If you call this fine, then I guess you'd figure a zombie with four limbs to be the paragon of health."

Despite his claims to the contrary, the talking head was quite spirited.

As athletic as Marie was, running at full sprint with two heads in her arms was a tough task. The heads alone were as heavy as bowling balls. As she fought the urge to throw away the one under her right arm, Marie squinted.

There was nothing moving on the streets of Akihabara under the morning sun. However, the city's clockwork devices must have caught fire. Flames rose up here and there.

It paled in comparison to the groaning that even Marie's ears could catch ringing from underground. It had been going on for a while now. It was surely the sound of the city breaking down.

"By the way kid, did anything happen to my handsome face?"

"You know that guy who sank into a blast furnace from that really old robot movie?"

"Did my artificial skin melt?! Bitch, what did you do to m—" This time, Marie slammed him against a guardrail. "Hey, you're being downright abusive!"

"Listen, Mr. Talking Head," she said, raising Vermouth to eye level. "Whether or not you end up stuffed in a trash can or tossed in a toilet all depends on my mood. And right now, I am feeling absolutely atrocious. When I was demagnetizing you, I seriously considered letting you boil to death just to let off some steam. Fortunately for you, I have the rationality of a world-class genius and the kindness of an angel. Be grateful that I decided to let you live. A shitty hooligan like you ought to swear loyalty to me while thanking me in tears, got it?"

"You're doing what some brute or demon would do," Naoto retorted, but Marie ignored him. She continued in a kind voice that would instill terror in the heart of a demon king:

"Serve me well. Otherwise, die."

*That's your raison d'etre,* she added silently.

"Oy, kid, is it just me," Vermouth muttered dejectedly. "Or is this filthy sow legitimately insane?"

"I see that you're fond of trash cans. Or do you like toilets better?"

"Calm down, old man. The answer is yes, but seriously, I'd keep quiet if I were you."

"Don't screw with me, you shitty brat! Come on, think about it rationally. I have the right to be mad, don't I?!"

"See," said Naoto. "Whether one has rights or not... is a matter of jurisdiction..."

Vermouth was impressed. "For how young you are, it seems like you get it. Let's share a smoke for reconciliation if we ever get out of this mess alive."

Marie snorted and kept running. They drew close to a place that had been known since antiquity as Mansei Bridge.

Large objects were shadowed against the dawning sky above. A truly gigantic pillar extended up as far as the eye could see. Surrounding it were a number of enormous discs, several kilometers in diameter, with small gaps in between. Discs of the other grids that made up Tokyo.

Amongst them, Akihabara had the lowest elevation. The connecting bridge led to the grid just above Akihabara. That was where they had to reach.

*So,* Marie thought as she turned around.

The Pillar of Heaven was blocking out the morning sun, casting a gigantic shadow over the ground. In its shade, Marie glared at the enormous mechanical spider arrogantly lording over Akihabara.

"Give me a short answer. That weapon is the culmination of electromagnetic technology... yes?"

"Is there some sort of meaning in asking such an obvious question, Princess?"

Marie stopped. She dropped the head under her right arm and stomped on it.

"I don't need your snide remarks. If you answer with anything other than a 'yes' or 'no' next time, I'll beat you to death."

"Yes."

"Good. Next question, what does that thing plan to do next?"

"No."

Without missing a beat, Marie grabbed Vermouth's head and prepared to pitch him overhand into the Kanda River. Naoto stopped her and not a second too soon.

"Calm down, Marie. Don't kill people in front of AnchoR."

"Oy kid, it's great that you saved me, but isn't your reasoning a bit strange?"

"I was a fool to try to rely on this schmuck for even a second," Marie growled, beside herself with anger. "Say, just to be sure, wouldn't AnchoR be able to do something about that thing?"

*AnchoR's overwhelming combat power stayed toe-to-toe with even RyuZU's Mute Scream,* Marie thought, but AnchoR looked down and shook her head.

"I'm sorry... Mother..."

"AnchoR is low on charge right now," Naoto cut in. "It's unreasonable to expect her to do something about that monster."

Marie understood.

The Perpetual Gear was an instrument that manifested perpetual motion through infinite heat. Even if AnchoR's input energy had no limit, her output energy certainly did. If she continued expending more energy than she could output, she'd eat into her Power Reservoir.

She was currently using her First Balance Wheel of Differences—her lowest gear. As long as she possessed the initial energy from her spring, she could continue to operate perpetually in this state. That was why she had been able to autonomously demagnetize herself.

However, after being seriously damaged in the fight with RyuZU and subsequently repaired, AnchoR had lost nearly all the surplus inside her Power Reservoir. If she continued exceeding her output by raising her Balance Wheels of Differences, she'd run out of energy in minutes.

*In other words, we can't resolve the situation by letting AnchoR deal with it.*

Marie groaned, shaking her head. "If we could at least read that thing's movements, there'd be some things we could try, but..."

"I'll say it again, Princess. What meaning is there in asking such an obvious question?"

"Shut up. I'll really toss you in the river, you know."

"I'm being serious here, Miss Self-Proclaimed Genius. The pieces are all there. If you can't figure this out I'll be disappointed, you know?"

" ... "

Accepting the challenge, Marie organized the situation in her head or tried to. She sighed.

*I'll admit it. I'm flustered right now.*

*Everything started with this talking head's shortwave transmission.*

*Chasing after the source of the transmission led us to Mie Grid's underground levels, where we discovered that enormous weapon.*

*That weapon was something that Shiga Grid's Technical Force, which had been conducting illegal research on electromagnetic technology in their home city, had created to ensure their survival. A weapon that could destroy the world.*

*Then we learned that the feds and Mie—Shiga's military of old—were about to engage in a large-scale conflict.*

*In order to mitigate that, we took the initiative and evacuated the population by giving advance notice of our terrorist attack. And after the coast was clear, we baited Tokyo's security force underground and had them intercept the enormous weapon.*

*Then... all we did turned out to be for naught. We failed. Between the strike powerful enough to pierce through a grid, and the EMP that followed it, Akihabara was completely wrecked.*

*Not only that, Halter is barely clinging on to life, RyuZU is seriously damaged and out of order right now, and AnchoR has insufficient energy to act. To top it all off, the city's been turned into a magnetic field. I'm completely powerless right now.*

*All of our plans were torn apart. All of our combat strength thoroughly neutered.*

Marie had yet to recover from the shock of that.

*The pieces are all there...? What is? It's no good... my head's going in circles. I can't collect my thoughts...* Marie bit her lip, seeming vexed.

Just then, Naoto unexpectedly raised his head. He had the same scary expression on his face that Marie had seen just a little while ago, only this time, his gaze was penetrating, as if he were saying with his eyes: "I can see everything you're up to."

He shot a piercing look at the enormous spider that towered over its surroundings, blocking out the sun.

"We don't need to do anything. Isn't that right, you shitheads?"

Marie turned to glare at Naoto, but before she could, Vermouth's laughter reverberated through the post-apocalyptic world that was Akihabara. AnchoR almost jumped with fright.

"Ha ha ha hah! This brat really is something else! Oy princess, you sure picked up an interesting kid!"

"What...do you mean?"

*Once again, things are proceeding due to factors I'm unaware of. Because, by relying on logic, there are some elements that I can't comprehend.*

Marie's brows knitted together, feeling a sense of anxiety.

"That thing is over there because it chose to appear over there," Vermouth explained. "And that is the worst-case scenario for the feds. The enemy queen has suddenly appeared out of nowhere and put their king in checkmate. It's terribly unfair, but regardless, the match is over."

*I don't get it. What did Naoto and this schmuck grasp to come to that conclusion?*

"Princess," Vermouth said, trying to stifle his laughter, "I feel bad for saying this, but you're nothing but a sheltered little girl after all. How cute."

"Wha—"

"On the other hand, this brat is... how should I put it? Despite his cute face, he's capable of some nasty thoughts. You've got what it takes to become a great scumbag, kid."

"I'm used to being called a pervert, but the word scumbag irks me a little," Naoto pouted, discontent.

"In short," said Vermouth. "It's just like the kid said: all they have to do now is sit and wait for the feds to self-destruct. It's checkmate."

**CLOCKWORK PLANET**

# ● Chapter One / 07 : 20 / Explorer

**W**HILE ALL HUMANITY had made a life atop "Y's" enormous gears, not all of those gears were the same.

Cities that had been important before the Earth's clockwork mechanization—the capitals of developed countries and major financial centers—possessed special mechanisms.

Tokyo Multiple Grid was one of them. It was the nucleus of Japan, formed from the composite of many city grids. As Japan's greatest population center, Tokyo Multiple Grid was at the forefront of politics, power, communications, education, industry, and culture. It was a composite city that could be considered a microcosm of Japan itself.

And within Tokyo, Kasumigaseki Grid was considered the political hub. It was an administrative city that housed both the National Diet Building and the buildings of the various government ministries. On a regular day, Kasumigaseki was simply a quiet city where civil servants of the various ministries solemnly went about their work.

Today however, the city was practically a war zone. And there was no end to the ongoing crisis in sight.

The staff of the Ministry of Defense and the National Police Agency dashed about with desperate looks on their faces. The scrambling bureaucrats in charge of the lines of communication worked their resonance phones to the fullest, shouting into their receivers. And, at the center of Kasumigaseki Grid where the building of the current ruling party stood, the Anti-Terror Committee was holding an emergency meeting.

"So, just what is going on here?" the prime minister inquired leisurely.

Having paid no mind to the great disturbance last night, he'd finally shown up to the dawn meeting and casually cut across the room to take his seat at the head of the table. Currently, he was looking about and sipping his tea absentmindedly.

"I heard there was some sort of terrorist attack late last night. I'm guessing the situation has been brought under control?"

"Prime Minister, with due respect, the situation is far more dire than you think," the chief cabinet secretary replied.

The prime minister scowled. "Don't tell me that there've been civilian casualties? That's not okay! I just formed my cabinet, you know! If my approval rating drops again because of this..."

"The situation is far beyond that. Akihabara Grid is currently not functioning."

"What'd you say?"

"Not only that, an enormous unidentified weapon owned by an armed group is currently occupying Akihabara."

"An enormous unidentified weapon...?" the prime minister muttered, his mouth agape.

"It's enormous: a super ultra-dreadnought class mobile ground weapon. The Seventh Aerial Squad of Yokosuka Grid deployed in the gray of morning to intercept it, but I just received news that they've been wiped out..."

The baffled prime minister started to look anxious. "Hey now, that's not okay. Tactical fighters are quite expensive, aren't they? We just cut the defense budget last year, you know. The media's going to have a field day with me."

"Like I said, the situation has progressed far beyond that, Prime Minister."

"Prime Minister, please listen to this man's explanation."

The secretary general of the ruling party pointed at a young man in his early thirties. He was tall and bony with tousled hair that he hadn't put much effort into combing. He was wearing jeans and a casual leather jacket which, overall, gave off a somewhat unreliable impression. His informal attire stood out all the more among the suit-clad bureaucrats.

"And you are?" the prime minister asked suspiciously.

"It's a pleasure to meet you. My name is Yuu Karasawa. I'm a civilian Meister. I was sent here by the Ministry of Technology as a consultant," the man responded with a slack smile.

"A Meister...?" the prime minister said dubiously.

The man presented his chrono compass as proof.

"Frankly, the situation at hand couldn't be worse," he continued with a pained grin after his identity was confirmed. "An armed group has taken over Akihabara Grid. If the enormous weapon invades other grids as well, the damage will surely grow even greater."

"What are we sitting around for then? We ought to overpower the terrorist scum without a moment's delay, no? Isn't that why we have a military?" There was an edge to the prime minister's voice that showed his irritation.

"It isn't so simple," Karasawa answered calmly. "Tokyo's security force discovered the enormous weapon deep underground and intercepted it late last night. They were entirely wiped out."

"Huh?"

"Furthermore, the fighters of the Seventh Aerial Squad that were shot down just a little while ago were in CzFG-11's, the newest model out there. Taking the skill of the pilots into account, that squad was the most powerful aerial force that the military possessed."

Karasawa paused to let that register.

"When we confirmed that they had been wiped out, we tried firing directly at the enemy with Tokyo's defensive cannon tower. All shells hit, but we were unable to deal any damage to the target's armor."

The prime minister stared at the man in mute amazement before turning to the Minister of Defense.

"Just what have you all been spending the yearly defense budget on? You can't even overpower terrorists?"

The Minister of Defense blushed. "With due respect," he answered in a low, restrained voice. "Our military armaments are limited to weapons intended for inter-municipal warfare. We do not possess a weapon with enough firepower to deal with a situation like this."

"Hey you, that's a problem. Protecting the city is your ministry's job, isn't it? Yet you're telling me that you can't even overpower mere terrorists!"

"Our role is to defend the country from a foreign invasion. An immensely destructive weapon suddenly appearing out of nowhere from within is entirely beyond expectations—"

"I don't care about the fine details," the prime minister blurted. "Can't you launch a cruise missile or whatever and annihilate it already?"

"The enemy possesses the anti-air capability to one-sidedly exterminate our newest tactical fighters, you know?" Karasawa interjected with a smile. "Not only that, it has plating that can withstand a direct hit from the defensive cannon tower. Surely, you're not thinking of launching an AMM against one of our own cities?"

"An...AMM?"

"An antimatter missile. In antiquity, a nuclear missile would have been the closest thing to it."

"Oh, I see... why didn't you say so from the start? You specialists are always so quick to resort to jargon. Anyway, that wouldn't work. It'd incur backlash from the people." The prime minister shook his head. "So, what does the military plan to do?"

"In short, overpowering the armed group with a head-on attack is impossible under the present circumstances," Karasawa replied assertively.

"Telling me that doesn't make it okay. This is due to the military's negligence, isn't it? The responsibility lies with—"

"It doesn't matter whom the responsibility lies with right now," the chief cabinet secretary interjected. He was reputed to have an iron-clad level of patience, but even he couldn't hide the irritation in his voice.

"Listen, all right? Because of this terrorist weapon, Akihabara Grid has ceased functioning. For all practical considerations, it's as though it's been destroyed. If we leave the situation as is, it'll only be a matter of time before the other grids are destroyed as well. We must deal with the situation immediately."

"Like I was saying, that's the military's jo—"

"The military cannot bring the situation under control. As such, we must consider the next-best option. Implementing it would require your authority as prime minister."

"Mine?"

"We must purge Akihabara Grid immediately. Please give us the authorization to do so."

The prime minister's eyes darted about in a panic. "What are you saying? There's no way we could do that!"

"There's no other choice."

Karasawa stopped smiling for the first time. Standing up, he raised a hand. "Ah, excuse me. As the technology consultant, I really can't recommend purging Akihabara as the countermeasure..."

The chief cabinet secretary turned around and glared at him with eyes like needles. "And why is that?"

"Because Akihabara isn't simply another city. Structurally, it's a critical component, necessary to keep Tokyo as a whole operating smoothly. If it's purged, the other grids will definitely be affected."

"But that's how a purge works, no?" the chief cabinet secretary answered sharply. "Thanks to that weapon, Akihabara might as well have been destroyed already. Won't the other grids already have been affected?"

"Yes, of course. Currently, the other grids are compensating by burdening themselves with Akihabara's workload. Nothing's going to happen today or tomorrow. However, they'll surely fail within six months' time if things keep up like this."

"Is there any prospect of repairing Akihabara as it is right now?"

"That depends on how badly it was damaged. As of right now, I can't tell you anything for certain. However, if we were to gain the full support of Meister Guild, I can't say that it'd be impossi—"

"Out of the question," the chief cabinet secretary said, cutting Karasawa off. "I can understand you wanting to play up your former employer, but clinging to such uncertain, wishful thinking and averting your eyes to the practical threat before us is simply irresponsible. Well, Prime Minister?!"

Karasawa tried to object, but the chief cabinet secretary ignored him while pressing the prime minister for a decision.

Seeing the secretary's intense countenance, the prime minister quailed.

"Uh... what about the residents?" he objected disjointedly, cold sweat oozing from his forehead. "We just tried to purge Kyoto not so long ago. If we try to conduct a compulsory purge of Akihabara now, wouldn't the backlash from the public... be something else?"

"Eight hours have passed since the incident began. The evacuation of the residents is already complete. It's a grid with a small population to begin with."

"Chief Cabinet Secretary! You're being too rash!" yelled the female Minister of Foreign Affairs. "There's still a chance that Akihabara can be repaired, right? Furthermore, the enemy's identity and objective still aren't clear. We should try negotiating first!"

"Is now the time to suggest something so complacent? We should take bold measures. There might be problems later, but we should prioritize resolving the situation at hand immediately, no?"

"Purging Akihabara wouldn't just be a problem for our nation! Other countries would react as w—"

"As long as the situation is promptly resolved, we can gloss over the purge any which way, no?"

"What kind of foolishness are you spouting?! That inclination to cover things up is exactly what brought about the downfall of the previous administration! If we adopt such a hard-line stance, censure from other countries will be unavoidable!"

"Dealing with that is *your* job isn't it?!"

"That's exactly why I'm telling you that I can't accept your resolution! We should try reaching for a peaceful solution first!!"

The chief cabinet secretary and the foreign minister shouted back and forth in an uproar. The prime minister, who was stuck between them, simply looked on nervously, the words, "What should I do about the next election?" written clearly on his flustered face.

*Maybe I chose the wrong job after the Meister Guild...* Karasawa groaned, sitting down and reclining in his chair. He stared at the quarrel that was far beyond his control and sighed in exasperation.

*Absolutely ridiculous.*

*The chief executive is incompetent, he has no proposals of his own, and can't make any decisions.*

*The chief cabinet secretary, who does accurately grasp the situation, is a proactive realist but his ideas are far too drastic.*

*The foreign minister is an idealist who, while she does understand the situation, probably can't offer a practical solution.*

*It's like nothing has changed in a thousand years. Actually, make that two thousand years. Or more. No matter how far you go back, politics has always been like this.*

*Even my old home, the Meister Guild, a nonprofit organization that operated beyond borders, was no stranger to politics like this.*

*Maybe this game of power is the true nature of humanity...*

Karasawa narrowed his eyes, enveloped by a sense of resignation. *Dr. Marie... are Dr. Konrad and the other Meisters safe...?*

He had an accurate grasp of the Akihabara Terror Incident. Actually, he was an accomplice who had assisted with the cleanup.

In his previous job at Meister Guild, he was in the first division of the second company's communications department. He had worked under Marie and had agreed readily when she came to him seeking help, but...

*Expecting me to be able to handle a situation like this is unreasonable, Dr. Marie,* he thought, making sure not to show it on his face.

*The existence of the enormous weapon may be one thing, but Akihabara Grid collapsing is clearly not part of the plan.*

*We failed.*

*I should probably try to contact her to discuss how to deal with the situation from here, but...*

Seeing the feud unfolding before him, Karasawa sighed for what might have been the hundredth time today.

"I wonder if I'm going to be paid overtime for this."

• • ● • •

The sun was already high in the sky, indiscriminately bathing the city in warm, white light. But, even in the middle of the day, there was a place that its light didn't reach.

In one corner of Ueno Grid was a soiled underground shopping district. It was supposedly a red-light district that bustled with nightlife, but right now it was just a deserted street, lined by shuttered doors.

There was only one place open at this time of day. Cheaplooking neon gears languidly flickered in front of the dirty flower decorations adorning the front of the building.

There was no front door, but you could hear lively music coming from the back. This place had been made so you couldn't see anything from the entrance.

Three people stood in front of the establishment. One of them, a petite boy, was quietly reading the sign aloud.

"The Ueno Strip...?" said Naoto.

The girl beside him lowered her gaze. An old poster pasted on the wall came fully into sight...

"150% true to life! The real deal! Pole dancers with everything exposed!!"

The picture was an automaton girl of about Marie's age. She was posed in such a way that the average person would find her of prurient interest. Which is to say the poster both depicted and described, in a patently offensive way, extreme sexual conduct. Lacking in any serious literary, artistic, political, or scientific value.

It was obscene.

"Ngh?!"

Marie reflexively turned her face away.

*I don't know what's what anymore. Actually, I do. Everything's filthy. Impure. You could even call it repulsive. I don't even want to think about how something can be "150% true to life."*

"Father...?" AnchoR asked curiously, still carrying RyuZU on her back. "What kind of store is this...?"

"Ah, it'll always be too early for you to know. I think it's best if we save that talk till you're a grown up..." Naoto replied, dodging the question. He whispered out of the corner of his mouth to Marie: "Hey... you're sure that this is the right address, right?"

"That...should be the case. Yes, indeed it should."

"But I mean—"

"Don't say it."

"No, I'm gonna say it. No matter how you look at it, this place is for those over eighteen, you know?!"

"Like I'd know anything about that! This is definitely the right address, okay!" Marie yelled, her face flushing bright red.

It was a back-alley sex shop, no matter how you looked at it. A special strip club, so to speak.

But it wasn't one where live human girls danced. No, it was a place of "refined" interest, where pleasure automata wore scandalous clothes, danced scandalous dances, and provided scandalous service. A debauched theater born from the degradation of modern society and the cultivated tastes of "elevated" men.

Marie wouldn't ever look at such a place, much less set foot inside it. However, though she checked over and over again, this was the rendezvous point that Konrad had designated in case of an emergency.

Someone came out from the back, perhaps hearing the commotion by the entrance. A classy old man wearing a well-tailored suit.

"Dr. Marie! I'm so glad you're all right...!"

Marie froze on the spot. It was Konrad. His characteristic monocle swirled with color as it reflected the neon gears. The combination couldn't have been more awkward.

"Dr. Marie, what happened?! Just what is going on—"

*That's exactly what I want to know. There's a heap of things that I should report to him and just as many things that we need to consult on. It's true that I'm relieved to be able to meet the old man, but frankly... because of the location, I can't bring myself to feel happy...*

She was assaulted by an intense feeling of lethargy.

"Um... Dr. Konrad. Er... this place has the equipment at least... right?"

"Of course. Don't just stand by the door. Come on in."

*As if it were an obvious question...*

Marie couldn't make sense of anything, but she did agree they shouldn't be discussing these matters in public, so she followed him on back.

She had to muster a significant amount of courage to step through the doorway.

Behind her, she could hear Naoto instructing AnchoR: "Keep your eyes on the floor. It'll be bad for your upbringing otherwise."

"Okay...?"

· · ● ● ●· ·

"Hmm. I see... It appears that the situation is more serious than I expected," Konrad said solemnly as he led the way.

But Marie wasn't paying much attention. Despite the gravity of the topic at hand, this carnal place filled with "ooohs" and "ahhhs" made it impossible for her to maintain a serious attitude.

The inside of the establishment was almost exactly as Marie had imagined, but still, didn't fail to surprise her.

It was dimly lit with red light, so you couldn't see very far. The automata dancing on the stage, however, were clear as day. 150% true to life, they worked the poles to the intense beats of some extremely loud, exotic music...

The real problem though were the leather sofas that sat along the walkway. They appeared to be customer seating and came with a partition screen that provided privacy from the outside.

*If that's the case, then why are there a pair of legs sticking out from the top? What kind of awkward sitting position is that?!*

*And why is the sofa creaking so much?*

*Hey, what do you mean, "I'm coming"?! Aren't you already here?!*

*Hwah? Some woman's underwear just flew over my head! Just what kind of miracle is that supposed to be?!*

*Such decadence. Such depravity. Such immorality!!*

Marie locked her eyes facing forward, her face flushed bright red. A nude, curvaceous automaton, her magnificent breasts on full display, brushed past with a sensual wink.

Marie's emerald eyes lost their luster. She was dead inside. Behind her, the fully-equipped pleasure automaton coquettishly smiled at Konrad as she drew nearer and nearer to a panicking Naoto. His eyes darted about, and he froze solid.

"Gyahuhwha?!" A soft hand caressed his butt, and Naoto let out a strange noise.

"Father," asked AnchoR, still obediently staring at the ground. "What's wrong?"

"A-ahh nono... Children shouldn't look!"

"*You* shouldn't be looking either! Heck, *I'm* not supposed to be looking!" Marie retorted, unable to put up with it any longer.

"Ha ha ha, relax your shoulders, Princess," Vermouth said flippantly from under her arm. "Is this your first time in a place like this? I heard that you're a terrorist now, no? No need to mind any silly laws at this point."

"That *isn't* the problem!"

*It's absolutely filthy!* Marie nearly shouted, restraining herself in consideration for Dr. Konrad.

Making their way past that unwholesome space, the gang entered a back room where a staircase led to an underground level. Descending the stairs, they walked through a hallway and came across a wide room.

"Here we are. Sorry, it's a little dirty."

The room Konrad guided them to was considerably more respectable than the upper floor. At the very least, there was nothing so conspicuously obscene. The lighting was a bright clean white and the loud music above was inaudible. The only things in the room were a simple bed, sofa, table, and some assorted basic necessities. There was a thick door in the back of the room. It seemed like the workshop lay beyond it.

Finally calming down, Marie let out a deep, deep sigh. At last, she could ask the question that had been burning inside her.

"I'd like to explain the situation but... could I ask you just one question first, Dr. Konrad? Why did you choose this place?"

Konrad looked puzzled. "Isn't it nice? It doesn't suit your tastes?"

"Did you think it would?" Marie replied coldly.

Vermouth cackled. "That so? It's a nice venue, don't you think? I'd love to visit this place again while equipped with my lower half."

"In that case, let me give you a coupon later. There's a discount for staying the whole day," Konrad said, smiling.

Vermouth grinned. "Despite your appearance, you know

what's good, gramps. If you could give me a smoke, as well, I'd be in heaven."

"Unfortunately, I quit smoking many years ago, you see."

"That's a shame. Smoking is a man's duty, you know."

"At my age, a good glass of scotch is more than enough."

"Dr. Konrad?" Marie shot a sharp look at the old man with the appearance of a gentleman.

"A close friend of mine owns this business," Konrad said, holding up his hands in surrender.

"A friend of yours?!"

"Yes, the owner is an old friend of mine. Once in a while I come here to tune up the showgirls for him and in return he treats me to a drink."

"Dear Lord, you were using your skills as a Meister on an establishment like this?!" Marie eyes went wide with shock.

Konrad laughed and shrugged his shoulders. "Business here has been quite good lately. Supposedly the girls' dancing has gotten better, which is why my friend gladly provided us a hiding place here today. And," he continued in a whisper. "This isn't something that you can go around telling people, but this place is also an auction house for illegal automata."

"Huh?"

"Well, it's a black market dealing in high-class automata sporting illegal parts marketed towards men. The authorities turn a blind eye to it because they have ties here themselves, so it's a perfect hiding place, and it comes with a workshop."

"Wow, politics sure are dirty..." Naoto grumbled.

Marie held her head and sighed. She felt so disgusted that she was starting to get a headache.

*No, he's right. There was the workshop in Akihabara Grid, too. It's remarkable that Dr. Konrad, an Englishman, has so many connections in Japan.*

*It may not be able to match a full-fledged workshop, but it's at least equipped with the basics. Beyond that, while there isn't any military-grade stuff here, there's still a ton of illegal parts and high-grade materials.*

*However, putting that aside... should this really be allowed? I'd always believed Dr. Konrad to be a fine gentleman. He's a senior clocksmith to whom I give my utmost respect, as well as a master craftsman from which I've learned a great deal.*

*But of all things, to think that that person was secretly a pervert like Naoto!*

That fact caused Marie such despair that she felt as if her legs would give out.

"Well...in any case." She shook her head, switching gears. *There are more important things than that right now.*

She held up Halter's head. "First, can I ask you to take care of preserving his mind? He's been magnetized...but if the brain inside is unharmed, then he should be fine if we just switch out his head casing, right?"

She didn't dare add: "If he's still alive."

*Halter's burning from the magnetism. It's a miracle that Vermouth is fine. If Halter's artificial body broke down before the life preservation mechanism could activate... I don't want to think about it, but it's possible that Halter's already brain-dead. As of right now, there's absolutely no guarantee that he's alright.*

Konrad nodded, appearing to have grasped Halter's situation. "Hmm... so he needs a reverse-transplant brain operation, yes? That's the specialty of one of my acquaintances, a back-alley doctor. I'll make the arrangements with him immediately."

"Please do. And also..." Marie hesitated a little. "Doctor Konrad, would you be able to get a spare artificial body for Halter? Within thirty-two hours... no, within twelve hours if possible."

"That's impossible even for me."

"..."

"Simply acquiring a military-grade artificial body right now would be exceedingly difficult. Dangerous even. Actually, to be honest with you, just before you guys arrived, some bureaucrats on an inspection run stopped by here. Even here. Keep in mind that this place does not sell any military-grade goods and that it also has ties with politicians."

"..."

"I suspect that the underground vendors throughout Tokyo are being exposed right now. Acquiring a military-grade automaton in this city would be impossible. The moment you get one, you'll be hunted down."

"Is that so..."

*Then, what should I do?* Even though Marie knew their hopes were slim from the beginning, she still felt crestfallen.

"First, let's connect his brain to a life preservation device,"

Konrad said gently, seeing Marie's countenance darken. "We can wait until that's done to consider what to do about his artificial body."

"Yes, please... take care of him."

Marie surrendered Halter's head over to Konrad, who swiftly set off, leaving the room. She slapped her cheeks with both hands.

*I don't have time to dilly-dally.*

She turned around and faced Naoto, standing in a corner of the room.

"Naoto, carry RyuZU into the workshop and put her up on a hanger. While you're doing that...I'll find some suitable parts to make an auto-fan, something to cool her with."

Naoto nodded but seemed unsure. "Right... but wouldn't cooling her with water or ice be faster?"

"Seriously... do they teach you nothing at school? If you cool something extremely hot too quickly, it'll crack or deform. RyuZU did what she did because she thought it was the right choice... believe in her."

*I know I'm stretching things a great deal, but...* It seemed like AnchoR noticed Marie's gaze, because she inadvertently raised her head.

"Mother?"

"Stop calling me that," Marie warned, looking away.

The built-in anti-magnetic shielding of Halter's artificial body was the world's best. His body had been designed to be able to function even in the mock ionosphere that the Planet Governors produced. At least, for a short period of time.

However, the enormous weapon's EMP had easily pierced that shielding and totaled his body.

Given that AnchoR and RyuZU were not only able to endure such a powerful EMP, but even demagnetize themselves on their own, there could only be one conclusion.

"Y" had anticipated electromagnetic attacks from the very beginning.

*This adorable little lump of absurdity that's currently tilting her head at me proves that. In that case, RyuZU should also recover once she cools back down—it may be ridiculous, but I'm convinced of it.*

"..."

*How ludicrous. Halter's artificial body, the culmination of the Breguets' full technological efforts, didn't stand a chance against that EMP, and yet, an antique doll that was made a thousand years ago is walking around just fine.*

*What exactly have we accomplished up to now?!*

Marie's heart was filled with disgrace, powerlessness, and above all, anger at herself for her weakness. She couldn't outwardly express it. That would be *too* disgraceful. Instead, she took a deep breath and locked away her melancholy. Steeling herself, she headed for the workshop.

"Ohh..."

Taking a look around, Marie found some surprisingly decent equipment. There was a device for machining automata parts, even if it was an old model. Not only that, but the workbench and automata hangers were quality ones that could withstand the abuse of a professional clocksmith.

*This might be the best there is for a personal workshop.*

"As expected from Dr. Konrad..."

For the time being, Marie decided to gloss over the fact that the equipment here was used for the dolls dancing on the upper floor.

"Oy Marie, is this hanger fine?" Naoto asked, following her in.

"Yes, that's fine."

"Roger. Well then, AnchoR-chan, I'll leave it to you."

"Okaaay," AnchoR cheerfully replied, hanging her sister's body up on a hanger that was close to the workbench.

Now, in good lighting, it was clear just how awful RyuZU's injuries were.

Her abdomen was the most damaged area.

Not only were her clothes melted, but even her artificial skin was damaged. The trauma had exposed her inner mechanisms, including her main cylinder. An entire bundle of extremely fine wires that served as her pseudo-nerves had been torn apart and were protruding outward from the wound.

She seemed to be missing several parts.

The deformation of her skeletal frame was worse than expected, too. Even if they restored her power, as she was now, she surely wouldn't be able to properly maneuver her arms and legs.

*If that's how bad things look on the outside, just how bad is the damage on the inside?*

Naoto watched over RyuZU anxiously. *Her injuries look far more painful than my measly burns, but more than that, there's something that's...*

"Father, Big Sister will be okay, right?"

Naoto crisply changed his expression into a smile. "Of course, silly. The reason RyuZU did what she did was because it was the right choice. So she'll be just fine! You don't need to worry, okay?"

AnchoR's shoulders drooped, and Naoto patted her head.

*The palms of your hands have awful burns too, you know,* Marie thought, sighing softly as she exited to the previous room. There was a first-aid kit mounted on the wall near the entrance. She opened it up, took out its contents, and returned to the workshop.

"Come over here, we have to hurry up and treat you, too," Marie said, holding up a syringe. "These are medical nanomachines. If you don't want to die from infected burns, then hurry up and take off your clothes and sit over there."

"Oh, thank you." Naoto obediently followed her instructions. His face tightened from the pain as he slowly took off his scorched clothes and threw them in a corner. He then sat down on the ground.

Marie readied the syringe—a cylinder as thick as a can of juice—by peeling off the film on its tip. "Just so you know, don't expect this to be some kind of cure-all. Without an artificial skin transplant or a skin graft, there'll always be scars."

"Not a problem. As long as I can move my hands, I'm happy."

Marie let out a sigh. Naoto's back was just as blistered as she had anticipated. Aligning the syringe against it, she applied pressure.

The needle thrust painlessly into his skin. Pressing down on the plunger, Marie injected an ample amount of medical nanomachines into the worst of Naoto's burns.

The nanomachines would keep his wounds sterile and even

assist in tissue regeneration until all his wounds were fully healed. Naoto may have been lucky that such materials were on hand, but in all honesty, what Marie had just done was a *test*.

The medical nanomachines were powerful, but they also caused extreme pain after injection. Marie had deliberately chosen not to mention this.

The intense pain of having nanomachines work their way into everything from one's bones and muscle fibers to one's skin and nerves should be unbearable enough to make an adult man cry out for mercy, but Naoto didn't let out a single groan.

*I don't think it's that his nerve endings are dead. His face is heavily twisted, and his fists are clenched and trembling.*

However, Naoto never verbalized his agony. Instead, he simply let out a deep sigh.

"Wait here, I'll see if I can find some clothes for you."

"Right, sorry for the trouble. Please do."

Feeling as if she had lost to him somehow, Marie left the room.

"..."

Naoto had moved RyuZU simply because his intuition had told him it was necessary to do so. The expression he wore and the words he said back then, and now his current stoicism, played over and over again in Marie's mind.

*I suspect that... no, I'm sure of it. There's no room for doubt. Had that guy, that gigantic fool determined that it was "necessary," he would have even cut off his own limbs without hesitation.*

A chill ran down her spine.

*That expression, that look of his, convinces me of it. It isn't resolve.*

*No, it's something else. That quality that lets him assert that his decision was simply a matter of course, for some reason, it really...*

Managing to find a change of clothes for Naoto, Marie returned to the workshop. She handed Naoto what appeared to be some sort of promotional item, a T-shirt with the logo of a store printed on it.

As he ran his arms through the shirt's sleeves, Naoto appeared to remember something. "Oh, by the way, what are you gonna do about that old man?" Naoto was looking at the head that Marie had offhandedly laid upon the workbench.

"Do you guys not have souls or something?" Vermouth said, seemingly discontent. "If you've forgotten then let me remind you: it wouldn't be strange if I died any second, you know? Hurry up and hook me up to a life preservation device, please."

Marie shook her head. "God, this guy is something else. Why are you and Naoto both so... meh, forget it." Marie changed the subject, ignoring the picture of the sexy-looking automaton with her legs spread wide open printed on the back of Naoto's shirt. "In any case, I can't let you sleep just yet. I still have things I want to get out of you."

"Give me a break would you? Wait, hey. Hey hey, wait you dirty sow! What the hell are you planning to do?!"

"I'm going to kindly link you to a suitable automaton. I'll install a life preservation device inside as well, so rest assured."

"You're seriously insane, you shitty bitch! You're telling me that your master plan is to connect me to a dutch wife?! What the hell do you take a man's dignity for?!"

"No such thing," Marie coolly asserted as she pulled a hanging doll towards the workbench.

Then she offhandedly—at least, that was how it looked to Naoto—plucked off the doll's head and plunked Vermouth's right in its place.

"Damn it. Is this crazy princess for real?!" Vermouth felt a chill as he glared at the self-proclaimed genius in front of him.

It wasn't his aversion to being transplanted onto a female body. He had no choice but to acknowledge that this sheltered little brat of a princess was indeed worthy of being called a genius.

Vermouth was terrified.

In the first place, full body cyborgs and automata were completely different machines. One was a reproduction of the very "essence" of the human body, while the other only merely replicated its "functions."

Put simply, automata did not have brains. Depending on the model, an automaton could continue to operate even after losing its head. Full body cyborgs, on the other hand, housed a live brain.

Because of this, artificial cyborg bodies were made to replicate the structure of the human body. If that wasn't done, the brain would reject the artificial body.

*And yet, this little brat managed to exchange an automaton's head with mine like it was nothing. Not only that, my brain doesn't feel out of place at all... and she installed a life preservation device before I even realized it. It's simply inhuman.*

"I see, so you weren't a ghost but a demon," Vermouth muttered, seemingly lost in admiration. "Sorry for the various things

I said, Princess. If you're a demon, it's only natural that you're lascivious— Gyaaahh?!"

Vermouth cried out from the pain of having all of his nerves connect to the automaton in one go.

"Now then," Marie said cheerfully behind him. "Let's sort out what we know about the situation."

· · · ● · · ·

The Anti-Terror Committee was in turmoil. As the gravity and danger of the situation sank in, the debate became rowdier and rowdier.

*We should resolve to purge Akihabara. No, we should try negotiating with the criminals first. How about reassembling the military of the neighboring grids and counterattacking? We should consider evacuating the residents first. We should consult with other countries and take a united response...*

Various opinions were given and refuted. They couldn't decide, and the meeting had yet to advance even one step closer to its destination.

A Minister of State, who was against the purge, raised his hand. "Fortunately, I don't think we have to worry about the Pillar of Heaven being attacked, considering its relative position to the enemy, no?"

"Are you still asleep?" the Minister of Defense spat. "So long as they have their main cannon, they can hit anything in Tokyo! It doesn't matter whether there are grids in the way.

If they want to, they can shoot right through any of the grids, just like they did with Akihabara! That thing intentionally turned up in Akihabara because it's the lowest grid of Tokyo, so that means that the entirety of Tokyo is in its firing range, understand?!"

"What in the world *is* that weapon in the first place?!" a different Diet member shouted, seeming agitated. "Whether we're talking about the power of its main cannon or how it invaded Akihabara from the deepest underground layer, aren't its capabilities simply too absurd?!"

He stood up and looked across the faces of everyone in the room. There, he noticed the civilian consultant sitting in a corner.

"You! Just what is the enemy armed with?!"

The consultant—Karasawa—tilted his head with a blank expression. "Are you asking me?"

"Who else is there?!"

"I'm glad to hear that. I thought I'd been forgotten," Karasawa said, smiling sweetly. He stood up, scratching his head. "Um, you were asking about the enemy's armaments, right? I'm happy to take a guess."

"Get your act together! What do you think you were hired for?!"

"With due respect, I was hired as a consultant on clockwork technology. I'm not versed in the field of electromagnetics, something that we all know violates the international treaty."

The meeting instantly fell into silence. The member who had questioned Karasawa was taken aback.

"Electromagnetic technology you say?" asked another minister, a pale expression on his face.

"Yes. I've carefully read through every single word of the report. There's no other possible explanation," Karasawa said crisply, his voice carrying through the silent room.

"First, as to their main cannon firing through Akihabara, I have absolutely no idea. However, I do know that what they emitted afterwards was an electromagnetic pulse. The armor that was capable of withstanding shots from Tokyo's defensive cannon tower is also likely a magnetic shield or something. And the fighter planes? That was probably a railgun."

Agonized moans of terror resounded from the committee.

"Umm, is there any chance at all that they're utilizing some sort of new clockwork technology?" the minister of state asked, desperately clinging to some last ray of hope.

"No. That weapon produced two phenomena that no clockwork mechanism could ever create: the magnetization of the entirety of Akihabara Grid and the nullification of Tokyo's resonance cannons. Those two things can't be explained with clockwork engineering, even by the current theories being researched by the Five Great Corporations."

*Considering the capabilities of certain composite materials, it's possible that the armor was just that. There also exist clockwork mechanisms that could produce something akin to the super-ultra high velocity cannon that shot down the fighter planes. At least, in theory.*

*However, nullifying the resonance cannons is simply impossible. If something can defy cracking from resonance, it wouldn't be due to its material. The only possible explanation would be that it has an outer membrane that can't resonate.*

*And keeping in mind that Akihabara Grid was magnetized, the most natural conjecture would be that the weapon had a magnetic coating.*

"B-but this should be outside your expertise as well! You can't say for sure, can you?!" the Diet member who'd first asked for Karasawa's opinion exclaimed.

Karasawa nodded with a frivolous smile. "Yeah, that's true. After all, if I were well versed in electromagnetic technology, that'd make me a criminal. It's technology that violates international law as set by the IGMO, you know? Since even researching it is forbidden, I think the real question is why a weapon that employs so much forbidden technology is in Japan. Isn't that far more important?"

The Diet member turned paler than paper.

*There's no way that such a thing suddenly appeared out of nowhere. The research necessary to create it must've began a long time ago. And probably in Japan at that. I'd bet anything that at least some of you know the truth behind what's going on...*

All present at the meeting were blown away by his revelations. An uproar ensued.

"D-do you have proof?!"

"That's right! Don't spit out irresponsible speculation when you don't even have any proof!"

"Please excuse me for that," Karasawa said placidly as he was crucified by everyone's gazes. "However, the threat that looms below us is an undeniable reality. I have simply given my thoughts on the matter as befitting my role as a consultant, nothing more."

The committee fell dead silent. However, within seconds, they began making remarks intended to sound out the truth from one another. As the committee was consumed by mutual suspicion, the meeting plunged even further into the depths.

*If I were to immediately report this matter to the IGMO, this country would be on the brink just from that.* Karasawa sat back down, entertaining that dangerous thought.

*If knowledge of this spreads worldwide, the international community would surely adopt harsh sanctions against Japan at the bare minimum.*

*Well, their saving grace is that the weapon is brandishing its spear against them... but honestly, will "terrorism" really serve as an excuse for this situation?*

The international treaty covered many different things. This was what Karasawa grasped from the present situation:

First, it covered the research, as well as use, of electromagnetic technology.

Second, the manufacture of any weapon capable of dealing grave damage to a municipal grid.

Third, the great expenditure of Earth's limited resources on any enormous product that didn't contribute to running the planet.

Fourth, the implementation of a cannon turret with a firing range of fifty kilometers or greater.

And fifth, it banned all of the above without special permission from the IGMO and prohibited the possession of such a weapon without a security council resolution.

Forget just the IGMO, these five facts alone trampled all over ten articles of the international treaty as written by the International Grid Security Council (IGSC), the International Electromagnetism Agency (IEA), and the World Resource Organization (WRO).

*But in the end, we're all birds of a feather.*

Indeed, every country had possessed illegal weapons of a similar nature since antiquity.

No nation abided by the rules. If there was one, it'd be an insignificant third world country. If nothing else, everyone trusted the rest of the world to violate the treaty—otherwise there'd be no need for the IGMO to have an inspecting body in the first place.

*It's precisely because of this unspoken truth that the penalty for the exposure of any illegal weapons always ended with mere sanctions. The real issue was that the rogue weapon wasn't under government control.*

*Frankly, things would be much simpler if that weapon had invaded a foreign country.*

*If that were the case, the situation would end with an international armed response. As extraordinarily powerful as that weapon is, it wouldn't be able to hold off the pressure forever. It would eventually meet its demise, succumbing to the difference in sheer numbers.*

*However powerful a weapon it may be, in the end, it's still just a single weapon of war. It isn't enough to sway the balance of power in the world and, tactically speaking, attacking with just a single unit severely limits your options.*

However, if such a weapon was pointing its cannon at its own country... then what?

The committee was switching gears. No longer satisfied with shouting at one another, they were now verbally lynching a Diet member with a suspicious background.

Watching the ensuing chaos, Karasawa inadvertently discovered the terrorists' endgame.

*I see. So this must be what the enemy was aiming for. Sons of bitches...*

· · ● · ·

"So you're saying that the feds and their military will self-destruct just by virtue of that weapon sitting there in Akihabara?" Marie muttered in a trembling voice. "And all the Shiga guys have to do is sit back and watch it happen?"

*You're telling me that weapon, or rather the people inside it, thought that far ahead?*

Vermouth confirmed Marie's suspicions with his gaze. "But if that conjecture's correct, then things will get troublesome. Ain't that right, kid?"

"Yeah. I mean, the Shiga guys have no intention of letting things end there."

"What do you mean by that?"

Naoto sighed, shaking his head. "I said that the weapon won't move... but at the same time it *can't* move."

"..."

"I don't know anything about electromagnetic technology... but it's not like it can just move without a power source, right?"

"Well yeah... the weapon should have a battery or generator of some sort," Marie muttered. "But..."

Naoto nodded. "That thing's power probably comes from gears."

"Huh?" Marie's jaw dropped.

*Is he saying that the weapon, equipped with technology antithetical to all clockwork devices, uses clockwork technology itself? But if that's the case, wouldn't it ruin itself?*

As question marks popped up all over Marie's face, Vermouth sighed.

"It appears they combined conductive gears with an insulator. So the weapon isn't simply a revival of ancient technology but a hybrid design that utilizes the best of both worlds."

Marie furrowed her brows. "It makes sense in theory... but is such a thing really possible?"

"They made it possible. That's precisely why that enormous object can still move after emitting an EMP," Vermouth sneered. "The mobile composite electromagnetic assault weapon, Yatsukahagi— that seems to be its official name. Feel free to laugh. After all, the ones who named it weren't the guys from Shiga but the feds."

"What'd you say?"

"In the blueprint my team found, the original proposal had

been thoughtfully attached alongside it. What do you think was written on it?"

Before Marie could answer, Vermouth spat: "'We hereby approve the research and production of a mobile composite electromagnetic assault weapon on the twenty-fifth of March in the 985th Year of the Wheel.' It came with the signatures of the prime minister, chief cabinet secretary, and minister of defense at the time, you know? What a riot, right?!"

Marie didn't find that the least bit funny.

"Well," Vermouth said, seeing her expression tense. "The power source of that enormous thing is no different from other clockwork devices. It uses spring generators that draw energy from gravity. I don't know how many it has in total though..."

"It has 1,033 of them. The sound they make is strange, but it's undeniably the sound of springs. And the enemy is currently recharging them."

Marie and Vermouth looked at Naoto in disbelief.

"That initial burst of light which caused that... what was it called, an electromagnetic pulse?" Naoto continued, paying no mind to their stares. "It probably used up all its power. I don't know why, but after that, it's been recharging. Sustaining itself on ten percent of its available power.

"Based on what I heard before we left Akihabara Grid, it'll take 71 hours, 32 minutes, and 12 seconds before it replenishes its full capacity. It's been five hours since then, so... there's roughly 66 hours remaining. It shouldn't be able to move during this time."

Vermouth was bewildered. "Oy kid, you've seen the blueprint?

No, that wouldn't be enough to explain how you know all that. Just who the hell are you, you bastard?"

"You said that for the next 66 hours and 30 minutes, that weapon can't move?" Marie pressed, ignoring Vermouth. "Are you certain?"

Naoto shook his head. "I'm not sure since I know absolutely nothing about electromagnetic technology. If it cuts off the charging to some of its armaments, it might be able to move sooner. Also, I don't know what it's been spending that ten percent on, but if it shuts off whatever's consuming that energy, the charging should speed up to the same extent, but that's not the problem."

"Wait... there's more?"

"Despite it being checkmate, they're still bothering to recharge the weapon," Vermouth interjected. "Do you still not get it, you sheltered princess?"

"...!"

Marie turned around to glare at him, but Vermouth merely laughed. "This isn't terrorism, it's a coup d'etat. Sure, they plan to wait for the feds to self-destruct, but from there it's on to phase two, whatever that may be."

At that moment, Marie finally understood. She was flabbergasted, dumbfounded. Her emerald eyes were as wide as saucers. There could only be one conclusion. The federal government was on its deathbed.

*So that's what Vermouth meant by "checkmate." Terrorism? This isn't anything so cute. They are on the verge of overthrowing the government.*

*No wonder they always get the better of us despite our crafty plans. Considering just how much time, how much obsession, how much endless spite Mie's—no, Shiga's—military of old must have put into their plan, it's only natural that we, reacting to an impending crisis, would be utterly crushed.*

*With that in mind, think about what you can do right now, Marie.*

*The enemy has the heart of Tokyo at knifepoint.*

*Akihabara Grid has been magnetized, so the control system bypass that we worked so hard to create is no longer an option.*

*And the cabinet is probably in total chaos right now, just as they planned.*

*As for what they plan to do afterwards, Naoto and Vermouth aren't sure either.*

*But at any rate, it's inevitable that the feds will self-destruct. And if other countries find out about that weapon... in the worst-case scenario, the IGMO might even consider an armed intervention.*

*If the use of Tall Wand, the anti-surface assault satellite, is authorized, then Tokyo will vanish from the Earth.*

*No, even if the international community doesn't take any action just yet, it would still only be a matter of time.*

*Best-case scenario: the Shiga guys succeed in their goal and seize control of this country.*

*If they're the ones in power, demagnetizing and restoring Akihabara might be possible, given their expertise in electromagnetic technology. However, in exchange, the entire world would view Japan as a rogue nation and immediately move forward with military sanctions.*

*In the worst-case scenario, the situation at hand is resolved through a foreign armed intervention.*

*That would probably be the quickest way to resolve things. However, that would also signify the destruction of Tokyo, something that would affect all of East Asia's grids and likely embroil the world in total war.*

*Such a horrifying possibility isn't so far-fetched, if I may say so myself. And...facing a situation of this scale, what can we even do at this point?*

*We've lost RyuZU and Halter, two big components of our fighting force, and AnchoR is currently without her supernatural combat capabilities. No, even if everyone was at a hundred percent, what could we do?*

*An imploding national government and an enormous weapon that complicates international affairs just by existing. Japan will surely end up in a stand-off with the principal nations of the world.*

*What could we, a few self-proclaimed terrorists, possibly do?*

*There's only one answer: absolutely nothing.*

The second Marie came to that conclusion, Naoto sprang to his feet, his face totally serious. "Hey AnchoR, let's go on a day trip somewhere."

"A...day trip?" The young automaton girl tilted her head, looking puzzled.

"Yeah, I mean, you haven't been able to do what you wanted to for a whole thousand years thanks to that cursed limiter, right? Let's go check out a bunch of different things," Naoto said, extending his hand towards her.

"Yay!" AnchoR grinned as she took Naoto's hand.

Marie stared at Naoto in disbelief. "Are your heart and nerves made of some sort of super tough alloy or something? What are you thinking? Are you planning to stroll around and shop?! You're one of the most wanted terrorists in the country right now!"

Upon seeing Naoto's gaze, she swallowed her breath.

She felt as if her heart had been clutched by something.

Naoto's eyes weren't wavering.

"Isn't it obvious?" With enough determination to rekindle Marie's fading hope, Naoto concluded: "I'm going out to do what I can."

· · ● · ·

"I'd like to order, please."

"Yeah! Yeah! Anything's fine! What is it?" Naoto nodded with a slovenly smile.

AnchoR happily beamed as she pointed towards a trinket shop two buildings down. "Can we take a look inside that store?"

"Any store is fine! If there's anything you want... heck, I'll buy out the whole store if you'd like!"

"Hey, Naoto," Marie called from behind him. She seemed to be looking through him rather than at him. She was out of sighs at this point. "I'll ask on the off chance that you actually have a good reason: what are you doing right now?"

"I'm doing what I should be doing right now!" Naoto

replied crisply, his gray eyes shining. "Everything that AnchoR-chan has wanted to do but couldn't all this time!! Now I'll grant all of her wishes with my own hands!! What else could there be besides that?!"

Marie didn't answer him. She simply smiled a dry, empty smile and looked up at the bright blue sky.

"The weather's nice today, isn't it? That reminds me, there was an ice cream shop I wanted to try. Maybe I should stop by before the sun sets on Tokyo," she muttered, her shoulders drooping. Her words were filled with calm resignation.

They were in a shopping district of Ueno Grid, situated immediately above Akihabara. The sign on the arch at the entrance read "Ameya Alley" in an old font. The street was filled with liveliness, almost as if the events of last night had just been a bad dream. It was daytime on a weekday, but there was no end to the number of people walking around.

Seeing the great amount of merchandise protruding onto the street and hearing the shouted deals from the stalls, Marie felt a strange sense of pity. None of the people around her suspected a thing.

After all, a gag order had been imposed. They knew nothing about the enormous weapon that had appeared in Akihabara this morning.

Marie had received a report from their mole, but even without it, she could have guessed that the government would take such a measure.

"An electromagnetic weapon that violates the international

treaty suddenly appeared out of nowhere in the center of Tokyo yesterday. Its goal is a coup d'etat, and even now, it's occupying Akihabara and putting all of Tokyo in danger of destruction."

*There's no way they could honestly report such a thing. The feds... no, not just them, anyone who would be inconvenienced by the truth will use their full authority to censor the news.*

*It was the obvious response.*

*We're talking about a national-level crisis, not to mention that it all stemmed from something that the feds sowed in the first place.*

*As Naoto anticipated and Vermouth stated, that weapon is a bomb that has dealt a lethal blow just by surfacing in Tokyo. It's obvious that it would spell bad news if the citizens found out about it, but it'd be even worse for them if the various member nations of the IGMO found out.*

*Really, how ironic. For the feds, there's a silver lining—thanks to the EMP, all the equipment that could prove its existence was silenced.*

On top of that, because Marie and Naoto had issued an advance notice of their own terrorist attack, Akihabara's residents had all been evacuated. Because of that, they had served to divert the citizens' attention as well.

Looking up, Marie saw a large street-side television reporting on the Akihabara Terror Incident from last night.

"Due to advance notice regarding a plot to freeze Akihabara, the city is currently under lockdown. The government has prohibited travel to the city to ensure the safety of all metropolitan residents. Furthermore, the government has announced that the identities of the terrorists have already been determined and that they have a promising lead on their whereabouts. Chief Cabinet Secretary Orihata remarked that..."

Of course, the feds hadn't actually discovered anything about Marie's group.

*It appears that even at this late a stage, the feds still want to hide the existence of the weapon from the populace. They must be idiots,* Marie scoffed.

*Once that weapon starts up again, the truth will be known. Not to mention that if even one scoop-hungry journalist ignores the lockdown and takes a news helicopter down into Akihabara right now, it'll all be over.*

*However... if Naoto and Vermouth are right, that's exactly what those Shiga guys want to happen.*

*The more the government tries to cover up the weapon that destroyed Akihabara, the angrier both their own citizens and other countries will be when the truth is exposed. If that happens, the populace and the rest of the world could become bigger threats to the current government than the weapon itself.*

*And what have the feds been doing in the meantime? Nothing but pointing fingers at each other in an attempt to shield themselves from blame.*

"*Hmph,*" Marie snorted, looking up at the sky through her sunglasses.

*Seeing yet another high-speed helicopter fly past,* she smirked. *I'd be willing to bet that one is a fleeing government official.*

"Playing the victim and seeking asylum abroad, huh? It's only a matter of time before knowledge of the situation spreads to the neighboring countries."

*In short, this peaceful and lively everyday scenery will end in a few more hours. What will befall all of Tokyo then is surely...*

"Fath... Mother, I'd like you to give me an order, please."

"Yes, yes! Papa will let you do anything you want. No, I mean Mama will!"

Marie slumped.

*Just...what am I doing right now?*

Mother wasn't Marie. That's not to say that Marie had ever accepted AnchoR calling her that in the first place, but in short—AnchoR was addressing Naoto, who'd replied with a sloppy, smitten expression.

Going out in public required them to disguise themselves. One might think that was all there was to it, but the process had been nightmarish for Marie.

The automata girls' makeup artist, who Konrad had introduced them to, had been a massive deviant. She was a gaudy woman who was the very picture of the term "lady of the night."

"Kyah!" she yelled the second that Naoto and Marie entered the dressing room. "How wonderful! Dr. Konrad! Can I really dress up these little cuties?! I'm gonna get serious, you know?!"

"Yes, I'm counting on you."

"Ufufu~♪ It's been so long since I dressed up humans! I'm dying to show off what I can do once I get my hands on them.♡"

An indescribable chill ran down Marie's spine. Naoto looked somewhat uneasy himself, at least at first, but...

In a dazzling flurry, the makeup artist ripped off Naoto's clothes, applied light makeup to his face, put a wig on him, and clothed him in a dress. Finally, she had him stand in front of a mirror.

"H-huh? Holy crap, could it be...that I'm actually pretty cute?"

Naoto had acquired a new kink.

As Marie was caught in despair, AnchoR's eyes glittered next to her.

"Father, you look cute... ngh."

Receiving AnchoR's praise, Naoto immediately snapped to attention. "I see! I see! So Papa really is cute! If AnchoR-chan says so then it's like God said so, so I guess I *am* cuuute ♡," Naoto yelled as he picked AnchoR up in his arms and spun joyfully right out the store.

*What an admirable pervert. I'm jealous even. I too wish that I could just forget everything and chase after butterflies right now...*

"Now then ♪, you're up next sweetie!"

"I'm just fine thank you!!" Marie rejected the poison fangs of the perverted woman with all the strength that she could muster. *Who knows what I'll end up looking like if I leave myself in this woman's hands.*

*You could say that managing to quickly rearrange my hair, snatch a pair of sunglasses, and find a suitable change of clothes before scrambling away to safety was the silver lining to that mess...*

"Seriously," Marie muttered, dispelling the cursed memory with a shake of her head. "What's everyone doing while a bomb that's likely to lead to a regional—no, an international crisis—is sparking right before our eyes?"

Apparently, Naoto heard her mutter with his sharp ears. "It can't be helped, can it? How can the people here make a fuss over something they don't know about? I was in the same position during Kyoto's incident until you showed up. That's just how it is."

"I'm talking about people like you—you total pervert!!" Marie shouted angrily. "You're in the group of people who know the truth, aren't you?! Worry a bit, won't you?! Actually, before that..."

Sensing that they were making a scene, Marie quickly lowered her voice. Still, she was unable to stifle her anger.

She glared at Naoto. "Have some restraint, would you? So you have a fetish for cross-dressing on top of everything else? I see that your disease has finally become terminal!"

Naoto had declared that he was going to do what should be done. The boy had displayed the resolve to accept any sacrifice necessary to that end.

*Yeah, okay. Considering that we might all be dead soon enough, I'll admit it. His decisiveness, his resolve, his unwavering pro-activeness... those are the things that I lack right now. Naive as I was, I was even moved for a second back there.*

*And yet, this was the action the pervert decided to take using any means necessary with his perverted pro-activeness and judgment, even going so far as to brave the risk of being discovered by our enemies. A fun and relaxed date in drag with a little machine girl.*

*If we weren't in public, I'd take him to the ground this very second and beat him until he blacked out.*

"Fath... Mother... is it... okay for me to want that?"

"My, what a cute stuffed animal that is! AnchoR-chan, you have great taste. Forget permission to want it, I'll buy it for you!"

Lost on cloud nine, the pervert and the doll paid no mind to Marie, who was doing her best not to commit murder.

*To be honest, even now, I'd still love nothing more than to drag him into an alley and beat him to death.* A different thought suddenly popped into Marie's mind.

"Hey, Naoto-chan. You're acting quite generous, but if I recall correctly, wasn't RyuZU the one who earned that money for you?"

Naoto tilted his head looking puzzled. "Yeah, what about it?"

"You're always calling RyuZU your wife, and yet you're going to spend her money on some other girl?" Marie looked at him as if he were scum.

"Stupid fool," Naoto countered. "RyuZU is my wife and AnchoR is my daughter. What's wrong with a parent spending money on his child?"

"I...get it now, so just do whatever you want."

"Sure, I would've anyway, even without you telling me to!"

*Really now, what am I doing?* Marie thought.

First, she detested how she couldn't do anything about the current shit-show. Second, it irked her that there was a multi-modal pervert enjoying a merry old date at a time like this. And third, and possibly most of all, it pissed her off that said incorrigible pervert—

"Oy, Mama! If you don't hurry up, we're gonna leave you behind, you know?!" Naoto yelled, waving at her.

—actually looked damn good as a girl. Every part of him.

Marie groaned and looked away. In the display window of a boutique shop she saw her own reflection. She looked like a teen-age girl from a foreign country. Her light-blonde hair was put up in a ponytail which showed off the straps of her thin, almost transparent camisole. She'd concealed her characteristic emerald eyes behind a pair of heavily shaded sunglasses.

Turning her eyes towards the pervert in front of her, she saw what appeared to be—if she turned a blind eye to everything she knew—a beautiful teenage girl. One that might be found on the cover of some fashion magazine.

Naoto was wearing a thin, blue summer coat over his dress and soft, high-laced boots. He had a childish but well-proportioned face and pristine, porcelain skin due to being such a shut-in. With the wig and the cat-eared hoodie as well... he looked like a real girl through and through...

That cherubic-looking girl was laughing as she walked alongside an even more cherubic-looking child—which one would be hard-pressed to believe was actually an automaton. They were holding hands.

*Who would ever think that they could be terrorists?*

In this congested crowd of people, the two of them gathered attention simply by walking together. All of the onlookers saw them as a pleasant sight for sore eyes.

*Yeah, why don't I just kill them? That'd be lovely.*

Without realizing that she was drawing plenty of fascinated attention from the crowd herself, Marie chased after the two of them.

• • ● • •

A nearby street television was playing a detailed follow-up report on the Akihabara Terror Incident:

"This boy is Naoto Miura, age 16. He is a prime suspect believed to be involved in the bootlegging of illegal military automata parts and the trafficking of illegally modified automata.

"Our experts have pointed out he likely has ties to the international armed organization Avant Ceglie. The suspect appears to have been attending Tadasunomori High School, a public school in Kyoto as a cover.

"However, it is extremely likely that the information in his family register is fabricated, so the police and the military are requesting those who may know anything about him to step forward."

A blown-up picture of Naoto in his normal attire was displayed on the gigantic screen. It must have been a picture taken of him on the rooftop last night, as Halter could be seen in the background.

Across the street from the public television, that very same villainous fiend of a boy—Naoto—couldn't keep from grinning.

"Wow, I'm really something else, aren't I? What's that supposed to be anyway? The backstory for the protagonist of a manga?" He shuddered as he sipped his cold vanilla shake.

"Well, yeah," Marie answered sardonically, stuffing her face with apple pie. "No one would believe them if they announced that the one who pulled off such a grand terrorist plot was just some high school student. It'd be humiliating for them if they don't play you up."

"Even so, didn't they put too much effort into it? I mean, what's this 'Avant Ceglie' thing about?"

"If I remember correctly, it's an armed organization that's having a grand old time in Europe. Some pretentious idiot called Cagliostro is the leader. In reality, they're just a small group that focuses on international fraud."

"Oh, I see," Naoto replied, not seeming particularly interested. He pouted. "Actually, all things considered, shouldn't the one on the screen be you, not me? 'An illegitimate clocksmith who participates in terrorist activities while attending school with a falsified family register.' When you think about it, there's someone here who fits that bill perfectly."

"Don't point your straw at me, pervert," Marie groaned, sipping her chocolate shake.

"The man beside him is Vainney Halter, age unknown. He is a full-body cyborg mercenary, and there are records of him being involved in many international conflicts. He also has a reputation as an infamous professional terrorist."

Marie's eyes widened. "Well would you look at that, they're actually reporting the truth on Halter."

"Wow, really? Old man Halter comes from that sort of background? Well, I guess it makes sense. He's tough enough to serve as a bodyguard for a walking bomb like you, after all."

"Who are you calling a walking bomb? Well, Halter's supposedly famous in that line of work, you know? Famous enough that the talking head knew of him."

"Two female students who were reportedly friends of the

suspect went missing around the same time. Their safety is currently a matter of concern."

The faces of a blonde-haired girl and a silver-haired girl—Marie and RyuZU—appeared on the screen. Considering that they were wearing uniforms, the pictures were probably taken from the school's student register.

Naoto looked dissatisfied. "The ringleader is treated as a victim while old man Halter and I are treated as international villains... Life's really unfair, isn't it? Well, whatever."

"It's probably karma for your everyday conduct as opposed to mine."

"I'm a saint compared to you." Naoto scowled, but his expression changed as he suddenly remembered something. "By the way, is this gonna be okay for you? They're displaying your photo on live TV when you should be dead, you know?"

"Don't worry. They'll never suspect that the girl in the picture is the 'deceased' Marie."

"Why?"

*Did you use the authority of the Breguets or something?* Naoto looked as if he wanted to ask.

"I can guess what you're thinking, but you're off the mark. I'm the one who severed my ties with the Breguet family, so there's no way I can borrow their authority." Marie narrowed her eyes slightly. "I... simply took the liberty of using my elder sister's cover. That's why it's absolutely impossible for anyone to catch me. Apart from her."

*And to be honest, when I think about what would happen if*

*she were to find out, I think I'd rather be caught by the military or the police.*

• • ● • •

Throwing her paper cup and wrappings into the trash can, Marie sighed. She left the restaurant and walked to where Naoto and AnchoR were waiting, musing over a question she'd thrown on the back burner.

*In the end, what does the situation look like right now?*

*Funnily enough, the feds are using our previous actions to their own advantage. It's incredibly frustrating, but at least there haven't been any civilian casualties thanks to our precautionary measures.*

*Who knows how many tens of thousands of people would have died from the initial cannon shot or the accidents following the EMP? Without Akihabara's evacuation, things could have been far worse.*

*In that sense, our actions weren't completely meaningless. That's the one thing we can take pride in. But now, it's being used against us. We've indirectly helped the feds cover up the incident and that's ultimately aiding Shiga's ex-military in their plans.*

*I find that fact simply—*

"Mother... I'd like you to give me an order, please."

"Huh, eh, what?" Marie jolted up, having lost her train of thought. AnchoR was right there in front of her, looking up at her with a worried face.

"Mother... you're crying. Please give me an order to help you."

*Crying? Me?* Marie inadvertently felt the corners of her eyes just to be sure, but they were dry. *As I suspected, even if "Y" was the one who made her, an automaton's an automaton in the end. She might not be able to process human expressions very well. Somehow, that feels like a relief... wait, why should I feel relieved?*

*Before Marie could answer her own question...*

"You're crying. You're saying 'help me.' That's why I'd like an order to help you, please."

"..."

Marie was *really* astonished. It hadn't been very clear to her until now, but Marie felt something like disgust towards AnchoR. But upon those words, that disgust had lost purchase and was now lingering inside her with nowhere to go.

*AnchoR's an automaton. There's no doubt about that.*

Marie could understand the psychology behind loving a doll as a doll. She thought dolls were cute as well. However, as a completely separate matter, the clocksmith within her still thought of *it* as just a man-made creation.

*Automata aren't human, in the same way that I'm not an automaton. In that case, is it weird of me to want dolls to act like dolls? No, it's common sense.*

*It's also only natural that I feel disgust towards her uncanniness. She's helped me realize that she makes me feel uncomfortable, something that I was previously unaware of.*

"Is...AnchoR not good enough to help you?"

*No. This is weird. It's impossible.*

Marie didn't know of any doll that acted like this. A human-

101

shaped automaton was expressing sorrow right in front of her, and it just didn't feel right. It defied any logical sense.

"Well, in that case, AnchoR—can you destroy that thing?"

*I shouldn't think too deeply about this,* Marie's intuition told her. Obeying that, Marie gave the doll the order.

"Would that help Mother?"

"Yeah, that's right. If you could damage that thing enough that some of its abilities are limited, the situation would change considerably."

*If I can use AnchoR to change things, that would be the best choice. If that enormous weapon is destroyed before the public finds out about the current gag order, the situation will improve greatly. At the very least, things won't go according to their plans.*

*Since we were the ones who broadcast the advance notice of our terrorist attack...*

*"Everything was just a terrorist plot that the government successfully subjugated." If that narrative passes in the public eye, then the situation will come to a better conclusion than where it's currently headed.*

"Well then, Father will help you, Mother," AnchoR replied with the smile of a pure and innocent child. "So don't cry, okay?"

Marie was dumbfounded. *What are you talking about?* Marie reflexively searched for Naoto.

"Wha... hey, Nao... wh-what's wrong with you?!" Marie barely managed to restrain herself from screaming. She rushed towards him, flustered.

Naoto was sitting on the ground by the roadside panting heavily, his face completely pale.

"Ah, Marie. Hey, mind getting me a migraine pill...? An anesthetic would be fine, too, as long as it doesn't make me fall asleep," Naoto said with a strained smile, his face covered in sweat.

Getting a close look at him, Marie finally realized...

"Hey... wait... what happened to your headphones?!"

"What the heck are you saying? They broke back in Akihabara..."

*That's right. He threw them away right in front of my eyes. But more importantly...*

"If you have the time to pamper a doll then go buy new headphones first! How stupid can you be?!"

Marie couldn't imagine the world that Naoto perceived, but even she could faintly hear the strange noises coming from below Akihabara.

*There's no way that Naoto doesn't hear that.*

*Actually, considering that Naoto has been talking to us through 100% noise-cancelling headphones this whole time, now that he's not wearing them, wouldn't the world be way too loud for him? Not to mention we're in the middle of a bustling street right now!*

Naoto shook his head with a weak smile. "I don't need them yet. If I buy them now, I'm not confident that I'll be able to stand not putting them on."

"This isn't the time to be saying stupid crap like that! Do you know how pale your face looks?! You look like you're about to die!"

"Ah! Please stop, Marie. The temptation is seriously hard for me to resist right now."

*The temptation? What?* Marie was confused by what Naoto was saying, but looking into his eyes, she found her answer. His gray, quivering eyes told her everything she needed to know.

*"If I lose focus right now, I'll immediately want to drive a screwdriver into my head and end it."* That's what his eyes were telling her.

"Once I find what I'm looking for, I'll go buy new headphones as fast as humanly possible," Naoto groaned. "Even without you telling me to. So please just get me some painkillers for now."

"A-all right," Marie nodded, overpowered by Naoto's resolve. "But what are you looking for Naoto?"

*There should have been a drugstore at the corner of the last street we were on...* Almost in two places at once, Marie looked around in a panic to confirm it.

In contrast to Marie, who by AnchoR's estimate had been "on the verge of tears," Naoto's eyes were filled to the brim with a fierce, almost uncontrollable determination.

"It's obvious," he said. "I'm looking for a way to win! Some way that we can beat the crap out of the ones who had the gall to do such a thing to RyuZU!"

• • ● • •

"Father, can you please order me to pet your head?"

"Oh, sure, sure! Father will recover in no time if you pet his head!" Naoto was happily playing with AnchoR. Throwing caution to the wind, he had taken painkillers. An entire pack of them.

*It's true that I was a little worried by his pained face.*

Except in the moments when he touched AnchoR, Naoto's face had been twisted the whole time. It wasn't simply due to the pain from his burns.

*Naoto should be feeling pain much greater than that right now.*

"..."

Marie looked down in silence. She was ashamed of herself.

*When all's said and done, Naoto has been doing what he said he would this whole time.*

*He's been doing what he could.*

*On the other hand, I've been simply standing around doing nothing, stuck worrying about things beyond my control.*

"Marie," said Naoto, looking up from petting AnchoR. "Just making sure but: Akihabara is one of the components that makes up Tokyo Multiple Grid, so it can't be purged, right?"

"Yes. While it isn't impossible for the system to execute its purge, all of Tokyo would be affected, so it wouldn't make any sense."

Clock towers governed the municipal functions of the grids, the core tower governed the clock towers, and the horological control tower (colloquially known as the Pillar of Heaven) governed every core tower in Japan.

Unlike the core towers, which extended deep underground, the Pillar of Heaven was an enormous structure that reached towards the heavens.

"It's easy to understand if you think of Tokyo as one big clock. If Akihabara Grid is purged, all of Tokyo might collapse along with it. If that happens, it might start a chain reaction affecting all of Japan. At the worst, all of East Asia could be devastated. That's how much of an effect purging Akihabara can have."

"In that case." Naoto smiled. "Thinking about it the other way, even if Akihabara Grid isn't functioning, it should still be possible to alter its current condition from a neighboring grid, right? Ah, thanks to you, Papa's all better now, AnchoR!"

"Really? You mean it? You still look like you're hurting, Father..."

"If it's for the sake of my wife and daughter, this level of pain is nothing! So, going back to what I was saying..." Naoto flashed a daring smile. "We can just heat it up or burn it if that's easier. Akihabara Grid, I mean, and that weapon along with it."

"..."

Marie stared in mute amazement. Words wouldn't come to her.

*The bypass we used when we broadcast our fake warning has been magnetized and is no longer usable.*

*Even if it weren't, that plan isn't as simple as Naoto's making it out to be. Given that our bypass is out of order, it should already be impossible to manipulate Akihabara Grid's municipal functions, but...*

"Even if one grid stops functioning, the neighboring grids will shoulder its functions and maintain the status quo, right? If the status quo can be maintained, then naturally, it should be possible to destroy it as well. Right?"

*Just as he said he would, this whole time the guy has been thinking of nothing but how to boil Shiga's ex-military alive.*

"So, have you discovered anything useful?" Marie asked, feeling half-relieved.

"Not yet. I've found several bypasses, but it seems like going through Ueno Grid alone won't have much of an effect.

"It's probably just like you said, Tokyo Multiple Grid is one system and the countless intertwined governing mechanisms are covering for Akihabara Grid's burden right now, but just one more... if I can confirm just one more thing...

"I'll beat them," Naoto snarled like a wounded animal. "And beat them until those bastards cry. Until then, I'm not going to wear any headphones."

Naoto sat AnchoR on his shoulders and rose with a carefree smile, as if he were a different person.

"But finding things that AnchoR-chan wants to do is important as well! She has to take back a thousand years' worth of desires! How could I make her wait any longer?! Alrighty, where should we go next, AnchoR! Should we check out some clothes? Although, the ones you're wearing right now are cute already! I have absolutely no complaints about them!"

"But Father... Mother asked me if I can destroy that..." AnchoR muttered from atop his shoulders.

Naoto whirled around in anger. "Marie! You were still saying things like that?!"

"Y-yeah... after all, if she can destroy it, then—" *It'd be a much quicker and easier solution than trying to heat Akihabara up through its neighboring grids.*

"That's a no," Naoto interrupted. "Absolutely not! What do you take AnchoR-chan to be, you walking land mine?"

*Well obviously,* the clocksmith inside her observed. *An*

107

*automaton that's the embodiment of absurd and unreasonable vio-*
*lence. Isn't she a weapon that was made precisely for times like these?*

"If AnchoR were in perfect shape, then yeah," Naoto continued before Marie could answer. "She could easily send that un-
seemly piece of junk off to the recycling plant. AnchoR's a strong
one after all, but..."

"Uhm... I'm sorry..."

"You don't need to apologize, AnchoR! There's no need to
listen to the babbling nonsense of a walking land mine. Especially
when she pretends not to know any better."

"Wha—" Marie reflexively tried to defend herself, but Naoto
glared at her.

"Didn't she say that she needs to recharge? I'm pretty sure I
remember that she was using her Twelfth Balance Wheel when
she was fighting RyuZU. If she used that right now, she'd only last
a few seconds. A few seconds from AnchoR's frame of reference,
to be clear.

"In any case, she'd have to revert back to her First Balance
Wheel after that, so she'd be left vulnerable in the same state that
she's in right now. So, even as powerful as AnchoR-chan is, do
you really think it's reasonable to ask her to destroy that stupidly
enormous piece of garbage in such a short amount of time?"

"That's..."

"In order to operate for a meaningful amount of time at her
greatest output, she needs to continue storing the excess energy
that her perpetual gear is putting out.

"Let's see..." Naoto paused to strain his ears. "It'll take about

160 hours. The enemy will become operational before that... so forget the convenient thought of making AnchoR solve everything. And, more importantly," he added with a hint of scorn. "Don't go and shove all the burden onto a child! Were you planning to just sit back and watch? How selfish can you be?! Aren't you ashamed? Frankly, I'm disgusted with you."

"Ngh!"

Marie trembled. Her blood was boiling. The words "humiliation" and "shame" could barely scratch the surface of the emotions that were broiling her brain.

"But Father... Is there any other way—?"

"There isn't. But even without another option, having you fight against that thing is rejected, denied, forbidden, and absolutely no good!"

"...O-okay..." Overpowered by Naoto, AnchoR fell into silence.

*What are they talking about?* Marie was irritated that the conversation had drifted away from her again. It was a pattern that she had grown to hate. Once again, things were being decided through alien logic and morality that were completely foreign to her. Left out of the picture, she could only grind her teeth in frustration.

"I'm sorry," AnchoR said from atop Naoto's shoulders, hanging her head down.

Marie's heart was pierced by the sorrowful tone of AnchoR's voice.

"Wow, Marie," Naoto said mockingly. "Making a child who's been depressed for a thousand years even sadder. Could this be the very peak of sadism?"

"N-no, that's not what I was trying to d—"

"I'm sorry, Mother."

"I told you to stop calling me that. Argh no, come on! I get it! I understand! I was wrong, I'm sorry! So don't make that face!!" Even Marie herself didn't understand what she was trying to say.

*Lamenting this, lamenting that, and in the end, coming up with nothing.*

*And to top it all off, I had the immature thought of resolving the situation by conveniently leaving everything to a little girl.*

*And while I've been trying to pass the buck, Naoto has been... no, even now, he's gathering as much information as he can. He's been practically killing himself to come up with a way to break the impasse we're in.*

*Now that I think about it, ever since the* EMP *hit, this guy hasn't stopped for a single moment.*

*And you, Marie Bell Breguet?*

*Just what have you been doing?*

"..."

Marie clenched her teeth so hard that it felt like her molars would crack.

*If I continue to become this pathetic at every little surprise, I'm really gonna come to hate myself.*

*Just how many times, how many hours, how many days, how many years am I going to twiddle my thumbs before I finally learn my lesson...?!*

"Naoto."

"Yeah, yeah, what?"

"Sorry, but I'll be heading back before you guys. AnchoR, can I leave this guy in your care?"

"If that's Mother's order..."

"It isn't an order. It's a request. I'll leave Naoto to you. If you guys are found by the police or the military, shake them off as best you can and return to base."

At that moment, for the very first time, Marie treated AnchoR not as a doll but as a comrade. Only AnchoR picked up on it.

"Okay, a request. It's much more important than an order..." Seeing AnchoR nod with a smile like a blossoming flower, Marie nodded as well.

Naoto didn't ask where she was going.

Marie didn't tell him either.

*My brain is finally working again after that fiasco with the EMP. That's all there is to it.*

*I'm simply going to do what I can—what I should be doing—without hesitation, I'm going to give it all I've got!*

· ·• ● •· ·

"Mother wasn't crying anymore," AnchoR said after Marie disappeared from their sight. "Father, you're amazing!"

"She's actually an amazing person too, you know," Naoto whispered to her with a somewhat ambiguous smile. "She's a genius."

"Ge-ni-us?"

"Yeah, it means she's a super amazing person."

"She's...more amazing than amazing?"

AnchoR's eyes opened wide. She hugged her stuffed animal and Naoto felt at ease. The two resumed their walk.

"Yeah! It's a secret that I said that though!"

He began to walk faster and faster, breaking into a jog.

"That girl wastes her time worrying about the strangest things, but when push comes to shove, she's a genius that always pulls through in a pinch. She's different from a guy like me."

*Geniuses probably have their own worries that only they can understand,* Naoto thought. *But even so, for a genius like her to waste her time stressing over trivial things is annoying, to put it mildly.*

*I mean, for someone to be so smart that they loop right back around into stupid, now that really is idiotic.*

"Well, it looks like I'm feeling a little better, so let's do what we can as well! All right, let's go somewhere that's a little further away next. Full speed ahead!"

"Okay." Atop his shoulders, AnchoR was lost in thought as the wind brushed past her face.

*My amazing father is saying that my mother is even more amazing than amazing. If the two of them are here, no one will have to die. Everyone will be saved and start smiling again. Big Sister, too!*

Feeling hope for the future for the first time in a thousand years, AnchoR smiled.

"…"

"Father, I'd like you to give me an order, please."

"R-right… umm, yeah, you see… there's a sporting goods store, over there, so…" Naoto wheezed, his voice began to flag. "C-could you buy me some water…and an oxygen can?"

Without the slightest paternal dignity, he slowly wilted until he was fully prostrate on the ground. Lungs heaving, he couldn't do anything but watch as AnchoR scurried off to the store.

● ● ● ● ●

"Excuse me, Prime Minister. What...did you say just now?" the Minister of Defense asked, his voice trembling. He spoke for everyone present.

The meaningless, fruitless conference of the Anti-Terror Committee was still going strong. The conference had been adjourned several times. It was now in its fifth meeting.

In face of what the prime minister—the representative of the ruling party—had just said out of nowhere, none of the committee members could conceal their astonishment or terror.

The prime minister shook his head, seeming dissatisfied with the committee's response. "It's just like I said. I was on the hotline with the IGMO just now, and I've just finished explaining the situation. And..." He took a breath before emphatically declaring: "I made an emergency request for the use of Tall Wand on Akihabara Grid."

The meeting room didn't erupt into a clamor. Just the opposite, everyone was flabbergasted. The room was filled with silence.

The chief cabinet secretary looked as though he had chewed a bitter pill. He stepped forward from behind the prime minister, who was puffing up his chest, full of confidence.

"The gag order is reaching its limits," he explained in a strained voice. "It's only a matter of time before our present situation is discovered by other countries.

"Once that happens, they will eventually propose the use of Tall Wand on Japan. Regardless of which nation brings it up, it's inevitable that all the countries of Asia will oppose it, in which case a war is likely to happen."

*We know that already,* everyone in the room thought at once. *At the very least, aside from the prime minister, everyone in this room should have swallowed that solemn truth.*

*Wasn't the purpose of this committee to decide what to do based on that premise, and isn't that also why we've been arguing at an impasse this whole time?*

"But," the chief cabinet secretary continued, everyone staring on in mute amazement. "If we request assistance with resolving the situation by reporting this national scandal ourselves, then it's a different story. We'll disclose all the information on the target that we currently have to the IGMO and have them destroy it along with the grid.

"As of right now, the militaries of the neighboring countries and Meister Guild are heading towards us as quickly as possible. This is the best action we can take to keep the damage caused by destroying Akihabara Grid to the bare minimum. This is also our best means of avoiding the worst-case scenario: a world war. That's the prime minister's reasoning."

The terrifying tone of the words made it apparent to all the members present how he really felt.

Everyone simply had one thought. It was a singular question

that, for a single miraculous moment, united the opinions of the committee members for the very first time.

"What the hell are you saying?"

*If it's a joke, it's in poor taste, and if it's the truth, that makes it even nastier.*

"Prime Minister!" the Minister of Defense bellowed. "Do you have your wits about you?! I can present countless rebuttals, and calling what you just did above your legal authority wouldn't be enough!!"

"It's an emergency right now," the prime minister replied, composed.

Everyone was at a loss for words.

"As this country's prime minister," he said, puffing out his chest. "I hereby declare a state of national emergency! The fate of the nation is in jeopardy right now. We don't have the luxury of waiting for the target, Yatsukahagi, to begin moving again!"

*He really did it! That god damn son of a bitch... ugh!* As angry roars filled the room, Karasawa felt a chill creeping up his spine.

*There's an utter fool here. Not the prime minister. He's not even worth mentioning. But I'm certain there's a god damn son of a bitch here, an utter fool who gave our idiot prime minister that insane idea. Who inflated our idiot prime minister's ego? Look at him, he really thinks he's the cock of the walk.*

*Here is what happened:*

*"Even if you stay quiet and continue observing the situation, in the end you'll be forced to take responsibility and resign. In that case, why not avoid that scenario by making an appeal to the citizens as*

*well as other countries, showing that you're a sincerely faithful prime minister? After the situation is resolved, you can evade responsibility by blaming everything on the previous administration that held power in this country for so long."*

*That's the nonsense that the fool crammed into the prime minister's head.*

*In the first place, do you think that if you request the use of Tall Wand, that the* IGMO *will answer with "Understood, it'll be delivered to you in thirty minutes," like a pizza or something?*

Tall Wand was the most powerful anti-surface weapon of mass destruction in known existence. It was made using the scientific theories from the ancient era. An orbital satellite, Tall Wand worked by dropping a rod made of heavy alloy at something on the Earth's surface from its platform up in space.

While there were no records of its use, Tall Wand was understood to possess a destructive power that could easily pulverize a city. Using it required a majority vote of at least three-fourths of the IGMO's executive committee.

*However, as there are currently seven Asian countries in the executive committee, getting a favorable decision would not be easy.*

*There's no way that this idiot, who I'm not even sure knows what kind of weapon Tall Wand is, has the diplomatic skills to get the* IGMO *to authorize its use in such a short time.*

*Which means this is all a part of someone's pre-arranged scenario. Everything's been scripted from the start!*

"Yes, you're right! A declaration of national emergency is in order! After all, Prime Minister, the nation will be left in ruins if it's left to an incompetent like you!!" the Minister of Defense bellowed, the veins by his temples popping.

Rebuked right to his face, the prime minister unsurprisingly responded in kind. "Watch your mouth, Mr. Tokita! Who do you think I—"

"Shut up! I have no intention of speaking with a traitor. In light of this national crisis, I hereby strip you of all your power by my authority as this country's Minister of Defense!

"As of now, the military will temporarily seize the authority of the prime minister!" the Minister of Defense continued shouting with the intensity of a conflagration. "At the same time, we indict you for inciting civil unrest as well as treason!!"

"Wh-what did you say?!" the prime minister—or rather, the ex-prime minister—yelled, looking startled.

"You!" the Minister of Defense howled, slamming a thick bundle of documents on the table in front of him. "Despite knowing of that illegal weapon's dangers, you gave it your tacit consent! The evidence that you tried to use it to strengthen your political foothold is right here!

"As soon as that plan failed, you conspired with foreign countries to greatly harm our nation just so that you could escape responsibility! This is none other than a breach of faith against our nation!"

"Th-that's a false accusation! What do you think you're saying?!"

"Your squirming is unsightly! The evidence is already in order! Play the tape!!"

The second the Minister of Defense said it, a video was projected onto the enormous screen hanging on the front wall of the meeting room.

It showed a somewhat dimly lit room. In the center was an old man wearing an aged military uniform. He was sitting in a chair. The lighting was too dim to make out the expression on his face, but the old man said indifferently:

"I'm sorry, Prime Minister, but you belittle us by trying to use us as a tool. If you're looking down on us as naive ideologues who fancy themselves revolutionaries, then you shall pay with your blood. We shall impeach those of you in the federal government and mete out our enmity and indignation on equal terms."

The short video ended, and the room was filled with commotion. It was a clamor of animosity and outrage directed towards the prime minister.

"Ex-prime minister," the Minister of Defense shouted in triumph. "This is the enemy's proclamation of criminal intent that our public security police found on your computer. Pretending to be a faithful public servant while concealing something like this is a joke, isn't it?!"

"I-I've never seen this video before! I know nothing of this!!"

"Shut it! We'll hear all your excuses in the interrogation room. Take him away!" Two military officers that had been standing behind the Minister of Defense stepped forward and tried to escort the ex-prime minister outside.

However, a Minister of State blocked their way. "With all due respect, Minister of Defense! I'd like you to hear what I have to say as well! Two weeks ago, a section of the military was given an order to go on standby, which resulted in a hole in Tokyo's security force's defenses! Isn't that the underlying cause of that terrorist broadcast from Akihabara?! Actually, who *but* the Technical Force of Tokyo's military would have the technology and knowledge to make that possible?!"

"Wh-what are you trying to say?!"

"Are you not currently playing the part of the hero in a situation you helped instigate?!"

"What nonsense! That's an insult that I can't let slide, you bastard!!"

"In that case, I'd like you to answer my question!"

At this point, the meeting was in such pandemonium that no one could put things back in order. Before Karasawa realized it, even the prime minister, who had been in the middle of being escorted out, was a part of the clamor again, set on repeating his own claims without a clue as to what anyone else was saying.

*There's no doubt about it at this point. Someone's definitely pulling the strings here...* Karasawa groaned, a step away from the center of the commotion. *Everything's simply falling into place too perfectly.*

*Whether it be the prime minister acting at his own discretion, a coup d'état by the military, or the indictment against the Minister of Defense, it all happened like clockwork.*

*Things will no longer end with just the collapse of the cabinet. It's only a matter of time before all the different factions of the federal government fracture and a civil war begins.*

*Is it the double agent from Shiga's ex-military described in the intelligence report provided by Dr. Marie? No, in this whole chain of events, the Akihabara Terror Incident was the one thing that the mastermind shouldn't have accounted for.*

That event had been an unprecedented miracle. Even having known all the details, Karasawa had doubted the plan was possible when he first heard it.

But now, even that unforeseeable miracle was being used as a part of the script.

*A monster who's successfully using even the magic of Dr. Marie's group against us. Is the identity of that monster really Shiga's ex-military?*

*I can't help but feel that isn't quite right.*

Taking a good look at the room, which was currently embroiled in chaos—Karasawa became reluctantly convinced: *I'm the only one capable of thinking rationally in this room.*

*Has the situation thrown them into disarray, or are these the true faces of our excellent elected officials?*

While hoping for the former as a Japanese citizen, Karasawa concluded: *At this point, I have no choice but to investigate matters myself... though it's extremely dangerous.*

*What can I do? I guess, it's my job as a consultant... No, actually, this clearly falls outside of the call of duty, doesn't it?* Karasawa shook his head with a bitter smile.

At the same time, his sharp gaze focused on one person. A suspicious man who, like himself, wasn't taking part in the commotion. A step apart, that man was currently trying to sneak out of the room.

*Well then, I guess I'll have you show me your tail, at least!* With a sly smile, Karasawa concealed his own presence and set off in the pursuit of the man.

· · ● · ·

Even after the sun set on the Tokyo metropolis, the city didn't sleep. In a complete reversal of how desolate it was during the day, the underground shopping center was now filled with lively voices and light from neon gears. Naoto and AnchoR returned to base, jostled by the crowd along the way.

As they entered the workshop, Vermouth, who had been left on a hanger, called out cheerfully: "'Sup, kid?! Wait, huh? What's with the cute dress? Where're your balls? C'mon, show me real quick. I'm worried that a bad mister will assault you."

"Someone like you, old man?"

"Hey now is that any way to address a lady? Not that this whole dutch wife situation was my idea. So what happened, kid? Ba ha ha!" Vermouth laughed as he tilted his head.

Naoto looked towards the workbench. His eyes had been locked there since he entered the workshop. There, he could see Marie's back as she repaired the heavily damaged RyuZU.

"How long has it been since Marie started working?"

It had been nearly seven hours since Marie had left Naoto and AnchoR and returned alone. During that time, Naoto and AnchoR walked all around Ueno Grid and even Sakuradamon Grid as well. Still, Naoto didn't think that RyuZU would have cooled down by the time Marie had gotten back.

"Yeah." Vermouth nodded, answering with a bitter smile, "I can imagine how you feel. Four hours. She's been at it like that for four whole hours."

"..."

"She wasn't twiddling her thumbs while she waited. She was making preparations, trimming replacement parts and assembling them. Once RyuZU's body cooled down... well, she's been like that the whole time."

Marie continued working. Most likely—no, without a doubt—she hadn't even noticed that Naoto and AnchoR were back.

"What a bad joke, right? Is what we're seeing even humanly possible?"

It was a terrible joke. Something that Naoto was intimately familiar with: the miracle he had had the privilege of seeing in Kyoto. The apex of an art form that could only be described as a divine feat.

It was like the air was grating. The physical laws of the world seemed to distort around the petite blonde-haired girl.

Screws, cylinders, wires, springs, gears... every single clockwork part in her vicinity defied gravity. Or rather, they flew up and returned to their proper places so rapidly and so precisely that it looked as if time were being unwound.

Raw materials were refined, nerves were tuned, and mechanisms were adjusted. She was like a conductor operating with a grace that could bring you to tears. The girl's breath, her blood flow, even her bones and muscles were all in splendid harmony. Marie was performing the symphony of a god.

*Is this really a living, breathing human?* Naoto began to doubt his own eyes. *Am I not seeing an artisanal music box of the highest order? An instrument made in the human form with an absolutely transcendent technique?*

"Father... is this 'genius'?" AnchoR asked quietly, watching Marie defy her human limits.

"Yeah, that's right. It sure is... goddammit." Naoto nodded, then gritted his teeth in vexation.

*Back then, I was simply moved. I even felt envious of how beautiful it was. I was entranced by her forceful, even violent technique. By a talent that felt like it could remake the world.*

*But now, I'm feeling something more. Jealousy, thirst. If she were repairing any other automaton, or maybe a core tower, then I wouldn't care, but... why is the person over there the one repairing RyuZU? Why is that person not me?!*

Suddenly, the melody broke down.

"Haa! I'm out of sugar! My chocolate, where's my chocolate... ah, there it is... hmm...? Oh, Naoto, you're back?"

Remembering to breathe, Marie fell over on the spot. She munched on a bar of chocolate that she'd taken out of her pocket and, noticing Naoto's presence, raised her head. Naoto nodded lightly. He still looked queasy.

"Yeah... I'm back"

"Mother... we're back."

"Yes, welcome back. Did you find what you were looking for?" Marie asked, seeing new headphones sitting atop Naoto's hair.

Naoto nodded.

"Yeah..." he said hesitantly. "But first, Marie, could I ask you a something?"

"What? Ah, do you mind if I answer while I work?"

"No, not at all."

Marie nodded and returned to the workbench. Her pace was slower than before as she was a little less focused, but even so she was still far faster than an ordinary person.

"What'd you want to ask?"

"Marie... how are you repairing RyuZU? You can't get compatible replacement parts for her from the stores, can you?"

"Aside from that absurd Imaginary Gear," Marie answered without slowing down. "I can fix the rest of her mechanisms one way or another. RyuZU was originally owned and kept by my family—the Breguets—you know? Do you have any idea how many times I analyzed and rearranged her parts to try to get her to operate? Even without her blueprints, I've memorized her mechanisms down to the arrangement of her nanogears."

Naoto stayed silent. Marie lowered her gaze to an object on the floor. It looked like a corpse but was really a thoroughly dismantled automaton.

"Fortunately, there are a ton of automata here that used high-grade materials for shitty, indecent purposes. Let's see, how many did I take apart in all?"

"Twenty-seven," Vermouth answered.

"Ah, yes, yes. After I dismantled twenty-seven automata, I had all the parts I needed."

"Hey Princess, try to be a little more thoughtful, eh? That

gramps Konrad was crying it was the end of the world, you know?"

"Like I care. These objects are evil," Marie muttered with a straight face. She turned around to face Naoto and pointed her screwdriver at him with a snap.

"Just so you know, my ears aren't as handy as yours. What I can do with the equipment available here amounts to nothing more than first aid. Making the final adjustments is *your* job, got it?" she said teasingly.

Naoto nodded slightly and looked away. While somewhat surprised by his reaction, Marie resumed her work.

"Ah, what about old man Halter?"

"*I couldn't get an artificial body for him. I'm putting his case on the...*"

*That's a lie,* Marie thought. *No, not exactly. It's true that I couldn't get an artificial body for him, but because of that, I tried hooking him up to a speech device instead.*

*But there was no response.*

*It isn't certain. But, even with a proper procedure, transplanting the brain pod into another artificial body would undeniably involve a fair amount of risk. Not to mention, considering what had happened, it wouldn't be strange if the damage reached his brain as well...*

"Could you give me a hand with this? I'd like three resonance-linking autonomous movements."

"Sorry, I can't make those."

"In that case, just the circuits would be fine, so make me—"

"I can't do that either," Naoto said as he shuffled off to a corner of the room and sat down. "What you're doing right now is way beyond my understanding."

"Now look here," Marie said, sounding a bit irked. "Shouldn't you have learned how to construct circuits in junior high? Why can't you even do something as easy as that? Have you never thought that throwing your school fees down the drain is wasteful?"

"Oyyy Marie," Naoto retorted, raising his voice. "I have no idea what you're talking about! But don't go underestimating machine enthusiasts! I've read through my textbooks so many times that they're all worn out, and who knows how many manuals I bought with the pittance of a fortune left to me. I don't even remember, myself!"

"You. Not. Remembering. Is *exactly* the problem here—tch! Don't say it like it's something you should be proud of!" Marie yelled back, matching his tone. "For God's sake! Why can't you do it when you have such handy ears..."

*Do you have any idea how many times I thought: "If only I had superhuman hearing like you..."*

*I wouldn't waste even a single second if I suddenly got it now. I would immediately get to work mastering it and show you all I can do with it, and yet you...*

Marie shot a resentful glance at Naoto, but he simply replied: "Good question. I'm mystified by it myself. Because, you know, no matter how many textbooks and manuals I read, I don't understand the things written in them!"

"Stop taking pride in something so stupid! I'll knock you down, you know?! Ahh, the poor trees that were wasted on you..." Marie sighed, feeling a migraine coming on.

Taking another bite of her chocolate bar, she stopped. Suddenly, a question arose in her mind...

*Why can't he do it?* She wasn't attacking him. She was genuinely perplexed.

*There's no way he isn't trying, I mean, we're talking about Naoto here! An idiot who loves, and only loves, machines—so much so that he fell in love with a mechanical girl. He even proposed to her for God's sake.*

*I could understand it if we were only talking about general subjects. This guy truly has zero interest in things that don't appeal to him. However, when it comes to machines, he should have been paying attention in technology class.*

*He gave up because he couldn't understand it?*

*As if. I can't imagine this guy giving up. Even just hearing him say that he can't do something feels out of place. I understand that much about this boy.* Marie was proud of this.

*Why can't he do it, despite having that level of resolve and such an absurd talent? It's not like he has a bad memory. He isn't hopelessly incapable either. In the first place, even if he could grasp all of RyuZU's inner workings, would that alone have been enough to fix RyuZU's malfunction?*

"Hey," Marie said, casting her doubt at Naoto. "Didn't you fix RyuZU up back in Kyoto? How did you do it then?"

"I just fumbled around inside her with my hands."

"Fumbled around... you say?" Marie repeated, dumbfounded.

"I don't understand the explanations written in the text-books, so I just fumbled around with her parts until the unpleasant sound I heard inside her went away through trial and error," Naoto answered with a sigh.

*Simply ridiculous. Does this guy not understand how complex of a machine RyuZU is? With that talent of his, he should understand. Even more so than me.*

*I don't get it. This guy has to be making some ridiculously basic mistake... wait.* Marie felt an indescribably chilling thought creep up. *Or perhaps, even though I think I get it, I'm actually the one missing something basic...*

"..."

Marie stopped thinking about it. It was a dangerous line of thought.

"I really don't get you, you pervert." She partitioned off her thoughts with a curse and changed the topic. "So, is that all you wanted to ask? What happened with things on your end?"

"Right." Naoto nodded. "That remarkably gargantuan tower—the Pillar of Heaven, was it? That isn't under the jurisdiction of the military, right?"

"Hm? That's right, it's under the jurisdiction of the Imperial Household Agency. Why do you ask?"

"The Imperial Household Agency? Then that means... ahh, I see." Naoto nodded.

"Japan is rooted in old traditions that began well before the planet was recreated with gears," Vermouth explained, catching wind of what Naoto was thinking. "No one can make a move there. Kid, you're Japanese, you should know what I'm talking about, right? A de facto inviolable territory. It's the perfect place to build what's literally 'the cornerstone of the nation' that governs the core towers at the nucleus of Tokyo's various grids."

"It doesn't sound that way to me," Naoto muttered, looking at him with a suspicious squint.

"Well, duh! That's nothing more than a pretext after all!" Vermouth cackled.

"What do you mean?" Marie asked, lost by their exchange. She gasped. "Naoto, just what are you thinking?"

Her voice was trembling a little.

However, the boy being asked looked bold. Naoto did not waver in the slightest. His gray eyes glittered, and his lips were curled in the smile of a kid that was up to no good.

Then he said something that made Marie doubt her ears, Vermouth explode into laughter, and AnchoR tilt her head.

"I'm just gonna skip to the conclusion, Marie. We're gonna take over the Pillar of Heaven. Or should I say, the Imperial Palace."

• • ● • •

Naoto had spent half a day looking for a way to win. Simply calling his plan outrageous wouldn't do it justice.

"So yeah, what do you think?" Naoto asked as he finished going over it.

"Hah ha ha hah! Oy kid! Oh, Naoto-chan! My eyes didn't deceive me! Your plan is as interesting as it gets! You're on your way to becoming a good scumbag. Actually, you might be one already!"

"Father...you're amazing!!"

Vermouth convulsed with wild laughter while AnchoR's eyes sparkled. Only Marie was left astonished.

"You... you aren't sane," she said, as if struggling to breathe. "Do you truly understand what you just said?"

"Well, yeah? Come on Marie, try recalling what happened," Naoto said as he raised his index finger. "Who was the first one to claim responsibility for the terrorism, us or them?"

*Us. We announced that we would freeze Akihabara.*

"Who's being taken as the perpetrator for this chain of incidents?"

*Us. Indeed, it's being reported on the news.* Marie gulped. A chill ran down her spine.

"So why not go ahead and answer all of their expectations by playing the part they gave us? Fiendishly at that. How about a name befitting a group that's related to that international armed organization, whatever it was? For example, Mr. Naoto Miura and His Merry Friends," Naoto said with a twisted smirk that didn't suit his baby face.

"We were responsible for everything."

It was exceedingly simple and straightforward "evil" that anyone could recognize. The creation of a convenient culprit, a scapegoat for everyone else to lay the blame on.

"If they want to put on a farce, then let's dance extravagantly to their tune. So much so that the enormous piece of junk is over-shadowed and we steal the show! Coup d'etats? Conspiracies? No one will be made to take responsibility for something that 'never happened.' After all, everything was caused by a random group of terrorists blindsiding everyone."

And all with just one move—just like how Shiga's ex-military put the feds in checkmate. But this time, they would be the ones put in a corner. Seeing Naoto's ominous sneer, Marie shuddered.

*The logic checks out. However, does this guy understand what that method would imply?*

"With this, we can jam them into the boiling crucible of Akihabara, and the firewood to fuel it will be the Pillar of Heaven."

*He does. He really does. He's suggesting it despite knowing the ramifications.* Discerning both reason and madness from the glint of his eyes, Marie finally understood.

*It takes a lot to make Naoto Miura truly angry. Even if someone made fun of him or cursed at him, it would be inconsequential.*

*However, there's just one thing that Naoto Miura can't forgive. One extra-large land mine that he has. And Shiga's bunch stepped right on it. Not once, but twice.*

*The first time was restraining AnchoR with that mask. The second time was wrecking RyuZU with that* EMP.

*I finally understand why Naoto was abnormally composed upon waking up after fainting. This guy completely snapped at that moment. He was possessed by an endlessly cool, stark rage.*

*It's just the same as his burns. If Naoto finds something to be necessary, he'll do it. He'll do whatever it takes to achieve his goals.*

*When you get down to it, that's all it is. But how many people would pay any and every price to achieve their goals?*

*Naoto Miura is scary.* Marie acknowledged that. But that wasn't all. Deep down Marie thought: *Naoto Miura is strong.*

Even though she thought it was a pointless, frivolous, and hypothetical, she still couldn't stop herself from thinking it.

*If I were ever to make this guy my enemy, would I be able to win? If I used all of my knowledge, my skills, my connections...*

*If I fully used everything I have at my disposal...*

"Naoto Miura's specs are no match for Marie Bell Breguet's." *That should be the case. But why is it that I can't imagine a world where I beat this guy?*

"Hey, Princess. I implore you from the bottom of my heart. I won't be spoiled and ask for a military-grade artificial body, but could you please switch me to another body that I can move in, at the bare minimum?"

Marie, who'd been at a loss for words, turned to face Vermouth. When she looked over, she saw AnchoR with her eyes sparkling and Vermouth looking like he'd found his resolve.

*Naoto is AnchoR's master. It's only natural that she'd obey him, but...*

"Are you seriously on board with Naoto's plan? Hell awaits us whether the plan succeeds or fails, you know?!"

*Even if everything does go according to plan, we'd still become "evil". Heinous, unsurpassable epic villains.*

*This man has no obligation or motive to take on that burden. He's just a spy who lent his services to some corporation for money.*

*He has neither a sense of justice nor any sort of creed. He's simply an outlaw that works for money. A criminal. I don't trust him, nor should I. That's the kind of man he is.*

"Didn't I say that his plan is interesting?" Vermouth answered without shifting his gaze away from Marie. "Does a man need a better reason than that?"

"..."

"You can't understand? Well, that's fine. But I'm serious. In fact, there's only been... yep, only one other time in my life that I was this serious."

"Just for reference, what was the first time?" Marie asked, her curiosity piqued.

"It was for some stupid dream," Vermouth replied, a bitter, cringing smile on his face. "I screwed up, though. Then as I was drifting through my second life as a cyborg, like a dead man, really, that runt over there—"

"Ah... I'm, sor—"

"—saved me. I remembered that I was alive, just as I was about to kick the bucket." Vermouth turned his gaze to Naoto. "Then, as fate would have it, when I woke up to my third life, this brat was here.

"A crazy bastard who says he'll crush anyone who rubs him the wrong way, no matter who they are. I'm 'in love.' I would very much like to have a front row seat. I want to see just how far this kid'll go. What kind of schemes he'll perpetrate."

Marie sighed. Exasperated, she gave Vermouth and Naoto a look that said: "I can't understand the two of you at all."

"Mother, are you scared?" AnchoR asked, looking up at her. "AnchoR will protect you, so..."

"What are you getting cold feet for, Princess? Hurry off to the dressing room and put on some lucky panties for your date tonight. This is the part where you're supposed to shake your ass to mark the start of our imminent counterattack, you know?" Vermouth laughed, egging Marie on.

"What are you saying Miste—Miss? Not that it really matters, but this won't be a counterattack," Naoto corrected, sounding exasperated. "After all, the feds were attacked by the guys from Shiga, not us. And Marie?"

"What do you want?"

"When you were a kid," he said with the bright, innocent smile of a child. "Didn't you ever see other kids desperately trying to make sand castles in the sandbox and think it'd be crazy fun to kick their sand hills into oblivion and run away?"

Marie remembered...

*When I discarded my identity as a Breguet and a Meister, when I decided to call myself a terrorist after thwarting the compulsory purge of Kyoto... back then, on the rooftop of that school, what did I say to this guy?*

*"We probably wouldn't be praised or thanked by anyone—"*

*"—but it would definitely—"*

Marie sighed with a bitter smile. She ran a hand through her hair and scratched roughly.

"You two really are hopeless boneheads aren't you?"

"But it sounds fun, right?" Naoto smiled.

She got the sense that her resolve was being dragged out and manipulated by Naoto's smile, but strangely, it didn't feel unpleasant. Marie nodded.

*I get it now, I'm an idiot, too.*

At that very moment, with the frivolous air of children plotting a prank, the crime that would be the first and last of its kind in scale was set into motion.

## Chapter Two / 05 : 17 / Disaster

THE DAY HAD BROKEN. A long and massive silhouette extended towards a dawning sky dyed blue and orange.

It was a tower. An enormous pillar that towered over its surroundings. It stretched from the surface all the way to the heavens. The Pillar of Heaven.

Looking down from above, you could see the enormous gear which the base of the pillar passed through. The "roots" of the pillar extended outwards below.

The pillar was in Sakuradamon Grid: the city with the highest elevation in Tokyo. It was a small city, only several kilometers in diameter, but as the Pillar of Heaven occupied the majority of its surface area, there were no civilians there.

However, at the center of the city, inside the castle that enclosed the Pillar of Heaven, there *were* a few residents. A family whose imperial lineage traced all the way back to the ancient era and those who worked for them.

A deep trench encircled the castle, isolating it even from its own city. It is the nature of gears to turn, and the same holds true for the world's cities, which rest upon them. This place was one of the rare exceptions. It was motionless.

In one quarter of the castle was a space adorned with vibrant greenery and water. The scenery wasn't artificial. It was a plaza filled with real nature. A hanging garden.

There was an observation deck at the edge that let you survey all of Sakuradamon Grid and more.

A young woman stood there, wearing heels and a light-pink, silken blouse under a hand-tailored black pantsuit. Her glamorous, flowing black hair reached all the way below her waist.

Given her looks and outfit, one might mistake her for a normal girl working an entry-level job after college. Only her eyes attested to something more. The young woman had keen, lucid black eyes that an ordinary girl could never have. They projected a will as tough as steel.

Her sharp gaze focused on the military deployed below, right before the castle gate.

The palace was under siege.

· · ● ● ·

For the most part, Houko correctly grasped the chaos and crisis befalling the nation.

*Yet, there is nothing I can do about it... that irritates me...*

"Things just will not go the way I want them to, huh? I'm so powerless," Houko muttered as she turned her gaze downward.

She pulled back her left sleeve, revealing a silver wrist watch. It was a plain, functional model. The letters "MARIE" were engraved on the clock face in a small, subtle font.

The time was 5:17. There was forty-three minutes left until the raid began.

Late in the night of February 8th, the Akihabara Terror Incident had occurred. An unknown, enormous weapon had appeared at dawn. The electromagnetic weapon stopped Akihabara Grid from functioning and annihilated the military forces that had gone to intercept it.

A national state of emergency was declared, and the prime minister was stripped of his authority. He was indicted for inciting domestic unrest and conspiring with foreign enemies. Furthermore, the Minister of Defense was accused of the same crimes.

Around the same time, a news station discovered the existence of the enormous weapon and reported the scoop.

Now that it had come to this. Riots had simultaneously broken out in all of Tokyo's grids. Upon learning that Tokyo was at risk of collapsing, the residents fell into a great panic. It didn't help that this followed right on the heels of the Akihabara Terror Incident.

The police, unable to handle the chaos, asked the military to declare martial law. However, a unit centered around a group of young officers had defected and thrown its entire chain of command into disarray. They had immediately attacked the garrison in Ichigaya Grid. After plundering the equipment in the garrison's armory, they closed in on Sakuradamon Grid and surrounded the palace.

It would later be called the Uprising of 2/8.

"At this point, we can't leave it up to the brass," a young captain said from his seat at the negotiation table. "Neither the government nor the military is even trying to fulfill its duties in resolving this national crisis.

"And that's hardly the end of it, considering that both tacitly consented to the research on electromagnetic technology which led to this crisis in the first place. The incident in Kyoto was just a few months back, and now this? We won't stay silent any longer."

*Well, he's right,* Houko thought. *At the very least, the upper echelons of the government and military are nonfunctional at this point. And it's also true that they were the ones who brought this about.*

"We don't have much time," the young captain added. "The threat of the enormous weapon is still looming, and the request for authorization to use Tall Wand has not been withdrawn.

"We must seize power swiftly and begin negotiating with the group behind the weapon. There's also diplomatic inquiries from various foreign countries to think about. However, for any of this to happen, we need a symbolic gesture to prove that we truly possess the authority of the nation, Your Highness."

*So you mean the Pillar of Heaven,* Houko thought. *His reasoning is correct in one respect. Even if they use military might to defeat the current administration, if no one acknowledges their legitimacy, they would be looked upon as rebels. The only ones who can do such a thing, even if it is just a formality, is us. The residents of the palace.*

*It's only natural that they wouldn't choose the bedridden emperor, and the imperial prince is still too young. That only leaves the one officially substituting for Father on the throne, me—Imperial Princess Houko Hoshimiya.*

*Just how convincing will that symbolic gesture really end up being?*

"This country has begun to rot! The situation must be rectified! I know there can be no excuse for intruding upon His Majesty's personal residence, but please, Your Highness! Could you lend us your hand for the sake of the nation?"

*From a personal standpoint, I understand how they feel. I even think they're right. If times were better, or if the situation were different, I might have bestowed them with the Imperial Standard.*

*However, reality is not as sweet as daydreams. It's obvious how I should reply.*

"It'd be pointless. I humbly refuse."

The young captain's face twisted. Houko gazed through all the captains that sat before her.

"I think it would be best if each of you cease this meaningless pursuit and immediately return to your stations. You have duties to uphold. You probably will not go unpunished, but I promise that I will write a formal petition under my name to lighten that punishment as much as possible."

"Your Highness! Please reconsider!"

"I have already given plenty of thought to the matter. This is my conclusion."

"We cannot afford to withdraw," the captain said in a low

growl, his face flushed red. "To be clear, we are prepared to use force if you insist on maintaining your position."

"There is no helping it. In that case, do as you like, Captain."

"Do...you think it's an empty threat?"

"No. I am sure that you have your own design. However, I too have beliefs and duties that I cannot afford to compromise."

And so, the negotiation broke down. After that, the rebels made several more inroads, but in the end there wasn't enough time.

6:00 AM on February 10th. That was the deadline that they gave her to change her mind. Then they would storm the castle...

"Here you are, Your Highness."

Houko turned around. There, she saw a small old man wearing a black tailcoat.

"Mr. Kusunoki."

"Given the present situation, it is dangerous for you to walk alone."

"Killing me would accomplish nothing. In fact, considering their goal, they would want to avoid me dying at all costs."

*Breaking into the palace with the sword is already dangerous enough. If someone in the imperial family dies, it would be impossible for them to assert their legitimacy to the people.*

"That might be the case for their leaders," Grand Chamberlain Kusunoki replied doubtfully. "But not everyone who is caught up in this momentary fervor is as wise as Your Highness."

"True." Houko nodded. "I wonder. If everyone were wise, would the situation have come to this?"

"I do not know. However, perhaps if someone like Your Highness stood at the top, then—"

"I wonder about that. In the end, I too am powerless." Houko smiled self-deprecatingly and returned her gaze to the deployed forces below the observation deck. Gazing fixedly at them, she muttered, "They too must be doing what they think is right."

"It is a gathering of fools. Breaking into the palace?! Absolutely blasphemous."

"Perhaps. Still, while we may call them fools, it is not like we can do any more about the situation than they can."

Kusunoki gasped. "Your Highness, are you suggesting that they are in the right?"

"No. As I said at the negotiation table, there would be no point in me affirming them. Doing so was out of the question as soon as they decided to revolt. Especially when there's a clear threat looming over Tokyo." Houko paused for breath. "Even if I hypothetically do agree with their position and therefore acknowledge their legitimacy, what would change?"

"Your Highness, that's..."

"I am not making light of my imperial authority. But even if the citizens accept it, how much respect would foreign countries—and those operating that enormous weapon—give to what would be, in the end, nothing but pretext?"

"According to the reports," said Kusunoki. "It is Shiga's ex-military, and their goal is a coup d'etat against the government. If that is the case, I do not think they would take the authority of the imperial family lightly, no?"

"Is that really the case? I am a little suspicious." Houko muttered, narrowing her eyes. "Speaking of reports."

"Yes...?"

"Have you made any headway regarding Marie Bell Breguet's whereabouts?"

Kusunoki made a conflicted face. "As you know, she is officially dead, so tracking her is very difficult. We have yet to get any leads. If Your Highness hadn't noticed the resemblance from that photo, we surely would not have even thought of her name."

"Still, it is certain that she was involved with the Akihabara Terror Incident in some capacity."

"Does Your Highness think that she holds a key of some sort?"

"I think she is the ringleader of it all," Houko said, wringing the guardrail with her hands. "Seizing an entire grid and manipulating it freely is impossible even for the clocksmiths of the Imperial Guard. I cannot imagine that a clocksmith in the security force could do it either. I do not know of any other clocksmith with the otherworldly skills necessary to pull off such a feat."

"If I recall correctly, she was your friend at school, yes?"

"Only for a month, but yes." Houko smiled faintly. "I had the chance to get to know her during my studies in Europe. I remember her well. She had a sense of justice many times the size of her small stature and burned with a passion like fire itself. And, of course, she was one of the best clocksmiths, if not the best, back then as well..."

"Are you suggesting that a person like that is the ringleader behind this disturbance?"

Houko shook her head. "I feel like the Akihabara Terror Incident does not fit with the rest of this, somehow. The coup d'etat would have succeeded even without it. Rather, was it not thanks to the proclamation of terrorism that all the residents were able to evacuate safely before the enormous weapon appeared?"

"Then is Your Highness suggesting that the Akihabara Terror Incident and the coup d'etat were carried out by different parties?"

"Yes. Of course, this is nothing but fuzzy conjecture. However, if it turns out to be true..." She paused. "There might yet be another incident. That is the feeling I get."

*Of course, that is probably nothing but my personal fantasy. It would be way too convenient for it to be true. I am not so naive as to believe that reality is as sweet as daydreams. Rather, I thought I was not, and yet...*

But just a mere ten minutes later—852 seconds to be exact—not just Houko herself, but the entire world would be reminded that a lack of imagination was what was truly naive. The world they were living in had never been cut and dry. They were, in fact, already living such a fantasy. Reality had always been stranger than fiction.

• • ● • •

At that same time, outside the palace:

Sakuradamon Grid was filled with a tense, imposing atmosphere. It was just moments before the scheduled raid. The soldiers felt the zeal of justice, pre-battle excitement, and, at the same time, guilt from the transgression they were about to commit. News helicopters peeked at the army surrounding the palace, moments away from waking from its dormancy.

The air was suffocating. Everyone present got that feeling...

"Ahh... finally, some fresh air after almost forty-eight hours. Exquisite. Actually, I am not equipped with any mechanism equivalent to human lungs, but even in spite of the riff-raff who have still yet to evolve past their flea-like brains, this invigorating sensation is most definitely real."

A small group slowly approached from behind the back lines. The one leading them was a silver-haired girl wearing a formal black dress. Her springy steps matching the graces of her good mood, she gave the impression that she might start elegantly dancing at any moment.

A cool, bell-like voice blossomed from her flowery lips. Her topaz pupils filled with vigor as she executed her first performance of verbal abuse in quite some time.

Behind her, a black-haired boy and a blonde girl were following at a leisurely stroll. Between them was a young girl wearing red and white armor. Nonchalantly, but full of confidence, they boldly advanced through the middle of the road.

The girl wearing the black dress turned to look at the boy with a smile that could enchant an angel.

"Master Naoto? Though I am merely a humble clockwork servant, even I should have the right and dignity to choose whom I pay my respects. My head is neither so light nor so cheap that I would lower it to those who even single-celled organisms would be nonplussed by. I would like to point out once more that I find this order exceedingly objectionable."

"Right, no, I get that, but see..." It seemed like they had had this exchange many times already. The black-haired boy nodded, looking fatigued.

"I understand your reasoning," the girl continued, as if she couldn't contain her discontent. "I see your point, shoddy as it may be: that I should take care to distinguish between the beasts who do not even comprehend the word 'man' in 'manners' and those who can at least do that. I will obey your orders, but nonetheless, I still find it exceedingly objectionable."

Catching on to her true voice hidden beneath that flowery smile, the boy replied with a bitter grin. "Yeah, we have to put on an extravagant show so please bear with it for now. I've even prepared a reward for you, so..."

"I am Master Naoto's property. Giving a reward to a follower... please remember your place." Her face was filled with glee contrary to her words. However, it was something that only the boy could detect.

"How about you AnchoR? Are you ready?"

"Yes, if that is Father's order... I mean, request... then..."

The boy patted her head, and the young girl in red and white nodded with a smile.

Lastly, there was the blonde girl smiling bitterly in self-deprecation. "Is the word 'nervous' not in your vocabularies? This is gonna work, right?"

Contrary to her words, her voice didn't sound all that anxious.

Perhaps the others picked up on that, because they replied with cheerful smiles.

"That depends on you, Marie. After all, there's no way that RyuZU or AnchoR will fail."

"Mistress Marie, I do not know if... well, if Master Naoto says it can be done, then it is only logical that even challenges that would confound the gods would prostrate themselves and yield. Of course, that is only *if* a certain dull-witted fool does not drag him down, but..."

"Fine, fine I'll leave it at that. Curiously enough, even your venomous tongue feels reassuring to me right now, RyuZU. Besides, this is the perfect opportunity to vent my anger and really cut loose."

A small-sized mobile weapon stood alongside a car as an impromptu barricade, blocking their way. As they approached it, the boy muttered and listened carefully to the sounds of the army encircling the palace.

"There are eighteen heavily armored multi-legged tanks and thirty-two heavily armored soldiers. As for the heavily armored and lightly armored automata... argh, distinguishing between them is too troublesome. Just know that there's sixty-eight of them altogether. There are ninety-eight cyborg soldiers as well."

"Marie," he asked casually, having easily grasped the full makeup of the force laying siege to the palace. "If the world's most powerful troops were here, how long would it take to annihilate this entire force?"

"Without causing any collateral damage to the palace

whatsoever? It would be near impossible, but let's see..." The blonde girl looked down slightly, considering.

She wasn't a mercenary or a soldier but a clocksmith. So like a clocksmith, she calculated and compared the capabilities of the opposing forces.

"Hypothetically, if your troops are seasoned in urban warfare and subjugation with the next-next generation equipment, and if there are lightly and heavily armored automata and cyborgs *as well*... with four companies, a conservative estimate would be fourteen minutes."

"In that case," Naoto answered, hearing that her estimates were based on an impossible premise in the first place. "RyuZU, AnchoR, your time limit is *seven minutes*. Easy-peasy right?"

"Master Naoto, I think Mistress Marie asks more than enough dumb questions for all of us. You need not join her."

"Destroy all... of that? I'd like you to give me an order... may I hold back some?"

"Sure, hold back as much as you can. Don't kill anyone. That's an absolute condition, got it?"

If there were any outsiders listening, what would they have thought? Would they have laughed their butts off? Maybe they'd chide this pack of cheeky kids for their ridiculousness.

"Well then, RyuZU, AnchoR. As planned: draw their attention *with a bang*. I'm counting on you."

"Understood. Excuse me."

Over the year, Japan had faced an unprecedented chain of incidents following the attempted purge of Kyoto.

The Akihabara Terror Incident, the Akihabara Magnetization Crisis, the Kasumigaseki Convention, the authorization request for the use of Tall Wand, the Uprising of 2/8, the Mutiny of 2/9, the Battle at the Palace Gate...

Now, as if to mock all of that, something happened. A massive upheaval that wrapped everything up as an *epic crime* perpetrated by a single terrorist organization.

That something was the last incident in this chain of events. A grand conclusion that tied all of the preceding incidents together under one neat name. It was also the very first of the incidents in a chain of numerous others that would shake the very foundation of this world.

It would later be known as the Uprising of 2/8, but it had another name. The Second Ypsilon.

In this year, on this day, at this hour, in this second...

5:59 AM Japanese Standard Time, on February 10th in the 1016th Year of the Wheel...

Hearing a loud rumble, the soldiers all turned toward the source. Toward a building that had been sliced up like a jigsaw and collapsed into pieces. Amidst the roar of the collapse, a clear voice sounded like a music box.

"Your attention, please."

Standing before the collapsing building, the girl in a black dress gave an elegant bow. Crudely mimicking her big sister's gesture, the young girl beside her in red and white armor bowed as well.

"How are you all faring on this day? I am the First of the Initial-Y Series, RyuZU YourSlave."

"U-umm... I'm the Fourth of the Initial-Y Series, AnchoR the Trishula, o-or the One Who Destroys. N-nice to meet you."

It all began with those greetings.

"Germs, failing to discern their place, always busy themselves with crude ploys. It is, to put it mildly, greatly comedic. Given my master's orders and a little bit of my own personal resentment towards what has been done to me, I am just *raring* to vent my anger on you, but..."

"U-umm... p-please let me apologize in advance... I-I'm sorry... ngh"

With the smile of an angel, the girl in black revealed two obsidian scythes that extended from beneath the hem of her skirt, while the other looked apologetic as she twisted her solid gear cube and pulled an enormous sword out of the void.

The people who'd just heard them name themselves doubted them.

"I am not sorry in the slightest," said the girl in the black dress with a smile, as if she didn't *need* them to believe her. "And though this is much too high of an honor for your pitiful brains, savor the supreme bliss of having heard my voice. As well as the *taste of dirt* in your mouth as you grovel in *worship of my name*."

"I-I'm sorry... ngh!"

Those who heard their words couldn't resist. They couldn't even figure out what was happening. It was an absurd turn of events. Impossible. Everything, down to the handguns of the armored soldiers, broke into pieces and fell to the ground.

Their existence overwrote everything that people knew.

Those living on the Clockwork Planet were once again forcefully reminded just what kind of world they lived in.

That reality could break past the boundaries of fiction as if it were nothing at all.

$$\bullet \ \bullet \ \bullet \ \bullet \ \bullet \ \bullet$$

"There are no facts, only interpretations."

Who was it that said that? In any case, it applies to everyone—even those who witness history being made firsthand.

Take for example Captain Sumitada Hikoshima of Tokyo's Central Intelligence Unit. He'd turned twenty-eight this year, a young officer who'd climbed through the ranks as fast as possible for someone his age.

The role of the Central Intelligence Unit was to process information about the military and support the operations of other units. Now the Akihabara Terror Incident had occurred, and an enormous unknown weapon had appeared...

"A joke, an absolute, complete joke! Okada died for something like this? Ghh!"

Captain Hikoshima slammed his fist onto the table in rage, shaking the canvas walls of the makeshift command center. Seeing the sharp, threatening look on his face, the other officers gulped.

First Lieutenant Tsutomu Okada had been his friend. A member of Tokyo's security force. He was deployed to intercept the enormous weapon and killed in action.

The chain of command fell into chaos, conflicting reports

surfaced on the situation, and many looked to Captain Hikoshima. He was roused to take revenge for his friend. That's when he learned of one of the military's top secrets: that research on electromagnetic technology had been tacitly approved and that the cover-up had ultimately led to the purging of Shiga. Their attempt to gain political ground out of the wrongs of their past had led to the current situation.

*My friend was killed by politicians scrounging for votes! Those bastards, I'll never forgive them.*

He couldn't leave this matter in the hands of his superiors. Watching them fracture into factions, trying to shove the blame onto each another... He gave up on them and contacted some colleagues he trusted.

All were promising young officers who had vowed alongside him to give their all for the nation. Captain Hikoshima's righteous indignation spread like wildfire, igniting the hearts of many of them. The result was this mutiny. This noble mission.

He was extremely disappointed in the princess's reply, but his friends had chided him, saying:

"You can't blame the imperial family for being conservative."

Captain Hikoshima understood it in his heart of hearts— there was no way seizing political power was right. They weren't on the side of justice.

*But we're in a state of national emergency, facing a crisis where the fate of the nation hangs in the balance. There are things which must be done, even if it means straying from justice. Why can't you understand?!*

*Given the true intentions of those inside that weapon, obeying the brass while they squander valuable time would be like committing tortuously slow suicide. We must consolidate our power and rally the military's forces. We don't have a second to lose.*

*But... attacking the palace just because of that? Ludicrous,* thought Captain Hikoshima, shaking his head. *We can't use the end to justify the means. In the end, this is nothing more than meaningless internal dissension.*

*We have neither the time nor the troops for something like this. I didn't want it to come to this, but I have to finish things up quickly.*

The hour of battle was drawing near. Just as Hikoshima was about to give a final warning to those inside the palace, an explosion rang out. Then a second, and a third.

"What's going on?! Who's the idiot that jumped the gun?!" said Captain Hikoshima, clicking his tongue. Someone had decided to begin the attack.

*This is bad. Starting the attack without a final warning will become a problem. Actually, an even bigger problem is the fact that there are idiots here who would begin the attack without orders.*

"The seventh squad has been wiped out! It appears that we're being attacked from the rear!"

"What did you say...?"

What the communications officer said next was even more shocking.

"The self-propelled artillery positioned in our right flank has also been destroyed!"

The captain's eyes opened wide with astonishment.

"I'm not getting a response from the second armored soldier unit! The third and fourth units have also gone silent!"

"Impossible, who are they?! Which squad is attacking us?!" he shouted at the communications officer, hectically trying to figure it out.

*The military brass? No, those incompetents are still engrossed in their blame game.*

*The mobile police squad? They don't have the luxury of attacking us. They have their hands full just trying to maintain public order.*

*SWAT? Impossible. They don't have enough men to assault an army of this scale.*

*In that case, the imperial guard force... tsk.*

The imperial guard were the Technical Force who managed the Pillar of Heaven. Hikoshima had judged their combat strength to be low.

*They're still the unit that's charged with protecting the Pillar of Heaven. Did I underestimate them?!*

*They likely used some underground tunnel beneath the palace to ambush us. In that case, what if we respond with our main force and send a flying column to storm the front?*

*It's different from what I planned, but with this, we can keep the damage to a minimum!*

"Give me a report on the scale of the enemy forces!" the captain yelled, turning around...

"Come again? Giving me an order... I see that you are quite bold. You are free to determine the value of your life at your own discretion, but if you think you have the right to aggravate me, you had best think again."

The clear voice of a girl was his only answer. That, and silence. The others in the command center had all fallen face-flat upon the table. Their large amounts of equipment had just been turned to scrap.

*What happened? When exactly? How?*

The wind lightly lifted the flaps of the slashed tent, and the scenery outside suddenly became visible. As Hikoshima looked about, he spotted the four-legged Komainu tank that had been positioned behind the command center. Or rather, what was left of it.

It was an unrecognizable heap of scrap metal. On top of it stood a girl in a formal black dress. Two scythes arched from under her skirt. She gave him a confident smile.

"Haaaaaah?"

Captain Hikoshima let out a questioning sigh. His eyes seemed empty. It was how humans reacted to an impossible situation.

"Hoooly... ah, well, so, I'm guessing that you're the one in charge?"

Whirling around, the captain saw a blonde girl who looked like she just happened to be passing by.

"Well, I can understand how you feel... I'm sorry, just... pretend that you were caught in a natural disaster or something, all right?"

Peeking inside the tent, the girl looked like she sincerely sympathized with him. She closed her eyes and made the sign of the cross.

Captain Hikoshima mustered all the strength he had.

"Wh-who...are you?"

"It'd be exceedingly tiresome to introduce myself over and over again. We've left one of your transmission devices untouched over there, so could you do me a favor and relay this to all of your troops?"

A violent gust swept through the command center. This time, the entire shredded tent was whirled up by the wind, and three heavily armored soldiers were knocked down in one blow before they had a chance to retaliate.

The girl in red and white armor, who had brought about this inconceivable tragedy, suddenly noticed Hikoshima.

"Ah, umm... nice to meet you. My name is... AnchoR."

"And I am her elder sister, RyuZU. We are Initial-Y Series automata. Thank you for your meaningless work. Have a nice day."

And just like that, they were gone. Captain Sumitada Hikoshima was left in a daze.

He had just borne witness to history. If someone were to ask him what had happened, I wonder what he would say?

Absurdly, unreasonably, off-handedly, his revolution—which had burned with righteous indignation—was incomprehensibly squashed before his eyes.

Would he describe it as a battle? An incident? No. It was a phenomenon that could only be described as an "accident" and nothing else.

At any rate, deriving meaning from it was not the job of a witness but a historian.

· · • ● • · ·

The scene was like one big punchline. It hadn't been a battle. One side was just completely mowed down. But it wasn't a natural disaster, either. It had simply been a massacre: another case of the strong trampling the weak.

"I knew what you guys were capable of... but really, your powers are totally unfair," Marie muttered in sympathy for the young officer.

"It's obvious that RyuZU and AnchoR would be capable of this much," Naoto replied with pride.

They were talking as they ran around the moat of the palace, making their way to its drawbridge. All the while, enemy forces were being annihilated around them. Yet another pair of lightly armored automata aimed their guns at them and were shredded as they talked.

About a second later, an artillery platform positioned several hundred meters away was annihilated in much the same way.

Both these cases were probably RyuZU's work. Marie couldn't be sure. She was completely blind to RyuZU and AnchoR's movements, but RyuZU moved at an ultra-high speed while also maintaining a defensive perimeter around Naoto. Anything that threatened him was minced to pieces, so the destruction in their near field of vision was most likely her work.

As for AnchoR...

"Oh, no... my kick... ngh," the girl said, flustered.

*From what I can see, I'm guessing she swung her sword but*

*couldn't bring the blade around in time to deal with the Komainu behind her, so she kicked it with her heel instead. She was probably trying to hold back as best she could, but...*

"Hey Naoto... Komainus are incredibly heavy. They weigh about 38.4 tons. Did you know that?"

"Really? That's surprisingly heavy!"

"Yes... they certainly are. And yet here they are flying through the air. Is this some kind of joke?" Marie laughed dryly, watching 38.4 tons of metal soar by. They weren't supposed to do that.

The C & S 22 Type 22 four-legged tank—Komainu, also known as a Guardian Dog. These multi-manned, four-legged tanks were jointly developed by Seiko and Citizen.

Even if they weren't at the level of the Five Great Corporations, they were still the two largest clockwork corporations in Japan and possessed advanced technology that received worldwide recognition.

Their current flagship model, the A-un, was the successor to the Komainu, but given the abrupt nature of the revolution, the rebels probably couldn't get their hands on the newest equipment.

However, Guardian Dogs were still masterpieces of design that had made their appearance on the modern battlefield. As a clocksmith, even Marie couldn't help but admire them.

Despite being manned, the units possessed a 360-degree field of vision. More impressive still was their loading capacity—in addition to the basic 1200mm cannon and 300mm auto cannon, they were also capable of fielding four additional armaments and possessed the ability to switch out their loaded configurations in real time during combat.

"Ah... ngh, Father, Mother, I'm sorry."

AnchoR flew in front of them so quickly that it looked like she had teleported. She casually swung the back of her hand, and Marie heard the burst of an explosion far above. A second later, Marie realized what had happened: *AnchoR effortlessly diverted a shell with the back of her hand...*

Retracing its trajectory, Marie saw the Guardian Dog that had fired it—its body was split vertically in two, and AnchoR was apologizing to its flabbergasted operators, still sitting in their positions, having their hair tussled by the wind.

Seeing such a spectacle, Marie couldn't help but put on a strained smile. Japan's military equipment was by no means shoddy. If anything, it was top of the line—which was especially impressive considering that they'd largely equipped themselves with domestically manufactured technology. However, all of that equipment had been reduced to this.

"Hey Naoto, think you could pinch my cheeks for a sec? I think I'm dreaming."

"Sure thing. Hey, why are you pinching back?!"

"Even absurdity should have its limits!"

"Oww... that's my line... God..."

Witnessing the tempest of violence firsthand, Marie finally understood. RyuZU didn't call herself the weakest of the Initial-Y Series out of humility.

"Looks like I should have taken the fact that RyuZU, the

self-proclaimed 'weakest' of the Initial-Ys, can cut through current-gen military weapons like butter a bit more seriously..."

*Now that I think about it, RyuZU had also casually, effortlessly shredded the Vacherons' latest manned weapon, the Goliath. That enormous spider shrugging off her attacks had been an exceptional case. The absurd truth is that it is perfectly natural for the Initial-Y Series to reduce modern weapons to nothing.*

*All the more so when they aren't up against the "weakest" but the "strongest."*

Seeing AnchoR mow down three Guardian Dogs with a single swing of her massive sword, Marie suddenly felt very tired.

"Hey, Naoto. What do you think 'Y' had in mind when he gave that child such incredible combat capability? Even aliens would turn tail and run if they saw a scene like this..."

Naoto looked confused. "Isn't that the point? AnchoR's here to make those who would threaten the Clockwork Planet scurry away in fear, no? You sure do ask some obvious questions sometimes, Marie. Wait, I found it." He had been searching for the enemy without his headphones this whole time. "The heavily armored automaton Cz35C Black Tortoise, there's no mistaking it. I found it."

They could just invade the castle now, humming away freely. However, that wouldn't be *good enough*. They had to crush the entire force before they could retreat.

Under Naoto's plan, they had to destroy all of the forces here as absurdly, overwhelmingly, and unreasonably as possible. In other words, at a speed that would be impossible for even the strongest military force in the world.

And there was one additional condition. "Okay, on to the next phase then!" Tightly hugging the brain pod she was carrying in her arms, Marie pursed her lips in firm resolve.

Multiple news helicopters darted about the sky, fearlessly covering the storm of destruction below. Confirming that one said news helicopter was pointing a camera her way, Marie raised her left arm and swung it in a large arc.

· · ● · ·

The imperial guard had established their emergency headquarters in the palace parlor. The upscale furniture had all been cleared, and various transmission devices and an enormous screen took its place.

Just minutes ago, the guard were enveloped in a heavy air, resolving themselves to honorably defend the palace to their last breath. Others in the palace trembled in hopeless fear. But now everyone's eyes were glued to the live footage being played on the screen.

"E-everyone please take a look at this incredible sight!" a female reporter exclaimed. She seemed astonished herself; her voice was unevenly shrill.

That was understandable. The video being captured was, indeed, truly incredible. After all, the military force that had surrounded the palace was being destroyed by "something" making its way clockwise through them.

"Their true identities are uncertain! H-however, one of them is... ah yes, that boy over there! There is Naoto Miura, the suspect believed to be behind the premonitory broadcast announcing the Akihabara Terror Incident! And according to eyewitness testimony, two automata who claimed to be from the Initial-Y Series have appeared during the incident as well. Oh!"

"What... is this?" Houko muttered, her eyes fixed on the screen.

"W-we don't know," replied a young officer of the imperial guard. "There shouldn't be any weapon capable of this, but..."

"Is the video being played in real-time? Is it not possible that it's been edited?" the princess asked cautiously.

The officer considered it.

"Since it appears this is indeed being broadcast on live television, no one would have the time or the technology to prepare such an intricately doctored feed. And not just that, no one would have had a motive to do so in the first place."

But of course. Who would gain anything from fabricating footage like this? It was all happening within a stone's throw of the palace. The people inside could likely confirm it with their very eyes. As long as they had a window, any effort to alter the video feed would be pointless.

"In that case, this video is accurate?" Houko asked.

The officer couldn't quite bring himself to express it in words. He nodded.

This was reality. Houko herself had almost forgotten how strange it could be.

Shuddering in fear, she returned her eyes to the screen and

noticed something. Beside Naoto Miura, a blonde girl looked directly up at the camera. Her emerald eyes were gleaming as she raised her left arm as high as she could above her head.

"..."

Houko inadvertently turned her left wrist over, revealing the face of her silver watch, engraved with the letters "MARIE."

"A-an anonymous tip has just come in! Wha? Ah, no, excuse me! According to the report, a-apparently, they're—"

As she listened to the announcement that followed, Houko's eyes widened. She was the only one that understood. The magic words that resolved everything.

"—the criminal group behind the Akihabara Terror Incident, and also the ones responsible for both the manufacture and the activation of the enormous unknown weapon that halted Akihabara Grid... The report appears to be yet another declaration of responsibility from the criminals themselves!!!"

· ◦ ● ⬤ ● ◦ ·

"Hoo! Hell yeah! Finally! Haven't felt alive without this suit, it just isn't the same without it."

On a rooftop near the place, a woman in a rubber suit smoked a cigarette. She stood by the edge, gazing at the boisterous scene below.

To be precise, she wasn't a woman. Strictly speaking, "she" wasn't even human. Nor was she a full-body cyborg or an automaton. The man who'd had his brain pod forcefully connected to the female automaton heard his name called over a resonance transceiver.

"Vermouth, according to Naoto, the target seems to be in a unit of five at two o'clock from your position," said Marie.

S-he stood up lazily, stretching his-her arms. "All right, as expected of the kid I'm in love with. Tell him that I'll stuff him full later as a reward."

"Naoto said: 'Stay away, I don't want to be infected by your gayness.'"

Vermouth cracked a bitter smile as he vaulted off the building's edge and leapt through the air. He jumped from one rooftop to another as he made his way towards the designated position.

Over the transmission, Marie seemed anxious, or perhaps unsatisfied. "I know it's too late to change the plan but... you really can pull this off right?"

*Damn right it's too late,* Vermouth sneered.

"What's the matter honey, getting cold feet? You're the one who tuned this body, you know. If you don't even have faith in your own work, then you're just as much of a bitch as I thought—"

"How am I supposed to have faith in it? I did the best I could, but that body isn't an artificial body. Do you understand what I'm saying? It wasn't made to be connected to a human brain!"

"Seriously?! That's news to me! In that case, would you mind telling me just one more thing, Princess? Who was the *bitch* that linked *my* brain to such a thing?" Vermouth spat, shutting Marie up.

She didn't need him to tell her that. She was well aware of it herself.

"There's no need to worry," he told her. "I'm feeling pretty good. You did a great job, Missy."

Vermouth wasn't lying. His body's shock-absorbing mechanism was cushioning his landings with ease. This new, lascivious body was that of an actress or a top model. It was typical for a love automaton. But miraculously enough, despite the difference in height, he hadn't needed to adjust much to get a feel for it.

The power output couldn't compare to a military-grade artificial body but, on the other hand, his new body was capable of some surprisingly supple maneuvers. Things that his original body hadn't been capable of. Perhaps because it was specialized for dancing.

He felt almost no lag in response time from this body. No one but Marie could have tuned it so well, even if they'd used high-grade parts for everything.

*I see. Sure enough, this is the work of a genius,* Vermouth thought.

"After all, despite being a lady love machine, it comes with such a big cock—"

"I'll really kill you, you know?"

Vermouth's jest was met with a freezing voice full of murder.

"No, but really, why'd you go out of your way to deliver me a package?"

"I didn't! It was there to begin with! I didn't want to touch the wicked thing, so I just left it!!"

Vermouth's eyes widened. He could just imagine how red Marie's face must be right now. "Oy, this is the standard model?

You've gotta be kiddin' me! So this is 'Cool Japan?' I mean, I've heard the rumors but... wow, the Japanese always live in the future regardless of the era, don't they?!"

He laughed, amused, but sensing an ominous air from his transceiver, he turned serious.

"You know," he said in a quiet voice, lighting a new cigarette. "These cigs taste great."

"What do you mean? There's no way you can taste with that body. Actually, that goes for your original body as well."

Vermouth laughed bitterly. *You don't get it at all.* As he jumped from rooftop to rooftop, he checked on his destination. Just as Naoto had said, there was a unit of five machines at 2 o'clock. Vermouth verified the target.

"Princess, people say crap like 'the air here tastes great,' but what does that actually mean?"

"..."

"Like air could have any taste. What they mean is that the air puts them in a great *mood*."

The heavily armored automaton Cz35 Type C Black Tortoise was made by Citizen. It featured both thick composite armor and heavy firepower. With a 40mm autocannon in each hand and a thermobaric buster on its shoulders, it was also equipped with a high-precision, high-speed artificial intelligence.

Vermouth couldn't help but crack a bitter smile at the fact that a young officer was able to field such a powerful weapon for his mutiny.

But it seemed like the commander couldn't get as many as he

had wanted. The manned units accompanying it were three Iron Demons and a four-legged tank, a Guardian Dog. Around their feet were several cyborg soldiers and lightly armored automata.

*Looking down at them, Vermouth recalled Naoto's demand. Let me repeat your order. Destroy only the AI of the Black Tortoise and eliminate all of the units supporting it without killing anyone.*

*Would that complete your order? Would you like some fries and a drink with that?* Vermouth stifled his laughter. *That brat gave a scumbag like me such an impossible task.*

"And yet...right now, these cigs taste like the best thing in the world!"

*"Only you can do this, no?" That's what that kid told me.*

"And what does that mean?" Marie asked, befuddled.

Vermouth kicked off from his rooftop perch and leapt downward. He descended in a zig-zag between the walls of the building he'd been standing on and the six-story building on the opposite side of the road. He made his way to the ground.

"I'll crush them for pissing me off!"

Vermouth puffed out a large breath of smoke, recalling the look in Naoto's eyes, and bit down on the filter of his cigarette with a daring smile.

"It means that there's no way I'll screw this up!" Vermouth sneered as he headed towards the battlefield, running out from the shadows of the buildings.

He charged toward a cyborg soldier who was vigilantly scanning the surroundings. Naturally, the soldier saw Vermouth.

"Wh-who are y—"

Bewildered by the sex automaton charging at him, the soldier readied his rifle.

But Vermouth accelerated even faster and closed the distance. At the same time, he threw out a kick. The tip of his boot connected with the rifle, causing it to spiral out of the soldier's hands.

As it flipped around, Vermouth grabbed it and fired. A gunshot rang out and a bullet pierced the right leg of the cyborg soldier. Passing them by, Vermouth unloaded three more rounds into the soldier's abdomen to incapacitate him.

As the enemy keeled over, Vermouth flashed a smile. "What do I look like to you? I'd very much like to know."

"There's an enemy here!!"

Hearing four gunshots, the other cyborg soldiers responded.

"Ah, nice, things will be easier if you all see this basket case of a dutch wife as an enemy." Vermouth laughed.

Enemies showered him with bullets from three different directions, but Vermouth kept his feet moving. He evaded the rain of fire with skillful, dance-like steps.

He was weaving through the blind spots, taking advantage of their formation to bait friendly fire. Vermouth continued advancing with a slick glide.

Though they were only shooting at him with rifles, if the body of the sex automaton caught even a single bullet, it'd be fatal damage. And yet, there was no fear in Vermouth's expression. He continued moving with a sardonic smile.

"I'll be borrowing your head for a sec, little boy." Vermouth stepped on the head of a cyborg soldier and leapt into the air. An armored walker stood before him: an Iron Demon.

Landing on its shoulder roughly eight meters from the ground, Vermouth clung on tightly. Although it was no match for a military-grade artificial body, he still possessed strength that far exceeded human limits.

Losing track of him, the Iron Demon assumed a cautious, defensive posture, but it couldn't find its target. Vermouth was very much aware of the fact that none of the eight cameras on an Iron Demon covered his position.

He stretched his hands out and, opening the hatch hidden by the machine's nape, pulled the emergency release lever inside, twisting it clockwise.

The Iron Demon stopped moving. As the sound of turning gears and cylinders rang out, the hatch to the cockpit parted like an opened backpack. The pilot looked like he had just graduated from a military academy.

"Huh?" The officer stared at Vermouth in blank amazement.

"Hey kid, that's quite the sexy car." Vermouth grinned, shoving the muzzle of his rifle right up the officer's nose. "By the way, did you know that this beauty's a single-seater? Shocking, I know."

Keeping his rifle firmly in place, Vermouth used his free hand to cram a cigarette into the pilot's mouth.

"Whaddya say you trade me this babe for that cig? I mean we're friends, aren't we? You can tell me your thoughts on your journey through the air afterwards, all right?"

Grabbing the head of the bewildered officer, Vermouth

forced him to nod, then pulled the ejection lever under the pilot's seat. A fwoosh rang out, and the pilot's screams echoed up to the high heavens as his seat blasted off.

"Thanks, mate." Blowing a seductive and unnecessary kiss after the pilot, Vermouth slipped into the cockpit. "Now then, guess I'll meet li'l Naoto's expectations and act like the scumbag I am."

Since the seat had been ejected, a portion of the steering system was lost. However, unlike a fighter plane, the cockpit itself was still there. Vermouth clutched the joystick and some torn wires. He could grasp the steering system of the Iron Demon with just that.

*If Marie saw these skills of mine, just what kind of face would she make?*

Vermouth went over the remainder of the mission plan. The armored walkers and four-legged tank in front of him seemed flustered. Vermouth scoffed.

*Hah! Can't even override your machine's friend-or-foe recognition, and turn this unit from ally to enemy? You juveniles aren't fit to be called amateurs.*

Despite having lost an Iron Demon, the enemy had yet to retaliate. A mechanism prevented friendly fire, and they couldn't use their armaments against the stolen Iron Demon until they changed it.

In much the same way, military automata like the Black Tortoise couldn't change alliance settings at their own discretion. For them to do that, they had to detect not just one but *two* attacks towards a friendly unit from the target.

In other words, until Vermouth attacked them twice, no one could open fire.

*If that's the case, how should I play this?*

*I have to crush the four-legged Guardian Dog. With the light plating of this Iron Demon, not to mention the incomplete controls, it'd be game over if that unit takes a shot at me.*

*In that case, I'll crush it in one blow and, right after that, destroy the Black Tortoise's AI. There's no other way.*

*If I can't take out the Guardian Dog in one go, the instant I land a second hit, the autocannons on the Black Tortoise will turn me to Swiss cheese.*

*That said, if I go for the Black Tortoise's AI first and the crew of the Guardian Dog manage to change its alliance settings, that's game over as well.*

*The best odds would be to incapacitate the Guardian Dog first, then take care of the Black Tortoise. After that, while they're pissing bullets all over me, I'll have to take out another two Iron Demons.*

*And without killing a single person. Easier said than done.*

*This mission makes the top ten in terms of difficulty in my career.*

*But...* Vermouth flashed a ferocious smile that looked out of place on a sex automaton's face. *It's fun as all hell.*

"Hey there, you piece of junk," he said, kicking the floor of the cockpit. "Know what Code D3 is?"

Naturally, there was no response. As the pilot's seat had been ejected, the unit recognized itself as unoccupied. However, even if there had been a response, the system would surely have answered no. After all, Code D3 was a combat order that Vermouth had arbitrarily named himself.

"You don't? Well, that figures. How about the one that the ghost princess taught me?" Vermouth operated the wires in his hands with precise movements. They controlled the Iron Demon's power output.

Before the mission started, Marie had taught him what to do.

"Release all limiters. In other words, shake those hips for me as hard as you can. Like your life depends on it. Got it, you pathetic virgin?"

As if responding to him, the few gauges that were left in the Iron Demon lit up. A countdown of the operational time left on the screen in front of him read "162 seconds."

"Hah, two and a half minutes for your first time? No need to worry, ya touched squirt. I'll show you a technique that'll make all the ladies come two minutes in!!" Vermouth let loose a rallying war cry from within the shaking machine.

"You have a disease," said Marie's voice through his resonance transceiver.

"Oh? What, you were listening in, ya little shrew? I'm hardcore, right?"

"Are you serious? I'll gladly stuff some sense into your head if you are, but—"

"Ha hah! Did you get confused? You're the one that gets stuffed!!"

Vermouth pulled on the wires like the reins of a horse, and the Iron Demon began to sprint. It unsheathed a high frequency oscillating blade with its right hand and charged towards the Guardian Dog.

Closing the distance at a speed near its functional limit, Vermouth smiled bitterly.

*AnchoR and RyuZU, those cheats dealt with them casually. But normally, a four-legged tank, even an outdated one, is a monster on the battlefield.*

*Challenging one with the capabilities of an armored walker is basically equivalent to suicide.*

But even if he didn't understand the unit's design like Marie, Vermouth still understood their weaknesses. There were three in a multi-legged tank: the supporting AI, the power spring, and the cockpit on the underside where the armor was thin.

However, the first two weaknesses were protected by sturdy armor that couldn't be pierced by the power he had. As such, the best option was to slip underneath the unit and kill the crew.

But Naoto's order had stipulated not killing anyone. Instead, Vermouth chose to go for its "fourth weakness" by process of elimination. It was a vulnerability that was present without exception in all multi-legged tanks. No, in all manned weapons. Cutting the steering control that existed in all human-piloted weapons.

That was also protected by tough plating, though not as much. The only part of the plating that was thin enough for his Iron Demon's blade to penetrate was the back of its waist. That spot was right above the cockpit.

Incapacitate the tank by piercing its armor without damaging the cockpit directly below it. He had been given this ridiculously difficult task.

*"Only you can do this, no?"*

Vermouth grinned. He pulled in the wires, and pushed the joystick all the way forward. The Iron Demon kicked off the ground and soared into the air, its boosters propelling it at maximum power.

The burst surpassed the unit's power output limiter and made the actuators cry out with strain. But that didn't matter. Vermouth adjusted the Iron Demon in midair and measured his aim.

Like driving a nail using a 14.2 ton hammer, The Iron Demon thrust its high-frequency oscillating blade into the back of the Guardian Dog.

"God daaaamn!!" Vermouth cursed loudly, feeling the impact of the strike through his body. "It fucking hurts!! So you're gonna contest the power of my cock, huh? You shitty mongrel!"

Vermouth roared as the recoil hit his hands. The blade creaked and distorted, but Vermouth continued pressing down as hard as he could.

"Just so you know," said Marie's voice. "The vulgar way in which you speak is actually the antithesis of hardcore."

"Ngh?!" Shocked by Marie's words, Vermouth choked on air as he finished his maneuver and jumped backwards. At the tail end of the swing, he felt the resistance against the controls give way. He figured that the blade had finally managed to go through, if only barely.

*As proof, the Guardian Dog's knees gave out, and it collapsed on the spot.*

*It should be out of order until it gets repaired. A few hours at the very least*, but more importantly...

"Wait, what?! Masterfully applying words like 'fuck,' 'shit,' 'damn,' and 'bitch' to a situation is what makes a man chic, isn't it?!"

Completing his swing, his Iron Demon's right arm burst apart. Its legs were damaged as well.

Meanwhile, all the automata adjusted their recognition from "ally" to "target for reevaluation" and focused their attention on him. At his feet, soldiers were showering his unit with bullets. Vermouth ignored them.

"Are you from America or something?" said Marie. "I mean, even the hooligans in gangster movies spit out more elegant lines these days, don't they?"

"Seriously?" said Vermouth, sensing the truth in Marie's fed-up voice. "So everything that bastard told me was a lie?! I'm gonna kill him if I find him in hell." Cursing Amaretto, his deceased colleague, Vermouth stared down the Black Tortoise in front of him.

*The instant I land a second attack, I'll be exposed to a shell-storm. So, of course, the target of my second attack is the Black Tortoise.*

Vermouth unsheathed the Iron Demon's remaining blade with its still functional left arm and accelerated forward. Ignoring the annoying malfunction reports popping up on his screen, he closed in on the Black Tortoise.

*Suck on th—*

His unit swayed heavily. One of the enemy's Iron Demons

had bodily tackled him. Even without adjusting the alliance set-tings, a tackle was possible.

"Fuckin' A! Looks like there's a virgin here with a working brain after all!" Vermouth growled through gritted teeth.

*Even though the enemy's unit is the same model, it's not much of a match for mine now that all the limiters are released.*

*It should be possible for me to ignore this guy and attack the Black Tortoise, but...I wouldn't have the precision to destroy the AI while being grappled from behind. I need to eliminate it first.*

Vermouth hesitated, but only for an instant.

"Hey, were you telling the truth earlier? Despite how it seems, I'm an authentic Neapolitan you know?! At least, I think so. On my family register... actually, I don't have a family register, or any memory of my youth, but it should be true, you know?!"

"Whatever the case, aren't you just a punk from the cesspools of society?"

Resolving himself, Vermouth spent his remaining free attack on the waist of the enemy Iron Demon.

"Oy bitch! Apologize to all of Italy! Italy is, you know, num-ber one in the world for luxury cars and ball games! And by ball games, of course, I mean bedroom sports as w—"

"Maybe you should just die."

The enemy unit collapsed to the ground, its power spring destroyed. However, at that instant, Vermouth felt himself sur-rounded by an artificially murderous intent. Naturally, that ap-plied to the prize in front of him as well.

"Ah... well, careful what you wish for."

The Black Tortoise turned its thermobaric buster towards him. Forget a direct hit, if his unit was even grazed by a shot, he'd have a guaranteed ticket to heaven.

"Vermouth?!" Marie cried out.

"Hey, bitch!" Vermouth shouted with his entire body. "There's no mistaking it, I'm an Italian after all. That's what my soul is telling me!!"

For a split second, he was staring down the barrel of the cannon.

"Fuckin' A!" he snarled. *I still have a chance to win.* Pulling on the wires, he wrenched his unit to the left. The shell from the thermobaric cannon flew right past him.

*I just have to stay out of this guy's line of fire! I can withstand the shots from the lightly armored automata for the time being but...*

"After all, it's screaming at me to act cool in front of a girl even at a time like thiiis!"

Vermouth intuitively moved his unit further left. Autocannon shells showered the spot where he had just been.

The attack came from the enemy's last Iron Demon.

"So you finally learned how to alter the alliance settings, eh? But I wanna thank you, you know? I truly appreciate it." Vermouth sneered, his unit veering left.

The enemy's autocannons howled as they chased him with continuous fire, while Vermouth swiftly made his way to the flank of the Black Tortoise.

He took a position where he could use it as cover from the enemy bombardment. Sparks flew as the cannon fire that had been chasing him hit the Black Tortoise's plating.

Vermouth snickered. "If you're gonna alter the alliance settings, change only the one you're supposed to. Let me guess, you've self-studied a billion times but never had any experience with an actual woman?"

All the automata in the area now also recognized the other Iron Demon as their enemy. *With this, there are only two I have to deal with.*

The Black Tortoise's AI hesitated, deciding whether it should prioritize the new enemy threat or the old one.

A momentary reprieve, but...

Vermouth curled his lips. He slid his unit to the rear and thrust his blade into the AI. Sparks scattered as his blade pierced deep inside the plating.

"On the battlefield, hesitating for less than a fraction of a second can be the difference between life and death. Was this educational for you, cherry boy?" The resistance disappeared. This was why Naoto had said this was something only Vermouth could do.

If only knowledge was required, Marie could have done it.

The weakest spot in the plating was where the processors and controls were positioned amongst the AI's bundled actuators. And Marie knew just how much energy was necessary to destroy the AI while leaving the rest untouched.

However, she wouldn't be able to execute the necessary actions in combat. What amount of power would be just enough, and what would be too much? Even if Marie could calculate the correct value, she didn't have the finesse to precisely apply it. Not while being fired upon in a commandeered war machine.

The Iron Demon's oscillating blade was massive, at two-and-a-half meters long. It was on a completely different scale from a clocksmith's handheld tools. If she were to accidentally destroy the unit's circuitry, they would have to make repairs.

*Just like cute li'l Naoto said, this is something that only I could have done,* Vermouth bragged to himself. He had experience destroying more than a hundred different models similar to the Black Tortoise.

Seeing it had ceased operating in front of him, he was certain.

*That should do it. I've destroyed just its AI, as ordered.*

*The only thing left to take care of is the enemy Iron Demon which, like mine, has been recognized as hostile by the enemy automata and the fodder on the ground. However, it'd be difficult for lightly armored automata to take down an Iron Demon by themselves.*

*In the worst case, the enemy Iron Demon could prioritize taking me down. The pilot could always try and figure out how to reset the alliance settings for his squad's automata after.*

*Furthermore, my unit's left hand is a mess, and it's lost both of its blades. Even if I get out, it'd be difficult to escape from the fodder with my current body.*

*In that case...*

"Still one more unit left on the hit list. Hey there, you piece of junk. Remember what I said about Code D3?"

Vermouth looked at the gauges. *Sixty seconds left, huh? Well, that should probably be enough.*

"Die for my sake," he muttered, tugging on a single wire and hooking it onto the lever by his feet. "See ya. We got along well, but pumping and dumping is my way of life. No strings attached."

"Really, you're the worst."

Chuckling at Marie's comment, Vermouth jumped out of the cockpit.

Immediately after, and at an aberrantly swift speed, the Iron Demon Vermouth had been piloting grappled the other and froze. Both units were locked in a hail of gunfire.

Meanwhile, Vermouth was assaulted by shells from cyborg soldiers and automata on the ground. If even one of their shots hit him, the commercial automaton body he was using would turn to scrap. However, Vermouth evaded the enemies' shots with graceful somersaults as he headed towards his destination.

Glancing at the sky, he zeroed in on his target.

"Welcome back, buddy. How was your flight? You promised that you'd tell me your impressions, right?" Vermouth smiled at the silhouette floating down from above. The pilot who had been forcefully ejected from the Iron Demon.

Vermouth untangled the parachute deftly and restrained the pilot.

"The car I borrowed from you broke down," he said nonchalantly. "It was definitely defective, no doubt about it. As such, give me back my cig please."

Vermouth snatched the cigarette from the pilot's mouth and took a drag.

"Hm? Does your mouth feel lonely? Try a taste of this then."

Vermouth swiped the handgun from the pilot's holster before

the man could react. He stuffed the muzzle into the pilot's mouth, locking his dropped jaw in place.

Now behind a hostage, Vermouth flashed everyone a big smile.

"Now then...if you don't want this guy's head blown off... even an idiot should know the drill, right?"

"F-fggh...ngggh." The hostage floundered about, but Vermouth's hold didn't loosen.

"You dirty little crook!" said one of the cyborg soldiers who had their guns pointed at the two of them.

"Haah? A crook? Reaaaally? That's weak, man. Yes, and?"

Crook. A cheat and a swindler but also a term that typically implied some manner of success at it. Vermouth chose to focus on the latter.

*Yeah, you're perfectly right*, he laughed.

Paying no mind to the countless guns, Vermouth took a deep drag of smoke and blew it out. The automata in the area couldn't fire at him, not with one of their designated allies in the way.

*Five, four, three...*

"Work on your vocabulary a bit more, pal. Hoo... aaaaaand zero!"

Vermouth's Iron Demon converted all of its remaining energy to heat and exploded. A shockwave of hot wind flew past with a thunderous roar. Shrouded by dazzling light, the enemy's Iron Demon collapsed with a hole in its abdomen.

Vermouth had set his Iron Demon to self-destruct in twelve seconds. It had converted the remaining forty-eight seconds of operational energy to heat. Just as planned, it was only enough force to destroy the abdomen of the enemy machine.

Confirming that the pilot had successfully bailed, Vermouth blew out another puff of smoke. "Hell yeah... the cigs today really are delicious. Mission accomplished. Oh."

His gun still stuffed into the pilot's mouth, Vermouth flashed the man a filthy smile. It was a total mismatch for his bewitchingly beautiful face.

"Give me a more fitting adjective next time, got it? Like, for example—"

A chain of black flashes broke out. All the fodder in the area was minced. Cyborg soldiers were incapacitated, automata made irreparable. Only assorted piles of humans and scrap metal remained.

RyuZU landed in the midst of the wreckage and scoffed. "What a cowardly, sleazy way of fighting. Really, I am impressed."

Vermouth laughed. He bumped the back of his hostage's head to knock him out and released him.

"You get it, dont'cha, Miss Dolly... yes, yes, call me 'honorable' in that tone of voice."

At that, Naoto, AnchoR, and Marie arrived.

"I can't believe it," Marie gasped. "You really pulled it off? With that body...?" Her voice was filled with true astonishment and relief.

It satisfied Vermouth. He took another deep drag with a smug smile. "What Missy, were you worried about me? So that's why you kept yakking over the radio. Let me guess, is it love?"

"Die, pervert. It was because if you screwed up, Halter would be in trouble."

"Hah! That so? So the Master's your number one, huh? Guess there's no helping it, I can't compete with him." Vermouth laughed and raised both hands in resignation.

"Confess your love for me, Missy!" he called out after Marie as she ran off towards the Black Tortoise. "If you screw up, I'll comfort you!"

*I managed to pull off a miracle. Now it's your turn to show me that you're the real deal. Or are ya really just a bitch?*

Picking out Vermouth's meaning between the lines, Marie smirked at his way of cheering her on.

*He may be an uncouth, infuriating man, but he did finish the job like he said he would.*

"RyuZU, AnchoR, and especially you, Marie, I'm counting on you. Okay?"

RyuZU curtsied, then turned and kicked off of the ground. She tore open the Black Tortoise's back plating.

AnchoR carried Marie up to the freshly exposed internal mechanisms.

"Mother, do your best... ngh!"

"Ugh, I told you to stop calling me that!" Marie grumbled. She put down Halter's brain pod and laid out her tools. Nodding, Marie opened and closed her fists to warm her hands up.

*I'll make Naoto's plan a success.*

*We have to destroy the entire enemy force absurdly, overwhelmingly, unreasonably, and at a speed which would be impossible for even the world's strongest army.*

*And, there's one more thing.*

As she ferociously began her work with Halter's brain pod in front of her, Marie recalled the details of last night's meeting...

• • ● • •

"Link Halter's brain to a heavily armored automaton?! What, are you screwing with me?!" Marie cried out.

As Marie listened to the plan—no, it was questionable whether this crackpot idea could even be called a plan—Naoto proposed a way to find a new artificial body for Halter.

Given his combat experience, Halter's absence hurt their overall strength considerably. However, connecting him to a cheap artificial body would actually be more dangerous.

Instead, Naoto figured that they could just seize the enemy's main weapon, the heavily armored Black Tortoise, and hook him up to that. But...

"Now look here, and I won't let you tell me that you don't realize this: human brains are things that control *human bodies!* A heavily armored automaton is completely different from an artificial body, which is made to be compatible with human brains!"

Despite having the most basic common sense shoved in his face, Naoto tilted his head in confusion.

"I mean... I think old man Halter can do it though, you know?"

"Because you figure Halter has experience operating manned weapons? Well yeah, of course he does. But that's completely different from having his brain linked to one! Have you ever taken in a panoramic image all at once? Like insects do with their compound eyes? Could you handle operating eight legs like a spider? The information that artificial skin and touch sensors send are completely different, you know? A human brain can't process that kind of information."

"Nooo? You're wrong about that, Missy," Vermouth interjected from a workshop hanger. "I feel like you're underestimating the brains of veteran soldiers. I'm talking about the ones who successfully trained themselves until their weapons became like their own flesh and blood."

"Don't be ridiculous. In the first place, there's no precedent for such a—"

"But there is. Countless examples, in fact."

Marie was left in mute amazement.

"If a human brain is directly linked to a weapon," Vermouth scoffed. "You avoid the inflexible algorithms of an AI, and you also avoid control lag, the major shortcoming of manned weapons. There are those who were forced to do it and those who chose to do it on their own, you know?"

Marie glared. "Don't screw with me! That's a violation of human rights! It's totally illegal!!"

"Hah hah! That one-liner's a masterpiece. To speak of human rights on a battlefield! Just where is this goddess who respects something like that? Because, unfortunately, I've never met her!"

Ignoring the flabbergasted Marie, Vermouth laughed sarcastically as he shifted his gaze. "So, brat. As I thought, your craziness is sublime. Besides, you only suggested this because you already figured it out, right?"

"Ah, so I guessed correctly?" Naoto said. "I had heard that the old man's artificial body was a verification unit, so I figured—"

"I love it. I love that scummy, keen perception of yours! On the other hand, I'm surprised that you don't know anything about it, Princess."

"What are you talking about?" Marie asked sullenly.

"I told you, didn't I?" Vermouth answered with a wide and exceptionally repugnant sneer. "There are those who chose to do it on their own. Master Halter is one of them."

"You must be joking," Marie muttered, practically holding her breath.

"I'm genuinely surprised that you didn't know. It's a famous legend in our line of work, you know?" Vermouth erased the sneer on his face and continued. "The Scarborough Fair Incident. Oberons. The absolute war machine Overwork. Only an imposter or an amateur scumbag wouldn't know of the legendary mercenary who performed a miracle. The Master hooked himself up *in the middle of combat,* you know?

"He linked his own brain!" Vermouth continued in a somewhat boastful tone. "On the spot! To the heavily armored automaton that he captured from the enemy!

"The Master supposedly said this back then, you know?" he shouted with pride. "That 'no AI can ever match the brain of a human who has survived the battlefield.' And with that, he destroyed twenty-seven heavily armored automata of the same model as his linked one and survived. He proved the truth of his words."

It was like someone reciting a legend of his favorite baseball team.

"That's a lie. If there were any such cases, there would have been papers written on the subject already, but there aren't any," Marie replied.

"Scarborough Fair was an unofficial operation. Something that happened before you were born, Princess. By the way, should I tell you why I was surprised that you didn't know about this when lil' Naoto managed to sniff it out? Listen, Princess. A verification unit basically means a test model."

The words truly made Marie choke on air this time.

"Savvy? Normally it might be a human rights violation, but what if the subject was someone who couldn't be more suited for the job?"

*Vermouth doesn't look like he's lying.*

*It's true that I don't know the original reason Halter was hired by the Breguet Corporation.*

*But, if what Vermouth's saying is true, then that'd mean that Halter's a test model...*

"Even theoretically," she said, doubling down. "That's impossible. If a military grade automaton feeds its sensory information into a human brain, the brain would be ruined."

"It's just as you say. That's the reason that such 'weapons' aren't mass produced. It's also the reason there are countless idiots who ended up forgetting their own names after trying to follow in the Master's heroic footsteps," Vermouth sneered. "Like me, for instance."

Marie stared at Vermouth. The man who had lost everything except his brain smiled impishly.

"I told you, didn't I? That I'm the Master's humble fan."

Marie sank into silence, then let out a deep sigh. "Very well. But I have a condition. If you call yourself his fan, then you should know the unit that Halter connected himself to, yes?"

"HS-FK2, 'Oberon'. It was an antique model even at the time. This country doesn't have them, and even if you did find one it'd be useless on a modern battlefield," Vermouth replied.

*She probably wants to use the same model to lower the risk as much as possible, but...*

However, Marie just muttered to herself and stared off into space. Satisfied, she nodded calmly.

"Oberon, huh? I see. I can see how it was possible. So Halter didn't actually go for broke without any consideration."

"Huh?"

"An Oberon. It's a model that has a 'flawed design.' It concentrates its control system and processors in one spot. In a live-fire test, it would shut down if it was hit in the back by so much as an anti-material rifle, so its back plating was reinforced. But because of that, its center of gravity became lopsided. So to stabilize it, the designers overloaded it with frontal armaments. That's the kind of failed creation it is."

Mouth agape, Vermouth stared at Marie. "Oy, don't tell me that you have the blueprints of all the weapons of the world?"

"Memorized? But of course," Marie affirmed, smirking. "Don't underestimate an ex-Meister, Mister Dutch Wife. If that's the case, we might be able to solve the problem."

"Err, what do you mean?" Naoto asked, tilting his head.

"It's true that concentrating a weapon's control system and processors in one place is a design flaw," Marie explained. "But it does have the benefit of making maintenance easier. There are quite a few weapons that employ this type of design...

"For instance, there's a model with a similar design currently in service in Japan: the Cz35C, 'Black Tortoise.' Naoto, can you tell where all the Black Tortoises in Tokyo are with those magical ears of yours?"

"So my hearing is magic now, huh? Like I could tell from just their model numbers? I need to hear their sou—"

"Okay, you'll know if one's turned on then, right?" Marie asked with a serious look. She repeated her query for confirmation. "Right?"

"Yeah. If there's one that's turned on, I'll find it." Naoto looked right back at her, nodding.

Evaluating his credibility from the expression in his eyes, Marie nodded in return. "I see."

*What am I doing? I don't have the luxury of doubting this guy's plan at this point. And doesn't Naoto always pull through?*

"Then that's what we'll target. We need to make the necessary preparations for connecting Halter's brain to that specific model. Vermouth." It was the first time she'd called him by his name. "Answer me honestly: what do you think the chances of success are?"

Halter was completely unresponsive. He didn't even make a sound when connected to a voice device. He was currently unconscious, essentially in a vegetative state.

*Will this really work? Will Halter really wake up?*

"Let me tell you something good, Ms. Marie Bitch Breguet." Vermouth flashed her a daring smile. "Soldiers live and die by the battlefield. Even if he did become your babysitter, his soldier blood will stay in him for the rest of his life. If the Master gets even a whiff of the battlefield..."

He paused for breath.

"He'll wake up, even if he's dead. And in the best possible way at that: by being in the worst mood ever."

• • • ● • • •

Connecting a human brain directly to a heavily armored automaton. Facing a task that any clocksmith would say was impossible, Marie laughed mockingly.

The high frequency oscillating blade that Vermouth had offhandedly thrust into the unit had destroyed the AI as planned. No more, no less. Perfectly. Precisely.

*He's a vulgar and irritating man, but it looks like he's not all talk. He did his job. He answered Naoto's magic with his own.*

"Well then... I'm up next, I guess."

Thirty seconds. That was the time limit that Naoto had given her. The maximum amount of time that AnchoR and RyuZU could lure the enemy to one spot while defending the group around the Black Tortoise from attacks.

"Sure! Just watch me! Piece of cake, I tell ya!!" Marie howled with a ferocious smile, deliberating putting on a show of confidence.

Time slowed down. At least, that's how it felt to Marie. Intensifying her focus, the clamor all around her faded away. She looked over what was in front of her. Tossing Halter's head into the air, Marie spread out her tools like a bird unfurling its wings.

Dismantling and removing the destroyed processors—2,876 parts in total—she finished all the necessary preparations. As Halter's brain fell before her eyes precisely 2.4 seconds later, the automaton's control system was prepped for a recreation of history.

*The operation itself is simple. Repairing RyuZU was much harder.* However, the nervousness she felt now was on a whole other scale. All the bones in her body creaked, and her muscles spasmed. She felt as if her blood were boiling.

If she messed up a single procedure or calculation, Halter would not wake up. That was an understatement. She would have put the final nail in his coffin.

In the face of such a terrifying possibility, Marie wore a mystifying smile. *It's doable. It's doable if you're the one who tries, Marie!*

She finished the preparatory cleanup, and Halter's brain pod fell back into her hands. 27.6 seconds remained. She swiftly yet carefully connected his brain pod to the control system.

*This'll take 7.6 seconds. From there, it'll take me 6.1 seconds to test the automaton's nerve circuits, 4.9 seconds to tune the control system's algorithm closest to human cognition, 3.3 seconds to reboot the unit externally, and at least 4.1 seconds for Halter to awaken.*

That added up to 26 seconds in total. The buffer she had to deal with any unexpected situations was less than two seconds. *Man, I have two whole seconds to spare!*

In that instant, Marie got the false impression that time had stopped. Her heart beat rapidly. Sound faded away. She felt like her body temperature had taken a nose dive. As her tension and focus reached their limits, Marie felt as if her very consciousness had ascended to a higher plane.

Touching something like the imaginary domain where only RyuZU was allowed to tread. Just like Mute Scream, it was the sensation of the interval between the present and a second later being stretched out infinitely.

The only difference was...

*My hands are so slow. Ngh! Get moving already!* Her body couldn't keep up with her mind in that infinite second. She felt heavy and slow, as if she had sunk into a sea of tar.

However, from the rest of the gang's perspective, her display was already in the realm of magic. All sorts of parts and tools danced in the air of their own volition before settling into their proper places.

It was as if there were special gravitational forces that existed between them, an orbit that dictated where they should go. If this spectacle wasn't divine, then just what was it?

"I can't believe it! Oy, li'l Naoto, is that girl really human...?" Vermouth muttered.

"Yeah, that's genius," Naoto replied. "See that, AnchoR?"

"It's more amazing than amazing! Mother's a genius," AnchoR said in admiration, turning around in the midst of a battle with shells, bullets, and enemies swarming her.

"Make no mistake, AnchoR. Those are the limits of a human," RyuZU responded. "At least for now."

RyuZU's voice seemed to harbor mixed feelings. With no regard for the things going on around her, Marie became sharper and faster, immersed in a level of focus beyond focus. In the depths of her trance, she recalled Vermouth's words:

*"I feel like you're underestimating the brains of veteran soldiers. I'm talking about the ones who successfully trained themselves until their weapons became like their own flesh and blood."*

*Yeah, it's true that I underestimated human prowess. I get what he was saying now. After all, my mind fully grasps all the machinery that my hands have just touched.*

*The gears, cylinders, wires, screws, springs hidden beneath the heavy-duty plating, the power mechanism that they constitute... I understand everything about them. Everything.*

*If I felt like it, I could name the kinds of parts being used in every one of its junctions, in what numbers, even the condition they're in. Forget that, this mechanism that I'm touching, this enormous power mechanism, too... Even this city that I'm standing on!!*

*Ngh!*

Marie perceived danger through her expanded consciousness. A self-propelled artillery roughly three kilometers away was about to bombard her position.

*It seems like the others haven't noticed it yet. They have their hands full dealing with the enemies close by...*

Marie tried to warn them, but nothing came out. She couldn't breathe. She was sinking into the sea of tar. Her ascended form remembered that it was perhaps human after all. Her honed awareness was dulling.

*No, I can't! Not yet!* She still had work to do. She needed another second to tune the control system... no, she screwed up. She needed two seconds to recover now.

There were eight seconds left. She pulled back her receding consciousness and continued to focus.

*Done!*

The unit began to reboot.

One, two, three... success. There were five seconds left. However, from the corner of her dulled awareness, she noticed that the self-propelled artillery had taken aim.

*This is bad. I don't have any more time. Move! Move move move move move move move. I said move! Halter!!*

She should have done everything correctly. However, the unit did not respond.

The only thing left to do was wait for him to wake up. That should have been the case, but...

The artillery fired. She even perceived the shell spinning in the barrel as it accelerated against the rifling.

*Why hasn't Naoto noticed?* She wondered, before immediately answering her own question. *He can't hear anything faster than sound*!

Marie finally remembered something that she should have realized much sooner.

*Estimated time left until the shell hits, twelve seconds. The trajectory is stupidly accurate. It's shooting towards me in a straight line. In twelve seconds, the shell will rip through my body and into the exposed internals of the unit where Halter's brain pod is, pulverizing him.*

She could see a clear vision of that future. However, in that instant, her footing shook. As her consciousness was pulled back into real time, she lost her balance. She was flung into the air from the impact of the shell that had landed to her side.

Marie just barely managed to comprehend what had happened. *The unit just barely dodged! Incredibly enough, it was just enough to make the shell that would have meant certain death miss me.*

The Black Tortoise rotated violently, its feet tearing up the earth as it nimbly caught Marie's body with its right arm. Then, with an unmatched accuracy and speed that astonished even RyuZU and AnchoR, the Black Tortoise vaporized the self-propelled artillery with the thermobaric buster on its shoulders.

Without even a momentary pause, it turned the wheels on the inner sides of both its feet, actually drifting as it traced a large arc and unleashed a volley with its 30cm autocannons.

The shells burst like a sudden shower, and yet, they had the precision of a sniper rifle. The Black Tortoise was absolutely annihilating the enemies that even RyuZU and AnchoR couldn't fully contain on their own.

"M-Mother!"

Marie was flung into the air in an abrupt maneuver, and AnchoR hurried to catch her.

The Black Tortoise continued its rampage all the while, as if it had gone mad. As it barraged the area with its side cannons... no, as it sniped targets with its fusillades, it spun around and around, its large legs plowing through the lightly armored automata in the vicinity.

"Hal...ter...?" Marie muttered, staring dumbfounded at what looked like the frenzy of a vengeful god.

The only thing emanating from the Black Tortoise that was connected to Halter's brain was stone-cold murderous intent. The desire to mow down and trample everything in its sight. There was no air of human emotion.

"Could it be that...I screwed something up?" Marie muttered in a trembling voice.

"Screwed something up?" Naoto responded with a blank look. "Wait, you screwed something up, Marie? The old man seems to be perfectly back to normal though."

"Huh?"

"Allow me to explain so that even someone like you, Mistress Marie, whose deficiency in mental faculties is enough to engender a sense of pity in others, could understand. So that even a monkey could make sense of it. Namely, please visit an eye doctor if it looks to you like any of his attacks are hitting us."

Marie turned to see RyuZU taking a break from her attacks to smile.

*It's true,* Marie realized. *We haven't been attacked by the Black Tortoise at all. But then, what is that terrifyingly systematic destruction all about?*

The Black Tortoise fired two shots from its main cannon, and heavily armored automata several kilometers away were hit and vaporized.

"Godammit! Which one of you bastards was the one who woke me up when I was sleeping so comfortably?"

Hearing the Black Tortoise—or rather, Halter—groan unhappily through the static of the external speakers, Marie's eyes welled up.

"Halter!" she yelled, trying to hide her truly heartfelt relief. "Halter, do you hear me?!"

"Aahh? Oh, it's you, Princess. What's going on here? Wait, what the... what's with this nauseating field of vision? Am I seeing through compound eyes? Oy, so you hooked me up to an automaton? What the heck have you been up to?" Halter muttered, the tone of his voice changing from angry to baffled as he grasped the situation.

"That's my line," Marie retorted with a teary smile. "Making me go through all this trouble. What the hell were you doing?!"

"Yeah, sorry about that... I was taking a little nap."

"A little nap...?" Marie repeated in shock. "Don't tell me that the reason you didn't respond when I hooked you up to a voice device was because..."

"Oh, that happened? No, see, when my sensory organs are cut off, I get really sleepy somehow. I'm sorry, really. Feels like I got some sound sleep for the first time in a long while."

"..."

Marie's body shook, emanating a menacing aura.

*Are you kidding me? This guy was sleeping like a baby while I worried my brains out? I'm going to slaughter him when this is over.*

"Missy, I told you, didn't I?" Vermouth interjected with a laugh. "That the Master would wake up in the best possible way: the worst mood ever.

"A soldier who's rudely awoken by a night raid loses all sense of rationality. He retaliates. His body and mind are strung to their limits. In other words, it's the perfect set of circumstances for him to perform a massacre. That's why one of the few rules that is actually respected on the battlefield is 'no night raids.'"

Marie sighed in frustration, not entirely satisfied with Vermouth's explanation. Meanwhile, seeing an unfamiliar face, Halter nimbly tilted his giant mechanical head.

"Oy, you're that greenhorn? What, did you awaken to that kind of thing?"

"Hardly. This little number is something that your princess gave me. Despite how it looks, it comes with a pretty big cock. If I felt like it, I could give the brat that I fell in love with a good dicking."

"Dear me," RyuZU interjected, her voice cutting like a knife. "Is this pervert a homosexual man—excuse me, a homosexual doll—as well?"

The scythes grated against the ground as RyuZU walked towards him.

"Calm down, Miss Dolly," Vermouth continued daringly. "It was just a figure of speech. I'm just looking forward to your master flipping this world upside down as one of his fans, that's all."

"Is that so? In that case, you are correct in your evaluation of Master Naoto. I shall interpret your statement that way and let you off the hook. But should you ever look at Master Naoto with lecherous eyes..."

"Give a guy a break, will ya? Jeez. I'm straight, okay? Oh, right, I guess you missed it. I gotta say though, that kid in drag—

Naoko-chan—was quite the jewel, you know?"

RyuZU froze. Like an old iron gate in need of oiling, she turned her head towards Naoto with an audible creak. "Have you finally awakened to that particular sexual fetish while I slept, Master Naoto?"

"RyuZU, I'm used to others looking at me like I'm utter trash, but you doing it seriously hurts, you know?! It was a disguise, okay? A disguise!"

"Father...had a lot...of fun. He was...cute, you know?"

"So, everyone except me and that magnified piece of patchwork over there witnessed it?" RyuZU asked, her voice trembling slightly.

Even Marie understood how RyuZU was feeling from the sound of her voice. *How novel. It's astoundingly hard to believe, but it appears that RyuZU is...sulking.*

Marie let out a sigh. "If a photo will do, I have one that the woman who dressed Naoto took. More importantly, right now..."

"Understood. I shall take it from you even if I have to kill you," RyuZU said with a wide stare, cutting Marie off.

*Ah, she's serious.* Seeing the intensity of her stare, Marie resolved herself for death.

Meanwhile, AnchoR was tugging on RyuZU's sleeve. "Big Sis... here..." AnchoR presented several photos that she had retrieved from her pockets.

RyuZU accepted them with trembling hands. She scrutinized and absorbed every last detail in them before hugging them to her chest.

"Ahh..." she sighed.

Having attained her prize, RyuZU quickly stuffed the photos down the collar of her dress with a smile like the Holy Mother. "AnchoR. Exceptional. Simply exceptional work, if I may say so as your eldest sister. Do you realize that you have just saved a human life?"

"You...aren't talking about my life, right?" Marie muttered in a trembling voice.

AnchoR flashed her sister a broad smile. "And... and also, I had a date with Father! It was really fun!"

The saintly smile disappeared from RyuZU's face. "Is that so? It was a lot of fun, huh?"

"Y-y-yeah...?" AnchoR nodded rigidly, feeling the sudden change in the wind.

RyuZU formed a smile with her lips, but her eyes were dead. "I see, that is good to hear, AnchoR. However, should you two partake in such activities without me again, I shall be forced to take the appropriate measures. So be warned. More specifically, measures of force. Discipline..."

"Oy RyuZU?! I won't allow any sisterly figh—"

"I-I'm sorry... but, I don't want to fight you, Big Sis. I would... probably win."

"What are you saying, AnchoR?! Obviously it is Master Naoto who'd be put to the sword."

"Wait, meee?!" Naoto cried out.

"It is with extreme regret that I must inform you of this, Master Naoto," RyuZU said, coldly looking down on him. "But while I can accept you having a 'sister sandwich,' I must be part of it. That is the most I can compromise."

"I-I'm so sorryyyy! I'm a failure of a husband to have gone on a date without my wiiife!" Naoto exclaimed, diving to the ground and prostrating himself before RyuZU's feet.

Halter sighed, watching this conversation from above. "Hey, could someone answer my question? What's the situation?"

*Oh, right,* Marie thought, shaking her head. Relieved at Halter's return, she had almost forgotten the situation they were in. Just as she opened her mouth to explain the circumstances, Naoto stood up to interrupt her. His answer was extremely concise:

"It's a *fun* situation."

Naoto smiled wickedly. "We're gonna beat the hell out of the fools who wrecked you, old man. We're gonna take revenge for what they did to RyuZU, and all of Akihabara, until they cry. And after that, we're going to stuff them in a crucible. We'll send anyone who gets in our way flying and silence all the loudmouths who think they know anything. That's all there is to it."

"I see," said Halter. "Well, that certainly sounds *fun* indeed. Do let me take part."

"That's why we put you in that unit. How do you feel?"

"Perfect. Thanks, Princess. I wouldn't expect any less from you. You did great work," Halter said, giving Marie a thumbs-up with the Black Tortoise's hand.

Looking up at him with an exasperated smile, Marie puffed out her chest. "But of course. Just who do you think I am?"

"Ha ha. Well then, Naoto. It seems like you're the commander of this operation, so what're your orders?" Halter asked with a low laugh.

Everyone looked at Naoto. Even Marie's ears perked up so that she wouldn't miss what he said.

*Naoto, RyuZU, AnchoR, Vermouth, and Halter.*

*When I first heard Naoto's plan, I thought it was idiotic. I thought it was idiotic when we decided to do it. Even after we started doing it. To be honest, I still think it's idiotic even now.*

*But for some reason, I feel like no matter what Naoto tells us to do, I'll believe that it's possible.*

Surveying the enemy force that encircled them from a distance, Naoto smiled daringly. "Hm, I see that you guys rounded up the remaining forces like I asked."

If they had left Marie behind and continued to subjugate the enemy, they could have kept the battle at a distance and, ironically enough, let her work more safely. They had paused their advance for thirty seconds because...

"To start things off, annihilate the 378 enemies here in the remaining thirty-eight seconds without killing anyone."

"Talk about anticlimactic," Halter chuckled. "That's a piece of cake."

Everyone smiled a little at his bravado. And so 22 seconds passed. That was the time it took for the gang to annihilate the weapons and armaments of the 378 man force.

After neutralizing all remaining threats, they entered the palace, and Naoto flipped off a news helicopter behind him.

• • ● • •

Opening the enormous gate, the gang passed into the palace. The passageway was large enough that even Halter could walk through it in his current form. Advancing straight ahead, the passageway led to a courtyard-like hall. There were people waiting for them.

Several tens of imperial guards stood poised behind a sorry excuse for a barricade, warily studying the intruders. Behind them were two slightly out-of-date armored walkers.

It seemed like they were aware of what had happened outside because they looked afraid of Naoto. Even so, they were hyping themselves up, as if to say: "We won't give up without a fight."

*What should we do?* Just as Marie thought that, a young woman came forward alone from behind the line of imperial guards. She walked straight to the front, brushing off the soldiers trying to stop her.

Marie smiled. *Thankfully it looks like she remembers me.*

"Wait here." Marie said, making her way to the front of the group.

They stopped within meters of each other.

Marie bowed elegantly. "Nice to meet you, Your Highness Princess Hoshimiya."

"Yes, I believe this is the first time we have met, Ms. Terrorist." Houko said, lowering her head in kind.

"Well then," Marie continued, after they had exchanged

spoken and tacit greetings. "Allow me to introduce myself. My name is Maëribell. The ringleader behind this country's current crisis, and the most nefarious terrorist in history is my boss."

Marie pointed a thumb over her shoulder at Naoto. He glared at her.

"Oy, you bastard!" Naoto howled. "You dodged responsibility just now, didn't you?! You're trying to make a contingency plan in case things go sour, aren't you?!"

Marie ignored him and smiled at the princess.

Houko seemed to be a bit at a loss. "Well then, Miss Maëribell. Have you come here for the reason I imagine?"

"It might be a little different." Marie shrugged. "We came here for our own sakes. That's all."

Houko furrowed her brows. "Are you really certain that this is what you want?"

"Of course. This is the path that we chose for ourselves. Also, I think you're misunderstanding things, so allow me to restate my position. That idiot over there is truly the ringleader behind this chain of incidents."

Upon hearing that, Houko's eyes widened. She bowed her head deeply to Naoto, as if to correct some sort of mistake. When she looked up again, she castigated the entire group in a stern, elegant voice, looking at each of them in turn:

"In that case, all you terrorists with whom this is my first meeting—allow me to express my sincere resentment. You wreaked unprecedented havoc upon this nation in your attempt to subvert it. Now you even threaten my very life for your own gain.

"I shall surely never forgive your nefarious crimes. I have conviction that you all will be met with due punishment one day."

Her obsidian eyes filled with a sharp, powerful will of steel. "Now then, pray tell: what do you hope to achieve?"

It was RyuZU who replied to those resolute words.

"Yes, let me see... For now, I think a deep cleaning of the palace is in order. Much like the *landscaping* of the grounds we did outside. Master Naoto?"

"Yeah, we've advertised ourselves plenty by now. Let's give everyone watching the last push. I'll leave it to you."

RyuZU bowed reverently, then touched the clock by her chest. If she had used this method from the beginning, it would have taken her a wink to annihilate the forces outside, but she deliberately chose not to. An advertisement should be easily understandable. An advertisement that no one could understand would be meaningless.

However, now that they had destroyed the outside forces in seven minutes and completed that "impossible" demonstration, all that was left were the two words that would perfectly top things off. RyuZU's formal black dress transformed into a white bridal gown.

"'Mute Scream'"

A display beyond anyone's understanding began and ended just as abruptly.

Six minutes and forty-eight seconds after Naoto's initial declaration, all enemy forces, both inside and outside the palace, were completely neutralized.

• • ● • •

"As we reported a little while ago, the criminal identifies himself as Naoto Miura—"

This news report was on live TV, broadcasting to the entire world. The footage was so compelling that everyone living in Tokyo, no, everyone living in the *world* was glued to the screen.

The ordinary citizens of Tokyo were obviously watching but so were the politicians who had been embroiled in their fruitless meeting, as well as the police and military who had been busy handling the unrest. Even foreign businesses were watching with astounded eyes.

Among those assorted groups of viewers, the military and the arms manufacturers took the footage the hardest. Of course they did. After all...

"Furthermore, according to testimonies from the survivors, the vast majority of the damage was caused by two automata who referred to themselves as Initial-Y Series—"

*This is it.* It was the report one person had been scouring the channels for.

*I see, the rebel army that had surrounded the palace was nothing more than a ragtag force in the end. Their leaders were delirious youngsters whose degree of proficiency was nothing to boast about.*

*As to the equipment, our reserves and old weapons made up more than half of what they have. But, even taking that into consideration...*

"I repeat! It's been an hour since the terrorist group occupied the palace, but there haven't been any confirmed casualties so far..."

Seven minutes. Strictly speaking, six minutes and forty-eight seconds. That was the amount of time it took for a terrorist group (whose numbers didn't even reach the double digits) to annihilate two battalion-sized military forces.

Had there ever been such a force in this world? It would be easy for an elite army to do something similar if they had more time and their lives were no object.

However, no one could produce such a result in so short a period of time. Those who understood military matters and clocksmithing knew this fact all the more.

And no matter how many times they replayed the footage in slow motion, they still couldn't get even a clue of how the terrorists annihilated the imperial guard. They had done "something" at a speed faster than even a single frame of video.

There were two in that group who called themselves Initial-Y Series automata. Legendary automata made by the one who had recreated this planet.

To ordinary folks, they were legendary things. Fairy tales, an urban legend. To those well versed in technology, they would be international treasures. If they really existed. Those well versed in politics knew they *did* exist but also that none of them were operational.

Still further into the dark side, those who knew secret intelligence and highly classified information (for example, people at the top of the Five Great Corporations) understood the truth.

That the Initial-Y Series existed, and if they were ever activated, they would become the most terrifying weapons in history.

The understanding among these different groups of people were either altered or made certain by the broadcast. The footage was impossible to reproduce with any current technology. That was the greatest proof that there truly were Initial-Y automata among the terrorists.

A noise suddenly flooded the live footage. At the same time, there was a severe quake centered around Tokyo.

All communication mechanisms in the area ceased functioning, and the resonance gears began to turn irregularly.

The gears of Tokyo's core tower, which coordinated municipal functions, began to behave in unprecedented ways.

It wasn't a malfunction. It wasn't a fault caused by degradation over time. Everything about the system's operation was normal. Only, for some reason, the mechanisms wouldn't obey the superintendent.

The people of Tokyo remembered a phenomenon that was very much alike to this: two days ago they had looked on, petrified in their helplessness, as they listened to a boundlessly cheerful claim of criminal responsibility from the devices all around them.

And now...

"Ladieeeeeeeeeeessssss annnnnnnnnnnnnnnd gentlemen!! As well as you insignificant others that I'll skip naming, do y'all remember my voice?!

"It's been a while hasn't it? Maybe a couple days? Did you miss me? Were you lonely, maaaaaaaan?

"Sorry for making you wait but check it! I've been stirring up trouble for a few consecutive days now! I love you baby baby babyyyyyyyyyyyyyyyyy!!"

Once again, the voice and face of nightmares was broadcast as the entire world watched on.

· · • ● • · ·

"By popular request! For all you nincompoops who fell in love with me after the last broadcast! Today's the grand reveal of my face, hee hee! Let me guess, you're head over heels, right? I'm such a stud, right?!"

As that maniacal voice prattled on, someone was pacing the transmission room of the headquarters of the current ruling party.

"Sure looks like they're having fun over there." Yuu Karasawa smiled bitterly. He understood the true intent behind this broadcast.

*Dr. Marie must be pretty upset. This is far too close to entertainment for her tastes. I've no doubt that her expression is something that she never wore during her time with Meister Guild.*

*If possible, I'd have liked to see it. Take a picture for posterity's sake, but...*

"Work work work. Good Lord, laborers sure have it hard."

Karasawa turned his gaze from the TV back to the plain door in front of him. It had no doorplate. Instead, the words "Transmission Broadcast Room" were painted directly onto it. It was not equipped for short-range transmissions, but rather for super-long-range ones that could reach the opposite side of the planet.

"Well, grumbling about it won't help. Guess I'll get to work... as a consultant..."

*This is definitely outside my official duties, though,* Karasawa thought as he took a short breath. Exhaling, he kicked the door with all his might.

"!!"

The door flung open with a boom.

As Karasawa entered without a moment's respite, a startled man jumped up and turned around. Karasawa knew his face. It was unmistakably the man who had skulked away from the conference room two days ago.

"Wha... who the hell are you?! What are you doing here?!"

"My, my, that's what I want to ask *you.*"

Unsettled, the man's face twisted into something ugly. Karasawa wore a cool expression and a soft smile.

"Would it be alright if I asked you where you sent that message? You know, as a consultant."

"I have no obligation to answer you, you bastard."

"Well, I guess I don't have to force you. I can find out easily enough if I just check the logs."

"You bastard, you don't have the authority to do either of those things!!"

"Yeah, maybe. But who'll hold me responsible?"

The man drew a handgun from inside his jacket. Seeing the

maneuver, Karasawa realized that the man was clearly a cyborg, and used to combat, although his body was disguised as flesh.

He aimed his gun at Karasawa in one slick movement and began to pull the trigger.

"Hey, sooooooo no offense, but I'm a little disappointed, okay? Heck, I feel bad enough to cry! I mean, I knew there'd be small fry, but I didn't expect you guys to be *that* weak. You minnows aren't even a meal! Or is my grand old gang a little too strong?! Sorry for that, seriously!"

*Clang.* The handgun fell to the floor.

"Really, it's just like Mr. Naoto Miura said, isn't it?" Karasawa continued, maintaining his smile. "Challenging a Meister with an artificial body of all things! You're selling us way too short, you know?"

Karasawa folded and put away the portable tools that he had instantaneously drawn. He looked down. At his feet was a groaning man who had just had his artificial body dismantled.

Karasawa picked up the man's gun. "Well then, I'll give you just three seconds, all right? Think you could tell me who you were communicating with? Using the ruling party's transmission equipment without authorization?"

"You bas...tard. How much do you know..."

"That's enough, thank you."

Without even a second of hesitation, Karasawa fired. Bullets hit all of the parts of the man's artificial body.

"Be grateful, all right? I'd rather just dispose of uncooperative people myself, but due to the request of a certain cute girl, I'm stopping short of killing you. I figure someone'll find you within the forty-three hours it'll take for your brain's preservation device to expend its power. Now then…"

Karasawa tossed away the emptied handgun.

"Time to find out why someone who clearly doesn't belong to the government is using the ruling party's transmission station, what they communicated, and to whom. Ah, I need permission, right?"

Karasawa scoffed and pulled the man on the floor up by his collar. He fetched his ID card to show the man, although his artificial eyes were clearly out of operation at this point.

"I'm Yuu Karasawa, a consultant hired by the Ministry of Technology. I'll be checking your transmission logs, all right?"

Karasawa violently shook the man by the collar to make him nod, then slammed his face into the ground with a smile. "Thank you for your cooperation."

The man wasn't even twitching anymore as Karasawa turned away.

Karasawa took out a mobile device from his pocket and connected it to the transmission equipment with the movements of a veteran Meister. Then, he waited for the transmission log to download.

"Ahh, by the way, I'm not an official employee of the Ministry of Technology. Once I find out who you were communicating with, anything more would be extra-professional work, so even if someone uses this room afterwards without authorization, it'll be considered your fault for failing to manage the premise properly, not mine. Don't think badly of me."

Karasawa tapped briskly at the terminal, and a notification that communication lines to the ruling party's headquarters had been opened was sent to eighteen different locations in the outside world.

"Now then, have I done enough to earn my pay?" Karasawa quipped.

He read through the log, humming to himself.

• •• ● •• •

"Honestly, I'm super disappointed at how easyyyyy it was to chew through the military. Despite us giving advance warning in Akihabara to round the military up in one place, they were destroyed! Annihilated! Eradicated! By just *one* of our toys?! What the hell?! Why're y'all such party poopers, maaan?!"

Inside Tokyo's military headquarters in Ichigaya Grid, the military's chief of staff trembled as he listened to the madman, his face flushing a furious red. Around him, other officers were slamming their fists on the table and cursing, but the chief of staff endured an even deeper rage, as well as terror. He bit his lip.

He couldn't refute Naoto's statements. The enormous weapon was occupying Akihabara even now, and the imperial guard had been subdued in an instant. How could he refute someone who backed his big talk up with action?

"And so! Because you guys are so weak and easy to chew through, it's starting to feel like a chore to follow through with the rest of the plan that I put together!"

The chief of staff shuddered at what the consequences of this broadcast would be.

*The world has already gotten word of the electromagnetic weapon. Now, there's this footage. At this point, knowledge of what happened in Tokyo has circulated throughout the planet.*

*For a threat as large as this, the ISS committee will surely authorize the use of Tall Wand. Even if the neighboring Asian countries oppose it.*

*Normally, the motion would require the permission of the Japanese government, but the prime minister's hasty request has still not been withdrawn.*

*Actually, considering that the government isn't even in full control of the military right now, and that there isn't even a functioning provisional government, the ISS might deem Japan to be in a state of anarchy.*

"So I'm thinking that I'll liven things up a bit, baby! C'mon now, everyone! Shake your booty and scream: yayyyyyyyyyyyyy!! You like me! You really like me! Thank you! Thank you everyone! To answer your expectations...I solemnly swear! Within three hours...

"We'll make the entirety of Tokyo collapse in a suuuuper flashy fashion! Yay!!"

Hearing those words, everyone in the military headquarters, no, in all of Japan...froze stock still.

*Three hours?* The chief of staff shot to his feet, gawking. *Did he just say three hours? The ISS committee wouldn't be able to authorize the use of Tall Wand in such a short time. Forget that, the weapon itself wouldn't be ready, even if it was authorized right now.*

But even this consideration was stopped dead in its tracks.

"Whoooooooooopsies, how rude of me! I completely forgot! I got so into things that I left my guest in the waiting room! Hey, come on dowwwwnn! It's time for the gueeeeeeest segment!!"

The camera turned at the boy's over-the-top gesture. A certain young woman came into view, bound in ropes. The chief of staff knew her face well. It was someone whom nearly all the Japanese people watching this broadcast had seen at least once before.

"Dear citizens, please listen calmly to what I am about to tell you."

It was the First Princess of His Majesty the Emperor, Imperial Princess Houko Hoshimiya. Arguably the most highborn woman in the country had been reduced to a pitiful prisoner.

Her face looked haggard, and her complexion pallid. Despite that, she resolutely raised her face to gaze into the camera and spoke to her subjects.

"These people have seized control over the grid regulating mechanism of Tokyo—of the Pillar of Heaven itself. I believe that this broadcast proves that fact beyond all doubt."

Hearing those words from the princess, the entire world froze still in mute amazement.

• • ● • •

Even the ordinary citizens of Tokyo understood what it meant. With just a touch of his finger, that villain could destroy Japan and all of East Asia along with it. This was now an international crisis.

"All of you in the military, please, pay no mind to my safety and promptly regain control of the Pillar of Heaven," the princess continued stout-heartedly. "These people are serious. Also, citizens of Tokyo, I beseech you to obey the directions of your officials and calmly evacuate the capi—ahh!"

The princess was yanked from behind and let out a brief yelp as she fell backwards out of the frame. In her place, Naoto Miura came back on screen and stuck up his middle finger with a sadistic expression.

"Hey hey heeeeeeey?! Uhhhhhh, Princess?! What kind of garbage do you think you're blurting out?! If you keep going off script, I'll string you up tortoise-style and have everyone watch me play piñata with my cock what the hell, old man?! What kinda cue card is that?! I've got my wife and daughter here, y'know?! Do you want my wife to skewer me in a family meeting?!

"Ah, right right, my wife and daughter are the two Initial-Y Series automata that made their debut in the news just now. How about it, they're crazy cute, right?! But I better not see any affiliated goods, I wouldn't be able to stop myself buying them! Please forward such business requests through my agency! Using their likeness without permission is forbidden! Absolutely forbidden!"

Nobody watching the broadcast even knew what to think anymore. The woman who had been on screen earlier was Japan's first princess. Although she had no political power, culturally, she was one of the most important people in the world. A symbol of the nation.

Even though she was technically substituting for His Majesty

the Emperor, who was currently bedridden, she was just as important as the Queen of the United Kingdom or the President of the
United States. She was a VIP. Nearly all Japanese people regarded
her as such, regardless of what region they were from.

Not to mention that the young, beautiful princess had acted
so courageously despite being tied up by fiendish terrorists. Even
citizens who were normally unconcerned with the imperial family, even foreigners, felt their hearts stir.

"Ah, hey, oy watch it! I'm telling you, don't kick me. Ugh,
gawd, you keep slowing me down. Man, this princess is a serious
party pooper. Oy, keep giving me trouble, and I'll fucking kill you,
got it?!" the terrorist rashly asserted.

Those who watched the scene unfold began to feel a strong
sense of solidarity in their swelling anger. Their minds rapidly
cleared to focus on just one thing: the unforgivable criminal had
laid his hand on someone sacred.

· · ● · ·

"I see... how impressive."

Inside Yatsukahagi, the enormous weapon bearing down
on Akihabara Grid, Gennai Hirayama muttered to himself. The
broadcast was displayed by the giant screen in the control room.

*It's clear what their intentions are.*

*If they just wanted it to be known that the princess has been taken
hostage, they could have gagged her. They need not risk letting her talk.
Yet, they let her speak freely because they didn't need to silence her.*

*At the very least, the military now has a pretext to end their infighting and unite against a common foe. The citizens that have fallen into a state of violent panic will probably obey the directions of the police to some extent as well.*

*And of course, the princess also functions as a hostage. At the very least, there shouldn't be any commander who'd ignore her safety and launch an attack on the Pillar of Heaven.*

*Even if they did, a raid would be a last resort. They'll surely wait the three hours. In that time, they'll... no, "Y" will work on gaining full control over the Pillar of Heaven. Easily, without anyone hindering him. He'll undoubtedly destroy this Yatsukahagi.*

*With that, Shiga's ex-military will disappear...and the only thing that will be left is a convenient "truth."*

"Ahh, how truly impressive. With that, they've taken away all our options."

"Y-your Excellency! We should immediately declare criminal responsibility ourselves!" the adjutant by his side yelled, flustered.

Gennai looked up at him with a calm expression. "Right and what would we say? That we have no relationship with them and that a coup d'état is our goal? Do you really think that there's anyone who would believe such nonsense?"

"Th-that's—" The adjutant faltered for a second but then shook his head. "H-however, if things continue like this, the capital will collapse within three hours, so either way...!"

"Calm down, Major. They have no intention of making the capital collapse. A trifle like this is within expectations."

*That's right, they have no such intention. What they did was take all the blame.*

*By taking on responsibility for the horrors and malice of the military—including ourselves, the government, and the industrial economy—they washed away the sins of the elite. And in doing so, they united everyone against them.*

*The reason they did it, when you get down to it, is to save this country.*

*They didn't even kill anyone in the military forces that they annihilated, and you're telling me that they'll make Tokyo collapse? It's obvious they're bluffing.*

Gennai recalled a legend of the ancient era. The story of a man who bore all the sins of humanity and was executed for it. Gennai bit his lip, growling. "So you want to play a messiah after playing God?"

"Y-your Excellency…?"

Gennai ignored the adjutant. "Answer me, what is our current charge?"

"R-right," one of the operators replied. "We're at 72% charge! Y-your Excellency, what would you like me to do?"

"Stop all power usage. Get back up to 82% charge within twelve minutes."

Everyone in the crowded control room looked confused.

*Just what would rapidly recharging accomplish at this point? More importantly, shouldn't we get out of Akihabara immediately?*

"Now then," Gennai murmured lightly. "How far have you really figured us out? Show me. I wonder if you realize that we still have some cards left to play, 'Y'!"

# ● Chapter Three / 07:15 / Liberator

**A**S FOR THE ATROCIOUS VILLAIN who had just thrust all of Japan into the depths of terror and thrown the rest of the world into a frenzy, the boy who had declared that he would wipe Japan off the map in an unprecedented indiscriminate act of destruction...

"Ahhhhhhhh... oh, yes yes yes... this happiness is what I liiive for!"

He was kicking back, enveloped by a feeling of safety and security as if he were in his own home. More concretely, he was rolling about with his face buried in the lap pillow of an automaton girl in a formal black dress, squealing in delight.

The automaton girl—RyuZU—sighed. "Master Naoto, with all due respect, I suspect that just about anything would make you very happy considering the simple brain you were born with."

"How rude, RyuZU!" Naoto countered, burying his face in her thighs. "And not just to me! Are you insinuating that there could possibly be a pillow more luxurious than your lap?!"

"Excuse me. It is the height of humiliation to be cornered with a sound argument from Master Naoto, but it is true that nothing in this world could match the value of even a lock of my hair. With that in mind, my lap pillow must be an awe-inspiring, ultimate treasure that would draw the envy of even the gods. It is self-evident that making use of my lap pillow is a peerless luxury. I apologize for my mistake."

Seeing their exchange, the little automaton girl in red and white armor pressed her index finger against her lower lip. "Father... I'd like an order please..."

"Yeeees yes yes! Dive right into papa's belly! C'mon!" Naoto spread his arms and looked up at her with a silly grin.

AnchoR dove into his belly with a *pomf*. "Tee-hee... Father, you're warm..."

"Kaaaaaaah!!" Naoto yelled, slapping his forehead. "No one else in the world is happier than me right now!"

"Well, Master Naoto, considering that you crushed the ephemeral happiness of the masses just a little while ago, that much is obvious. Even in absolute terms, considering you get to monopolize the ultimate works of art that are AnchoR and my-self, it does not really matter how happy the rest of the world is, does it?"

It was just as she said. In the present moment, Naoto was rising beyond cloud nine.

"Hohh... the great one who brought me as well as RyuZU and AnchoR into this world," he prayed to no one in particular. "Whoever you are, I love you!!"

Leaving that syrup-smeared, drippingly sweet microcosm as it were...

The Pillar of Heaven. Just as its name implied, Tokyo's alpine central management tower pierced the heavens. Right now, the twentieth floor was enveloped in as much tension, if not more, than during the battles that had taken place just a little while ago.

"Dr. Konrad!" Marie yelled. "Everyone else, too! How does the sensitivity feel?!"

The eighteen automata that were working hurriedly on the insanely detailed mechanisms turned around and answered her in unison with a thumbs-up.

They weren't the responses of AI but of the eighteen clock smiths remotely controlling the automata used for maintenance in the Pillar of Heaven.

The automata had been modified for remote control and were being used by Marie's associates scattered throughout Tokyo—by way of the transmission station in the ruling party's headquarters.

They were the same Meisters who'd lent Marie their hands during the Akihabara Terror Incident. Their skills were top-notch, even compared to other Meisters.

Currently, they were doing minute work remotely through a relay station, a setup which limited their senses as clocksmiths. Even so, under Marie's command, they were able to work as one and showcase a manual finesse far beyond the understanding of ordinary people.

The imperial guard were clocksmiths themselves. They serviced the Pillar of Heaven's mechanisms daily and could become an immediate asset to the Meister's Guild if they joined it. But if they saw this sight, they would probably cry and submit their letters of resignation, saying: "From now on you're the ones in charge."

"Ahh, it's going well on our end too, Missy. Good grief, so this is the skill of a Meister? I can't get enough of it." Vermouth grinned.

Then... the voice of an old man came out of the same voice-box. "Dr. Marie, don't mind me. Most likely, this body is the most stable one here in terms of sensitivity."

Vermouth sneered, controlling only his mouth while the rest of his body was operated remotely by Konrad. "Well duh, gramps. This body's sensitivity is the best 'in many ways,' right?"

Indeed. Though she didn't want to admit it, Marie couldn't help but agree with Vermouth. His transceiver was a unique, custom-made article that Konrad had personally installed in the love automaton before Marie had used it as Vermouth's body.

To begin with, the resonance devices (in other words, non-contact coupled movements) required an element that was particularly difficult to create.

Made with liberal use of an extremely precious material, and close to 100% pure, these specific devices were super-long-distance resonance gears. Their maximum range was about forty kilometers, give or take. You could erect a building in the most expensive district of Tokyo for the price of just one of these valuable gears. And furthermore, for personal use, you would need at least two of them: one for sending and one for receiving.

Normally, there'd be no need for super-long-distance transmissions. The world was already thoroughly equipped with wired infrastructure. If you went through several relay stations, you could send a message to the opposite side of the Earth through a series of short-distance jumps with almost no latency.

The only ones who would have use for something like this would be a small number of corporations, militaries, and high-ranking government officials. People who needed to regularly exchange information that they couldn't risk being intercepted.

However, they had another use. And that functionality was most likely the true reason that Konrad had one installed into a love automaton.

Super-long-distance resonance gears had three merits: distance, confidentiality, and information processing power.

Transmissions that went through relay stations obviously shared bandwidth with other users. As such, depending on how much traffic there was at any given time, the number of resonance gears you could couple at once were limited, and the precision which you could operate an automaton remotely was also limited.

With super-long-distance resonance gears, the amount of information that could be exchanged was far greater. For example, it would be possible to receive information from all five senses at once.

As to why Konrad not only had such an extremely expensive device but had installed it onto a love automaton... thinking about it made Marie's head hurt.

"But it's proved to be fortunate now. Don't think too deeply about it, Marie," Marie muttered, trying to persuade herself.

Seeing her expression, Vermouth grinned. "Hey Missy, did you know? These super-long-distance gears were originally developed not for distance but informational throughput."

"So?"

"Sex is always the driving force behind everything in this wor—"

"Dr. Konrad, please shut him up. Please. I'm begging you." Marie cut the conversation short and returned to her work.

*Now that I think about it, something's felt off ever since the emergency rendezvous point turned out to be that strip club. No, stop thinking about it...*

"Everyone," Marie announced, refocusing. *"We're eighteen seconds behind schedule! Work faster!"*

*There's no time for this right now...*

*The military probably won't notice, but if they discover we're using a relay station to remotely control the service automata, they could copy the signal and interfere with our work.*

*In the worst case, they might even be able to trace the locations of the Meisters helping us.*

*We have to get as much done as we can now before...*

"Miss Maëribell."

Called by her fake name, Marie looked up and saw a young woman—Houko—standing in front of her with a stiff expression.

Marie kept working, typing on the processor console connected to the Pillar of Heaven's control mechanism but prompted Houko to go on with her eyes.

"There is something that I have to ask."

"..."

Marie could imagine what she wanted to know. She turned her gaze towards Naoto, who was frolicking with two legendary automata right next to her.

Houko followed Marie's gaze. "Where did he procure the blueprint of the Pillar of Heaven?"

"Such a thing doesn't exist. Does it?"

"No. That is why I am asking. Your group clearly grasps the structure of the Pillar of Heaven, more so than the people who regularly maintain this place. Although you are the one supervising the work, he was the one who gave out the instructions to begin with."

"..."

"As such, I can only think that he obtained the blueprint somehow."

"That's wrong. You said it yourself, such a thing doesn't exist. But regardless, this guy didn't know the structure of the Pillar of Heaven until he came here."

"Do you think I can believe that?"

"No. But that's the truth."

Houko pressed Marie for an answer. "Are you telling me that this boy fully grasped the structure of the Pillar of Heaven just by listening carefully in silence for six minutes?"

· · ● · ·

*Impossible*, Houko thought.

The Pillar of Heaven was the literal backbone that supported all of Japan. It far exceeded core towers and clock towers in terms of both scale and complexity.

As such, even the Department of the Imperial Household didn't fully grasp its structure. It had taken the country over a thousand years of analysis just to make a rudimentary diagram of its structure, and even that rudimentary diagram was classified higher than other state secrets. Not even the prime minister was clued in as to where it was kept, much less given permission to copy it.

Even so, if you were to obtain that diagram, you still couldn't hope to fully grasp the structure of the Pillar of Heaven. It was just a fragment, merely scratching the surface of its design.

*And yet, you are saying that he managed to do so just by listening carefully for only six minutes?* Houko could feel her complexion pale, something chillingly cold creeping up against her spine. She had felt it before when she learned of these adorable automata's capabilities firsthand. But, in a way, the sensation this time was far more extreme.

*Is this boy not far more dangerous than "Y's" automata?*

"I understand you having misgivings about this," Marie said, as if she'd guessed what Houko was thinking. "But I'm sorry, I can't explain it. Could you maybe do me a favor and pretend you didn't see anything?"

*"I cannot,"* Houko asserted.

*The reason I allowed them free rein in the first place was because I thought that it would be for the nation's good. In other words, I did so to use them. So they would take on the hate and blame for the country being on the brink of collapse and to learn what the perpetrators of the Akihabara Terror Incident intended to do with the Pillar of Heaven.*

Houko herself wasn't a layman when it came to clocksmithing. She had formally studied it during her study abroad. Though she wasn't as good as a Meister, she was a licensed Geselle.

She had planned on observing their procedure, techniques, and sources of information for the sake of the nation's security. Trying to make sure that such an incident never happened again. She went along with them with those interests in mind, but...

"..."

Houko narrowed her eyes. *How did they do it? Is it this boy? This exceedingly average-looking boy? If he really can grasp the structure of the Pillar of Heaven just by listening, what countermeasure could possibly be taken?*

*If it's the truth, then this boy in front of me is—*

"He is someone who cannot be allowed to exist. A grave threat to national security."

Marie sighed. "Rest easy. Or so I'd like to say. I very much think that there's a scientific explanation behind how his hearing works, but even I don't understand its principles."

*In other words, his ability is something that cannot be replicated. So, as long as he disappears, something like the Akihabara Terror Incident will never happen again.*

As Houko was considering that, Marie lowered her voice. "Let me warn you. I'm guessing that you're probably thinking of ways to kill this guy once he's served his purpose here, but..."

Before either of them could go any further, a black scythe was nestled against Houko's throat. That scythe, of course, belonged to RyuZU.

"If you truly wish to end your own life, then please take half a step towards me. If you do, then I promise that I will provide you with the most painless euthanasia in the world."

The automaton's topaz eyes showed no hint of emotion, just like those of a doll. The smaller one in red and white next to her also looked at Houko with an expressionless face.

"If you do bad things to Father, I'll do bad things to you."

"Whahh? Huh, wait, what's going on?" the boy said with a blank expression, seemingly the only one who didn't understand what was happening.

Houko sighed. *It would be senseless to die for this.*

"I apologize. That was improper of me. As for your offer, I am quite fine, thank you, so I would appreciate it if you would retract your scythe," Houko said, taking a step back.

RyuZU quietly retracted her scythe.

"Do you get it now?" Marie asked.

Houko nodded with another sigh. "Yes. Unfortunately, it looks like there is nothing that I can do. I will think more on possible countermeasures at a future date and set things aside for now."

· · ● · ·

*Looks like she gave up for now, thank goodness.* Marie placed a hand over her heart in relief. She was surprised to see Houko take out a small device, something that looked like a choker. As Marie looked on, puzzled, Houko put it on and smiled sweetly.

"Now then, it has been a long time, Marie."

Houko's voice was completely different. The choker was a voice changer. It appeared that she had prepared it beforehand to make sure there would be no record of the princess and a terrorist speaking intimately with one another.

*Thoroughly prepared as usual,* Marie thought with a smile.

"Yes. It's been a while."

"I am happy to see you again. This should be the first time since attending your funeral, I think."

"Yeah, though that coffin was empty, and I was actually in another country."

"I knew you were alive. But even so, I thought that I would never get the chance to see you again..."

The imperial princess and the younger Breguet daughter would have had opportunities to meet each other. However, there would have been no such chance for Maëribell Halter to do the same. Unlike Marie, with her colleagues and fellow Meisters, an imperial princess couldn't just meet whomever she wished.

It was too late to do anything about it now, but the outcome still made Marie feel lonely.

"Yes. I'm glad that we were able to see each other again." Lowering her eyes, she added: "You're still wearing the watch I gave you."

"Of course. It is a precious gift, the work of a dear friend. After

I parted with you, this watch has always been with me, sharing every minute.

"When I heard that you had lost your life in Kyoto Grid," Houko went on, grasping her left wrist with her right hand. "I was unbearably grieved. For you to lose your life in my country of all places…that is what I would think. I know this is very much late, but I want to say that I am sorry."

"There's no reason for you to apologize. It was something that I decided to do myself."

The computer in front of Marie made a mechanical popping sound. A metal belt—a punch card, with countless holes punctured through—streamed out from the top of the console.

"Moreover, I didn't decide to come here because this is your country. Regardless of where the malfunctioning grid was, I'm sure that I would have done the same thing. That's my job as a clocksmith." Marie slid her finger across the belt, reading the contents of the punch cards as if it were Braille.

"You are right," Houko muttered, sounding a little lonely. "That is the kind of person that I remember you to be."

Just then…

"Hey hey, why are you friends with the Japanese princess, Marie?" Naoto casually cut in from behind them as he lay sprawled out with his head on RyuZU's thighs. It was a simply voiced, spur of the moment, question.

Marie sullenly clicked her tongue and slammed her hand on the console. "Naoto, it's bad manners to interrupt a conversation, you know?"

"Ahh, sorry 'bout that. So anyways, why?"

"She and I are school friends," Houko replied. "We got to know each other pretty well when I studied in Europe for college. It wasn't as long as you might think though, since she finished all her requirements and graduated in one month."

"One month?!" Naoto squawked, his eyes wide open.

Marie shrugged. "If I hadn't been playing with Houko, I would have been gone in a week."

"Come now! That makes it sound like I was bothering you, you know?"

"Isn't that more or less the truth? Are you going to claim otherwise when you were the one dragging me around everywhere?"

"That is a good joke, Marie. I am quite sure that you were the one who had the most fun running amok. They still talk about what happened back then to this day, you know?"

Marie and Houko rekindled their old friendship with that exchange. However...

"I mean, I'm no expert, but shouldn't there be attendants or something who follow along when the princess of a country studies abroad? Also, of all people, why was Marie the one you happened to befriend?"

Marie raised an eyebrow. "Look here you. The Breguet Corporation stands at the top of the world as one of the Five Great Corporations, and our family originated from French aristocracy. I was the daughter of that noble family, you know? What problem could there be with me associating with the imperial princess of Japan?"

Naoto was making a face that showed he hadn't thought of that. "In that case, could it be that the reason that old man Halter calls you 'Princess' is..."

"What about it? It's a simple fact."

"I thought it was sarcasm."

"Like that could be the case. He obviously calls me that in praise of my overflowing intelligence, noble blood, and overall aura of elegance."

Naoto's face turned serious. "Sorry, I don't understand what you're saying. Was that supposed to be a joke?"

"I'll have you *thoroughly* explain just what you mean by that later," Marie growled, glaring at Naoto.

Houko chuckled. "You have changed a little, Marie. No, perhaps this was your true nature all along. I am a little envious."

"Houko?" Marie cocked her head in puzzlement.

Houko didn't explain. Instead, her tone turned serious. "By the way, would you guys kindly tell me now? What do you actually plan to do by gaining control over the Pillar of Heaven?"

"That's... you're right, I guess you ought to know." Marie nodded. "How much do you know about the enormous weapon that appeared in Akihabara?"

"I do not have any proof, but judging from the circumstances, it is clearly an electromagnetic weapon of some sort. From the intelligence reports, I gather it's controlled by Shiga's ex-military, who are trying to execute a coup d'etat."

"As I'd expect from you." Marie nodded in admiration.

"So it is true then?"

"Yes, Akihabara was magnetized due to that electromagnetic weapon. If things continue like this, I don't know whether it'll be possible to repair the grid even if the weapon is taken care of. So..." Marie paused. "As this idiot had suggested, we plan to throw them into a crucible and boil them alive. Akihabara will be the crucible, and its temperature should rise to roughly two thousand degrees."

Houko's eyes opened wide.

*She really is smart,* Marie thought. *It looks like she understood our scheme with just those tidbits of information.*

Heat all of Akihabara up, including the grid itself, until everything in the city reaches its Curie temperature. Under Naoto's plan, the enormous weapon would be eliminated and Akihabara would be demagnetized all in one go.

"..."

Marie remembered something.

*The first thing that Naoto said back in Akihabara Grid was what he would do with the ones who fired the EMP...*

*Even though he shouldn't have had any knowledge about electromagnetic technology, he said: "I'll stuff the ones who dared to do this in a kettle and boil them alive."*

*Even though, at the time, he shouldn't have known that things can be demagnetized with enough heat. This guy has always, consistently, all the way through...*

Marie turned towards Naoto.

"Master Naoto..." said RyuZU, who had been stroking Naoto's hair. "I am sincerely sorry."

*Was that an apology I just heard? Did RyuZU really just sincerely, unsarcastically apologize to someone?* Marie was astounded. She fumbled her hands, nearly hitting the wrong key on the console. Even Naoto was surprised.

"RyuZU?" he asked with wide eyes.

"Simply because I couldn't safely demagnetize myself, the hands and shoulders in charge of the planet's fate are..." RyuZU quietly felt the tips of Naoto's fingers, his palms, and then his shoulders with her dainty, pale hands.

Those were the places where Naoto had been scalded when he carried RyuZU to a cool place on the floor. Though his wounds weren't festering (thanks to the medical nanomachines) painful-looking keloids still lined his skin.

Marie was concerned about his burns as well. *The cramps and the pain should disappear within a week, but as for whether he can regenerate enough of the nerve tissue necessary for the delicate touch of a clocksmith... I can't say. I have no idea how well his wounds will heal.*

Marie couldn't complain, even though Naoto was messing around at a time like this. He had already done plenty, and he deserved to rest.

"..."

Feeling like she lost for the umpteenth time in these last few days, Marie sighed. She recalled what Naoto had been like when she first met him.

*He was just an ordinary boy who endlessly whined about the situation that he found himself in, and yet...*

*While I nearly broke down after the* EMP, *he didn't stop for a single second. He has continued taking the best course of action since then.*

*The best course of action indeed. Seemingly without any concern whatsoever for the price he has had to pay.*

Even when Akihabara was magnetized, all modern technology became unusable, and when the people they trusted the most were broken. Halter, in Marie's case, but in Naoto's... RyuZU was probably more important to him than his own life.

In the midst of that awful scenario, Naoto had managed to follow his intuition and move RyuZU, despite her burning up hot enough to melt the metal floor.

Without any sleep or rest, he endured agonizing pain from his burns, the kind that could leave you wishing for death. And all the while, he reassured AnchoR and went around the city trying to find a key to turn the situation around.

*And this is supposed to be an ordinary boy? A mere amateur? What a bad joke,* Marie thought through clenched teeth.

*Just how much am I going to rely on the power and determination of an ordinary boy, an amateur?*

*And in comparison, just what I have done? If Naoto hadn't pulled me along, I might very well be in Akihabara right now, still wallowing in despair.*

*On top of all that...*

"It's fine as long as you're safe, RyuZU. I think stuff like this is what they call the proof of manliness? Ha ha."

*Even now, he still has his headphones off.*

That way, he would immediately notice if anything changed suddenly. Despite the cold beads of sweat dotting his forehead, he answered RyuZU with a gentle smile.

*That's supposed to be an ordinary boy? Don't make me laugh. That...is what I've always aspired to...*

"Oh, but if you feel sorry for me, then how about giving me a reward for my efforts?! More specifically! What I mean is..."

"I see, Master Naoto. You are telling me to serve as an outlet for your hopelessly twisted sexual desires, yes? Understood."

"That's wrong! Uh, I mean, yeah, you're wrong... I mean, not right now, yeah... I'll leave that for another time, I think..." Naoto babbled as his nostrils flared.

Marie hurriedly reversed her previous thoughts.

"Ahhhh! Yeah!" Naoto continued, completely ignorant of any broken pedestals. "Not 'right now!' So, going back to my date with AnchoR..."

"To bring that up again right now, Master Naoto, I see that you are quite an admirable masochist. I understand now. Seeing that you wish to be spanked, where would you have me do it?"

"Gee, could you let me finish?! I-I didn't want to leave you behind either! That's why I got you a present..."

"This is what Father gave me!" AnchoR beamed.

Cutting Naoto off with the smile of an angel, she opened up her hand for RyuZU to see. On her finger was a shiny ring.

"Master...Naoto? I am having a little trouble understanding. Just how intensely are you hoping to be spanked?"

"Put your scythes away, please! I'm begging you!! Take a good look! It's on the middle finger of her right hand, see?!"

RyuZU turned her gaze back onto AnchoR. AnchoR was looking at the ring on her hand joyfully.

"Father made this for me. He said that... it's a good luck charm... to help me stay true to my own will..."

"It's also supposed to protect against evil spirits. That's what the salesperson said when I asked him. But, well, I thought that if that's the case then it'd be better if I made one for her myself. It was while I was shopping around to find a gift for you, you see! Now then..."

RyuZU tilted her head, looking slightly lost. With a smile, Naoto revealed a small box from his pocket and opened it in front of RyuZU. Inside was a silvery, lustrous *ring*.

"For my reward... could you give me your left hand without asking why?"

"..."

"It doesn't really have any special meaning until I put a matching one on too, so you don't have to worry about that... or is this still too much to ask?"

RyuZU didn't answer. Her expression didn't change either. She simply nodded and held out her left hand.

Naoto smiled gleefully. Perhaps he caught a delicate change in the sound of RyuZU's internal workings, despite her indifferent outward appearance. Something that no one else could hear.

"Thanks, RyuZU." Naoto put the ring on her left ring finger.

"If you think having me accept this reward for the excessive care you showed to me, your follower...then I am sorry to say, but..." Contrary to her words, RyuZU tightly gripped the ring that had just been fit onto her finger.

*I have to add this to the list,* Marie thought.

*This is yet another thing in his list of accomplishments up to now. He probably made it while I was busy repairing RyuZU, giving Vermouth a new body, and preparing Halter's brain pod.*

*Even in his downtime he was doing something productive, making this ring.*

"Ordinary, my butt," Marie murmured. "As if someone like you can be called ordinary."

· · ● · ·

Houko listened to the conversation between the boy and the automaton. They had just exchanged a traditional confirmation of love that has been repeated trillions of times on this planet.

Houko didn't know what it felt like to love a machine. But she could tell that the boy was serious and that the automaton could answer his feelings.

Those were the only two things she understood.

*But, this is not enough. I must get to know this boy better.*

"Excuse me," she called out with that thought in mind. "May I ask you a couple of questions?"

"Eh? Uhm, yeah..." Seemingly surprised, the boy raised his head. Houko could tell that he was nervous despite the arrogance he had shown.

*It appears that he is simply not used to others striking up a conversation with him.*

Houko smiled sweetly. "My name is Houko. I believe you are Mr. Naoto Miura, right? Would it be all right if I called you Mr. Naoto?"

"Er, yeah. Sure."

"Thank you. Excuse my rudeness, but could you answer two questions for me?"

"Uh, err, what do you want to know?"

"The automaton next to you, whom you treasure a great deal, was injured by the enemy. Is that why you want to destroy the enormous weapon? For revenge?"

Naoto looked confused. "Eh, revenge? Hm... no. That's not it. They made AnchoR do horrible things and hurt RyuZU, I'm going to make them pay the price for that, I guess."

"Make them pay the price... is that not revenge?"

Out of his element, Naoto made a complicated face as he tried to answer. "No, it's more like... I want to settle things or square things up. No, that's not it either. I don't like putting it that way, I'm not sure why. It's complicated. Argh, basically, in short..." Naoto paused for a breath. "I want them to pay their dues, right? That's it."

Houko tilted her head. "Their dues?"

"I can't explain it well, but..." Naoto rubbed his forehead. "Eating at a diner then leaving without paying is messed up, right? Don't you think that...if someone can't pay, he shouldn't have ordered something in the first place?"

"So you are saying that, given they ate already, they should pay for their meal?"

"Right right. That's it. That's how I feel," Naoto said with a smile, looking refreshed.

Houko nodded. "Thank you. Then, for my second question: With a talent like yours, would it not have been simpler just to purge Akihabara?"

"Huh?" Naoto's eyes widened.

"If cleaning up that enormous weapon is your goal, then wouldn't it be easier to just make it sink into the earth along with the city? Is that not so? You would not have had to brave such dangers in that case."

"Uhmm." Naoto looked a bit lost. "I mean, I heard that Tokyo as a whole would be damaged in that case, no?"

"Yes. As you say, Mr. Naoto, if Akihabara collapsed then all of Tokyo would probably collapse, but what of it?"

Naoto was left speechless.

"I had assumed," Houko continued, watching Naoto with a steel gaze. "That you would stop at nothing for the sake of your goals. And yet, you did not choose the most efficient method. Why?"

"But...I mean, only the ones operating that enormous weapon are responsible. Everyone else has nothing to do with it, right?"

"..."

*I see, so that is why he did not choose to purge Akihabara.*

*He said that he would have them pay the price. In other words, he would not seek payment from those who did not owe him anything.*

*At the same time, it also means that he would not hesitate to pay the price himself.*

*I understand why he has not killed anyone up to now. It was not that he respected human life. And it was not that he considered the impact his actions would have on Japan either.*

*He is simply seeking payment from the entity that harmed something precious to him. For that, he is prepared to pay any price. That is all there is to it.*

*I see.*

*—If I make him an ally, he would probably be the most reliable companion there is. But if I make an enemy of him, I would have to risk being sunk into the ground along with the nation.*

Houko smiled, nodding. "I understand clearly now. As I thought, you are not one to be trusted, Mr. Naoto."

"Ehhh?! That's your conclusion after my explanation?! Did I say something strange?!"

*Indeed, how could I possibly trust this boy? He would purge Tokyo without hesitation if he concluded that it was a necessary price to pay. At the very least, he has both the means and the nerve to do so.*

*Letting a person like him roam freely with neither a leash nor any contingency plan would be immensely dangerous, but...*

"However," Houko said cheerfully, keeping a smile on her face. "I also clearly understand now why Marie trusts you."

"Huh?"

"Hey, what the heck are you saying, Houko?!" Marie cried out, while Naoto looked blank.

"Because, you are a very 'fair' person," Houko said with conviction.

*Or perhaps this boy is actually a terrifyingly avaricious and selfish human being.*

*But at the same time, I am convinced that he is "fair" through and through. He would not approve of "unfairness." He would not tolerate injustice. He wouldn't think: "I want this, but I don't want to pay the price for it."*

*"If you want something, then pay the price for it." This boy holds himself to that doctrine as well. Obtaining something for free... an unfair thought like that would probably not even cross his mind.*

*In short, it is just a question of whether he thinks it is worth it. If he does, then he would proceed without hesitation. That is probably just the sort of person he is. Whether the price be his own life or the lives of other people.*

*For this reason, I should not involve myself any further with this boy and my dear friend.*

Leaving her personal feelings aside, the imperial princess would surely end up thinking about how best to use them. That line of thought would always linger in the corner of her mind. Naoto's power was simply too enticing for Houko to keep herself from doing so. To keep herself "fair."

"Frankly," RyuZU spoke up suddenly. "I am astonished. I never once considered that there could be someone aside from Master Naoto whose is not completely unobservant."

Houko chuckled at the questionable words of praise. "It is my honor to receive your praise. If a masterpiece of the great 'Y' says so, then I suppose there is hope for me yet."

"Mistress Houko, was it?" RyuZU continued. "May I give you a word of advice?"

"Yes, what is it?"

"I would advise that you choose your friends better, as frankly, someone like Mistress Marie is hardly worthy of associating with you."

"N-now you look here—"

However, Houko stopped Marie with her hand, smiling at RyuZU.

"In that case, Miss RyuZU was it? I have a word of advice for you as well. I do not know what you have against Marie, but refusing to acknowledge someone's brilliance simply because you do not like her speaks badly not only of yourself, but your master as well, understand?"

"..."

As RyuZU was taken aback, the tip of her nose paled. She opened her mouth, seeming to want to say something but closed it again. She then lowered her eyes and reluctantly nodded.

"I shall take your advice into consideration."

RyuZU's response made both Naoto and Marie's eyes widen in unison. Their astonished faces were saying one thing: *she managed to make RyuZU submit to her?!*

"Hey," Naoto began. "Marie, old man Halter's always calling you 'Princess,' but..."

"But what?"

"Well, I was just thinking that real princesses sure are charismatic aren't they? I mean, really, everything about her is just on a whole other level."

"Oh, yeah?" Marie put on a threatening smile. "Maybe you could care to explain to me a little more specifically what you are trying to say, Mr. Naoto?"

"Her brain, face, chest, height, as well as her character and air of refinement... I could go on if you wish, but..." RyuZU answered in Naoto's stead.

"Now. You. Two. Look. Heeeeeeeeeeeeere!!" Marie exploded.

Houko tried to stifle her laughter.

· · ● · ·

"We're about to reach eighty-two percent charge!" the operator reported in an excited voice.

Gennai nodded placidly.

"Your Excellency," the adjutant standing next to him said impatiently. "Could you kindly tell us what you plan to do now?"

Gennai glanced briefly at the adjutant's face but didn't answer. Instead, he asked: "What do you think of this world?"

"Huh? What do you mean by that?"

"It's been a thousand years since the Clockwork Planet was created. The manmade world functioning right before our very eyes. Even so, no one has been able to decipher, much less reproduce its technology." Gennai sighed. "Do you think that understanding something like this as 'science' is acceptable?"

The adjutant made a quizzical face. "It's true that there are still many mysteries regarding the clockwork technologies involved in the planet's functions but... as they do in fact exist, wouldn't it be truer to science and technology to make use of them regardless?"

"You're exactly right. Your view couldn't be more correct. Making use of things that operate on principles which no one understands because they're there? Indeed, that's science. But do you know what?"

"Your Excellency...?"

Gennai smiled sardonically. "It's been thirty thousand years since humans obtained fire. Yet, it was only ten years before the planet was remade that we discovered that fire is actually a type of plasma. A form of electricity.

"That means that for the 28,928 years before we unraveled that natural phenomenon, we were using fire without even knowing what it was. Truly scientific, right?

"But do you realize those are two completely separate matters? In other words..." He paused for a breath. "The Clockwork Planet is not a product of nature. It is a man-made object."

"That's..."

"You see, this universe was made by some kind of god, perhaps one called coincidence. Exposing and making use of its laws is science. Technology. It's theory, it's theorem, it's logic! But can I ask you one thing? By what 'science' was this man-made planet created?"

The adjutant couldn't help but feel daunted by Gennai's question, or rather, his sudden verbal attack and tone of voice.

"S-still..." he countered, gathering himself. "It's certain that 'Y' made this planet."

"Indeed, it's just as you say. And that's exactly why I shall assert that 'Y' wasn't human."

Seeing the fanaticism in Gennai's eyes, the adjutant gulped.

"That figure," Gennai continued, paying him no mind. "'Y,' drew his blueprint based on theories that didn't exist!

"Super technology? Unknown technology? You're telling me that a single genius invented all this, and after a thousand years of trying there's still no one who understands his theories?

"It'd be slightly more believable if you told me it was the technology of an advanced prehistoric civilization or aliens... but unfortunately, I don't love fairy tales enough to delude myself with such a fantasy."

*I can understand trying to analyze natural phenomena that we have yet to explain. That is the knowledge that humanity has continuously accumulated throughout its history.*

*But... to decipher the principles behind this man-made product that we're standing on?*

*That doesn't make sense. That's the opposite of how things should be. As such, the one who drew the blueprint of this planet must have known theories that no one else knew.*

*How this planet is said to be made is most definitely not within the realm of science.*

*And just where was "Y" supposed to have gotten his theories from?*

*Not only that, but the native ability of the automaton called AnchoR—Perpetual Gear...*

*A perpetual motion mechanism? It's ludicrous! You expect me to accept such a fantasy as technology? Don't screw with me!*

*Such a mechanism can only work according to physical laws that can't possibly exist. It is a rebellion against the universe itself!*

Before Gennai knew it, the eyes of everyone in the room were on him. Their gazes revealed that they were confused, perplexed, baffled, maybe even terrified.

"We have continuously tried to analyze the Clockwork Planet for a thousand years," Gennai shouted angrily. "And yet, we have still failed to fully grasp it! Not its fundamental principles nor the many functions that we still don't even have theories for! Well then, Major, would you tell me your thoughts on the matter?"

"Your Excellency..."

"Where did 'Y' find the principles behind this gigantic machine that humanity has yet to comprehend, even after a thousand years of trying?"

No one could answer.

Thirty-one years ago, when Gennai was busy trying to fuse clockwork and electromagnetic technology together on the federal government's orders, he realized something.

Although humanity might never have unraveled all the secrets of the world, it had once been one step away from uncovering at least a portion of them. That was what he himself was now researching: electromagnetism, a field through which humanity once tried to define the universe.

However, all of that knowledge crumbled away. On the day that the world was remade, everything changed. And, when the federal government purged his city to cover up the truth, everything collapsed.

That was when all his existing theories had been thrown out the window. That was when he understood, better than anyone else, that the ones who really rewrote and rebuilt the world were humanity.

Only humanity didn't change whatsoever, even after the world was remade. Ironically enough, humanity was the one thing that even "Y" couldn't change. On that day, inside Shiga's collapsed core tower, Gennai became convinced that "Y" wasn't human.

*Humanity doesn't change. It can't change. Only he was able to disprove all assumptions and arrogantly, insolently turn the whole world upside down.*

*There's no way that that was the work of a human. In that case, I can accept it. Whether "Y" was a god or a demon, as long as he was a monster that transcended human intellect, then there's no way that we mediocre humans could do anything to him or his creation.*

He had resigned himself and gathered his troops together to survive. Even if defying a god like "Y" would be a sin, Gennai wouldn't simply let himself be crushed by the other mediocre members of his species without a fight. He took over Mie, continued his research there, and at last, built the electromagnetic weapon that could destroy the world.

Upon which, he fell into despair once more. He had come to understand that the weapon, his brethren chasing after revenge with him, and even he himself were all nothing but ordinary people.

*Whether you realize it or not, in the end we're all dancing in the palm of "Y's" hand. How pointless...*

And so, tired of it all, he retired.

*In the end, we mediocre humans have no way to oppose transcendent beings. As such, I was disappointed by history and thrown into despair by the world. I thought that it'd be fine if I lived out the rest of my life in resignation...*

*Until I met that boy touting around one of "Y's" automata.*

"Sure," he had said a few days ago. "If you would first be so kind as to humor a story that an old man has to share."

An Initial-Y Series had suddenly appeared in the deep underground layers of Mie Grid, at the dwelling where he had decided he would die. And it was one worth talking to, unlike the Fourth.

Gennai recalled the story of "Judgment Day," an ancient myth. Supposedly, God would stand before mankind on the day of the apocalypse and lend his ears to their questions and their justifications for the life they had led.

*If that happens, then I'll be able to hear God's answer.*

With that faint hope, Gennai had raised a question:

"I'm referring to the riddle of 'Y's' existence. Where did they come from?"

*Was he or she a god? A human?*

*Are we truly in reality, or is this a dream?*

However, the automaton had brushed him aside.

"Are you done with your foolish questions? If so, I would like you to give me back my invaluable time."

Her stone-cold topaz eyes mocked him.

"Please do not take this too personally, I can see that you had the misfortune of being born with a brain smaller than a tick. Not that I can empathize. Do realize though, that labeling something you do not care to understand as the work of a god due to your own sloth comes naturally to the masses.

"I am sure that to foolish humans, 'Y' must be a lofty figure worthy of being called a god, but confusing reality with fantasy is proof that you can no longer grasp even basic truths. With that in mind, it would probably be for the best if you immediately received the appropriate medical care," RyuZU had said with a smile, but her voice was full of disgust.

"Are you fooling with me?" Gennai scowled, glaring at her with his moss-green eyes. "You call my questions foolish? A thousand years after 'Y' remade the planet, humanity still has yet to decipher the technologies he used!"

"That appears to be the case, yes. I can clearly remember 'Y's' face when gasping in disbelief at his own creation."

"Through all those years, how many scholars and clocksmiths dedicated years of their lives to arriving at the truth?! Though I may not have been worthy, I too was one of those people. Many a great person devoted his life to unravel this work of a god, and all of them were defeated. You dare scoff at that?"

"Not at all. Quite the opposite, I value their effort."

Gennai shut his mouth.

"But," said RyuZU. "As you said yourself, they were losers."

"Yes, you're right. I once thought I had hit upon something, but that too was an illusion in the e—"

"That was when you 'came to an end,' yes?" RyuZU interrupted him coolly. "And so you wasted your previous hard-fought, praiseworthy work on idleness..."

Judging that the automaton was toying with him, Gennai was on his feet before he knew it.

"Answer me! What was 'Y' thinking when he remade the world?! Why did he throw us onto such a vague and inexplicable, absurd, and incomprehensible contraption?!"

"You're an annoying grandpa, aren't you?"

It was not the automaton who replied but the boy who had fainted just a little while ago and had been resting on Gennai's bed. Now he was glaring at him.

"Master Naoto," the automaton girl chided. "You should still be resting. I will make this old man prepare an elevator for us, so—"

"Forget it, RyuZU," the boy said as he slowly got up and shook his head. "I overheard the conversation. This is a waste of time. Let's leave this guy to his own devices and find another way to return to the surface."

"You won't be able to reach the surface, you know. The current won't flow to the elevator unless I give the order," Gennai said sharply.

"Current? What's that? Well, then hurry up and give the order or whatever! RyuZU and I don't have time to waste."

Gennai raised his voice. "I'm not done talking yet!"

The boy scowled. "Look here, gramps," he said in an irritated tone. "We're busy, okay? We've got AnchoR-chan's case to take care of, which by the way, I'm off-the-walls pissed about! Turn the elevator on already, or else—"

"What, are you going to kill me?" Gennai challenged. Part of it was his pride as an elder against an insolent youngster, and part of it was backlash against having the question that he had risked his life for being treated like the idle musings of a doddering old man.

"Huh?" the boy said blankly. "Have you finally gone senile, gramps? As if killing you would get the elevator moving. Turn the elevator on, or else..." Naoto paused, then declared, with eyes that didn't harbor even a single shred of doubt, "I'll turn it back on myself. Elevators are those boxes that can rise so long as there's a wire pulling it from above, right?"

And then, just as easily as he divulged the location of the elevator, Naoto described its structure. Gennai was thrown into silence. He remembered that the boy was the master of an Initial-Y Series. It was "Y's" legacy. The newest addition to mythology. An automaton that had been made by a god.

Gennai knew of their existence. He had seen the Fourth in operation before as well. However, this automaton wasn't the Second, the Third, or any other in the series—but the First: YD01 [RyuZU]. Gennai belatedly recalled that no one had ever gotten past the First's Master Confirmation.

"Boy." *I was asking the wrong person*, Gennai thought as he turned to face Naoto. "Let me ask you a question. Depending on your answer, I might be willing to turn the elevator on for you."

The boy turned around silently.

"Do you not have doubts about this world?" Gennai asked,

staring straight into the boy's gray eyes. "This world that has mercilessly rebuffed all of humanity's attempts to understand it?"

*Living atop of this arcane, vague, and completely illogical planet... do you really have no doubts at all?*

Immediately after, Gennai was thrust into a reality that he had never wanted to know. Truth is always stranger than fiction. The most merciless, outrageous, simple, and boring answer was the correct one. Despite thinking that he had no hope left to lose, Gennai despaired for the third time in his life.

*The boy was unmistakably human. At the very least, he looked human, he spoke a human language, and he acted as humans do.*

*And he saw through everything, including my despair, and said to me of all people:*

"You're free to keep calling yourself a loser and wasting your life away grumbling here if you want. But you see," Naoto answered with disdain in his eyes. "You paint with far too broad a brush, geezer. Who do you think you are to speak on behalf of all humanity?"

"..."

"Don't lump us in with yourself."

*In other words: "Don't lump us in with someone who gave up. We won't despair."*

*That's right, he spoke of what it means to be human.*

Gennai sat back down in silence. Leaning back in his rocking chair, he let out a deep sigh.

"Very well. I'll tell someone to turn on the power for the elevator."

The boy's expression changed in a flash. "Oh? Jeez, gramps! So you're a reasonable guy after all! All right RyuZU, let's go!"

"Please wait, Master Naoto. You will faint again from a lack of oxygen if you run."

*With that little ruckus, the boy and the automaton rushed out of his home.*

*What a joke,* he thought as he saw them off with cloudy eyes. *That boy clearly possesses unique eyes that can see through the illusions draped before humanity and yet he had the gall to ask me why I can't see what he sees.*

*So he might be human in appearance, true. Those who babble that God made man in his image are numerous.*

*However, that human-looking genius, whether he be a shapeshifter, superhuman, a transcendent being... a god or a demon... he coolly asserted what it means to be human, despite not being human himself. He said it without any hesitation.*

Gennai sneered. The target of his maddeningly seething hatred had been right before his eyes.

*So you pretend to be a human, you arrogant, foolish god. In that case...*

"We'll meet again, boy. Or rather..." —"Y" *in the guise of man...*

A shrill beeping noise rang out. A window popped up on the wall monitor's screen and began to flash. His mind returned to the present.

Gennai turned towards the operator. "What just happened? Answer me!"

"Ah... r-right. We've just reached eighty-two percent charge..."

"Good."

Gennai nodded and stood up. He looked out over the entire control room, at the faces of his subordinates crammed inside.

They were the faces of comrades that had been following him since he worked on electromagnetic research in Shiga Grid, as well as some of the sons that they had raised in Mie.

For someone without any relatives, he could even call them family.

*None of them matter,* he thought.

*If even the planet we stand on is something ambiguous and uncertain, then in the end, the people before me right now are also nothing but an ephemeral dream.*

*If you really are a god, then I'll let you kill me.*

*But should you turn out to be a mere human, then I'll have you know your limits. A mediocre human, just like the rest of us.*

*I'll have you know the sin you committed when you defied that limit in remaking this world. I'll make you take responsibility for causing mankind to stagnate for a thousand years. When justice is served, you will perish in despair from your newfound knowledge.*

"Good work, everyone," Gennai announced with a mix of indignation, hatred, and resignation. "Let me give you my 'instructions.'"

Just then, an ultra-high-voltage current that could easily carbonize the human body ravaged the inside of the control room.

· · ● · ·

Naoto sprang up like a coiled spring. Eyes wide, cold sweat pouring from his body.

"Master Naoto?"

"Hey, what's going on with you, Naoto?"

AnchoR, who had been lying on Naoto's stomach, also looked up at him in confusion. However, he didn't have the luxury of answering them. A dangerous sound was ringing. His eardrums, his intuition... frankly, all of his senses... were screaming danger.

*This isn't just a threat to my life, it's something even more sinister. It's something I've never heard before... no, wait, I have heard this sound before!*

"Oy... Are you kidding me?!"

*Like I'd forget this sound,* Naoto seethed, *To think I'd have to hear this rank, disgusting, sickening sound again.*

"What's wrong, Naoto? The bypass will be finished in just a bi—"

"Marie!!" Naoto barked. "Gather all the clouds! Immediately! To the south of where we are! Get on it!!"

Marie must have seen something in his expression, she wasted no time in acting.

"Ngh! Did you hear that everyone?! Gather the clouds at six o'clock from the twentieth floor! Commencing weather manipulation!"

There wasn't room for doubt. Questions would have to wait. Marie was already furiously typing on the console's keyboard.

Naoto listened to the mechanical sounds of the Pillar of Heaven adjusting the temperature and humidity of its outer shell.

As the atmosphere creaked and trembled, a massive amount of steam was produced, but...

"Ahhhhh, God damnit! It's no good, we won't make it!! Everyone ruuuuuuuuuuuun!!!"

Naoto's desperate cry reverberated throughout the huge floor. Exactly five seconds later, the light of destruction arrived and blew everything away.

# ● Chapter Four/07:35/Progressor

THE LIGHT SURGED UP from under Tokyo and pierced the Pillar of Heaven. Looking up at it from the rooftop of the ruling party's headquarters, Karasawa stroked his chin, at a loss.

"Oh man, I was too late..."

He'd been just about to contact Marie's group to tell them what he had learned from the transmission log that he'd pulled from the station.

"What should I do? The pay I get as a consultant won't be enough to cover this!"

*Even though it's my policy not to do any more than what I'm paid for...* Karasawa thought with a bitter expression on his face, he was still clutching the phone in his hand.

He leaned against the rooftop fence and let out a deep sigh.

*I should have noticed. Dr. Marie reported that the enemy performed a successful override of the Master Confirmation of one of the Initial-Y Series before.*

*So why didn't they, being researchers of electromagnetic technology, use the technology present on that device?*

*Not to mention, with what the logs seem to imply...*

"It's way too risky for me to hold on to this information alone."

*I did a good job decrypting the correspondence between Shiga's ex-military and their accomplice, but now that it's come to this, I wish I hadn't found out.*

"Whether or not the coup d'état succeeds, the goal of the one behind it all remains the same: the purge of the capital. Really, what are we going to do about this?" Karasawa muttered to no one in particular. A cold sweat broke out across his face.

Just then...

"..."

Karasawa pushed himself silently off the fence. He wasn't surprised. When he got hold of this information, he knew that sooner or later it would come to this.

*I had wanted to give Dr. Marie, my savior, this information, but...*

"So you're already here, huh? Jeez, you guys may be scoundrels but I have to admit you're capable," Karasawa sighed.

Raising his head, he saw the person... no, the thing... that had appeared by the entrance to the rooftop. Karasawa couldn't clearly make out its figure, but he could just see a shimmering existence by the entrance.

Optical camouflage.

"A portable model? Not even the Five Great Corporations have successfully developed something like that, you know? As a consultant, I'm certain of this."

Karasawa smiled and tilted his head. "Say," he began cheer-fully. "If you don't mind, could I ask you something? How much do you make?"

The shimmer didn't answer.

*Yeah, no surprise there.* Karasawa smiled bitterly. *These guys aren't the type to waste time saying stuff like "any last words?" or "what have you found out?" or "say your prayers..."*

If the shimmer belonged to the group that Karasawa had got-ten information on, the presence would already know that he had nothing left to say. They should already be well aware of what information Karasawa had gotten hold of and also that Karasawa was an atheist.

In response to the murderous aura closing in on him, Karasawa undid his collar. Placing his right foot one step back, he took a stance.

"All right. Let's both do our jobs. Hey, did you know? In this country, uncompensated overtime is just the way of life? Long live the labor force," Karasawa muttered sardonically as he sized up the enemy before him.

*My enemy is most likely a cyborg with cutting-edge equipment. The brain probably belongs to a professional hitman. Meanwhile, I'm just a mere consultant with a single pistol and some portable clocksmithing tools... How many seconds can I survive? I wonder.*

With an inward sigh, Karasawa clocked in overtime on a mat-ter of life and death.

· · ● · ·

*What just happened?* Marie struggled to breathe as she looked around, dumbfounded.

*Everything's gone. Everything. That blast of light broadsided us and swallowed everything. There's nothing left.*

The central mechanism had melted like glass candy touched by fire. A wide, gaping hole had been bored into the floor, the walls, the ceiling...

The light had pierced through the outer shell of the tower, melting the floor and vaporizing the mechanisms in its way.

The holes all had ugly, jagged edges due to the brief liquidation of the surface materials. Marie sank to the floor right next to one such gap. If she had been just a second slower in evading the light, she would have been vaporized.

She looked around with trembling eyes. Houko was right next to her. The enormous Black Tortoise that Halter was operating was resting alongside the tower wall, with Vermouth on the ground at its feet. She also confirmed that Naoto, RyuZU, and AnchoR (who had been in a safe place to begin with) were fine.

But she didn't see any service automata. They had all been working where the light shot through, and it appeared that they had been unable to escape.

*But at the very least, it looks like there weren't any human lives lost.*

Now that she knew that, a question popped into Marie's head. With a trembling voice, she asked aloud: "What was that... what the hell was that supposed to be?!"

Her shout vanished through the gaping holes in the walls.

No one answered. No, wait.

"We were shot at," Naoto answered.

"What'd you say?"

*I don't understand. Shot at? By whom, with what? Why?*

"We were shot at by their main cannon!" Naoto yelled, seeing Marie befuddled. "The same piece of shit gigantic cannon that tore a giant hole right through the middle of Akihabara! Are you deaf?!"

She could hear him. At the very least, she understood the words.

"Why?! Why would they shoot at us?! Their goal is a coup d'etat, isn't it?! If Houko was... if the members of the Imperial Family were hurt, who would be there to confer the right to rule Japan?! No, before that..."

Marie jumped back to her feet and paced, waving her hands in disbelief.

"If they destroy the Pillar of Heaven, Tokyo would collapse and take them along for the ride, you know?! Hell, all of Japan might collapse!"

*That wouldn't be a coup d'etat. It'd be nothing but terrorism and the worst kind at that, suicide bombing. This is different from what we thought. Things aren't adding up. I don't understand why they took such an action...*

But it seemed that even Naoto couldn't answer her question this time. The only sound that could be heard was the wind gushing in from outside.

"It is indeed possible to dampen the power of a maser cannon by randomizing the directionality of the microwaves through the use of the refracting properties of steam," said a man's voice, resounding through the floor.

"An apt response to our assault, I must say. Cursedly so, in fact. But how could you tell that our main cannon is a maser cannon? I'd very much like to hear your answer."

His voice sounded composed, almost mechanical.

*Where is his voice coming from?* Marie wondered. *It isn't from the speakers, nor is it coming directly at us.* She looked around, trying to find the answer, and quickly realized that the entire floor was vibrating to transmit his voice.

"I'm sure you survived that, yes, 'Y'?" the voice continued. "Or should I say, Mr. Naoto Miura?"

Everyone's gaze turned towards Naoto. Everyone but RyuZU. Seeming to have recognized the voice, she and Naoto were the only ones looking down through the gaping hole in the floor.

Far below, they could see the pea-sized silhouette of the enormous weapon in Akihabara Grid.

"This voice... don't tell me it's the gramps from that time?" Naoto muttered in a daze.

"Naoto! Explain what's going on!! What the hell is a maser canon?! Who is this voice?!"

"How should I know what the heck is a maser or whatever?!"

"My, if it isn't the old pile of bones that we happened upon while we were still stuck underground," said RyuZU. "I am speaking to those squawking remains of a loser who fancied himself the wise hermit when he was really just a shut-in, yes? Well, to what do I owe the displeasure of having to listen to your grating voice once more?"

"Oh, but of course... you probably instinctively knew what you should do to protect yourself without really knowing why...

"You see, there was a device a long time ago called a microwave oven. This maser cannon works on the same principle. Likewise, I am projecting my voice by using electromagnetic radiation to make the walls of the Pillar of Heaven vibrate. With that in mind, I'm afraid that this will be a rather one-sided conversation. Do forgive me.

"Now that I think about it, I haven't introduced myself, have I? My name is Gennai Hirayama. I'm the leader of this coup d'etat. Setting that aside, I am sure that you are all wondering why I fired upon the Pillar of Heaven."

"Gennai... Hirayama..."

Maric engraved that name into her memory. *Yeah, you're right. After all, should the Pillar of Heaven fall, the only thing that would await you is death.*

"Well, I'll keep it short. About the coup d'etat... to be honest, it doesn't matter to me. The subordinates that I dealt with were certainly burning with righteous indignation, though."

*It doesn't matter to him? No, before that, what does he mean by having "dealt with" his subordinates?*

"We'll prove the superiority of electromagnetic technology to the narrow-minded world we live in," Gennai continued. "A world that won't recognize any technology other than clock-work technology. And, in our just cause, we'll rectify the federal government's offense in throwing us away like trash. That was our proclaimed mission but..." Gennai paused. "I was certain that we would fail."

"..."

"The premise was flawed from the very beginning. The world has long known the superiority of electromagnetic technology. Don't tell me that you are naive enough to believe there's a single country in the world that would uphold that shallow facade of a treaty and abandon such a capable tool."

*That's true,* Marie thought. *Even Japan, a country that is extremely timid on the international stage, was researching an electromagnetic weapon. There are surely at least one or two secret research facilities in every country.*

"As for overthrowing the federal government, the goal itself can be easily accomplished. But should our electromagnetic weapon become public knowledge, a world war would await."

There was no way other countries would ignore such a clear threat. They would surely eliminate it by any means necessary. With their own concealed electromagnetic weapons, should it come to that.

"My subordinates seemed to think that, with this weapon and its electromagnetic technologies, we'd be more than capable of holding our own against the rest of the world. Youth sure is a scary thing. I retired to the underground precisely because I couldn't dedicate myself to such an extent, but..."

Gennai changed gears. "That's when I realized that there was something far graver than this nation or the lives that were stolen in Shiga. Far more arrogant, insolent... the identity of the one that twisted this world beyond hope!"

His composed voice waivered for the first time.

"Naoto Miura. No, 'Y.'"

Naoto raised his head. His thoughts were impenetrable, and his gray eyes stared into space.

"You recreated our very universe, rejected the path that humanity had carved for itself, and bent the world to fit your own view. That's exactly why I must test you once more."

Marie had no clue what Gennai was talking about. However, she could sense wrath, hatred, and a hint of resignation in his voice.

"Show me what you've got. If you can stop me, then you aren't human after all. If you can't, then repent for your arrogant sin in bending the world to your will as I pull you down into hell. I'll teach you what us mediocrities who crawl through the mud are capable of, you wretched monster."

Silence fell.

The voice had stopped speaking. Breaking through the dumbfounded silence, Halter tilted the head of the Black Tortoise.

"So, Naoto. What kind of joke is this?"

"Hey, boy," Vermouth spoke up. "Just what kind of crazy abuse did you hurl at that guy for him to flip out like that? Shit's insane! Mind teaching me for future reference?"

Naoto shook his head, dumbfounded. "Huh? But I didn't really say anything to him. I just gave some short, apt replies to the comments he made... right? I mean, did I say something strange to him, RyuZU?"

"Not at all. You simply told him a few exceedingly obvious things. Now then, what could he be angry about? Perhaps he is simply testy due to menopause?"

"Don't fuck with me!" Marie shouted at the top of her lungs, unable to bear the situation any longer. "Like I'll let Asia collapse just because some old bastard has menopause!! And Naoto!!"

She pointed her finger at him. "Who was the loudmouth that called me a walking land mine?! We're in this situation because you walked through a minefield and somehow managed to step on every freaking one! Did you ever think that maybe you're the problem?! You're a magnet for trouble, you walking time bomb!!!"

"I mean, you can say that, but asking someone to correctly identify and avoid the sore spots of a loony old man like that is way too much to ask, you know?! You heard him! He's obviously pretty far gone!!"

"Father? What was that grandpa saying...?"

"Ahh, you don't have to make sense of his ramblings, AnchoR. I don't think anyone gets it really," Naoto replied with a hollow voice.

Marie felt a chill run down her spine. *Is it just my imagination?*

"A-at any rate, I'm gonna organize what we know about the situation!" Shaking her head, Marie dispersed the growing dread gnawing at the back of her mind. "Naoto, how long will it take that thing to shoot its main cannon again?"

"I...don't know. But, it probably shot at us with about eighty-percent charge just now. With that in mind, it should be at about... thirty-percent charge, I think?

"I should warn you, I don't know its precise structure, so this is just my guess. It might not be able to fire until it recovers at least eighty-percent charge, or maybe it can fire again at fifty-percent charge, I really don't know! There's no basis for me to judge!"

"Very well. Let's assume the worst-case scenario. How long would it take them to recover fifty-percent charge?"

Naoto held his head. "I'm telling you, I don't know. It's already weird that they were able to get to eighty-percent charge so quickly to begin with. I told you in Ueno, didn't I?! That it'd take sixty-six hours! It's only been roughly forty-six since then. There should have been nearly a full day left! That prediction turned out to be totally off the ma—"

Marie seized Naoto by his collar. Her blazing emerald eyes glaring. "We can only rely on your ears and intuition right now! Answer me intuitively! What's the shortest amount of time it would take for them to fire a second shot?!"

"Seventy-two minutes. There's no way...that it can be any quicker than that..."

*If this guy says so, then it must be true. We don't have any other frames of reference aside from his senses right now. So we'll just have to base our estimates on the figure he gave. We've got seventy-two minutes. That's it. That settles it.*

*And that is by no means a long time. In this situation, seventy minutes may as well be seventy seconds. Let's take a deep breath and deal with the problems one by one.*

"Halter," Marie asked the Black Tortoise. "How much time do you think we have left before the military stops twiddling their thumbs and sets out to regain control of the palace?"

"If you want me to be frank, they'll probably be storming in any second now. After all, there's no longer any guarantee of the princess's safety."

"Argh, God! Everyone just wants to stand in my way!" Marie stamped her feet furiously.

However, Houko took a step forward. "Actually, it should take the military at least forty minutes to get here. No matter what miracles they pull off, it should take at least that long."

"Eh?" Everyone focused on Houko.

"The enormous weapon quickly annihilated Tokyo's security force," Houko continued, facing everyone's gaze head-on. "That caused the government to break apart, which in turn caused infighting to break out in a total of eight locations in Tokyo.

"The first through the fourth army corps commenced emergency mobilization to subjugate the rebellion upon the request of the metropolitan police and are currently engaged in battle. The two battalions that made up the main force of the rebel army besieged the palace, but they were eradicated by you all, yes?

"To put it plainly, the constituent parts of Tokyo's military have either lost their fighting strength or are currently not under the normal chain of command.

"Assuming that the military used your recent broadcast as an opportunity to reunify itself, it would still need to reorganize its available forces, draft a strategic plan, and decide on who should take the lead as supreme commander. They would also have to summon the reserve forces should reinforcements be necessary.

"Even if there is an officer who has the capability, will, and popularity to handle all these things swiftly, considering how much time has passed, it will take at least another forty minutes. That should be the absolute lower limit.

"Although," Houko smiled tenderly. "I think if there were such a convenient person, then the situation would not have come to this in the first place."

Marie stared at Houko in astonishment. "You don't have any political power, right?"

"Naturally. I am a woman in the imperial family after all." Houko beamed.

*What a waste. If she were born in an earlier era, or even into any other family in Japan, she might have ended up leading this nation one day.*

"Very well," said Marie, dispelling the tangent. "Let's use that figure as a guideline. So, we don't have to worry about the military storming inside here for at least another forty minutes. Meanwhile, setting up a barricade and having Halter and Vermouth defend it should be enough to hold the imperial guard at bay. In that case, what's left is..."

The biggest problem of all. Which was precisely why Marie had hesitated to even bring it up.

"So the question is... in the seventy-two minutes that we have until the weapon fires its main cannon again, how can we connect the bypass that will allow us to destroy that gigantic thing from the Pillar of Heaven?"

*After all, the shot just now evaporated the linkage that we'd nearly finished building. We're back where we started in terms of the bypass, not to mention...*

"With eighteen fewer pairs of hands to help at that... ha ha..."

Marie could only laugh. Eighteen outstanding Meisters controlling eighteen separate service automata had spent more than an hour working on the bypass together. Along with Konrad, who had synchronized with Vermouth's body, and Marie herself. With how badly things were damaged, they had to redo the work of twenty people with just two and in less time than before.

*It's impossible. This joke's in terrible taste. No matter what kind of plan I draw up in my mind, none of them will make it in time. However, I don't have the luxury to hesitate.*

"Naoto," Marie shouted into the silence, broken only by the blowing wind. "We're going to remake the bypass! Tell me how this place is structured again!"

"Hey Marie, do you even know what you're saying?" Naoto laughed shakily. "How the heck am I supposed to hear the sounds of vaporized gears?"

Marie gulped. That short comment hinted at an ordinary boy on the verge of breaking. Marie felt like everything was absolutely and positively over. No ifs, ands, or buts. It was as if a god had just announced the end of the world.

• • ● • •

The floor was enveloped by the abnormal noise coming from the Pillar of Heaven, the wind, and time—ticking away on the clock. Miraculously, or perhaps cruelly, the device had survived the blast.

Everyone was silent, not knowing what to do. Marie sat on the floor, staring fixedly at that clock. Four minutes had already passed.

*A tenth of our remaining time has already fruitlessly gone by.*

"Would it be too late to start evacuating the metropolitan residents now?" she muttered.

"I think it would be impossible," Houko replied, sitting next to her. "At present, there is no one who can oversee the task of informing the residents and evacuating them. Those who are sharp should have begun to escape long ago... although whether or not their efforts will be enough to save them is another matter."

"Yeah, you're right. I know that as well, but..."

*I couldn't stop myself from asking anyway,* Marie sighed.

"Hey," Naoto asked AnchoR and RyuZU. "Would you two at least be able to save yourselves?"

"Out of the question," RyuZU replied immediately. "In case you have forgotten, Master Naoto: I cannot escape and leave you behind. If this fact has already slipped your mind, then I suspect that you have a severe case of amnesia."

AnchoR clung to Naoto and wouldn't let go. "AnchoR doesn't want to either! AnchoR won't leave Father!"

*Escaping from here is impossible,* Marie thought. *Gennai Hirayama had fired upon the Pillar of Heaven with the intention of destroying it.*

*Thanks to Naoto's intuition, we managed to limit the damage from the first shot, but with so many clockwork parts erased... forget linking up the bypass, we can't even manipulate the weather anymore. Defending ourselves from the next shot is impossible.*

*So what'll happen then?*

*First, the Pillar of Heaven will break and collapse. That would be enough to trigger the start of a severe calamity.*

*Next, the entire capital will cease functioning and collapse down into the core of the planet.*

*And, should Tokyo collapse, all of Japan might follow. Should that happen, all of Asia and eventually even the entire Clockwork Planet might suffer fatal damage.*

*Run away? Try as you might, you still wouldn't be able to escape the consequences. And no matter how much I think about it... there's nothing we can do to stop it.*

Marie ran her trembling fingertips across her lips. They felt dry and withered. There was a creeping unease crawling up her spine and yet, at the same time, she felt a numbing terror floating around her temples.

*What is this...?*

*It's despair.*

*It didn't start here. I've been despairing for two days now. Ever since I witnessed that* EMP, *a power that could destroy the world.*

*Back then, my heart froze along with all the clockwork. My will's been broken for ages. I've simply been clinging to the magic that is Naoto.*

Marie prayed with her parched, frozen heart as she asked: "Naoto, can't AnchoR and RyuZU destroy that weapon?"

"Maybe," Naoto replied with a lackluster voice. "But they'd definitely be wrecked in the process. I'd rather let the entire world collapse than let that happen, but..."

Naoto scratched his head furiously. He bit his nails with an expression that Marie had never seen before.

*He knows,* Marie thought, *that if this continues, it'll only be a matter of time before the same fate befalls the two of them just the same.*

*He knows that, but he still can't bring himself to give them the order to attack. He can't resolve himself to abandon RyuZU and AnchoR to save the world, but he can't just abandon the world either.*

*That's to be expected. He's only human. He worries, hesitates, and makes mistakes like the rest of us.*

*He isn't some convenient magic that can grant any wish.*

Only understanding such an obvious fact now, Marie's gaze fell to her feet. Just then...

"Father." AnchoR stood up. "Please, give AnchoR the order..."

"No." Naoto shook his head sternly. "Absolutely not! Please, don't make me repeat myself..."

"But, but... if this goes on..."

"Yeah, I know, I know okay! Please, AnchoR, let me keep that as our absolutely last resort," Naoto begged. "I'll do something about the situation. I definitely will."

However, Marie noticed something unusual. AnchoR's small shoulders were trembling as she took a step back.

"No..."

"Eh?"

Naoto tried to look into AnchoR's eyes, but she had looked away.

"I'm sorry, Father. I can't... obey that order."

"AnchoR...?" Naoto muttered, dumbfounded.

A shockwave struck the room. AnchoR leapt, flipped in mid-air, and dove head first through the gaping hole in the floor. She was heading straight down toward the enormous weapon.

"AnchoR!!" Even as Naoto called out, she wouldn't stop. The red and white figure shrank to a speck. Naoto turned towards RyuZU. "RyuZU! Bring her back immediately!"

"I...am not capable of physically stopping AnchoR once she has taken action."

"In that case... nghhh," Naoto groaned. "Then tell her to wait for just another sixty-four minutes! Please! I'll definitely find a way to take care of the situation before then!"

"Understood," RyuZU said, bowing elegantly.

The skirt of her black dress fluttered. However, she stopped suddenly and turned around.

"Mistress Marie, may I have a word?"

*"M-me?"* Marie stuttered, taken by surprise. *What could it be? RyuZU's never said anything to me of her own volition before...*

"I simply wish to inform you that I have decided to consider the princess's advice post-haste. Personally, I am quite certain that this is nothing but a waste of time, a small vain hope but... that said, though I may be flawless as a servant, I am not reluctant to admit that I am not completely omnipotent. I am the most modest among my sisters, after all."

"Oh, really." Marie nodded. *Don't you mean the haughtiest?*

RyuZU straightened her posture. "Mistress Marie, Master Naoto is always reading your regrettable mind. You would do well to remember that a theory is ultimately nothing but an idea that has been selectively compiled into a clear text for the convenience of sharing with others. The truth has never been universal, unchanging, or fair. Which is precisely why I find it terribly difficult to admit this, but..."

RyuZU paused for breath. Her topaz eyes reflected Marie's image in them.

"You are right," she said. "And so is Master Naoto. But at the same time, you are both wrong."

"Right... but wrong...?" Marie parroted in a daze.

*I can't get a handle on what she's saying.* However, RyuZU's words reverberated within her heart.

*In the end, who's really the one that's making a fundamental mistake?*

RyuZU bowed with a cool, composed face. "Feel free to push your lacking brain to its limits in considering what I have said, Mistress Marie. Well then, I am a bit short on time, so excuse me."

RyuZU turned on her heels and dove straight down through the gaping hole, leaving Marie behind. Everyone stared at Marie, silent, and frozen still.

Naoto stood up. "Let's get to it, Marie."

*Get to what?*

"I mean," she muttered, still trying to grasp RyuZU's words. "What can we possibly do?"

"That's obvious. We're gonna do something about the situation."

"I'm asking you what that is!" Marie yelled. "You said it yourself didn't you?! There's no way you can hear the sounds of gears that have been erased. There's nothing we can do! We're just gonna 'do something about the situation'? No such convenient magic exists, you know?!"

"So what?!" Naoto's angry roar reverberated through the floor. "So you're just gonna give up?! So you're just gonna kick the bucket without trying?! Yeah, if you want me to admit it, then I will! I have no clue what we should do!!"

Naoto seized Marie by the collar and yanked her up off of the floor, gray eyes full of anger. She couldn't breathe.

"Listen, stupid! Do I really have to remind you?!"

"About...what?"

"About what kind of woman you are!"

Marie's shoulders trembled. Naoto's grip on her collar was forceful, tight.

"You... you're always spouting your ideals with that proud, haughty, insolent, and naturally condescending attitude of yours," he said, his face twisted by rage. "And yet, when push comes to shove, you immediately give in to the pressure like jelly!

"The very second things don't go your way, you start grumbling as you think yourself into a corner. Then you self-destruct and take everyone else down with you! That's why you're a walking land mine!!"

"Are you lookin' for a fight?" Marie reflexively replied in her normal tone.

"But!!" Naoto paused for breath. "You're a woman who'll never believe that something's impossible, aren't you?!"

Marie's eyes widened. For a moment, she couldn't comprehend what he'd said.

"God damn it!" Naoto ranted, shaking his head irritably. "Why do I have to say something like this for you?! It pisses me off! I mean you're a genius, right?! Yeah, sure, so maybe I can do something that no one else can! But it was your talent that put my ability to use, wasn't it?!"

"..."

"Wasn't that the case in Kyoto? What about Akihabara? Well, wasn't it?! I couldn't have repaired AnchoR or RyuZU in time without your help, and old man Halter wouldn't be here if it weren't for you! We probably wouldn't even have been able to escape Akihabara without you!!"

"..."

Flooded by the rage in Naoto's words, Marie ceased thinking. She blinked twice. Naoto kept on shouting like a madman.

"Tell me Marie, please! With your brain, skills, and talent... why do you always give up so easily?!"

What she sensed from his words, though baffling to her, was envy, jealousy...

"If you're just gonna let it rot, then hand it over! Just give me that talent of yours. Hey, Marie, are you listening?!"

*Talent? Did you just say talent? Someone with a real, magical, godlike ability that no one else can imitate is pestering me, of all people, about talent...?*

"Naoto?"

Unable to understand, Marie raised her hands up. She wrapped her hands around Naoto's, still holding her up by the collar, and touched the scorched skin where he had been burnt. As she felt the bumps of his scars, Naoto released his grip.

"Marie..."

Like a flame that had burnt out, all the energy left Naoto's body. She suddenly noticed the large teardrops that had formed in the corners of his gray eyes. They looked like they would fall any moment now.

*Ah. As startling and unbelievable as it is... it seems like this idiot seriously envies me. I can't understand it one bit. I don't know why he would envy the talent of someone as brittle as me, but he does.*

The moment Marie understood that fact, she felt a welling fire light up in her heart once more. As proof of that, she swung her right hand with all her might.

*Slaaaaaaaaaap!*

"Ugeh?!"

Naoto's left cheek rippled with a cracking sound. As he recovered, Marie greeted him with her left hand just the same.

*Slaaaaaaaaaap!*

Naoto's right cheek rippled with the full force of Marie's might.

"Ugwah?!"

Naoto was left in shock with two swelling cheeks. Marie seized his collar and pulled herself up. On her feet, she rammed her knee into his solar plexus.

"Oof?!"

She slithered behind him and hooked his foot with her own, pulling him into an armlock at lightning speed. She proceeded to put him through the wringer. Literally.

"Hey, wait, time out! S-stop you idiot! Something's gonna dislocate!" Naoto stomped his feet, struggling to get free.

Marie ignored his plea.

"What kinda stupid bullshit did you think you were spouting in my face!! Huh?!" Marie roared. She felt her body temperature rise with agitation. "Like you're one to talk! You're the one who's letting an absurd talent rot!! If you can't even use them properly, then give me your ears!"

*If I had this guy's hearing, just what kind of amazing things could I do?*

*What if this guy had even a modicum of skill as a clocksmith?*

*Just how many times do you think this absurd wish has crossed my mind?!*

"Yeah, damn it! I would if I could!" Naoto shouted back. "If that'd help resolve anything about the situation then I'd give them to you right this second!!! Otherwise..."

He paused for a breath.

"Give me your talent! Figure out a way to do so! Right this second!!"

"Yeah sure, why not?! I'll do just that!!"

Marie yelled back at him, and Naoto glared at her. Seeing his expression, Marie finally understood.

*"The grass is always greener on the other side."* Just as I'm jealous

*of him, he's jealous of me. We both envy and desire the other's gifts. Upon that realization, their whole argument became ridiculous.*

*Yeah! I'm done. I'm done, okay?! That's enough worrying, brain, thank you very much!*

*That's right, now that I think about it, everything is odd. Ridiculous. Why do I, the noble Marie Bell Breguet, have to count on this idiot, this incorrigible pervert, this crazy bastard who sees a completely different world from the rest of us, to drag me around and show me the way?!*

*That's gotta be wrong. It should be the other way around!*

*Everything's pissing me off! I can't help but be mad myself, and everyone else as well!! All you shitheads in the world should just die! Die die die!!*

*Everyone's just doing as they damn well please! How dare you shitty good-for-nothing inferior creatures trouble me without my permission! Prostrate yourselves! Kneel!*

*And, and... huh? What was I thinking about again?*

Marie released Naoto from her grip.

"Right right, yes, right! Why don't I just teach you?! If I do that, we can break through this shitty situation!!"

Marie's joyous yell gathered everyone's attention. *It's simple,* Marie thought.

"When you break it all down," she announced. "If Naoto had my technical skills, we could do something about the situation. He'd be able to grasp the structure of the surviving movements of this floor and make a new bypass for them. Conversely, if I had Naoto's hearing, I could do the same thing. Isn't that right?

"And so," she continued. "If I were to summarize why this shitty situation has us at our wits' end, it's because of one simple factor: the situation is so severe that if Naoto and I split up, we wouldn't be able to finish in time."

Marie turned around to see the idiot scowling at her as he nursed his aching joints.

"That's why we're gonna go with the give-and-take principle, Naoto."

Marie returned to a thought that she had dammed up in the back of her mind. *Who's really the one that's misunderstanding something fundamental?*

RyuZU's words dashed around and around in her mind.

*Damn it. I absolutely don't want to admit it, but as hard as it is to believe...*

Marie took in a nice, slow breath and looked around herself.

Houko was there. Halter was there. Vermouth was there. She could sense Konrad's presence in Vermouth as well. And finally, Naoto was there, right in front of her.

Gathering all of their attention, she announced: "Your hearing doesn't lie, so I'll teach you how to make the most of it. In return, teach me how to perceive things like you do!"

· · ● · ·

"How to make the most of my hearing?" Naoto repeated in a daze.

"You said it before, didn't you? That no matter how many

times you read over your textbooks and manuals you can't under-stand what they say. It's because what they say contradicts what you know intuitively from your hearing, no?"

"Y-yeah…" Naoto nodded.

"Then it's simple: the textbooks and manuals are wrong. What your hearing's been telling you was right all along."

"Huh?!" Naoto cried, flustered. "W-wait a second here. I read the latest editions of technical manuals, you know?!"

"I'm sure you did. That's why…what's mistaken is our current understanding of clockwork technology."

*I…admitted it.*

Marie trembled at her own words.

Houko, Halter, and Vermouth all seemed to stay their breath.

"Dr. Marie," Konrad said in a fearful voice through Vermouth's voice box. "Please excuse me for interjecting, but what do you mean?"

"Exactly that. The clockwork theories that we learned are wrong."

Marie could sense Konrad gulping.

*It's to be expected,* Marie thought. *Admitting that modern clockwork theories are wrong automatically implies a rejection of all the knowledge and skill that we've engraved into our very flesh and bones.*

*However…*

"Naoto's sense of hearing allowed him to fix RyuZU's imagi-nary gear and precisely determine where the abnormality of Kyoto's core tower lay. It is undoubtedly correct. So if something contradicts that hearing of his, it must be wrong," Marie said, staring intensely at Naoto. "Although I'm ashamed to admit it, I don't understand how your hearing works. But the one thing that I *can* say is: that ability of yours is not simply good hearing."

"So...what exactly are you getting at with all this?" Naoto asked, bewildered.

"You *know* the answer to things," Marie asserted.

"I know...the answer?" Naoto parroted with a baffled expression.

Marie nodded. "The answer always comes to you first. You know how things should be, how mechanisms sound when they are functioning normally. If that weren't the case, you couldn't possibly grasp the movements of tens of trillions of fine parts. It should be fundamentally impossible. You vaguely describe your ability as hearing the discord in the sounds of mechanisms, but your answers are much too precise.

"No modern clockwork theory was written with senses like yours in mind," she continued. "In the end, that's why you're always left with no choice but to find the answer through brute force."

*Indeed, it's no wonder that he couldn't do his schoolwork or read blueprints. If the work he was assigned, and the blueprints he was shown, were "incomplete" in the first place—they would only confuse him. Because Naoto knows the "full" picture.*

"That's why I'm going to give you a lesson. I'll probably be the first one to do so. I, Marie Bell Breguet, am going to teach you a curriculum tailored especially to you. So get the earwax out of your ears and listen carefully..."

Naoto gulped. He straightened his back and gazed intently at Marie. He looked serious, as though he didn't want to miss the slightest gesture, much less a single word.

Marie nodded lightly and began.

"Break things apart and analyze them yourself. Class dismissed."

"Huh?" Naoto scowled, his disappointment apparent on his face. *Are you messing with me?*

"If you can already see the answer," Marie continued. "Then all you need to do is break the problem apart and work backwards toward the original question."

"Work backwards...?"

"To give you a metaphor, you probably...no, certainly...*hear* how the orchestra should sound before they even start playing."

"..."

"And when the orchestra finally starts, you become disappointed at their shitty sound. So, you pick out the sounds of all the different instruments, all the individual musicians, and fix all the wrong notes until it becomes the song you were supposed to hear. Know what I'm talking about?"

Naoto stayed silent, but if you looked at the astonishment written on his face, the answer was clear. His expression said: "how could you describe what it's like so accurately?"

"What you need isn't the blueprint of a mechanism but the score of the symphony of its gears. As you perceive things completely differently from us clocksmiths..."

Marie paused and shook her head.

"Actually, it might not even be the score that you need but pictures of their waveforms. At any rate, you perceive gears in a completely different way from normal humans. That's the real answer behind the discrepancy between the manuals and your senses. What you see is how the gears move together, their music. Their flow."

*Hmm, yes, it's the same as light, for example.*

*Light behaves like both a particle and a wave.*

*It's said that the question of whether light is really a particle or a wave gave scientists in the ancient era a lot of trouble.*

*So, if we were to apply that to clockwork... what modern clockwork theory considers purely "particles," Naoto perceives as "waves."*

*Without having been taught by anybody, he naturally hears them as sound. And, as absurd and irrational as it is, his interpretation is correct.*

*Just like how light is both a particle and a wave. If you think about it that way, it all makes sense.*

*It would explain why Naoto, despite having the talent to grasp the structure of clockwork mechanisms more accurately than anyone in the world, can't understand even elementary theory.*

*This disgustingly talented boy was taught things that are completely wrong. For Naoto, all of our modern clockwork theory is nothing but shackles. Of course it is. It's obvious that'd be the case. It has to be, by definition.*

*How could he possibly reconcile what he intuitively knows about how clockwork behaves as waves with how they behave as particles if he was only taught the latter?*

*And that's exactly why Naoto doesn't need to understand modern clockwork theory but simply to understand the basis of what he hears.*

"You don't need to worry about repairing or assembling mechanisms. Just break things down and work backwards from there."

Naoto could envision perfect images of clockwork inside his head. If he took that image, which wasn't even a micrometer different from the real thing, and reverse-engineered the process by which he mentally constructed it... the result would be his own personal blueprint of the mechanism.

Naoto watched Marie eagerly as he finished taking her lesson. His eyes expressed a jumble of respect, admiration, and envy. It was the same reverent gaze that she'd had received countless times during her time in Meister Guild.

To have Naoto look at her like that made her feel ticklishly proud. But, at the same time, she also felt humiliating defeat. Pushing those complicated feelings aside, she forcefully declared: "Now then, it's your turn to teach me!"

$$\bullet \ \bullet \ \bullet \ \bullet \ \bullet$$

*I'm no genius at all,* Marie admitted with a calmness *that surprised even herself. I'm just an imposter who desperately tries to keep up the appearance of a genius because of my pervasive inferiority complex.*

*A real genius would be my older sister or my father. Or the aggravating, perverted bastard in front of me right now.*

*I have some talent. I also put in the effort. So I get results.*

*But that's all.*

*I can't go beyond that. Even if I can use what someone else created better than anyone else, I can't create anything new. I can't make the impossible possible. What's impossible for everyone else is also impossible for me.*

Because she understood that better than anyone else, Marie defined herself as such:

"I'm a woman who'll never believe something's impossible."

It wasn't out of stubbornness or pride. It was a self-imposed rule that she couldn't compromise on if she was to be someone she could be proud of.

And now, to uphold that rule, Marie chose to reject all the common sense that formed the basis for her understanding of the world

*Now then, gather your resolve, Marie.*

*What you're about to be told is an understanding of the world that works on entirely different assumptions.*

*Just what will he tell me? What will he teach me? And will someone as measly as me truly be able to comprehend it?*

She shook her head to dispel her doubts.

*No, Marie. It's not "will I," it's "I will."*

*Just how does this superhuman before me see the world? You don't have to understand all of it. Just a fragment or a piece would be plenty.*

*I'll swallow anything, no matter how absurd it is. Then I'll demonstrate my new understanding with my own hands. I will!* Marie worked herself up as she waited for Naoto to speak.

Naoto told her in one breath: "I think you already understand, Marie."

"I...already understand...?" Marie repeated, raising an eyebrow.

Naoto nodded. "You've already mastered it... my not-so-special little trick, that is. You've had it down for a long while now. You proved that when you connected old man Halter's brain pod to the Black Tortoise, didn't you?"

"What are you talking about? That was just because I happened to know the blueprint..."

"Really?" Naoto sighed. "You're telling me that you were able to make a modification that you had never done before, in that short amount of time, without even thinking about it?" His gray eyes brimmed with admiration. "You can see it already, Marie. The outcome. The future to reel into reality."

She was about to reflexively deny it. She shook her head.

*He isn't mistaken, didn't I just admit that to myself?*

*Naoto Miura knows things that he shouldn't have any way of knowing.*

*I don't understand the theory or implications, but it's been proven.*

*In that case, if Naoto says I can do it, then he's right. I can do it. The man who embodies the qualities I admire most is attesting my ability. What could possibly be more reassuring than that?*

Marie became certain.

*Naoto Miura simply happens to have ears that are slightly keener than the average person. Just as he says, it's a slight variance that lies within the standard deviation of all humans.*

*If one were to treat his hearing as a superpower simply because modern equipment can't compete with it in terms of precision—...*

*Marie Bell Breguet, if you really wish to claim that is the right way to look at things, then show me a piece of modern equipment that can do a better job than you at anything clockwork-related.*

*In the end, it's just a little trick of his. A mere difference in aptitude.*

*However, when that slight variance meshes with a honed intuition, the human brain surpasses reason.*

*Didn't Halter prove that?*

*Doesn't Naoto's existence prove that?*

*Haven't I proved it myself plenty of times?!*

The image that flashed in her head made Marie's eyes stretch wide open.

"I get it now. We're complete opposites from each other, aren't we? In everything."

"Opposites?" Naoto muttered, perplexed.

Marie gazed into his eyes. She was certain.

*That's right, opposites.*

*Marie Bell Breguet starts by gathering all the facts about a scenario and tries to deduce the answer from there.*

*Naoto Miura starts with the answer he's looking for and tries to reverse-engineer a scenario that'll make it a reality.*

*In that case, it's just a difference in methodology. What I need to do is simple. I just need to work backwards from the answer.*

"Naoto," Marie said with vigor, raising her head. "Tell me the structure of the main circuits and movements of the Pillar of Heaven. Basically, anything you've heard that sounded important. I want you to tell me the outcome we need."

"Sure...I guess. I'm not confident that I can express it well in words though," Naoto replied with a troubled expression.

Marie smiled ferociously. "Just tell me. I'll decipher, memorize, and digest everything you say. What, are you implying that I can't? How impertinent!"

Seeing Marie like that, Naoto's eyes turned serious. He nodded. "All right then, Marie. I'm not as smart as you are, and I'm not that good with words. But, I'm sure you'll be able to understand even if no one else can, so I'm just gonna tell you my impression."

"Right." Marie almost added: *bring it on,* but swallowed those words and bit down on her lip.

"Marie, please listen carefully, then forget what I'm about to tell you."

"Eh?" Marie stumbled at Naoto's contradictory words.

"You don't have to memorize what I'm about to tell you," Naoto continued, paying her no mind. "But don't forget it either. Just listen to everything I say, but don't listen too deeply, all right? Think about it, but don't think about it. Acknowledge it flowing in one ear and let it flow out the other."

"…"

"Everything is right but at the same time wrong. What seems contradictory is in fact true. Right is left and vice versa. There's nothing here, but at the same time, that nothing holds everything."

"…"

"You don't know, but you know."

"Say that again…?"

"You know, but you don't know."

"Hey…"

"You don't remember, but you do. All right, let's get started."

"Wait…"

The temperature of Tokyo's grids can't be manipulated from the Pillar of Heaven—but they can be. All the floors and all the components that make up this tower work together. They're a single unit—but at the same time they're their own backup.

They flow from above to below, from below to above, from right to left, from left to right, from front to back, and from back to front again, as one block. If you just ignore the physical media, then what you're really left with is a flow of pure energy. Governing mechanisms are both nowhere and everywhere: in other words, there are some here, too.

The gears that have been lost are still missing. They won't ever come back, but at the same time, the other gears that are left will shoulder their burden. **What we should do is not try to work around that fact** but take the direct path instead.

Satisfy the conditions. **Trick the mechanisms.** Stop the balance wheels from turning, stretch the springs, twist the escape wheels, remove the hooks, drop the anchors, and raise and lower the needed gears. Then restart the balance wheels and align them with the pendulum.

Lower the rotational speed of the 86,754th set of mechanisms all the way to the pace of the 96,040 set so that they match the turn rate of the 36,396th gear and keep them there at that speed... Reconnect the transmission gears then connect the 457th gear to the 3,360th wire and lower all the escape wheels. Lower the amplitude of the swing of the anchors from 4,634 units to 3,053 units. At the same time, connect the 1st through the 3,530th set of mechanisms directly to the 406,464th set right below them.

If you synchronize the operations of the fifteenth floor to the eighteenth floor, you can control the energy that flows up from the set of springs at the base of the tower to the rest of the tower.

With that, you can have the energy that powers the twenty-second through the twenty-eighth floor shared with the twenty-first floor and through that reach the twentieth floor as well—where the difference engine lies. With that, you can then seize control over the power mechanisms that power Tokyo's various grids.

So, ignore the missing mechanisms on the twentieth floor and draw power to the floor anyway. **Then, stop.** Restart the transmission gears and increase the turn rate of all sets of gears.

It isn't the weather or the temperature that we'll try to change, but the flow of energy. We're not going to induce weather phenomena by setting the right conditions but create them directly instead.

Find some numbers that'll let us bend the laws of physics to our will. You don't have to calculate them; just find some values that you like. Whatever you choose, they'll be the right ones. But at the same time, they'll be the wrong ones.

So, to make up for that, we're going to put some other mechanisms to work. Cut all the wires in the 35,350th set of mechanisms and then reverse the direction of the gears of the 457,060th set. **Let energy pass through those mechanisms without any being lost.**

We'll reverse the output and input of energy and use both, which will allow us to retrieve the energy we need for a split second. Synchronize the turn rates of all the sets of mechanisms from the fifth floor to the tenth floor. Raise their turn rates from 3,535 rpm to 4,540 rpm and make sure to tune them so that this increase doesn't cause any problems.

The mechanisms that'll need tuning are in the 3,500th set of the 3,356th block. Take safeguards to prevent the mechanisms from falling apart. Break them yourself. Turn the movements themselves. If you do just that, the mechanisms will rearrange themselves without needing any further help from you.

Before we resort to brute force, the gears will subordinate themselves to us willingly. Force the 5,356th set of mechanisms to operate until they break down. Then, continue letting the broken parts operate anyway so that they break down even further. That'll safeguard against the other mechanisms falling apart.

Tracing the connections of that set will lead you to the aroma box on the twenty-ninth floor. Reel in the box and have it replace the broken set. Have it turn both regularly and irregularly, redefine how it should normally function. Seal the gaps and wring heat out of it. Transmit that heat to the twenty-sixth grid of Tokyo. The characteristic turn rates of the mechanisms in its core tower are 3,430, 3,035, 3,056, 3,053, 3,124, 3,394 rpm. Clockwise.

Though the two towers aren't connected by wires, we can use the coupled movements between its core tower and the Pillar of Heaven to transmit the heat instead. We have to raise the frequency of the twenty-sixth's grid's vibrations geometrically while keeping the frequencies of the surrounding grids the same.

The terminal movement on its first floor will serve as our reference. Nothing can be left approximate. Scale the values down for size but be sure to keep the ratios the same.

**And lastly, something for you to think about—if clockwork contraptions won't work with even a single gear missing, then how is this planet even running at this point?**

"Marie...are you awake?"

"Huh...?"

A hand waved before her eyes. Marie choked on air. *What did he just do to me... what the heck did he just say...?*

"All right, seems like you're awake. Did you memorize it?"

"Wha... huh? Memorize what?" Marie tilted her head, still unable to properly articulate her thoughts. *I do get the vague impression that he just said a lot of things to me, but...*

"Alrighty then. I see that you have it memorized."

"W-wait a second now?! What did you just do to..."

"I told you that I'd give you my raw impression, didn't I? So that's exactly what I did."

"W-wait a second. You said that I have it memorized! I don't have a single clue what you just said to me, though..."

"You do," Naoto asserted as if it were indisputable. "Look, Marie. You've not only memorized the blueprints of the products of the Breguet Corporation but of all the weapons and machines throughout the world, even RyuZU. Isn't that right?"

As Marie nodded blankly, Naoto sneered as if to pay her back for her condescending attitude.

"If you weren't aware of it then let me enlighten you: that's something that should normally be impossible."

Marie's eyes widened.

"I told you, didn't I? You've already mastered my little trick. The only difference between you and me is that you see it with your eyes while I hear it with my ears. Ah, and I'll have you know that I've got RyuZU's structure memorized down to her last wire, so you better not think you're the only one!"

As Naoto stood before her, haughtily puffing out his chest. Marie remained silent, gazing at him dumbfounded.

*She thought about the meaning of his words. Is it really that I "remember" it? Or do I "know" it?*

"Don't worry," Naoto said, as Marie tried to hazily think her way through that question. "If my impression came across as words, then you definitely understand what I said."

"Really...?"

"You definitely remember what I said. You don't remember, but you do. There's no doubt that the Marie I know, the genius that you are, must have understood everything about this floor."

"Where are you getting the confidence to think that?"

"I don't think that. I know that. The way you memorize things, it's a little embarrassing, but I'll tell you why I admire and even respect you." He paused for a breath. "We're the same in this regard and only this regard. You don't 'memorize' clockwork structures, Marie. You simply abstractly grasp them somehow. That's why I thought that I might be able to do the same thing."

Naoto gave her an embarrassed smile.

"Don't worry," he said with an expression that Marie had never seen on him before, a gaze of trust and conviction. "Believe in yourself."

Naoto stood up. He picked up some tools that had been scattered on the floor and headed towards his station. Marie gulped down the saliva that had built up in her mouth, then slowly stood up, following his example.

She picked up some tools and let her feet naturally lead her to her station. There, her hands suddenly froze. She worried.

*Frankly, I don't understand a single thing that Naoto said to me. What should I do? What would let me understand his words? How should I approach them?*

As Marie followed that train of thought, she sneered.

"Hah," Marie scoffed at the Marie Bell Breguet who had been twiddling her thumbs and basking in despair, unable to move.

*But I'm different now.*

Naoto, the unquestionable genius and hero that he was, her ideal self that she had always yearned for, had asserted with full confidence... *I should believe in myself.*

*The image of a hero that I've kept in my heart since childhood is going out of his way to assure me of that.*

*Perfect.* Marie smiled ferociously. *For now, just this once, I'll take his word as collateral and show him that I can enter the world that he sees just as easily as he's asking me to!*

"Four, in... three, out..." Marie muttered as she submerged herself in absolute focus with a breathing exercise.

She was aiming for the focus she achieved for just a moment when she connected Halter's brain to the Black Tortoise. The domain that she had set foot in then, a place where she could undoubtedly grasp an entire grid.

"Three, in. Two, out. Two, in. One..."

She closed her eyes, the external sounds around her faded from her consciousness. By erasing all extraneous noise from her mind, everything became clear. Fully immersed, she apprehended a vivid image with her inner eye.

A deep cavern was before her. It was a dark, unfathomable place with a gate that had been broken open and just left to settle. On the broken door was an engraved warning.

"Abandon hope all ye who enter here."

*I see.* Marie chuckled bitterly as she became certain: the literal hell that lies beyond this gate is the world that Naoto sees.

*"Abandon hope." Hope, you say?* Marie smiled. *Forget abandoning it, I already lost that unreliable gift ages ago. In that case, I'll replace my hope with the "greed" and "pride" that'll allow me to pierce the veil and bring light into this world.*

*Just those two "deadly sins" are more than enough to dive into the hell that awaits me!*

Marie took a step forward. However, before her foot could land, the meager amount of reason she still possessed warned: "If you dive into this world you'll never be able to return."

*I'm prepared for that. But, is this really...the world that Naoto showed me?* That slight hesitation broke her concentration. She opened her eyes and looked around nervously. Naoto had already begun to work.

He started, as usual, by staring into space and straining his ears. Then, slowly but surely, he began moving his hands without hesitation. What she saw was a right and proper clocksmith. She became certain. Naoto transformed.

*His hands aren't as fast as mine. His work isn't as polished as a Meister's either. He picks up the wrong tool from time to time, but...*

*because he doesn't hesitate for even a single instant when deciding which parts he should adjust, in the end he's working much faster than a newly certified Meister.*

*Actually, he hasn't undergone any transformation at all,* Marie corrected herself. *That is his true form. That's the reason I unconsciously detested him. Because, he's a bona fide...*

*"Amateur?" As if. You're a bona fide genius, Naoto. I know that better than anyone else... tch...*

The fire in her heart swelled and roared into a hellfire that could burn everything to ash. *I'm gonna catch up to that! I'll do whatever it takes!!*

She became immersed in her own mind and saw the cavern before her once more. Her world should have become silent, however...

"Say, Marie." A vivid voice resounded inside her mind. Squinting against the darkness, she saw Naoto turn around to face her. He was standing firmly deep inside the cavern. Hell.

"What are you acting scared for?" Naoto extended his hand towards her teasingly.

Marie flared in red-hot anger. "Don't get cocky, punk. Keep your hands to yourself! Don't worry, I'll catch up and send you a flying kick right this minute!!" Marie howled as she broke into a vigorous dash. She ran after him at full speed.

And so, she dashed straight into hell. The instant that she did, time stopped.

*Ah, I see. Indeed, I've felt this before. Whenever I was fully immersed in repairs or focused on something, this is how I felt.*

*Feeling like a fish swimming freely in a dream. My consciousness expanding limitlessly towards omnipotence. This much is familiar to me already.*

When Marie opened her eyes to reality, the world looked completely different. Everything had changed. Looking up, she saw a set of gears chugging along as usual, but now she could see their force, their movement, their flow, their directions... as a jumble of wind and color.

She could see things she shouldn't be able to see as wind.

She could sense things she shouldn't be able to sense as color.

What Marie saw as color was most likely what Naoto heard as sound. He perceived the vast amount of information that constantly assaulted his brain through synesthesia. The vast amount of information now assaulting Marie's brain was drowning her in a sense of euphoria.

The relationship of the parts were as wind and the laws of binding physics were color. Stirred by this extraordinary sense of omnipotence, Marie thought aloud: "Man, so I really was a genius after all."

She recalled the despair and absurd delusion that had filled her in Akihabara. *Ahh, looks like there's hope for me yet,* Marie sneered, picking up one of her tools.

*Turns out that the false impression... no, the sense I got that "everything is an illusion" was right. Everything I saw back then was wrong.*

*Or perhaps it'd be more accurate to say that I could only see the surface of the world, just as inside movements normally aren't visible due to the casing. Indeed, I've cleared away the veil. This is what the world looks like after you peel away its outer membrane.*

Marie had abandoned all her assumptions of the world. Now she was certain.

*Whether it's the "irregularity" of Naoto being able to grasp the structures of the core towers and even the Pillar of Heaven...*

*Or the "irregularity" of Vermouth being able to fight so well with a body that shouldn't have functioned...*

*Or even the "irregularity" of me being able to successfully link Halter's brain to a heavily armored automaton...*

*Actually, that's not all... now that I've cleared away my assumptions, everything I have simply accepted to be true up till now...*

*I can see that everything in the world is both "irregular" and "normal."*

*Non-contact coupled movements? Nanogears? Clockwork AI that's capable of replicating human thought? Everything, absolutely everything, is "irregular." According to common sense, such things couldn't possibly exist...!*

*Most likely, the people who fathomed the principles behind such things did so subconsciously, or perhaps they created those things by dipping their fingertips into the "interior of the world." In the same way that I'm now seeing it, they made the impossible possible through their own ability and fabricated the explaining theories after the fact.*

*All theories, sciences, and technologies work like that.*

*First there's a replicable result, then comes the theory that humans try to forcefully frame it with to explain it.*

*Once a phenomenon is understood, it becomes obvious. So there's something that can't be explained with our current theories? So what? That's nothing new.*

*The Earth used to be flat.*

*After observing the stars, formulating equations, and creating the field of astronomy, people came to understand that the Earth was a globe. They came to know that it was not the sun that revolved subserviently around the Earth, but the other way around... so then, what was reality like before those facts were proven?*

*Was the Earth flat? Were we the center of the universe?*

*No, reality's been the same all along.*

*And yet, throughout history, our world has constantly been "remade" by we humans ourselves, through our human perspective!!*

*Because of the work of someone who was juuust a bit of a madman, just a little bit ahead of his time, the Earth was remade once more, this time with gears. That happened a thousand years ago...*

*However, does that really mean that the Earth wasn't a clockwork contraption before?* Marie smiled. *Thanks to my newfound senses, I'm beginning to doubt even that.*

*"Y" is supposed to have said: "I'll show you all our world reproduced with gears." In that case,* Marie thought gazing at the whirling, colorful scenery around her, *would this not be the true form of the interior of the world?*

Marie moved her hands. She sharpened her focus and invoked an image in her mind. Her accelerated thoughts wrung out knowledge from the vast amount of compressed information that her senses were feeding her. What she could do was aligned with what she knew she should do.

"See? There's no way that you can't do something I can. Ain't that right?" Naoto said in a lively voice. He had sensed Marie's transformation from the sound and from her aura.

"No, duh…! Who do you think I am? I'm Marie: a genius who makes the impossible possible. I'm a god! The woman who'll have you completely beaten and crushed one day!"

*Yes, I know. I can only see what I'm seeing right now because you are showing it to me. However, I'll definitely show you that I can find my way back now that I know the feeling!*

The two of them exchanged smiles and let their instincts and intuition take over. After that, Marie began a performance that exceeded the limits of human reason. Any explanations of theory would have to wait until afterwards.

• • • ● • •

AnchoR stood at the edge of Ueno Grid, looking down at Akihabara below. The enormous clockwork monster was reflected in her red, glistening eyes. She reached for the cube by her chest.

"Stop right there," someone called out to her from behind.

AnchoR didn't bother turning around. After all, she didn't have to turn to know who it was and what she had come to do.

"Don't stop me, Big Sis," she said in a firm voice.

"No," RyuZU answered. "I will stop you, because Master Naoto asked me to."

"Father said that AnchoR can do what she wants, yes?"

"Acting freely and acting selfishly are two entirely different things. If a child confuses the two, then it falls to the parent to scold and correct her. You are making that very mistake right now, AnchoR."

AnchoR slowly turned around. "Then... in that case, what else can I do?"

RyuZU didn't answer.

"If I don't destroy that," AnchoR continued. "Everyone will die. AnchoR's the only one who can do something. AnchoR can't do anything but destroy. I'm different from Big Sis..."

RyuZU took those words head-on. Lowering her gaze, their topaz and ruby eyes met.

"That's where you are wrong, AnchoR," RyuZU said, taking a breath.

"Huh?" AnchoR's eyes widened. *What's Big Sis saying? Destroying is all AnchoR can do. I was the only one specialized for battle among us.*

RyuZU took a step towards her and bent forward to get a better look at her face.

"I shall repeat myself as many times as necessary. You were not made for such a reason. What 'Y' expected from you is not such a base and simple thing."

"..."

As AnchoR stood rigid and confounded, RyuZU put her arms around her and hugged her.

"As 'AnchoR,' who received her decree to serve as 'the one who destroys,' you are surely the strongest."

"Yeah, that's why...AnchoR can only des—"

"That is exactly what you are misunderstanding. Both why you were expected to serve as 'the one who destroys' and why you were given the name 'AnchoR.'"

"Why...AnchoR was...?"

RyuZU pulled away and patted AnchoR's head tenderly. "However." She smiled bitterly. "Your feelings are not wrong. That is why I will not stop you."

"Big Sis...?" *I don't understand. What is Big Sis trying to say? What is AnchoR misunderstanding? What is the right thing for me... for AnchoR... to do?*

"Your feelings are right and something to be praised," RyuZU added as AnchoR became confused. "However, you ought to believe in Master Naoto... and Mistress Marie as well I suppose, but only as a footnote."

She paused for a breath.

"Wait until things truly cannot wait any longer."

•  •  ●  •  •

"Hey, gramps... you're a Meister too, right?" Vermouth muttered, watching as Marie and Naoto demonstrated a divine feat that surpassed the limits of human reason.

The voice of an old man answered from the same mouth as the one that had asked the question. "Yes. Technically you could say that."

"Mind telling me one thing? Is that what a Meister is supposed to be? 'Cuz, if that's the case... and this is coming from someone who gave up everything human about him except his brain, mind you... they are far less human than..." Vermouth couldn't bring himself to complete the sentence.

He felt a sinking terror.

"With due respect, Mr. Vermouth," Konrad said. "Those who proudly called themselves Meisters before those two would only embarrass themselves."

*Humans do have limits,* Konrad thought. *They say "human potential is limitless," but wax poetic as much as you like, reality won't budge.*

Konrad had seen many promising, talented young people in his time.

*They all certainly brimmed with intelligence. They would pick up knowledge as a sponge picks up water and master it. Make it their own. By inheriting the accumulated learning of those who had come before, they were able to advance into territory that no man had yet to reach.*

*But even so, they too would eventually reach a wall somewhere along the way.*

Frustration, complacency, satisfaction, overconfidence, loss of motivation... it would be too unreasonable to dismiss those reasons for people ceasing to improve. It was simply human nature. The result of being spoiled by the taste of earlier success.

*Because that's what humans are. Thinking men always hit a wall somewhere. Despite having limitless potential, humans will seal away their possibilities somewhere along the line. Because if they didn't, they'd be crushed by that very same potential. They'd end up destroying themselves, even. Because they'd go mad.*

*However, Marie has already transcended such human fragility,* Konrad thought. *She'd never crack. Never fold. Despite suffering many defeats along the way, she has always continued to move forward, and by doing so, she has already reached a place that could be called the peak of this world.*

At least, that was how it looked to Konrad. And that was why the sight before his eyes was baffling: that small girl had willingly broken her own back and abandoned everything she knew. She'd wrung all the water out of her sponge and decided that she would advance forward no matter what.

She'd given everything to chase after a boy who occupied territory unknown to Konrad. No, it was territory that was most likely unknown to everyone who lived on this planet.

"Dr. Marie, just how far do you plan to go, I wonder?" Konrad muttered with admiration in his eyes, as if he were looking at something far away in the distance.

Vermouth sighed. "How should I put it? Seeing something like this firsthand makes me want to challenge the dream that I had almost forgotten. They say that boys will always be boys, no matter how old. Is that why I feel this way? What do you think, gramps?"

"Hmm...I see what you're saying. To be taught something by a youngling at this advanced age... I guess I still have a long way to go. Thinking about things from that perspective, I cannot help but feel excited. Even now, I am wondering what I will become capable of in the future."

Vermouth laughed bitterly at that bright voice. "Yeah, I'm expecting lots from you, old man. Make me the best Dutch Wife ever. And this time, one that's truly on the level of Little Miss Y-Series."

Konrad didn't show any displeasure at being teased. "Hmm? Do those words mean that you can sense it?" he asked curiously.

"Nah. I'm just someone who's been able to survive this long solely on gut instinct."

Vermouth looked down at his artificial body. Or, more precisely, the body of the love automaton that Konrad had made. "I simply can't imagine that someone like you, who did such a thorough job on a mere love automaton, wouldn't feel anything after seeing automata like that."

"Well, it's not really a big deal. I had forgotten about it after all," Konrad said in a reminiscent voice. "It's a story from when I was in my twenties."

"Now *that's* gotta be some ancient history."

"Back then, there was a greenhorn who'd gotten carried away, hogging the label of genius all to himself. He was being fussed over as the youngest Meister in history, you see."

"Oh, are you talking about yourself?"

"It's great that you can read between the lines. Well anyhow, that greenhorn was summoned back to his homeland one day, where he received a request directly from the incumbent queen. Something to do with an automaton that the royal family had always kept hidden away. It wouldn't operate. If I recall correctly, the engraving on her neck read 'Y. [BezEL].'"

"..."

Vermouth sank into silence.

"He couldn't believe it," Konrad continued with a bitter laugh. "The equipment that was available back then...nearly half a century ago...certainly wasn't as advanced as the equipment that we have today. But seeing the terrifying, awe-inspiring, godly piece of art was like seeing an entire core tower compacted into an automaton the size of a girl. And that greenhorn's pride couldn't help but be smashed to pieces. He swore that, one day, he would create an automaton to surpass it."

"Is that why you've worked as a clocksmith all these years?"

"Hardly." Konrad laughed bitterly. "I said that I had forgotten about it, remember? Well, surprisingly enough, it might have still been stuck deep in my heart somewhere, but...'to challenge the Initial-Y Series once more,' hmm? It's not a bad dream."

"Sure, why not. Challenging a dream from your younger days, right? People do that all the time. It's called a bucket list." Vermouth laughed, his shoulders shaking uncontrollably.

However, he soon found himself looking at the clock on the wall and turned serious. "Leaving that aside, forget surpassing the limits of humans. It looks to me like they've even surpassed the limits of gods. What do you think, gramps?"

"Yes, indeed. However, even at this pace, it's still a fifty-fifty chance whether they'll make it in time."

There was less than three minutes left. Naoto and Marie had done in thirty seconds what would normally have taken dozens of clocksmiths an hour.

*But will they really be able to make a new bypass for the Pillar of Heaven when it's been damaged so severely?* Konrad wondered.

*That work would take at least a month, even for ten dozen clocksmiths. And they mean to do so in just a hundred and eighty seconds? It should go without saying but, should they accomplish this, it would be a feat that surpasses even divine work.*

• • ● • •

The prescribed time came. The seventy-two minutes were just about up.

"It can't wait any longer," AnchoR said, standing up. "Well, Big Sis, AnchoR will be going now..."

She touched the swaying cube by her chest. With a creak, the gate to AnchoR's armory appeared in thin air. Reaching in, she dragged something out of it, but it wasn't a weapon. It was a teddy bear. The one that Naoto had bought for her two days ago.

Pulling the ring off of the middle finger of her right hand, AnchoR handed both it and the bear to RyuZU.

"AnchoR doesn't want these to be dirtied or broken, so...hold on to them please?"

"I...shall keep them safe," RyuZU said, accepting them. "AnchoR, if you were truly serious, I think you could move even faster than myself under Mute Scream. You could still stand to wait until at least seventy-one minutes and fifty-nine seconds have—"

"Sorry, Big Sis. AnchoR won't wait that long," she replied with a shake of her head. "AnchoR has fulfilled Father's request. So...

it's fine now. AnchoR will put an end to everything so Father and everyone else can rest easy."

AnchoR turned around and looked down at the target awaiting her in Akihabara. The sinister, enormous thing that was trying to kill the ones she loved.

She stared down at the thing which she had decided to thoroughly, mercilessly destroy, and took a deep breath. Once again, she touched the cube dangling by her chest.

As the spring unwound, all of the energy in her Perpetual Gear was converted into kinetic energy.

"AnchoR," her elder sister called from behind her.

But AnchoR didn't turn around. Instead, she took a step forward. Toward the battlefield. So that she could fulfill her purpose...

"AnchoR," her older sister repeated. "When you return, I imagine that Master Naoto will educate you on a side of yourself that you are not aware of. So, while I will not tell you to play it safe...

"All the same," continued the elder sister that AnchoR was so proud of. "Come back in one piece. And if you do not intend to do so..." RyuZU paused. "I will bring you back with me right now. Even if I have to punish you a little."

AnchoR bent her lips into a sorrowful frown. "Sorry, but AnchoR's too strong for Big Sis to stop."

"Oh? I wonder about that. It is true that you are my proud younger sister, but it seems that you are getting a little carried away. Perhaps some *reeducation* is in order..."

"..."

"Past, present, or future, there is not a single automaton anywhere in the universe that surpasses me. Nor has there ever been a younger sister anywhere that surpasses her big sister."

"Hee hee," AnchoR chuckled and nodded.

She kicked off from her perch and leapt down towards the magnetized Akihabara Grid that lay 1,500 meters below...

The intense wind caused her hair and clothes to flutter, but the girl in red and white continued to fall.

"Definition Proclamation," she declared in a tone that was different from her usual stuttering. More composed. Mechanical. "The Fourth of the Initial-Y Series, AnchoR, the One Who Destroys."

Announcing her transformation, she confirmed her status.

(Condition check—all green. All mechanisms are operating normally under the First Balance Wheel of Differences.)

(All armaments in working order. All conditions for running at full throttle cleared. Limiter released.)

(Warning: Power Reservoir is only 6.1% charged. Calculating projected run time... calculations complete.)

(At full-throttle mode in the Twelfth Balance Wheel of Differences, maximum run time will be 3.2 seconds from your own frame of reference. Do you still wish to proceed?)

AnchoR ignored the warning.

"Inherent ability: 'Power Reserver.' Initiating transformational sequence."

She declared mutiny. From this moment forward, she would violate the laws of physics.

She visually confirmed the distance to her target, the mobile composite electromagnetic assault weapon, Yatsukahagi. It spanned 320 meters in height and 932 meters in length.

(Heat source detected from its central actuators. Use of electromagnetic technology confirmed.)

For an instant, AnchoR felt someone laughing deep within her. Far far away from her own consciousness.

*Good grief, that's as far as they've gotten in a thousand years?*

As AnchoR puzzled over the voice inside her, her combat algorithms analyzed the target.

(Enemy armaments: electromagnetic pulse radiation, railgun, maser cannon.)

(Equipping phased array radar and infrared sight. You are currently within the enemy's firing range.)

(The target utilizes magnetic shield plating. Judging by the fact it repelled the First's scythes, it is estimated that necessary force to neutralize it will require running on the Eleventh Balance Wheel of Differences at minimum.)

"Enemy threat level classification: 'Black.' Initiating Shift to the Thirteenth Balance Wheel of Differences"

The girl's body flared up. The laws of physics were contradicted. The air grated, and friction was born.

"Beginning transformation. Shifting to the Second Balance Wheel of Differences."

The disk that had been inactive inside AnchoR—the automaton in the Initial-Y Series designed for combat—began to turn. The mechanism resembled a clock. Its hand jumped to where "II" was engraved, then "III."

"Shifting to the Third Wheel. 'Bloody Murder' can now be activated."

The girl's glossy black hair spread out in an arc behind her, being stained blood red. Her pure white armor turned black and swelled, enveloped by an ominous web of red lines.

"Shifting to the Fourth Wheel. The Fifth. Sixth, Seventh, Eighth..."

Her transformation accelerated. She could feel time breaking, creaking as it distorted under the violent heat emanating from her body. Each time she shifted gears, her perception of time stretched out in a square function.

"Ninth, Tenth, Eleventh..."

She felt the hand of the clock within her make its way nearly full circle. AnchoR resolved herself to execute the "alternative method" that she had informed her master about a few days ago.

When AnchoR ran on high output, her available armaments became extremely limited. But the same was also true for the enemy. Either way, it was not a problem, as she didn't have any other means available to her.

"Shifting to the Twelfth Wheel. Deploying armaments LB01, BC08 from the armory."

The cube by her chest twisted. A sword made of gears taller than she was materialized in her right hand. Eight floating orbs emerged from behind her, following her movements.

And then... the girl's chest blossomed. The clothes covering her chest unraveled and her artificial skin tore asunder, her ribs forming into a vessel in her disheveled state. The twisting cube continued to accelerate without restraint to a speed extremely close to that of light. It slipped into the recesses of the girl's vessel along with all of its infinite heat.

"Removing precautionary limits by my own will."

Inside her body, the hand that had been pointing to "XII" violently trembled. It twisted and turned, shaking as it ran out of control. Finally, as countless cracks formed along its surface, it broke.

That instant, AnchoR knew: *Today's the day that I wake up from my eternal dream.*

"Shifting to the Thirteenth Balance Wheel of Differences. Starting self-destruct."

Eternity burst into flames. And within those flames, the girl was reborn as a woman. Her limbs grew, as did her hair. It harbored an enormous amount of heat and flowed down her back like a waterfall. As her armor melted away, a gorgeously pink, velvety dress wrapped around her freshly reformed limbs.

"Chrono Hook. Initiating output of imaginary power by means of the Perpetual Gear. Materializing."

The world had fallen still, and the beautiful young woman declared a second set of apocalyptic words of which, of all the Initial-Y Series automata, only she could say:

"'Still Weight.'"

She said it in the tone of an obituary that she had written for herself—her final farewell. Her Perpetual Gear, the material manifestation of eternity, came apart. And yet, at the same time, it continued to turn.

Reality denied the fantasy of an eternal girl, forcing her to awaken from her dream. But that awakening demonstrated one simple fact. The absurd truth that, in exchange for her own demise, there was nothing in the entire universe that the Trishula could not destroy.

It was simple really.

Unlike the First, who manipulated time by entering into imaginary time, the Fourth wrenched open a rift by letting her infinite heat do the work. Just now, AnchoR had cut all the power she was using to protect herself from the friction, inertia, gravity, and recoil which resulted and raised her output to levels that would cause her own body to disintegrate.

It was enough for her to continue to run at maximum output, just as the name of the Perpetual Gear implied, perpetually. Until the moment her body, her frame and all her parts, reached their limit and broke apart.

Leaving behind the contradictory symphony of demise, the beauty revolted against the universe, tore apart the chains of physics, and compressed the world around her as she dived through the air.

· • ● • ·

AnchoR charged into the compressed world.

Normally, the eight floating orbs behind her functioned as small autonomous support units. However, AnchoR had them resonate with her Perpetual Gear, raising their output so high that they began to volatilize. Under its influence, the eight orbs became a pseudo-booster, spouting invisible flames.

With the help of those eight powerful sources of propulsion, AnchoR accelerated. She charged towards the target at a speed unperceivable to machines, much less humans. She entered effective range.

AnchoR was holding her giant sword before her with both hands. The edge of its blade was lined with molecular gears that began turning at ultra-high speed.

Normally, those gears would be able to shred through anything, regardless of how hard the object was. However, inside an almost perfectly still moment—this little crevice between zero and one second—the gears weren't able to synchronize. If she forced them to do so anyway, they would vaporize like the orbs.

That was why AnchoR raised her sword, took her aim, and swung with all her might. Relying on the endurance of the blade, her invisibly fast swing, and the natural laws of physics...

*Go through... ngggghhhha!*

"!!" With a grinding sound, the blade went through.

—No. My apologies, sound did not actually propagate inside this space. Thus, AnchoR relied on the pressure against her hands for feedback as she continued her attack.

Pointing her eight orbs towards the site of the incision, AnchoR "threw" them. Blazing forth, the orbs crashed into the incision point at a speed faster than the speed of light.

They released an enormous amount of energy as they did so

and, disintegrating upon impact, their heat tore away the electro-magnetic coating on the armor plating, vaporizing it.

With that, a hole large enough for someone to pass through finally opened, and AnchoR charged inside, storming into the interior of the Yatsukahagi with considerable momentum behind her...

*Ngh...!*

She crash landed as about twelve of the thirty-plus shock absorbers throughout her body broke.

Her frame screamed as all the fine parts in her body were crushed.

*My gyro-correctional control system is still fine. That's good enough!*

AnchoR paid no mind to the damage. Standing up, she dashed—or rather, glided—through the insides of the Yatsukahagi. Shaking off the fetters of gravity, she leapt and even "landed" on the wall as she continued to glide.

The instant she arrived at her first objective, her right foot broke from the immense heat-strain and the impact of stopping. Her frame twisted as her shock absorbers burst in two.

Various parts throughout her body were melting away, despite withstanding the heat from when she had demagnetized herself. By now, AnchoR was emanating heat far greater than the Curie temperature of any part of her body.

She ignored it. Rapidly closing in on the barrier wall, AnchoR swung her giant sword. The slash tore through space-time itself and instantly turned the barrier into plasma, vaporizing it. Before that plasma could scatter, AnchoR accelerated even further by kicking off the wall. Again, she sensed damage to her foot but ignored it all the same.

Inside the room beyond, she found 31 of the 1,033 coils that Naoto had mentioned. They were enormous cylinders made of spirals of fine coils producing a vast amount of electromagnetic energy.

*Ah....aaaaAAAaaAAAAAAAahhh!!* Letting out a soundless battle cry, AnchoR shook off the pain signals coming from the linked mechanisms in her arms and mowed through everything in the room in a single strike.

"..."

The only human inside the weapon—the only organic heat source—didn't move a bit. He couldn't. He probably couldn't even perceive what was happening.

Inside Still Weight, AnchoR had no way of measuring the difference between the time outside and the time in her vicinity. However, not even 0.24 of a second had passed between the moment she severed the plating, and now, when 809 coils had already been destroyed.

It would still take more than 0.3 tenths of a second for the first impact to propagate, Gennai's brain to perceive it, and for him to become aware of the signals of the shockwave passing through his body.

"..."

AnchoR took another step forward. Each time she did so, her manipulator took on further fatally irreversible damage. With every other step, the heat from the impact caused yet another layer of her actuator to melt away.

Even so, AnchoR continued to swing her giant sword until her right arm was torn off from the recoil. It flew off at the elbow, along with her giant sword, and landed still clinging to the hilt in the opposite direction of her swing. The blade lodged itself in the wall at a speed which exceeded even the enormous weapon's railgun.

AnchoR removed her severed right hand from the hilt and dislodged the sword with her off-hand.

*Hah.......AH aaaah...AAAAaaaaaaaaaaAAAAAAAAHHH!!*

She swung with all her might once more.

Explosions burst forth as space itself was torn apart. The impact was powerful enough to rip a hole through time, and matter disappeared into the rift. The marks of destruction rippled outward like a cleansing storm, as heat and pressure washed away the wall and everything else in the room behind.

Light was generated from intense heat, and the impact made a frozen roar. Unable to withstand the backlash, AnchoR found herself slammed against the wall. The shockwave's vibrations scorched the sealed space around her, and AnchoR realized that her gyro was so beat up that it couldn't even absorb that anymore.

Even so, she advanced to the next room like a revenant...

"..."

*It hurts...so...much...* Her mental endurance had finally reached its limit.

She had been operating at a truly unobservable speed, cleaving open the enormous weapon's plating faster than light. And she hadn't stopped there, mere instants later, she was plowing through the interior of the weapon, mowing down everything in sight.

Destroying the 932nd coil, she finally felt her own demise coming. Her gyro had already melted away. Her left leg had completely ceased functioning from the knee down, her right forearm had torn off, and even the giant sword that had made an astonishing display of endurance had just vaporized.

Her thought processors were in shambles. Her failed mechanisms had been squashed by the natural laws of the universe. AnchoR had lost practically all of her mobility. Even so, she arrived at her goal.

"Ah... AaaaaaaaAAAAAAaaAAAAHHH!!"

She screamed her defiance silently as she bashed the door with her remaining fist. Her powerful punch pierced through with a force that caused several coils in the room behind to explode.

As the broken pieces paid their dues to gravity, she heard her own scream and the noise of the destruction.

She came to realize that she was no longer moving faster than real time.

*It hurts, it hurts, it hurts, it hurts, it hurts, it hurts...so much... aggghhhhh! Father, Mother, Big Sis, please, save me! I don't want to...*

Her survival instincts cried out in a moment of weakness before her reason could check it. But before she could waste time feeling ashamed, her reason rallied and coolly analyzed the situation.

*There's no longer any difference between my own temporal reference frame and that of my surroundings. In that case, how many seconds has it been since I began the attack? Or has it been minutes by now?*

*There are still power coils that I haven't destroyed, and I have no idea just how many I have to destroy for this weapon to stop. But, if I want to be a hundred percent sure, I have to destroy them all or else...everyone'll...*

"Ah ah...aghhh."

Not even her vocalizer was working. She was near her limit. With neither the time nor the luxury to hesitate, AnchoR crept along the floor towards the heat sources of the remaining power coils.

This was the first time that she had ever used Still Weight, a maneuver of demise. It was something that allowed her to fight with force to spare even when she was nearly at zero power. It was literally her last resort.

There was no way to know how many seconds she could stay in that mode. However, her understanding as a combat unit was telling her that, despite it all, the current state of affairs was still preferable to the alternative. That, by operating in the Thirteenth Wheel, she had been able to do 18.2 times the damage she would have been able to otherwise. Had she stayed at the Twelfth Wheel, she would have run out of power after only destroying the outer plating.

*None of that matters,* her heart howled fiercely. *If I can't even destroy something like this... then why was I even... ngh!!*

She swung her fist and felt her remaining arm being crushed. But in return, everything in sight followed suit.

*This isn't good enough! Even though you made respecting my free will the requirement for my Master Confirmation, if you didn't make me strong enough to protect those who would try to give it to me, then why, did you...even...make...me?!*

*Tell me...why...*

AnchoR cursed her own creator as she advanced, even as the voice inside her screamed. She had lost both her arms. Her left leg had melted, and her right leg was straggling. The total number of nuclear power reactors she had destroyed was 1,008.

*Just...twenty-five...more...*

It was impossible. With all the power she had expended during Still Weight, opening up her armory would be difficult.

Even if she could produce a weapon, she had no arms left to wield it with.

Nearly all her sensory mechanisms were malfunctioning. Noise mixed with her distorted sight. Infrared sensors that had barely survived her rampage picked up a massive heat source...

She was certain that she had just seen a clump of concentrated heat in an area around two hundred meters from where she was. Her mind quickly abandoned its despair as it reverted to a stoic, calculating, weapon.

*Assuming that the main cannon of this weapon fires by concentrating the energy generated by the coils... if I destroy that concentrated heat source, I'll definitely at least be able to stop it from firing!*

*Break!!* AnchoR prayed through clenched teeth as she pumped her full strength into her half-broken right leg. She didn't worry about landing. The only thing on her mind was breaking through the wall before her.

As she launched herself, AnchoR realized something. The heat source in her sight had become completely still. Her personal frame of time was expanding again, pulling away from its surroundings.

*This will probably be the last thing I ever do,* she thought with a smile. With her remaining leg, AnchoR accelerated through the gap in time.

Her broken body flared up with the friction against space itself. Confirming that her body temperature had risen once again, she felt relieved. *I was able to accelerate. Even after all I've put my body through, it's still listening to me.*

This last spurt was surely like how the light from a candle flickered before it burned out.

Her remaining foot melted off from the impact of kicking a hole through space-time, but her expanded consciousness perceived the wall as strangely far away, somehow, as she collided with it.

Just like a cannonball, AnchoR pierced the wall with her scorching heat and into the block behind it. However, she became disoriented and lost control of her speed, helplessly crashing into the wall at the other end of the room.

Like a puppet that had had its strings cut, she dropped to the floor with enough force to bounce back up, but ultimately, her body fell prone.

*Not...yet...*

Even after losing all her limbs, AnchoR still continued to function. Her neck creaked as she raised her head stiffly to look at what was around her.

She was inside a small hall that was reminiscent of a temple or a church. In the middle of this area, buried in gears of various shapes and sizes, the floor bulged up, forming a dome.

Enshrined there was an enormous crystal cylinder, made up of countless shafts, bearings, and spheres. Its glass coils traced a spiral that had the god of lightning imprisoned inside.

*If I...destroy, that...*

Rallying all of her remaining will, AnchoR began to move. She inched her way forward by jerking her torso pitifully, like a slug.

*It hurts. It hurts it hurts it hurtshurtshurtshurtshurts.*

As her thoughts scrambled with the pain coming from her broken sensory mechanisms, anguish jarred her entire body. In that agony, her mind came to focus on a single question:

*Why does an automaton like me, one made for combat, need to feel pain...?*

And just as she asked herself that unhelpful question, a shock ran through AnchoR's entire body as a hole bore through her.

"How unsightly. To think that you're supposed to be one of 'Y's' masterpieces. Have you no shame?" The voice of an old man sounded above her head.

*It's Gennai Hirayama,* she recognized with hazy consciousness. However, at this point, she couldn't even turn to face him with her near-ruined body.

"Or is it that, surprisingly enough, electromagnetic technology works on 'Y's' dolls as well?"

*I can't move.*

*I can't move can't move can't move, (error), (hang up), (error), (error), (error...)*

"Hmm. That might just be the case, considering that you couldn't make it in time. I've already finished inputting the command to fire the main cannon."

(ERROR.)

"It'll fire momentarily. It's your group's loss."

"..."

Gennai looked down at "Y's" legacy convulsing on the ground. "Now then, if you would excuse the cliché, I figured something like this might happen, so..."

He held up the pistol in his right hand. It was not a regular mechanical gun. It was equipped with electrodes.

"This is a portable railgun that I prepared for the legacies of 'Y.' I never thought it would actually be effective though. I suppose this just goes to show that it's always a good idea to at least try and prepare what one can."

Gennai took aim. AnchoR continued to spasm. The muzzle of his portable railgun was pointed right at her head.

*Pwoosh.* The bullet accelerated forward at hypersonic speed, leaving its sound behind in its wake.

· · ● · ·

"Linkage complete! Marie!"

"I'm done here too! Everyone, prepare to evacuate! We're going to activate the bypass!"

At seventy-three minutes and fifty-two seconds, Naoto and Marie finished seizing control of a grid beside Akihabara.

It wasn't the work of gods but of man transcending human limits. They had managed to put together a new bypass quickly, despite the heavy damage to the Pillar of Heaven.

Even if a detailed schematic was available for reference, just grasping its structure would surely have taken a normal clocksmith more than a week. But even so, the time limit had simply been too merciless.

"Ain't no need for preparations! Our only option's to show our pursuers our fine asses and jump down that hole! Hell, wanna say hi on the way out? They've just dropped by to throw us a going away party!" Vermouth yelled sarcastically, spraying a volley of bullets over the barricade.

Before him were older mobile weapons and various other armaments that the military had gotten their hands on. They'd been closing in on him in waves.

*Houko acted like she wasn't really expecting anything of them,* Marie thought. *But it seems like there're still some soldiers with a backbone in the remnants of Tokyo's military after all.*

They were a mishmash of imperial guards and units that had rushed from other grids. They weren't even properly rallied when they came charging in, fifty-minutes after Naoto and Marie began work on the new bypass.

Normally, sending your forces into battle in one wave after another was a huge mistake but, with RyuZU and AnchoR absent, it was a tough fight for Vermouth and Halter to hold the position.

Really, the two of them should be praised for having held the intruders back until now. However, now all of them were feeling apprehensive.

It was already past the time limit. Two minutes past the earliest possible time that Naoto had determined the main cannon of the enormous weapon could fire.

Indeed, it should be the earliest possible time now. It could be that the cannon would take more than eighty minutes to recharge itself, but it was just as likely that it would fire at any moment.

But there was something that made Naoto even more anxious.

"Damn it. AnchoR, RyuZU... I'm begging you guys, please be safe..."

It was possible that the reason the main cannon hadn't fired was thanks to AnchoR or RyuZU's sacrifice. Perhaps both of them had laid down their lives. Naoto had no way of knowing.

*The only thing I can do is pray that this two-minute delay doesn't turn out to be the most expensive two minutes of my life...*

Meanwhile, Marie rushed to finish the final adjustments.

"Listen!" she yelled to Houko. "I'm gonna raise the temperature of Akihabara Grid's base to two thousand degrees Celsius and the immediate area of that weapon to thirty thousand degrees, all right?!"

*Am I insane? Her own words terrified her. But to be honest, even at a temperature like this, I'm still not sure it will actually be enough to destroy that enormous weapon.*

Shaking her head, Marie dispelled her doubts.

"The temperature-regulating mechanisms around the enormous weapon have already been put on standby, so it'll only take a moment to release their heat. But it'll take about thirty seconds to transfer enough heat to Akihabara Grid's mechanisms to demagnetize them! Houko, after thirty seconds have passed, use this console to stop the process. With that, the bypass will be discarded and the temperature will begin dropping back down."

"Yes." Houko nodded. "I understand."

"Oy, Marie! You're still not done?! Hurry the hell up!" Naoto yelled impatiently.

"I know! I'm starting it right now," Marie yelled back.

Just as she was about to press enter, she wavered.

*It's true... I've felt it... the knowledge of something I shouldn't be able to know. I cannot deny seeing something I that shouldn't have been able to see.*

*I had accepted that I wasn't a born genius, so I resolved to become one anyway. However, despite my success... no, precisely because of it... I'm still merely human.*

*And yet, right now, my finger is resting on a button that, if pressed, might lead to the destruction of the world.*

*Is this really gonna be all right? Could I have made a mistake somewhere? Was I presumptuous in thinking that I could pull this off?*

*This is the first time I have ever taken on a job like this. I had to rely solely on my intuition. The mechanisms of this tower were like no other I've seen.*

*We haven't even tested it! Hell, it's more likely that it will fail than work.*

*And yet, am I really going to press this button? If this goes wrong, Tokyo will go down. And with it, the entire country.*

*Down the line, it'll inflict fatal damage to the planet itself.*

*I could end up being the greatest mass-murderer in all of history. That's the kind of weight my fingertip is resting on.*

Marie's teeth clattered. Her fingertips went numb. Her brain was scorched with nervous excitement. She couldn't collect her thoughts. She felt like she might faint.

*There shouldn't have been any mistakes. It should be fine.*

No matter how forcefully she tried to make herself believe that, the fearful doubt wouldn't leave her.

A question suddenly popped up in her head.

*What made the ones executing this coup d'etat pull the trigger on their plan? What could it have been that thrust them toward taking such a precarious action, one that could destroy the entire world?*

"Oy, Marie, hurry up! What are you squirming for? Do you need to pee?"

*Ah... so that's it.*

"This is the second time you've shown disregard for your life. I swear I'm gonna beat you to death after this! Grrrr!!"

*It was anger.*

Marie smashed the enter key with her fist, and the Pillar of Heaven rumbled with a deep groan. Marie stood up, no longer caring to worry.

*This should work. Akihabara Grid should be able to withstand the heat. At the very least, this is how "Y" solved the problem of magnetized mechanisms. Those two automata prove that. In that case, this should be fine! If it's good enough for "Y," then it's good enough for me!*

Turning around, Marie found Naoto playing with the computer in merry spirits.

"All right! Well then, y'all're bein' a bit of a nuisance so back off a bit 'kay?"

*Tap.* A brisk, satisfying keystroke. The atmosphere beyond the barricade bellowed, jolting everything around with the force of an explosion.

The tempestuous, raging wind floored the units of Tokyo's military as it vortexed into a localized whirlwind inside the passageway, causing the walls to shake and rumble.

It was an ultra-small, limited version of a downburst.

Then, another tap.

"Everyone! We're gonna escape through the hole in the floor. Whoa!!" At that moment, a fierce updraft gushed up through the giant hole.

"Oy, Naoto," said Halter. "How're we gonna escape through the hole in the floor again?"

"We're gonna jump, of course."

"Do we have parachutes?"

"Nope, that's why I generated that wind." Naoto stood at the edge of the abyss and measured the updraft blowing through. "If we free fall from here, we should be able to ride the wind and descend all the way down. Probably."

"Probably?"

"We'll be fine. Relax. It's all about your attitude. Don't give up hope, old man."

"Seriously? I mean, I guess I should have asked how we were gonna retreat beforehand, but still, you've gotta be joking," Halter groaned. If he were in his own body, he would surely have slapped his hand onto his bald head and started rubbing it in exasperation.

It was about sixty kilometers from here to the ground. Not even Vermouth and Halter could possibly land unscathed, much less Naoto and Marie. However, Vermouth patted Halter's unit lightly and leapt out through the air.

"Well, I'll be going ahead! GeronimoOoooOOooOOOooo-OooooO!!"

The pitch of his voice bent with the Doppler Effect. Halter's visual sensors clearly captured the powerful updraft breaking Vermouth's fall. He was descending towards the ground as if he were gliding.

Naoto had also been listening carefully to hear Vermouth's descent.

"Great, looks like it works. All right then, I'm up next! I...can... flyyyyyyy!!"

Watching Naoto go, Halter followed. Having resigned himself, he leapt into the center of the wind tunnel with a sigh.

Marie turned to her dear friend.

"Well then, I'll leave the rest to you, Houko."

"Right. Rest assured, I will frame you guys as the most heinous criminals on Earth," Houko answered with a smile.

*This is probably our final farewell,* Marie thought. *She's the princess of a country, and I'm a nefarious terrorist. There'll be no way for us to meet directly ever again.*

*The two of us will forever walk parallel paths. I don't regret my decision, but I do feel a little...*

Just as Marie's expression turned cloudy, Houko held up her left hand. On her wrist was a silver watch...

"..."

Marie smiled and began her charge. As she passed Houko, still holding up her left hand, Marie slapped her palm. Then she leapt into the air and down the hole.

Right after that, the military broke through the barricade.

• • ● • •

"Wha??"

Gennai let out a short cry of astonishment. The bullet that had been accelerating to hypersonic speed stopped dead in its tracks. Two sharp scythes had caught it.

"Obeying orders faithfully is the duty of a follower," the girl in a formal black dress announced in a singsong voice, black scythes flashing as she spoke.

Immediately after, Gennai's right hand, which had been holding the gun, was severed.

"But never the less, looking after one's younger siblings is the duty of an elder sister," RyuZU said as she curtsied gracefully.

Gennai's twisted face showed his amazement. He had lost a hand, but his expression was not due to pain.

"Impossible... why didn't it fire?!" Gennai yelled violently, his face twisting with hatred.

"Because the scheduled firing of the main cannon never went through," RyuZU answered with a smile. "I came after my younger sister through the entrance she opened up and, along the way, I destroyed, I think, around eighteen power coils.

"Judging from how unsightly your face appears right now— and truly it is an expression worthy of being displayed in a museum with the title of 'The Fool'—it appears that my actions have thrown a wrench in your plans. Just knowing that puts me on cloud nine."

"Big...Sis...why..." AnchoR called out in a feeble, distorted voice.

Lowering her gaze, RyuZU found AnchoR perforated and limbless, and knitted her brows together. She exhaled and swung one of her scythes with a swish.

*Bam!*

The back of the black scythe pounded AnchoR's head once. Immediately, AnchoR stopped melting away as her body returned to the eternal dream of a young girl.

"It hurts... wah... Big Sis... hit me..." AnchoR cried as her beaten body writhed and sobbed.

AnchoR hadn't noticed her own transformation. She hadn't noticed that RyuZU's black scythe had severed The Thirteenth Balance Wheel of Differences linked to her Perpetual Gear, either.

RyuZU forcefully disengaged her Still Weight mode. If her aim had been just a little off, AnchoR would have ceased to operate for all eternity.

"I do believe," RyuZU replied coolly, so as not to let her younger sister realize the dangerous bridge she had crossed. "I said that I would punish you if you didn't intend to come back, yes?"

"Ah......augh....uuuu..." AnchoR moaned meekly, looking guilty.

RyuZU smiled sweetly on seeing that but immediately returned to a serious expression.

"So I couldn't win," Gennai groaned, wheezing and holding his bleeding wrist. "In the end huh...ngh..."

"Against whom? You have not lost to anyone." A glint of scorn surfaced in RyuZU's topaz eyes. She gracefully, but sardonically, curtsied. "If you think that a loser who had defeated himself from the very beginning ever had a chance against Master Naoto... my, I fear that such a grave delusion would be enough to tempt me to *downsize* you until you are a little more *portable*."

She paused for a breath. "Normally, I would have activated Mute Scream to chase after AnchoR, but in this case, there were two reasons why I could not do so. And because of this, I have ended up in the predicament of having to suffer your vulgar gaze, for which I very much expect your deepest apology."

Gennai remained still, as if he couldn't move. However, RyuZU paid that no mind. She crouched down by AnchoR's side.

"The first reason is that I would not have been able to bring AnchoR back."

Once AnchoR was in Still Weight, not even RyuZU's Mute Scream could catch up. However, as AnchoR continued to disintegrate, her speed gradually dropped. If RyuZU had touched her then from within Mute Scream, she could have ended up destroying AnchoR with the force of objects in different axes of time colliding.

As such, though she wasn't showing it, RyuZU had chased after AnchoR at full force immediately as she had begun her decent. Though she had headed straight after her younger sister, it still took quite a bit of time to catch up.

"And," RyuZU continued. "The second reason is that I simply could not bring myself to be so merciful as to let you die without you even realizing it."

RyuZU broke into a wide grin. She sensed a change in the atmosphere. The ambient temperature was rising. "It looks like your hard work paid off, AnchoR."

"Huh...?"

RyuZU smiled. *So you have not realized it yet. Because of you, Master Naoto and the rest were not only able to survive but to succeed. You should ask Master Naoto for lots of praise later.*

Keeping that thought to herself, RyuZU turned to face Gennai once more.

"Now then... Mr. Clanky Old Bones. If possible, I would love nothing more than to literally stuff you inside this crucible and savor the sight as your flesh burns, your blood boils, and your eyes burst until I reach my own thermal limits. But..."

RyuZU paused and lifted AnchoR in her arms. "Although it could not be further from my own inclinations, Master Naoto has decided that murder is bad for AnchoR's upbringing. Further still, there is a certain girl who has asked for the authority over your life and death."

Punctuating that statement, RyuZU's black scythes dashed forward. In a flash, all the weapons and devices that were on Gennai's person were minced to shreds. The back of the black scythe warped like a whip and bashed the back of Gennai's head.

"Ngh?!"

Gennai fainted before he could even react, and RyuZU deftly hoisted him up with her scythes.

"I will have to clean these later. Even though I had taken as much precaution as I could by cutting off his hand quickly... they have still been sullied by a faint amount of his blood, skin, and oils. Well, at the very least he will not be squirming about now. That would feel even grosser," RyuZU said to herself, turning around.

Holding AnchoR gently in her arms and suspending the old man with her scythe, she retraced her steps at full speed.

"Oh, and in the case that I do not make it out fast enough, and you end up dying a horrible death by flames, please be understanding. Accidents happen, yes?"

Just a few seconds after RyuZU and her passengers left the area, a sun was formed in the center of Akihabara Grid.

Reaching two thousand degrees Celsius around its perimeter, and thirty thousand at its center, immense heat engulfed the enormous weapon along with the rest of Akihabara Grid. As the ground burned away, the magnetic charge present in all the clockwork in the grid was shorn away by flame.

## ● Epilogue / 00 : 00 / Saver

IN THE MOONLIGHT, the sound of the ocean filled Ariake Grid, the port district facing Tokyo Bay. The artificial island, known since antiquity as Odaiba, along with the port facilities that had originally been made as a defensive barrier around the heart of Tokyo, were aligned with Ariake Grid, turning in the opposite direction at exactly the same speed.

There, in a shipyard filled with warehouses, was the place that Naoto and friends had designated as their rendezvous point.

"AaaaanchoRRRR... uuuuuuUH?!"

Naoto screamed as if the world had come to an end. And who could blame him? AnchoR was truly a shock to behold. She was limbless, and even her torso had scars on it.

Naoto tossed aside his luggage and sprang towards AnchoR, who'd been placed on a large table to sleep. Standing behind him, Marie gulped.

*Such terrible damage. No matter how you try to downplay it, she's been totally wrecked. Normal automata in this condition would be scrapped without a question. Just making a new one would be cheaper than the repairs. Well, for normal automata anyway.*

Holding her breath, Marie shifted her gaze to Naoto.

He was touching AnchoR with trembling hands. He nodded lightly.

"It'll be okay. She hasn't been fatally damaged. Just barely. I have AnchoR's structure memorized down to the placement of every wire, so if it's me and you... she can definitely be fixed. Haaaaah..."

"I see. That's good to hear. Truly."

As Naoto's legs gave way in exhausted relief, Marie felt the same feeling well up from the bottom of her heart. She didn't feel uncomfortable around the girl anymore. As Marie was trying to figure out why, Naoto raised his head.

"Thanks, RyuZU. For stopping AnchoR."

RyuZU bowed elegantly. "I only did what a follower should do. And, if I were to add, what an elder sister should do when younger sister was abasing herself."

"Don't worry, I'll take care of your injuries too, RyuZU. Being a big sister is tough, isn't it?"

RyuZU caught her breath in astonishment. Not because she was amazed that Naoto picked up on the damage that she had sustained herself. RyuZU was elated to see her pride in her master, the absolute best that she could have, grow even greater.

More than knowing that she would be repaired, Naoto had just asserted that he would repair her injuries himself. RyuZU bowed again to express her joy.

"I'm... so-rry..." AnchoR said feebly.

Hearing her intermittent, distorted voice, Naoto frowned. Marie lowered her gaze. Before either of them could say anything, AnchoR continued.

"An...choR...could-n't destroy them all...even...though... that's all...that AnchoR's...good for..."

Even though the only meaning in her existence was as a destroyer, an annihilator, she had acted on her own. Betraying even her own master's orders. And in the end, she couldn't even destroy all the things she needed to.

As Marie looked into her eyes, a thought reflexively popped into her head. Before her reason could come into play, she found her instinct yelling: *that's not true. The way you see yourself is definitely mistaken...!*

"I want... an order..." AnchoR looked to be holding back tears as she looked at Naoto and Marie with her scarlet, wavering eyes.

Her voice and expression were akin to that of a child realizing a mistake that could not be undone. She was bewildered as to what she should do. What she wanted wasn't orders but punishment. A way to atone.

"Yeah," Naoto replied immediately, in a tone that suggested he understood. "Well then, here's my order, AnchoR..."

Naoto took a deep breath.

"Puff out your chest and say: 'I did my best so I want you to praise me.'"

AnchoR eyes widened. Her scarlet eyes wandered to RyuZU, who simply closed her eyes as if to affirm Naoto's words.

"An-choR...did...her best...?" the hurt girl muttered between gasps.

"Ain't that right! AnchoR's the hardest worker in the world!"

AnchoR wheezed. After a slight pause, she turned to look at Marie. "Does, Mother...also...think it's okay for AnchoR...to ask... for praise?"

"..."

Marie obeyed the first impulse of her heart and walked towards the little girl. As she did so, she realized something.

*Being called "Mother" doesn't irk me anymore.*

Reaching down, Marie gently caressed AnchoR's face. It was the sensation of burnt artificial skin. Wrapping her arms around AnchoR's shoulders, Marie pulled her in and rocked her back and forth as she might rock a baby. She heard the creaking of AnchoR's spring as it wound.

*I'm disgusted with myself for thinking that this poor child was nothing but a tool of terrible destruction. Such a young child successfully fought to protect us. Of her own volition and until she became this beat up. And yet, she's questioning... honest to God, she's actually wondering whether it's okay for her to be praised. From her expression, it looks like she could break down at any moment.*

*And you're telling me that this is just a doll without a soul? Give me a break! I'm sick of that kind of thinking!! The me who thought that should just go fucking die!!!*

"Thank you for working so hard, AnchoR. You really did your best, didn't you?"

*Though it pains me to admit it,* Marie thought with a bitter smile, *I feel like right now... I can somewhat understand why one might propose to an automaton.*

*They're just dolls. Mere algorithms. If you simply stop at those preconceptions and dismiss automata as such, then aren't humans nothing but a calculator made of proteins and biological signals?*

*If a human wants to question whether automata have hearts, then he should find proof of a human heart first.*

"Uuh...wahh...ngh..." AnchoR cried feebly in Marie's arms.

Naoto patted her head. However, he then sternly narrowed his eyes. "But also, AnchoR, you're gravely misunderstanding something. I do have to scold you a little bit for that."

"Huh...eh?" AnchoR sniffled.

"You said that the only thing you can do is destroy. But that's not true at all."

Feeling confused, AnchoR remembered something. *"When you return, I imagine that Master Naoto will educate you on the side of yourself that you are not aware of."*

"AnchoR," Naoto began. "You're a clever child, capable of protecting everyone and bringing smiles to their faces. A girl like you can't be called violent no matter how powerful she is. Rather, she's *strong.*"

Violence versus strength. AnchoR blinked twice, seeming not to understand the difference.

Marie suddenly recalled something. "The trident Trishula, the symbol of the power of the god of destruction, Shiva..."

*And as I recall... and I'm sure that Naoto doesn't know this, but he understood it anyway. Or rather, he realized it.*

"What the three hooks on Shiva's trident symbolize are 'will,' 'wisdom,' and 'action.' Only when all three of these traits come together can one rule the world as a force of justice, as one of The Holy Triad, as Shiva did. It's an old myth that used to be passed down in Asia."

"So that's why AnchoR can't exert her power except by her own will, right?"

"Ah..." AnchoR gasped. Her eyes widened.

"Because she's a kind and clever child. Because her power to destroy is a power to *remediate* things. It is the same when repairing clockwork. Before you begin, it's necessary to first correctly *disassemble* the device. That isn't violence, it's strength," Naoto said with a gentle smile. "RyuZU said so too, didn't she? You ought to listen to what your big sister says, you know? AnchoR is an anchor. A force to keep things steady. I'm sure that's why 'Y' gave you that name."

AnchoR's eyes trembled and her lips quivered. She turned to face Marie. "AnchoR...isn't bad?" she asked timidly. "Isn't Mother...afraid of...AnchoR?"

*Immense shame washed over Marie. So she knew. She saw through the fact that I've always been afraid of her. The wall that I built around my heart, regarding her as a product, a thing, because she's an automaton...*

Overcome by feeling, Marie kissed AnchoR's forehead, then she kissed her eyelids, her flushed cheeks, and her perky little nose. Her voice trembled with emotion.

"How...could I...possibly...be afraid of you...AnchoR?!"

"…"

*Knock knock.*

"Hey Missy, did'ya know? Moviegoers'll get bored watching tear-jerking scenes if they go on for too long, no matter how quaint."

Rudely interrupted, Marie rubbed her teary eyes and turned around with an expression that could belong to the devil himself. Vermouth had opened the door partway and stuck his head through before knocking on the wall.

"So can we move on to the next scene already? A thrilling escape, perhaps? Like maybe how we're gonna get out of here, for example."

"Do you even need to ask? By boat. And, if this bores you, then scram."

"Fair enough, you've got me there. But I'll admit I was kinda hoping that we'd be water-walking next, I mean, we just finished freaking sky-walking, you know?! Well, hopefully after all that, our stunning adventure won't end tragically with us being shot to shit aboard a ship that we took our sweet time getting to sail!" Vermouth laughed, but his eyes were dead serious.

*It's been eight hours since we left the Pillar of Heaven. It should be common knowledge by now that the vicious terrorists have escaped.*

*There's no doubt that the land routes have already been blockaded, but even sky routes and sea routes... actually, considering where that enormous weapon appeared from, even the deep underground layers have probably been blocked off with inspection points.*

*If a suspicious ship appears out in the open, it wouldn't be strange for it to be shot down without warning.*

"It'll be fine," Naoto answered in Marie's place. "In another... four to six minutes? A tornado will *coincidentally* occur in this area and we'll pass right through the eye of the storm."

"Ooh, now that's a sound escape plan. Who thought of it?"

"Who else but Naoto would think of something so preposterous?"

"Yeah, you're right, ha haah! I knew you wouldn't disappoint me, kid! I really should stuff your butt up later as a reward..." As Vermouth was in the middle of his vulgar jesting, he was knocked over by RyuZU's scythe.

A short while after that, the shutter of the warehouse was raised as a white oceanic cruiser slowly came in to dock. Its hull was quite large, boasting not only a kitchen along with its cabin rooms but also a simple workshop. Completing its docking nice and steady, two men disembarked onto dry land.

"Ahh, humanoid bodies really feel the best after all."

"Hello there, Dr. Marie. Looks like we're a bit late. Sorry to have kept you waiting."

The ones who had come down from the ship were Halter, who had returned to a human-sized artificial body, and Konrad.

Marie greeted them both. "Please, Dr. Konrad. Don't be sorry. Really, you did so much for me this time. Although I nearly started to despise you because of some recent revelations, and to be honest, I still haven't let that go, but..." she said with an unamused stare.

Konrad simply smiled, letting her critical remarks go in one ear and out the other. "Not at all. The work was immensely stimulating and definitely something from which I profited as well."

Marie smiled equivocally, then looked at Halter. "Really though, I'm impressed that you were able to find a replacement artificial body for Halter."

"Indeed. Due to the turbulence, this country was temporarily under de facto anarchy. And wouldn't you know it, I was able to acquire quite a few items during that time, as it were," Konrad cheerfully answered.

*"Definitely something from which I profited." I hope he isn't just referring to things like this artificial body,* Marie thought, her smile stiffening. *However, it's not like we could escape with Halter connected to that Black Tortoise, so I can't really complain, considering that I'm the one who made such an impossible request in the first place.*

"I must say that this one feels a bit cheap compared to the one I had before though. This face too... I'd like to do something about it later," Halter said, rubbing his cheeks.

His face looked completely different from before. It was slender and youthful, and his physique looked a bit lanky, perhaps because his new body had fewer muscle gears. The only thing his new body had in common with his old one was the bald head.

The sunglasses and his gray suit were also reminiscent of his old self. It felt off, like someone was cosplaying Halter rather than actually being him.

"True, I suppose." Marie shrugged. "But any artificial body on the market right now will feel inferior when compared to an eighth generation model made by the Breguet Corporation, you know. You should be glad that you were able to obtain a body at all. Also, isn't it better for you to keep your new face as it is? I mean, your old face has been all over the news."

"Nonsense. That face was something I worked hard to sculpt. It's what I calculated I should look like at my age if I was still human, you know. Like I'd just give it up now because it's the face of a criminal. Just what do you take the pride of a suave middle-aged man for?" Halter asked, sounding disgruntled and stroking his bald head.

"Hey, by the way," Vermouth interjected. "Ain't there a replacement artificial body for me as well? I think I've lived long enough as a hermaphrodite."

"Why don't you just stay in that body for the rest of your life? I don't see the problem."

"Hey bitch, this may come as a surprise to you, but this body isn't even a true artificial body, you know?!" Vermouth shouted, then, finding himself looking down at his crotch, he added: "Although, I'm not gonna lie, I'm very much pleased with this fine specimen dangling here. I wouldn't mind keeping it when it comes time to part with the rest..."

"Rest assured, Vermouth! I'll make sure to attach it to a wonderfully haphazard place on an astoundingly ugly artificial body for you! Thank you for reminding me just what sort of filth you truly are!!" Marie looked gleeful. Like she might pounce on Vermouth at any moment to dismantle his entire body.

"Hm, well," Vermouth said, surveying their surroundings. "So now that we've got our escape ship and we're finally gonna use it to get the hell out of here, can I ask one final question?"

He looked towards a corner of the dock. Everyone followed his gaze to the old man who had been left aside until now. Gennai Hirayama, the true mastermind behind the chain of events, was sitting silently in a chair. He'd even been forced to crudely attend to his own wounded wrist. They hadn't even bothered to restrain him.

"Hey Princess, why's this geezer here?"

Vermouth and Halter exuded the same dark, stone-cold, murderous intent.

"Eh? I told you guys that I would stuff him in a boiling crucible, didn't I? One of the steel drums around here should do the trick, let's see..." Naoto began to look around for a suitable container.

"Before we began the operation," Marie replied, ignoring him. "I asked RyuZU to try to capture the mastermind alive if possible."

Halter slapped his forehead loudly. "Look here, princess," he said, looking down at Marie with an earnest expression. "It's normal to have qualms about killing someone, but you know that letting this guy live will just lead to further problems down the road, don't you?"

Indeed, having a counter-witness when they were trying to claim responsibility for this entire chain of events might be a problem. Fortunately, everyone in Shiga's ex-military, aside from Gennai, had already been killed. Marie wouldn't have had the resolve to kill them herself.

"If we just kill this guy, everything'll be settled. Heck, want me to do it? Once you get used to erasing corpses without a trace, it's as easy as puffing on a cig. If you give me just ten minutes I can let you choose between six different ways of killing him. Ranging from the merciful all the way to a war crime."

*So this is the mind of someone who's spent his entire life at war, huh?* Marie sighed to herself, feeling a chill run down her spine. She sized up the two men before her. "It's true that I didn't feel completely comfortable letting him bake inside that weapon. I'd be lying if I said otherwise, but..." She turned to Naoto with a serious expression.

Naoto had still been half-seriously... no, plenty-seriously... looking around for a fitting steel container. Noticing Marie's gaze, he turned around.

"Well, if you want me to be serious then I'll be serious, but..." He paused. "First of all, letting this gramps live is not a problem. I mean, someone will kill him even if we don't."

Marie looked confused. Meanwhile, Halter, Vermouth, and even Konrad and RyuZU, looked like they easily agreed.

"I see. You have a point."

"If it became known that the remnants of Shiga's military had attempted a coup d'etat, we're not the only ones that would be inconvenienced."

"Whatever he testifies, he'll be made out to be one of us and sentenced to death in a rigged trial. And that'll be the end of that."

"I imagine that he will have his lips sealed much quicker than you say. There is no problem at all in letting him live for now."

Seeing the reactions of the three people and one machine to Naoto's words, Marie's face stiffened.

*Why are such dark thoughts always the first thing that pops into their heads?*

Naoto continued to press the point. "If you'd like some additional reasons, well, he seemed to be after me in particular, and I want to know why. Also, if I had ordered AnchoR and RyuZU to leave him there, I feel like I would have been ordering them to murder someone, and that didn't sit right. And finally, if I had to give a third reason..."

Naoto paused and looked down at the old man. "I think there's probably someone further up the food chain, y'know?"

*What...?*

Everyone frowned in skepticism.

"True, there were some things that didn't seem to fall into place," Halter said. "But what's your basis for claiming that?"

"Huh, I mean, just think about it. Isn't it weird how someone like him—who hates 'Y' so obsessively—purposefully chose not to use AnchoR-chan, one of 'Y's' legacies? Why didn't he use the electromagnetic technology he's so proud of to override her Master Confirmation? If he was truly calling the shots, don't you think it would've been poetic for him to use his beloved electromagnetism to take control of AnchoR and use her for his revenge?"

Everyone gulped. It wasn't just Marie who had overlooked that. It was a fact that even those used to the battlefield hadn't seen.

*Had AnchoR been in perfect condition, it would have been a cakewalk for her to destroy the Yatsukahagi. Of all the contradictory actions that this man took, letting AnchoR take the bait and pursue*

*RyuZU, who couldn't even damage the weapon, was the one that makes least sense.*

Basking in their gazes, Gennai lifted his head. Among all the features of his face—his white hair, white beard, and paper-white complexion—only his moss-green eyes were moist and glistening with enmity.

"Indeed, impressive." Gennai's voice was dry and hoarse. "Truly, you were impressive to the very end, 'Y.' You loathsome god."

Naoto sighed, fed up. "You're still goin' on about that, huh? I have a name, it's Naoto Miura. Don't tell me that you really went on this rampage 'cuz the menopause made you senile old man."

"If the world were destroyed every time someone went through menopause, there'd be a riot," Marie retorted with half-closed eyes. She looked down at Gennai. "You've called Naoto 'Y' the entire time. What's up with that?"

Seeing his dark, murky, green eyes look up at her, Marie flinched.

"Marie Bell Breguet. The young genius clocksmith and the absolute treasure of the Breguets. To think that you wouldn't understand, what a disappointment you are..."

"What are you..." Marie began to mutter.

But Gennai shifted his gaze elsewhere. He studied Halter, Vermouth, and Konrad in turn.

"You lot should have been with 'Y' when it happened, yes? I can hardly believe that each and every one of you could be so dense as to not realize anything from seeing that absurdity, that magic he performed, firsthand.

"This boy is not human," he asserted, staring Naoto in the eyes.

"No, seriously, what the hell are you sayin', you geezer?" Naoto retorted.

"You all should have seen it," Gennai continued, ignoring his protest. "The sight of this boy easily twisting and recreating this world. Do you seriously believe that someone capable of such a feat could be a mere human, a mere clocksmith?"

Marie gulped. Halter, Vermouth, and Konrad also put on stern expressions. They couldn't bring themselves to simply dismiss this old man's words as a joke. Not after witnessing Naoto work in a manner that surpassed a god.

"I have nothing but questions for this Clockwork Planet, as well. Because there is absolutely no way that a human could ever have recreated the world with gears... ngh!

"An impossible existence and his impossible technology!" he continued, his voice raising violently. "In the midst of my uncertainty, wondering whether this world even truly exists, I thought that I must make my despair known. Prove our mortal limits as man. I suppose you can call that my motive if it so pleases you."

Gennai fell back into his chair. He lowered his gaze to the wound where his right hand should be.

"Well, things ended in my defeat though. I suppose it just means that, in the end, man can't hope to defy a god. If you're going to kill me, then hurry up with it. In the end, this world is nothing but an illusion, a fabrication that the arrogant god over there is showing us. I have no regrets whatsoever."

Gennai offered them his life without passion or remorse. His voice sounded dry, fatigued, and defeated.

"..."

*If I had heard those words a few days ago... in Akihabara, when everything was broken by the electromagnetic pulse, I might have agreed with this old man,* Marie thought.

*During that despair, that loss of faith, when I sensed that everything in the world was an illusion, I might have.*

*But, I know better now.*

*What I felt back in the Pillar of Heaven wasn't something to fear.*

With that understanding and conviction, Marie declared: "Don't fuck with me."

The words flew right out of her mouth. Gennai raised his head and glared at Marie with his dark, murky eyes, as if to challenge her. This time, Marie didn't flinch.

*It's true that the world is covered in illusions.*

*The Clockwork Planet itself peeled off a thin layer of that illusion when it was made. Naoto Miura simply happens to hear the sounds of the world from one layer deeper in.* Now Marie understood that principle well.

*The world allows for contradictions.*

*Common sense, preconceptions, modern theories... those things are nothing but one layer upon all the layers of illusions blanketing the world.*

*At the very least, the universe as observed by the human eye is undoubtedly an incomplete picture and our study of physics a defective framework.*

*With that in mind, if I shift my perspective. Both RyuZU's Imaginary Gear and AnchoR's Perpetual Gear apparently operate without question. They both appear to be fully consistent with the nature of our universe.*

Inside the world that Naoto had shown her, everything was simply natural.

*This world truly does exist as a fabrication, but by no means is it a fake conjured up by some sort of convenient magic.*

Even the modern theories of clockwork technology that Marie had reasoned must be wrong weren't directly contradicted by anything in her newfound experience.

*The fine line between those two ways of understanding the world was simply so thin that one could miss it.*

That was why Marie was being so assertive. That was why she *could* be so assertive. And funnily enough, Marie's answer wasn't so different to someone who'd spoken to Gennai before.

"If you just want to sit there and drool out complaints after declaring yourself a loser, then you can do just that. It's your freedom to believe what you want. But see..."

Gennai's eyes opened as wide as they could. Marie glared into those dark, murky, moss-green eyes.

"The subject in your statement is far too encompassing. Who gave you the right to represent all of humanity, huh?! So..." She paused for breath. "Don't lump us in with yourself. We won't ever give in to despair like you."

Marie's emerald eyes were filled with silent flames.

"Don't you dare think for a moment that a loser like yourself, who gave up all on his own, has any right to determine the limits of humanity."

Out of the corner of her eye, she could see Naoto standing next to her, smiling.

Gennai heaved a heavy sigh. "I see. So 'Y' was two people all along." His lips twisted into a sneer as he faced Naoto and Marie. "You two can sing the praises of man all you want, but I'll never acknowledge it. Bumping into boundaries is the true nature of humanity. As if the two of you, who can manipulate the world without any experience, much less understanding of that fact, could ever understand what it is to be human."

His eyes were still murky as he stared them down.

"Being able to taste only the smallest of victories after an infinite number of pathetic and humiliating defeats... playing dirty, using any and all means, reaching down into the abyss no matter how deep in filth and disgrace one sinks... *that* is what it means to be human. Even if the victory achieved isn't even one's own."

Gennai paused for a breath. "Yes, for example, *that* person *there* is truly human."

Breaking the quiet that had descended over the dock, an immense volume of sound rolled forth.

"What's going on?!"

As everyone looked about their surroundings, they discovered the cause. The resonance communication device equipped in the dock had suddenly turned on by itself. Someone was forcing a connection from outside. And, before anyone could act, the line was connected.

"Ha ha hah! Can I assume that you're referring to me, Mr. Gennai?"

· · ● · ·

*Who is that?* everyone wondered upon hearing the voice of a man.

Gennai was the one person smiling quietly. Seeing his reaction, Marie made a conjecture. However, before she could share it with the others, the man revealed the answer: "Right, I suppose you could call me the mastermind behind this chain of events. Does that make things a little easier to understand?"

"!!!"

Hearing that almost made Marie yell. He was the mastermind! The one pulling the strings behind Gennai. The existence that Naoto had suspected. She could hardly have expected that such a person would contact them of his own accord.

They couldn't hide their astonishment if they tried.

"Ahh, right, right!" the man said casually. "Would you mind opening the window for me before this shocking revelation paralyzes you completely?"

"The window, you say?" Halter repeated suspiciously.

"I promise that it's not a trap or anything! Come on, hurry! You'll end up missing it!" the carefree, but also thoroughly malicious, voice urged.

*This couldn't get any fishier.*

Although she understood that, Marie exchanged glances with

Naoto. He nodded. She turned to the window and undid the lock. It was tight with rust. She pushed it open, and the salty sea breeze brushed past her face.

"I don't really see anything noteworthy..."

A thunderous roar tore through the night sky.

The sudden crash nearly made her lose her balance, but she quickly recovered and stuck her torso out the window to look up at the sky. Something had broken the sound barrier. It left a silver streak in the heavens.

Marie strained her eyes to make out the object that was flying off into the distance.

*Tactical fighters?* Over twenty fighters were flying in formation through the dark, cloudless sky as they disappeared into the distance.

*Just where could they be... no, more pertinently... they were fighters that I didn't recognize...*

The moment that realization entered Marie's mind, the mastermind completed her thought.

"So, did you see it? Amazing right? What just flew past you is a new Vacheron product!"

Marie turned around and yelled in a startled voice, "The Vacherons?!"

Flashes of light blinded the sky.

A few seconds later, the sound of a gigantic explosion that completely dwarfed the earlier sonic boom rocked everything around them.

"That's right! They are one of the anti-electromagnetic

weapons that I had prepared for just such an occasion! Their target is the half-broken Yatsukahagi, but as of right now, the only ones who know that are you guys!"

With that, Marie understood. *In other words, what I felt just now was the sound of that enormous weapon being pulverized by the Vacherons' latest fighters.*

"This was the best presentation ever! I'm thankful for your cooperation! Eh? What'd you say?" The voice paused, then immediately let out a malicious laugh. "Ha ha ha, let me thank you again! It appears that, with just that brief demonstration, the Japanese government is already being flooded with inquiries from neighboring countries!"

"You...!!" Marie growled, her eyes threatening.

*To unveil an anti-electromagnetic weapon at a time like this, when the threat of electromagnetic weapons has just been publicly demonstrated... it's obvious what he's aiming for.*

*The stock of the Vacheron Corporation had crashed and remained in a slump. With this one play, it will fully recover!*

*Even as the Japanese government cleans up the situation and begins the work of reconstruction, it won't be able to avoid intervention from corporate interests.*

*However, that implies that...*

"I take it this was the goal of you Vacherons from the very beginning!" Marie shouted, shaking in indescribable fury.

Anti-electromagnetic weapons? As if something like that just so happened to be in development and was ever so conveniently completed today.

You had those fighters prepared for "just such an occasion?" Yeah, right! They're something that you prepared for this specific demonstration!

These guys had planned to manipulate the coup d'etat and instigate a crisis that they could then resolve. That is what those fighters were made for!

And their only reason in doing so? Just to push their own products... bastards!

"Ha ha hah, never!" the mastermind replied nonchalantly, trying to stifle his sneering laugh. "Although it's a great honor, you think far too much of me. I'm not capable of seeing the future. This was simply me using one of various potential scenarios to my full advantage. Although I will say..." He paused for a breath. "Even if I can't see the future, there was never any need, because you guys were still dancing in the palm of my hand this whole time, ha ha ha ha!!"

*This, guy...* Marie's body chilled. Her mind had gone past fury. Her fists were trembling in terror.

For all their actions to be used like that... even the amazing miracle they had pulled off in the end...

Naoto glared at the transmission device. "Don't lie out your ass with that creepy voice of yours, old man."

"Oh ho?"

*A...lie?* Marie looked at Naoto.

"As if you actually anticipated all of our actions," he continued. "We were in the palm of your hand? If giving us AnchoR-chan was a part of your plan, then we're dancing with a pretty generous hand."

*That's true.* Marie gulped. *I almost let myself buy into the bluff of this self-proclaimed mastermind.*

*It's just as Naoto says. If he was the one who ordered AnchoR to escort Gennai's forces, what reason could he have to purposefully gift her to us? He ought to know full well how ridiculously powerful she is!*

"So you're just someone who wants to start a war by making Tokyo collapse so that you can sell weapons. Actually... that doesn't explain everything. You still have something up your sleeve..."

Naoto stopped and turned around to look at Marie. She recalled what she'd heard several weeks ago in Kyoto from the mouth of a certain Technical Force officer that she had captured.

*"I heard that the incident in Amsterdam two years ago was instigated by you guys as well!!"*

*The rumor that Meister Guild deliberately sabotaged core towers in order to analyze their technology is... don't tell me...!*

"I see," Halter cut in, appalled. "If the coup d'etat succeeded, your stock value as a collaborator in the underworld would rise. If it failed, you would be in the prime position to sell weapons that could counter the electromagnetic weapon. And, if things went exceptionally well, Tokyo would have collapsed and you could analyze the technologies of its core towers and the Pillar of Heaven from the ruins. Not to mention the fact that the collapse could trigger a war, in which case you'd be swimming in business. You're the very picture of a scumbag aren't you?"

"Ha ha ha, shall I just say that I'm honored to receive your praise?" the voice sneered in response.

Marie was astounded. *What's with this guy? Just how would your mind have to be wired to be so thoroughly corrupt? Where is this guy coming from?*

Suddenly, she had an epiphany. "You... you're not a Vacheron! Who the hell are you?!"

It triggered something in Marie. Her rational mind followed her intuition.

*This supposed mastermind is acting like he's an executive of the Vacheron Corporation, but there's no way that could be true.*

*The Five Great Corporations have immense influence, yes, but...*

*In the first place, clockwork technology could be considered the lifeline of this planet. Its very foundation.*

*Our world's economy runs on clockwork. And because of that, one could argue that the Five Great Corporations who own and profit from that technology have more power than even the IGMO.*

*However, those in a position to execute a grand scheme like this are extremely limited in number.*

*First, such a person would have to have status equivalent to the heads of the Five Great Corporations. And second, he or she wouldn't have to mind the risk that such a grand, heinous deed could be exposed and utterly ruin them. In other words, such a person would have to be suicidally mad.*

*Not even the Vacherons are capable of purging cities and instigating wars for the sake of analyzing or seizing technology. Even if such things didn't bother the conscience of their executives... there's no way they would give such a plan the green light. Not considering the risk of their scheme being exposed and its substantial consequences.*

However, the self-proclaimed mastermind merely jested at Marie's question. "Ha ha ha! Who am I, huh? I've never even thought of that. After all, I don't get to introduce myself to others very often.

"By the way," he asked, before Marie could shout at him again. "Do you know what you guys are being called? In the twelve hours since you broadcasted the footage of you taking over the palace, there isn't a person left in the world at this point who doesn't know who you are…"

The man snickered. "They're calling you the 'Second Ypsilon.' As in, the second coming of 'Y,' you know?! They think that 'Y,' who once saved the world, has now come to destroy it! Man, what a truly cool name! Being nameless myself, I can't help but feel a little envious!

"However," he continued in a calmer voice. "In the end, 'Y' was just an incomplete 'X.' A relic really, wouldn't you agree? With that in mind, let me try giving myself a cooler name…

"I'm Omega, and I'm someone in the same business as you guys. Only I'm a *real* terrorist."

Marie engraved that name into her heart. *Omega. It's probably a half-assed name he chose just now, but that doesn't matter.* Marie's very soul was telling her that he was the enemy they must defeat.

"Well, feel free to go ahead and think of me as a member of a cliché evil organization," he continued jesting, oblivious to her resolution. "Oh, and by the way, while it's true that having the Fourth taken by you guys was regrettable, in the end it's only one weapon. Now that I've seen that its perpetual operation is nothing but false marketing, I no longer have any interest in it. If you're so enamored with that antique piece of trash then you can have it! Ha ha ha ha ha ha ha ha!"

"Keep that grating voice of yours inside your damn mouth, you bastard!!" Naoto shouted, hearing Omega convulse with malicious laughter. Then, for some reason, he stared up at the ceiling and howled: "Rather than babble garbage from up there, why don'tcha come down here and say it to my face! Ya goddamn coward!!"

"Pfft..." Omega laughed after a momentary pause. Shrilly, as if his sides had split. "Ha hah, ha ha ha ha ha ha ha ha ha ha ha ha ha ha ha ha hah.... whew!!" He sounded as though he was wiping tears from his eyes. "I found it hard to believe, but I've just confirmed it firsthand. I see, you really can 'hear things' can't you, Mr. Naoto?! I mean, logically, that had to be the case for you to do everything you have done, but to think that such a power really exists... man, the world truly is an interesting place isn't it, Mr. Gennai?!"

Marie gasped. *Crap! She'd realized it all too late. The reason this guy deliberately made contact and talked for so long... was to discern the truth of our trump card, Naoto's ability!*

"Sorry for having said such a mean thing, Mr. Naoto," Omega continued merrily. "You are truly interesting. I'd take the opportunity to study you before even a masterpiece like the Pillar of Heaven.

"As an apology, I won't try to take the Fourth back. Though if I'm going to be honest, it's extremely painful for me to let you have it, as I haven't had the time to figure out how her Perpetual Gear works yet. I sincerely apologize for my provocative words."

"Fuck off. AnchoR has been mine since the inception of the universe. Go to hell."

*"Naoto! Why did you... ugh!"* Marie shouted. *I get that you wanted to tell him off, but wasn't revealing your ability to him a mistake?*

"The hatch has been closed."

"Eh...?"

Those sudden words from Naoto made Marie shut her mouth.

Naoto continued to glare threateningly up at the ceiling. "He's in a large stealth bomber that's circling at twenty thousand meters right above where we are. If it was a just a regular bomb, RyuZU could easily take care of it with Mute Scream, but from what I heard, it sounded like that resonance cannon that AnchoR used."

Marie's eyes stretched wide open. "A resonance cannon? What are you talking about?! A resonance cannon couldn't possibly have a firing range of over twenty thousand meters!!"

That was over three times the effective... no, the current theoretical limit.

"Then it's gotta be something akin to a resonance cannon. What I can tell you for sure is what he's saying between the lines." Naoto paused, still staring angrily up at the ceiling. "'Where am I? If you answer correctly, I'll let you go. Otherwise, you're dead.'"

Marie gasped.

*That's absurd! She almost spat the words out reflexively, but she swallowed them back down. No matter how absurd it seems... if Naoto says so, then it must be true.*

*In that case, we just escaped death by a hair's breadth, on account of this madman's "leniency."*

*Probably because leaving us alive is more "convenient" for him, as well.*

*He plans to use us, and there's nothing we can do about it.*

"Impressive," the mastermind sneered, as though he'd been waiting for Marie to reach that conclusion. "You're right on the money. I wouldn't expect any less from you, Mr. Naoto!"

"Toying, with us... ghh!!" Marie knitted her brows. Her voice was trembling. The intolerable humiliation was making her lose her cool.

*Just how long has it been since someone made such a fool of me right to my face?*

"Well, having you guys around should make it easier for me to operate from the shadows, after all!" the man continued cheerily, as though he was savoring Marie's rage. "So, all you ladies and gentlemen in the grand international terrorist organization known as Second Ypsilon, I'd be extremely grateful if you would kindly do more flashy things in the future! But, before I go, I'm going to correct two misapprehensions you've made, Mr. Naoto Miura."

Omega paused to clear the air. "First, you taking the Fourth really did fall within the scope of my plans, okay? Because the prevention of Kyoto's purge couldn't be explained without some sort of magic being involved, I prepared some bait of the highest quality to lure that magic out. Ha ha, I'm glad that you found it to your liking! True, it was a valuable asset, but investing it really paid off!"

A chill ran down Marie's spine.

*That means that he really did reel us in, just like Naoto said. Since when, from where, and to what point exactly was he pulling the strings?*

"The second is that, while it's true that I was proposing a game of life or death to you guys, Mr. Naoto, I'm still perfectly fine with having everyone but the contestant who gave the correct answer die, you know?"

Marie's chill became a clear and sudden fear of death.

"Shit. Get down!!!" Naoto screamed.

Marie reflexively obeyed his order. Halter, Konrad, and Vermouth did the same. RyuZU adopted a combat posture. Gennai was still smiling.

A moment later, his head exploded.

"Wha?!"

Skull fragments and blood splattered everywhere. The smell of rusted iron reached Marie's nose. A second later, a gun fired somewhere far away.

*He was sniped!*

Marie clenched her teeth, and Naoto turned around in a fluster to see what had happened.

*This isn't good,* Marie thought. *The next target...*

"..."

".......?"

*They...stopped?*

• • ● • •

On the roof of a certain skyscraper, from where one could see all of Ariake Grid's port...

"Haah...I never imagined that I'd survive. Looks like I shouldn't write off my good luck! Well, I don't think there's any doubt that I worked far more than I'm paid for," Karasawa quipped to himself.

He gently twisted the tool he had thrust into an object the size of a motorcycle and some fine parts within broke. After the clattering sound of disengaged gears spinning in neutral, the device fell silent.

It was a long-barreled machine draped in a black cowl that gave off a dangerous air. An automated sniper rifle used for assassinations.

Karasawa destroyed the "assassin's" AI by thrusting a tool into a gap in its light armor.

"Rather, this kind of work is completely outside of my role and responsibilities. Well, I guess I could think of it as paying interest on the debt I incurred in the past. Most importantly, Dr. Marie appears to be safe and sound so why sweat the... ugh!"

Karasawa let out a small groan. He held his abdomen, and blood began to drip down between his fingers.

"Good grief, will I be able to get worker's comp for this? Ha ha, as if... sure is tough working for an organization that flouts labor standards."

Although Karasawa had narrowly managed to repel his assassin, he hadn't escaped unscathed. His right arm and several of his ribs were broken, and he'd taken two bullets in the abdomen. By his own diagnosis, he was a patient with severe injuries, in need of at least a month's rehabilitation.

*The one silver lining is that my wounds aren't so bad that my only hope is to become a cyborg...but if I don't treat them soon, my life's definitely gonna be in danger.*

Karasawa turned around, panting heavily. "I've gotta choose my next job... more carefully..."

*I ended up finding out things that I shouldn't have, and although I turned the tables on my assassin this time, if this keeps up, not even my good luck will save me. I need to disappear ASAP. That, or I'm going to need protection.*

*For the time being, the leads that look promising are... how about that Japanese princess? I already know just how much fun a workplace can be when there's a beautiful and capable woman running things, thanks to my time in Meister Guild.*

"As for Dr. Marie and the rest... well, they should be fine. The enemy is a bunch of clowns who let even a weakling like me escape, after all. I'm sure Dr. Marie and her friends can overcome anything... whoa, there."

Pulling back his drifting consciousness, Karasawa smiled gently. He swallowed down the clot of blood that had made its way up his throat.

"Ugh, shit, this is really bad. Before I worry about finding new work, I oughta... let's see, the closest back-alley doctor should be... ah, right. Well, let's get this over with."

Dragging his battered, wounded body, Karasawa disappeared into Tokyo's underworld without a trace.

· · ● · ·

Far off on the horizon, the sun was setting. Lying sprawled on a chair on the ship's deck, Marie took in the red-orange hue of the sea. It was warm, and the sea breeze that brushed past at intervals felt refreshing.

Looking up through her sunglasses, she could see the silhouette of the Equatorial Spring that covered a large portion of the burnt orange sky. As she tilted her head slightly to the side, she saw a man fishing by the edge of the ship.

"Halter, could you toss me a can of juice?" she called out to him.

"Sure thing. Does orange juice sound fine?"

As Marie nodded, Halter took out a can of juice from the cooler and tossed it over his shoulder without turning around. Catching the can in mid-air, Marie pulled the tab with a whoosh.

As she enjoyed the sweet, cool taste of the juice, Marie flipped the switch of the resonance radio on the table next to her chair and found a news report.

"Once again, regarding the Uprising of 2/8: As of right now, there are still no leads as to the whereabouts of the criminal group commonly known as Second Ypsilon. For those who are just tuning in, this is the name of the group who raided the palace, took Her Highness Houko Hoshimiya hostage, and seized control over the Pillar of Heaven on the tenth of February. Experts agree that the enormous weapon utilized by the terrorists possessed electromagnetic technology, and countries around the world have rushed to purchase the newly released anti-electromagnetic weapons that the Vacheron Corporation had been developing..."

Marie snorted. "In the end, everything went exactly as that son of a bitch wanted, huh..."

"Not only that," Halter sighed. "But with this development, quite a few countries will now have access to technology to counter electromagnetic weapons. They've all implicitly affirmed that they suspect each other of possessing something similar to 'our' spider..."

He kept watching his line and still had his back to her.

"It's not a problem for now," he went on. "But once the commotion from this latest incident dies down, this new development might spark other things. And, if even a single one of those sparks turns into a full-fledged conflict, our enemy's going to make a killing."

Sighing at Halter's words, Marie changed the radio to a station from another region where the commentators were having a conversation.

"In short, I believe that it was Princess Houko's courageous actions that ultimately led to the foiling of the terrorist plot.

"After all, if she hadn't risked her life to make a plea to the military, the Second Ypsilon wouldn't have felt pressured to speed up their plans and fire at the Pillar of Heaven.

"And, if they hadn't done that, their enormous weapon wouldn't have overloaded and self-destructed."

"Regarding Princess Houko, I heard that she took the lead in handling the aftermath once she was freed by the military, is that correct...?"

"Yes, exactly. Not many people know this, but Princess Houko is a certified Geselle who has studied abroad in Europe. I think it's safe to say that it was thanks to Her Highness assuming leadership of the imperial guard's Technical Force that the emergency repairs to the Pillar of Heaven's structure were able to narrowly succeed in making the entire system safe again."

"Looks like that princess is doing well for herself, huh?" Halter said cheerfully.

Marie nodded. "Doesn't surprise me. Although she's usually restrained by her position, she's actually well suited to be a leader."

*It was reported that the Meister Guild had begun to survey the extent of the damage done to the Pillar of Heaven, she reflected. And restoration work for the various grids that had been damaged were also proceeding smoothly with aid from the biggest players on the international stage.*

*As it stands, Houko is being treated as the savior of the nation. She's expected to hold much more influence over the government in the future, as well. Although much of that is because the ruling party has completely lost the trust of the populace.*

"And what an act she put on!" Marie continued, her mood improving at the thought of her friend's bright future. "I'll admit, hearing her condemn me, a dear friend of hers, as a 'self righteous, arrogant, egotist who must not be placated' made me a bit sad."

"Ain't that more or less the truth?"

The voice that came from above her head immediately dampened her mood. Marie lethargically raised herself and turned around.

"Hearing you say that makes me murderous rather than sad, Mr. Ringleader."

Naoto was wearing a comfortable Hawaiian shirt with shorts and sandals, but he had an exhausted expression on his face. RyuZU was standing slightly behind him, looking as unconcerned as usual in her formal attire.

Then, seeing someone walk out of the cabin, Marie relaxed.

"Ah, AnchoR! It's finally over, huh?"

"Ah, Mother...!" AnchoR smiled back as she slowly walked over. She now had provisional limbs again.

*As expected of Naoto,* Marie thought with a hint of admiration.

AnchoR had been basically totaled, not to mention that the materials that had been used to make her were all custom-made. There was no way that a getaway cruiser like this would have the raw materials necessary to make serious repairs.

As such, the arms and legs that AnchoR was using right now were equivalent to temporary prosthetics designed for automata. Marie had scrambled them together by disassembling the Black Tortoise that Halter had been using and salvaging its parts.

However, no matter how much Marie inspected and analyzed AnchoR's body, unlike for RyuZU (whose blueprint she had memorized) in the end, only Naoto could truly grasp AnchoR's structure.

Even just implementing those artificial limbs and linking them up to AnchoR's various senses so that she could at least perform some basic movements had required Naoto to spend the past two weeks inside the cruiser's workshop.

However, in spite of his strenuous efforts, it seemed that he couldn't get her new limbs to fit her all that well after all. AnchoR was tottering as if she couldn't quite get her bearings.

Marie pouted. "Took you long enough. Just how long were you planning to make her wait, you punk?"

"Buzz off. In the first place, I wanted to truly repair her, not put a bandage over things like this."

Indeed, what he had done couldn't be called a repair. It had merely been first aid, a stop-gap measure. Even so, it was something that Naoto wouldn't have been capable of before. Although he had used his ears to repair something before, putting something together with imperfect substitutes was something new.

*To be honest,* Marie thought, *I have no idea how he was even able to get those arms and legs working. In theory, what I made should have been flawless replacements, yes. I can attest to that. But really, AnchoR's nanogears and pseudo-nerves were all distorted by heat, and some were even partially melted. Not a single part of her body was as it originally had been. And there was damage from Gennai's shot as well. But even if that hadn't happened, the repairs should have been as difficult as can be.*

*Yet Naoto was able to mend those distortions through brute force. When we discovered that even her main cylinder was damaged, things felt hopeless, but Naoto overcame even that with some splendidly delicate repairs.*

*Of course, it took time. Two weeks, even with Naoto's ears and his newly awakened clocksmith skills. However, just how many years should these repairs have taken normally?*

*Would such a job have even been possible…?*

*It's not like he had cutting-edge equipment at his disposal. He did it all aboard a shabby cruiser swaying along the open sea. In a room that could be at best called a workspace, never a workshop.*

Marie didn't feel confident that she could have produced the same result given the same environment and the same amount of time—not yet, at least.

Getting up from her long chair, Marie rushed to AnchoR's side and gently supported her awkward steps. AnchoR was wearing a white blouse that they had put over her small body like a dress.

"Hey, oy!" Naoto cried out as Marie pinched a corner of that blouse. "Don't you take that off her! Her artificial skin'll—"

"Don't lump me together with a pervert like you. Now then, AnchoR, come this way. Rest with Mommy over here and enjoy the refreshing breeze."

"Okay, let's do that…" AnchoR nodded, smiling as Marie hugged her shoulders and slowly guided her to the deck chair.

Ever since the Pillar of Heaven, Marie's attitude towards AnchoR had shifted. She'd been tenderly doting on her with the sweetest smiles. However, there was someone who wasn't all too happy about that.

"Hey! Stop right there, oy!! You think I'll just let you nab my daughter away?!" Naoto yelled.

"Huuuh?" Marie scoffed. "Like AnchoR could be left in the care of a pervert like you. Don't worry, I've taken it upon myself to raise this girl into a proper lady."

"A lady?! Did you of all people just use that word?! Screw off! If she's left to you, it'll be the birth of another walking land mine!"

"And? If she's left to you and RyuZU, it'll just be the making of another pervert. Think calmly on which alternative is better for her future."

"The hell? No matter how you look at it, having another Marie is far worse for the world! Gahhhhh, I don't want to imagine an AnchoR-chan like that!" Naoto held his head in agony as he thought about it.

Ignoring his antics, Marie sat down on the deck chair with AnchoR in her lap. Naoto turned to whine to RyuZU, who was standing right next to him.

"RyuuuuuuuZU!! Marie snatched AnchoR away from us, you know?! What's wrong with our justice system?! Why does custody always go to the mother?!"

"With all due respect, Master Naoto, even if the universe were to be flipped upside down, Mistress Marie could never be your wife. I will not allow it," RyuZU replied with a cold gaze.

"Ooooooohhhhh?! Of coooooooourse! How could I have forgotten?! My wife is RyuZU!!! Wait, what?! Then this makes even less sense. Why is Marie getting to challenge me over AnchoR's custody?!"

"Again, with all due respect, Master Naoto, I have to ask: Are you dissatisfied with me as a wife in some way?"

"Now hold on a minute there RyuZU, is it just me or are you taking Marie's side?!" Naoto yelled.

RyuZU thought for a little while, then shook her head. "Certainly not. I simply thought that if I am going to be cuckolded by my own little sister, then I might as well let her go. So if you can promise me that will never happen, then perhaps we could work something out."

"What?! RyuZU, what are you even... we're not on the same page here at all, are we?! A-AnchoR?! Who's better, me or that walking land mine over there next to you?!" Naoto cried in desperation.

Marie hugged AnchoR close. "Of course, I'm better! Right, AnchoR?"

"Ah, eh..." Caught in the middle of the spat, AnchoR looked troubled.

"Oy, stop right there," Halter cut in, unable to watch any longer. "Asking a child whether she likes Papa or Mama better? That's downright awful. You're both classic examples of bad parents."

"Don't imply that we're married!!" Naoto and Marie screamed in unison.

Still making a troubled face, AnchoR opened her mouth hesitantly. "AnchoR likes...Father..."

"Heeeeeellllll yeaaahhhhh!"

"Wha?"

Naoto roared, pumping his fist triumphantly while Marie was left in visible shock. However, AnchoR continued with a carefree smile:

"But AnchoR likes Mother, the one who's with Father, too..."

"..."

385

"Father's...an amazing person. And when Mother's with him, she smiles. AnchoR likes Mother when she's smiling."

"..."

After a long silence, Naoto raised his head, determined. "All right, why don't we decide who's more fit to be AnchoR-chan's parent once and for all?"

"Huh?"

"The one who repairs AnchoR and RyuZU so they're back to their original state shall be awarded custody over AnchoR. No complaints about that, right?!"

Marie smiled smugly. "Have you forgotten, Mr. Naoto? The parts that AnchoR was made with? And RyuZU as well for that matter. They are all exceptionally rare materials, yes? Gee, I wonder if you can obtain materials of the same grade when you don't even have the connections and influence that I do?"

"Pfft, I'll just show off in another way then. So, what do we need to do to get our hands on those materials?!"

Marie snorted snobbishly. "There's a chemical engineering plant like those used for cutting-edge industrial research right in the Breguet Corporation's backyard. All I would have to do is ask and they'll send me the spare parts we made for RyuZU with atomic precision, but..."

Her smug face froze.

"Crap, there aren't any spare parts for AnchoR?! Ugh... now that it's come to this, my only option is to raid my family's weapons factory back home!" Marie moaned, biting her nails.

This time, Naoto was the one snorting with a smug smile.

"That means we both have a fair shot! All right, I've decided our next destination! We're gonna raid the Breguet estate! Wait, hold on. Why do we have to raid your house?"

Naoto tilted his head with a blank stare. Marie made a face of disgusted amazement at his stupidity.

"Do you seriously think that my father is such a happy-go-lucky fool that he'd simply say 'Sure, of course,' if I said, 'Well, I know I'm an internationally wanted terrorist now, but could you please let me use the Breguets' assets?!'

"If the Breguet Corporation becomes suspected of aiding terrorists, it'd be a huge blow. It's obvious that he'll shoot me the moment I show my face! That's why we're gonna preempt that with a raid instead! By the way, we'll also have to raid at least another one of the Five Great Corporations to make the attacks look indiscriminate. Ah, yes, we might as well take this opportunity to raid the Vacherons. They'd serve perfectly. If not as a smoke screen, then as a punching bag for me to vent my anger."

Naoto nodded and gave her a thumbs-up. "All right then, let's go with that! AnchoR-chan, make sure you don't miss any of Papa's gallant actions when we get there!"

"Mama's gonna drive how great she is into this good-for-nothing's brain, so make sure to watch closely, okay AnchoR?"

"Hmm? Okay!" AnchoR was completely lost by the sudden developments, but smiled and nodded. It looked like her parents were enjoying themselves.

Halter slapped his forehead. "Oy! More importantly, if you two really plan to go all the way to France on a scrappy boat like this, then I'd like to ask you to review our present location first. And look at what's behind us while you're at it."

Marie let out a fed-up sigh, brushing AnchoR's hair. "What, another pursuer? They're so damn persistent! Seriously, who do these guys work for?"

They'd already been attacked three times in the last two weeks. Although they'd successfully repelled those attacks without trouble, they were starting to get tired of it.

"Who knows," Halter replied apathetically. "We're in the Bay of Bengal, so take your pick from Myanmar, Malaysia, or Bangladesh."

Marie turned to see what was behind them. There, a high-speed destroyer and a group of small automaton boats trailed in hot pursuit. The enemy ship and automatons appeared to be faster than them, and they were getting closer by the second.

"Oh, those guys! Yeah, that's the Thai Coast Guard. I've been chased by them in the past," Vermouth piped up, bending over the guardrail.

"Oy, oy... why is the Thai Coast Guard out here in these waters? We're about to reach the Indian Ocean. This is definitely gonna turn into trouble," Halter groaned, running a hand over his head.

"Trouble for us or for international politics?" Naoto asked blankly.

"Interna—"

"So, it's irrelevant then," Naoto immediately declared.

He booted up the thermobaric buster that they had salvaged

from the Black Tortoise. But before he could finish, he had another thought.

"Oy, Marie, I just had a good idea. Let's commandeer that destroyer," Naoto suddenly proposed, all smiles.

Halter groaned. "Are you seriously thinking of getting across the Indian Ocean on a warship? That'd make us stand out far too much, no matter how you look at it. It'd be like waving a big old flag to alert others of our presence."

"Meh, it's not like people have been having trouble finding us as it is. Besides, we're not gonna sail across the Indian Ocean. We're gonna dock at Thailand."

Marie sank into thought while Halter knit his brows together doubtfully. Only Vermouth responded with a joyful smile.

"I like the sound of that! The Thai people are great, y'know? The women are beautiful, plus, they've got variety! I'm sure 'Naoko-chan' would be welcomed with open arms in Thailand, no matter what he's packing!" Vermouth laughed.

Marie sighed. "Well true, that's not a bad idea. It pisses me off, but I have to admit that you're on the ball, Naoto."

"Oh ho? What's that? You interested in the ladyboys, Missy?"

"I mean we can head for France by land if we make port in Thailand. Don't lump me in with you, pervert," Marie replied, shooting him a threatening gaze.

"Taking a land route from Thailand? What's your reasoning?" Naoto asked, tilting his head.

Marie nodded. "I'm referring to Krung Thep Mahanakhon Amon Rattanakosin Mahinthara Ayuthaya Mahadilok Phop

Noppharat Ratchathani Burirom Udomratchaniwet Mahasathan Amon Piman Awatan Sathit Sakkathattiya Witsanukam Prasit," she said in a single breath.

Naoto furrowed his brows. "Sorry... why are you chanting a curse again?"

"That's the official name of the Thai capital, Bangkok," Marie answered readily. "There was a time in the past when Bangkok—Thailand's multiple-grid metropolis—fell into dysfunction. At the time, Meister Guild intervened and got Malaysia, Myanmar, Vietnam, and Bangladesh to sign a treaty to adjust their borders with Thailand so that Bangkok's grids could receive functional support from the neighboring countries.

"Put simply, that turned Thailand's national borders into a colander, causing a number of black-market trade routes to develop. So, we should be able to find parts to repair AnchoR and RyuZU easily enough. Then we can head up north from there."

"Man, I really don't get politics..."

"Well, in essence," Marie declared with an exceptionally ferocious smile. "All you have to know is that we should sink all the automaton boats, knock all those aboard the destroyer unconscious, capture their ship, and nonchalantly sail it to dock at one of Thailand's military's harbors."

*Looks like Naoto's influence has taken its toll,* Halter thought. Of course, he would never say that aloud, he could only imagine what kind of reaction he would get.

"Ha hah! It might be tasteless of me to ask, but just to make sure, you're saying that we should play pirate in the face of this barrage of cannon shots, right?! Y'all understand just how well equipped that destroyer is?!" Vermouth yelled shrilly in excitement.

"Six 15-centimeter autocannons, eighteen cruise missile silos, a hundred and twenty-one men aboard it, and twenty-eight aerial drones to top it off!" Naoto replied just as excitedly. "Easy peasy, right?!"

"Yes, yes, I love it!! You're totally insane!! Well then, I'll be turning our ship around. Let's commence the attack!!" Vermouth yelled, turning the cruiser's steering wheel.

"By the way, Mistress Marie," said RyuZU, seeming to suddenly recall something and paying no mind to the commotion. "I have something that I need to tell you."

"I'm getting nothing but bad feelings about this, but what?"

"Right." RyuZU nodded. "No matter how much of a fuss you make, Mistress Marie, AnchoR's master is Master Naoto. Because of that, AnchoR cannot be separated from Master Naoto beyond a certain threshold of distance, so keep that in mind."

Marie's eyes widened. Her vision shook. The dismay nearly knocked her off her feet. *What?! So basically, If I want to own AnchoR...*

"I-It'd mean that I'd have to stay with this pervert?!" Marie cried out in despair.

"Hey you guys," Halter retorted, sounding fed up to the bottom of his heart. "You seriously haven't forgotten that all of us are internationally wanted terrorists now, right? We're all gonna be stuck together from now on whether you guys like it or not."

"No way, I can't believe that!!" Naoto and Marie screamed in unison.

Halter sighed heavily. *"What I can't believe is how stupid you two are, jeez."*

*You guys are making me feel like the idiot for being the only one sweating bullets over the considerable fleet we're up against right now.*

Halter turned towards Vermouth, who was steering at the helm of the cruiser. "Speaking of which, so just how long do you plan to tag along with us, greenhorn?"

"Jeez, Master! We're literally in the same boat here, is there really any need to be so cold, my cyborg brother?" Vermouth laughed flippantly. "Well, my intention is to go my own way once we set foot on land, but before I do, I'd like to ask you guys to return me to a proper artificial body. Abandoning me as I am is much too cruel, isn't it?" Vermouth pointed to his glamorous body, his blonde hair waving in the wind.

Halter nodded. *Gotta admit, I'd ask for the same thing in his position.*

"And well, even after we part, if anything interesting ever happens, just know that I'll come running. I mean, this kid's antics are just too fun to pass up, y'know?"

*I figured as much,* Halter thought, shrugging his shoulders. He kicked open the metal box sitting right next to him. *Thunk.* Inside was a bunch of treasure... or so he wished. Rather, it was stuffed with all kinds of ordinance, ranging from small firearms to large artillery. Halter rummaged through the box. He pulled out a large single-shot gear launcher and set it on his shoulder.

"Hey, Marie," said Naoto, seemingly recalling something. "We should give a warning before attacking, if only as a formality, right?"

"I guess you're right. Let's see. I struggle a bit with my Thai, but..."

"Oh? I'm surprised to hear that Little Miss Genius actually has something she's bad at. In that case, leave it to me," Vermouth teased.

Marie scowled. "So you can speak Thai?"

"I mentioned that they're a 'great people' didn't I? I'm an ex-spy you know? Don't look down on us."

"Losing to you at something has gotta be the second most irritating thing in the world. Once we land, I'll master the language immediately, right in front of your eyes."

"Feel free. So? What should I tell them?"

"Let's see... 'Please surrender your ship to us obediently without resistance. You'll all probably be court-martialed for surrendering to a single cruiser but don't worry. We'll be sure to leave you all in such a pitiful state that you can just tell them it was the Second Ypsilon, and they'll let you off the hook.' Something like that?"

"Okay, don't get wet at my linguistic mastery, now." Vermouth snickered. He took a deep breath and yelled into the cruiser's bullhorn in Thai:

"Test test. Hey, you, the destroyer over there! You must be feeling pretty discontent being ridden by a pack of virgins, right?! Well I'll make you moan with my top-notch hip-pounding. So loud that you won't ever want another man inside you, so wet your deck and wait for me! I'm coming all the way to your bridge! Those pathetic virgins aboard you can just plunge into the ocean while covering their shrinkage in shame!"

Immediately after, their cruiser was showered with a hail of cannon fire. Marie hit the deck to the sound of the bombardment. Shells hit the water, and columns of ocean splashed up all around them.

"What did you tell them?" Marie asked suspiciously.

"I simply translated what you said," Vermouth replied with a straight face.

Halter let out a deeply-fatigued sigh. "Yeah, I'm sure you did. Seems like this greenhorn failed to properly convey his good faith to them. Well, I guess you can't really expect to convey something that wasn't there to begin with."

"Hah haah! Translating is hard y'know, Master!" Vermouth yelled. There wasn't a single shred of regret or remorse in his voice.

The barrage of cannon fire tore through the sky and dropped into the ocean, producing violent waves that rocked their cruiser perilously. All the while, the sounds of the explosions shook the air all around.

Despite the tension of the situation, Marie seemed to be enjoying herself. "Last call! Vermouth, you take the helm! Approach the enemy vessel at max speed while evading its barrage! Halter, you're in charge of our rear! Sink the automata boats with the gear-launcher and that machine gun!"

Naoto also gave out his orders. "RyuZU, once we get close enough for you to jump across, knock out everyone aboard that destroyer. AnchoR-chan, you sit back and watch as Papa gallantly commandeers the steering mechanism of that ship!"

"Certainly," RyuZU said as she bowed.

"Father, Mother, do your best!" AnchoR cheered with a smile.

• • ● • •

*I wonder if Naoto and Marie have even noticed the complete and indisputable truth,* Halter thought, watching them give out their orders. *That they're already equivalent to gods on this planet.*

*Can they truly be called human anymore? How they see themselves is irrelevant. Regardless of what they think, ordinary people will treat them as gods. Hence why we've already been given the moniker Second Ypsilon—the second coming of "Y."*

*It's to be expected that the world won't leave them alone. There's no way that people would brush off gods who exist in reality, especially after seeing the miracles that they perform. Naoto and Marie have grown...*

*They practically broke into divine territory in a single leap, and then went on to fly right over past it. It felt not only nostalgic, but exhilarating, to witness them realize such incredible feats. Things that I myself aspired to in my younger days.*

*But on the other hand, the tinge of unease that accompanied that excitement has also only continued to grow. If I feel this way, it must mean that, as expected...*

"I guess I've gotten old," Halter sighed, muttering the words with a sense of deja vu.

He turned towards RyuZU. She was readying herself to activate Mute Scream. To end everything instantly, as Naoto had instructed.

"Hey, Missy. RyuZU."

"I do believe I have already warned you not to address me so casually before, but yes, what is it?"

"Do you think this is something that 'The Gear of Fate' proscribed?"

RyuZU turned quiet for a moment, then smiled elegantly. "Although I am not equipped with the functionality to measure such a thing…" RyuZU paused to turn her gaze ever so slightly upward. There, she found the Equatorial Spring turning in the sky far above.

"Which direction does that spring appear to be turning to you?" she asked.

"Clockwise, I'm quite sure."

"Is that so? However, if you head just a little further south from here, cross the equator and look up again, surely you would answer counterclockwise."

Their cruiser was still shaking. If even one shell hit their ship, it would be blown to pieces. Despite that, RyuZU continued as calmly as if she were looking up at a clear blue sky.

"There might well be as many subjective truths as there are observers in the world. But even so, there is still one indisputable fact: that spring is turning. Is that not the only thing that truly matters?"

*An automaton who can philosophize on the relative nature of reality.* Halter couldn't help but question whether an automaton's view of fate could apply to the human condition.

*But at the same time, she's credible exactly because of who she is. RyuZU's an automaton that can move inside Imaginary Time. She's proof that even the supposedly indisputable reality of time is really nothing more than a subjective truth.*

*No matter how it's twisted, or how it's bent, or even if it begins to turn in reverse...you cannot deny that it is still turning all the same. So, that's what fate is.*

Before his eyes were two idiot wonders with the power to change the world. They were currently having a grand old time in a hail of cannon fire.

"Quit dilly-dallying, Halter! We need you to help! You should at least be able to operate some artillery, even with that crappy body, no?!"

"There ain't much ammunition left for the thermobaric buster y'know, old man! Do your damn job!"

"Well, would you look at that. Perhaps you should get to work as they say, Mr. Junkbot."

*Good grief.*

Halter couldn't help but laugh. "Well, If this is the guidance of Lady Fate or whatever, I guess I'll go along with it."

With that, he shouldered the gear launcher and aligned it on the target.

He couldn't help but think of the day the world had ended and had been reborn in gears. Standing before history in the making, as witness to the second advent of that epic event, he thought: *I guess no matter how old I become, I'll always be just another brat like those two.*

Halter rubbed his slippery bald head with a tired smile and gently pulled the trigger. *Click, clack, click, clack.*

The gears turned and turned.

Systematically, mechanically, inexorably.

They marked the march of time just by fulfilling their function.

Even if a clock were to stop ticking, it wouldn't matter.

Even if the cogs of time became broken or twisted, they would surely continue to turn.

Systematically, mechanically, inexorably.

*Click, clack, click, clack.*

The gears simply continued to turn in the direction that they ought to.

Just who had determined that they ought to turn that way, not even the gods could say...

**O**N A CERTAIN DAY of a certain month, at a certain location, the voice of Editor S—excuse me—the Honorable Judge S resounded.

"The defendant, Tsubaki Himana, shall step forward."

The prosecutor, Kamiya, read out his charges: "The accused did nothing for six months with the plot that I, Yuu Kamiya, had passed over to him at the beginning of the year—"

"Objection!" Himana shouted in his own defense.

He felt like he'd heard the quote "a man who is his own lawyer has a fool for a client" in some foreign drama on TV before. Unfortunately, he had no allies present, nor did he really have any basis to deny that he was a fool.

And so, he continued in a strong tone: "Your Honor! The prosecution is wantonly trying to slander my character! It's true that I received something back from him at the start of the year, but you can't call it a plot! Not when it fit on a single piece of A4-sized paper! In addition..." Himana paused to glare at Kamiya. "I strongly contend that Kamiya should also be charged if the purpose of this trial is to determine whose fault it was that the manuscript was delayed!"

The prosecutor shook his head and sighed as he offered his rebuttal. "Your Honor. With regards to the matter at hand, in the first place, the content of the third volume was originally intended to fit in the second volume, and yet, here we are. From that fact alone, I believe it goes without saying that my plot outline for the third volume was more than elaborate enough."

"Objection, objection! The content that was originally intended to be put into the second volume was greatly altered when it was decided that the volume would be split into two! This was done to conform to the cliffhanger that I wrote for the end of the second volume! To suggest that the plot summary was already prepared is a blatant lie!"

"You were the one who changed the original plot! Take some damn responsibility and fix the plot holes that you created yourself!"

"You already told me that! And when I did just that, the story ended up falling apart immediately! Do you deny it?!"

"Don't admit your own incompetence so boldly!! Why can't you just come up with alterations that don't lead to plot holes?!"

"Hah! Your Honor, did you hear that? Kamiya was the one who told me that he'd leave the editing of the plot of Clockwork Planet to me. When I had asked him for help, he replied: 'NG*L's workload is killing me right now, so ask me later.' This was clearly a breach of contract—"

The courtroom flared white-hot with drama. Claims were being thrown out from both sides! Alas, who does the fault rest with?! What would be true justice?! In full swing, they continued to exchange lines in a heated debate (the contents of which have been omitted) just like actors in a courtroom drama!

"Are you two done screwing around yet?"

"Yessir."

Hearing the cold tone of The Honorable Judge S—excuse me—Editor S, Kamiya and Himana kneeled humbly and in unison. Matters like crime and punishment, or who was right and who was wrong, were all summarily answered with: "Both of you are guilty."

It was an awful script. But well, one could argue that, at its core, a courtroom drama is nothing but—

"I don't care about the fruitless blame game you two have been playing. More importantly..." Editor S paused after declaring the pure and unadulterated truth. He took out the cover of the manuscript and pointed to one spot. "Right here, why does it say 'secondary author' instead of 'co-author?'"

Author: Yuu Kamiya, Secondary Author: Tsubaki Himana

Himana looked away. "Ah, well, you know how... you often hear about artists breaking up due to 'creative differences?'"

"Why are you talking like a band that's just broken up? What's this air of newfound enlightenment?" Editor S quipped with an unamused glare.

"Creative differences, huh?" Kamiya replied bravely, inevitably turning in the other direction as he did so. "Now isn't that a convenient way to put it? It's been a nonstop cycle of me fixing all the plot holes that pop up ever since Tsubaki started writing volume one...

"This went on again and on again and, before I knew it, I was the one coming up with the developments, the settings, and even the text itself down to every single line of dialogue. Ultimately, even a considerable amount of the narration was my own.

"When I realized all this, I was shocked. It led me to think that if Tsubaki can be called a co-author, then we might as well add your name to the list of authors as well."

They turned their eyes on each other and began harmoniously in unison: "We had other candidates too, like 'Yuu Kamiya with Tsubaki Himana.'"

"Yeah, there was also 'Kamiya featuring TSUBAKI' and 'Yuu Kamiya with help from Tsubaki Himana... haha, just kidding!' as well."

"Haaah, well, I do apologize but I'll have to interrupt this report of past buffoonery that is somehow occurring with entirely serious faces. I'll pretend I didn't hear that on account of you both having the sense not to choose any of those in the end. Though, if both of you agree that it was Mr. Kamiya who wrote practically all of this volume, then why not just remove Mr. Tsubaki from the list of authors altogether?"

"I would have loved to do that... but the problem is that I can't say that Tsubaki didn't contribute anything either," Kamiya continued with eyes like those of a dead fish, still kneeling on the cold floor. "Aside from offering interesting ideas, he almost completely rewrote my parts. But, I guess you can say that when the developments of the story become as grand and convoluted as they did, reining things in just ends up being my job, somehow."

Hearing that, Himana gazed up at the heavens with exactly the same look in his eyes.

"Yeah," he muttered. "The volume could barely be called co-authored at that point. That's why we came to the conclusion that, in the future, if we can't divide the work of each volume up exactly fifty-fifty, then there's no choice for us but to finally accept that we'll have to assign separate roles for one another."

"In summary," Kamiya began, and Himana: "We learned that some things which haven't been attempted, aren't that way because they haven't been considered. But rather, it's because they're a bad idea."

"That can't be true. There have been those who think of something and only realize that it's impossible after attempting it. After all, I see two such people in front of me right now," Editor S said in tired amazement.

The two in front of him had expressions of Zen-like peace. He looked like he was having trouble coming up with the words to express himself, as if a migraine had come on, but somehow managed to form coherent sentences in the end. "You two turned the manuscript in way too late. Could it be that the two of you are idiots?"

*You're just figuring that out now?!* The two gasped in genuine shock. However, just as they were about to voice that thought, they swallowed the words back down, noticing Editor S's piercing gaze.

Editor S sighed, looking worn out. "Umm, so just hypothetically," he asked. "How would the two of you handle things if Mr. Tsubaki were the one who ended up doing most of the work for the next volume?"

"Eh? In that case it'd be just as you would expect."

"We'd simply credit Yuu Kamiya as the secondary author next time then."

"What happened to the talk of assigning separate responsibilities to each other?"

Editor S rubbed his temples. The two answered with great pomp and circumstance and even with a certain sound effect added behind them for a little extra drama:

"Assigning separate roles to each other. It's true that we did say that we would do that... buuuuut!"

"We didn't go so far as to say *that we've decided* how we'll divide those responsibilities up yet... diiiid we?"

Unintelligible muttering ensued in the background, making the ensuing silence feel all the more tense.

"Looook here now, you two. I'm about to slap both of you guys sideways, even being as kind and gentle a person as I am," Editor S said with a smile, glancing back down at the manuscript in his hands. "Well, fine. I don't really mind as long as the manuscript is turned in on time. So, where are things at for the fourth volume—"

A strong, cold wind blew right in his face. As he looked back up, there was no trace whatsoever of the two who had just been there. They had left two stuffed animals behind in their seats, as if to suggest the animals would take their place.

Facing that fact, Editor S sighed very deeply. "If only they would show that kind of total unity of mind and spirit in their work as well..."

HER JACKET
COMES WITH
A HOOD

I HAD THOUGHT THAT I'D DEFINITELY DO THIS ONE DAY, AND NOW I'VE FINALLY DONE IT...

THE STUNNING, MYSTERIOUS GALACTIC BELLE NAOKO-CHAN (BEAMING FACE).

THIS CHARACTER DESIGN IS SOMETHING I DREW UNDER A SPELL WONDERING, "HMM, WHAT WOULD NAOTO LOOK LIKE IN DRAG?" BEFORE I WAS EVEN INFORMED OF THE CONTENTS OF THE THIRD VOLUME. BUT I NEVER THOUGHT THAT IT WOULD ACTUALLY HAPPEN IN THE STORY. I WAS SHOCKED (SMUG GRIN).

# No.3
## CLOCKWORK PLANET
# DESIGN FILE

# DESIGN FILE
## CLOCKWORK PLANET
# No.4

ANCHOR IN HER STUNNING ADULT MODE.
HER HEIGHT IS JUST A LITTLE SHORTER
THAN RYUZU.

I TRIED TO MAKE HER LOOK BOTH ANGELIC
AND DEMONIC. HER COMBAT STRENGTH IS
LIKE THAT OF A HIDDEN BOSS WHO'S
STRONGER THAN THE LAST BOSS BUT
ALLIED TO THE PLAYER INSTEAD.

OR, AS I LIKE TO CALL IT, SIMPLY AWESOME.
AN AVATAR OF UNFAIRNESS WHOSE FIRST
STRIKE IS BOTH UNAVOIDABLE AND DOES
THE MAXIMUM AMOUNT OF DAMAGE THAT
THE GAME ENGINE CAN HANDLE WHILE
STILL IN THE CUT SCENE.

I DESIGNED HER WITH THE IMAGE OF A
CUTE ULTIMATE BOSS.

## STILL WEIGHT ANCHOR